SUNSTORM

BALLANTINE BOOKS • NEW YORK

SUNSTORM

A TIME ODYSSEY: 2

ARTHUR C. CLARKE
AND STEPHEN BAXTER

Published in the United States by Del Rey Books, an imprint of The Random
House Publishing Group, a division of Random House, Inc., New York.

Del Rey is a registered trademark and the Del Rey colophon is a trademark of
Random House, Inc.

Library of Congress Cataloging-in-Publication Data
Clarke, Arthur Charles, 1917–
Sunstorm / Arthur C. Clarke, Stephen Baxter.—1st ed.
p. cm.—(A time odyssey ; 2)
ISBN 0-345-45250-X
1. Space and time—Fiction.   I. Baxter, Stephen.   II. Title.

PR6005.L36S86 2005
823'.914—dc22   2004062354

Printed in the United States of America

Del Rey Books website address: www.delreybooks.com

2 4 6 8 9 7 5 3 1

First Edition

Book design by Julie Schroeder

SUNSTORM

PART 1
A BALEFUL SUN

1: RETURN

Bisesa Dutt gasped, and staggered.

She was standing. She didn't know where she was.

Music was playing.

She stared at a wall, which showed the magnified image of an impossibly beautiful young man crooning into an old-fashioned microphone. Impossible, yes; he was a synth-star, a distillation of the inchoate longings of subteen girls. "My God, he looks like Alexander the Great."

Bisesa could barely take her eyes off the wall's moving colors, its brightness. She had forgotten how drab and dun-colored Mir had been. But then, Mir had been another world altogether.

Aristotle said, "Good morning, Bisesa. This is your regular alarm call. Breakfast is waiting downstairs. The news headlines today are—"

"Shut up." Her voice was a dusty desert croak.

"Of course." The synthetic boy sang on softly.

She glanced around. This was her bedroom, in her London apartment. It seemed small, cluttered. The bed was big, soft, not slept in.

She walked to the window. Her military-issue boots were heavy on the carpet and left footprints of crimson dust. The sky was gray, on the cusp of sunrise, and the skyline of London was emerging from the flatness of silhouette.

"Aristotle."

"Bisesa?"

"What's the date?"

"Tuesday."

"The *date*."

"Ah. The ninth of June, 2037."

"I should be in Afghanistan."

Aristotle coughed. "I've grown used to your sudden changes of plans, Bisesa. I remember once—"

"Mum?"

The voice was small, sleepy. Bisesa turned.

Myra was barefoot, her tummy stuck out, fist rubbing at one eye, hair tousled, a barely awake eight-year-old. She was wearing her favorite pajamas, the ones across which cartoon characters gamboled, even though they were now about two sizes too small for her. "You didn't say you were coming home."

Something broke inside Bisesa. She reached out. "Oh, Myra—"

Her daughter recoiled. "You *smell* funny."

Shocked, Bisesa glanced down at herself. In her jumpsuit, scuffed and torn and coated with sweat-soaked sand, she was as out of place in this twenty-first-century London flat as if she had been wearing a spacesuit.

She forced a smile. "I guess I need a shower. Then we'll have breakfast, and I'll tell you all about it . . ."

The light changed, subtly. She turned to the window.

There was an Eye over the city, a silver sphere, floating like a barrage balloon. She couldn't tell how far away it was, or how big. But she knew it was an instrument of the Firstborn, who had transported her to Mir, another world, and brought her home.

And over the rooftops of London, a baleful sun was rising.

2: THE PEAK OF ETERNAL LIGHT

Mikhail Martynov had devoted his life to the study of Earth's star. And from the first moment he saw the sun, at the beginning of that fateful day, he knew, deep in his bones, that something was wrong.

"Good morning, Mikhail. The time on the Moon is two o'clock in the morning. Good morning, Mikhail. The time is two o'clock and fifteen seconds. Good morning . . ."

"Thank you, Thales." But he was already up and moving. As always he had woken to within a minute of his personal schedule, without need of Thales's softly spoken electronic wake-up call, a schedule he kept independently of the Houston time to which the rest of the Moon was enslaved.

Mikhail was a man of routine. And he would begin the day, as he began every day of his long solitary watches in this Space Weather Service Station, with a walk into the sunlight.

He took a quick breakfast of fruit concentrate and water. He always drank the water pure, never polluted with coffee granules or tea leaves, for it was water from the Moon, the result of billions of years of slow cometary accretion and now mined and processed for his benefit by million-dollar robots; he believed it deserved to be savored.

He clambered briskly into his EVA suit. Comfortable and easy to use, the suit was the result of six decades' development from the clumsy armor worn by the *Apollo* astronauts. And it was smart, too; some said so smart it could go out Moonwalking by itself.

But smart suit or not, Mikhail worked cautiously through a series of manual checks of the suit's vital systems. He lived alone here at the Moon's South Pole, save for the electronic omnipresence of Thales, and everybody knew that low gravity made you dumb— the "space stupids," they called it. Mikhail was well aware of the importance of concentrating on the chores necessary to keep himself alive.

Still, it was only minutes before he was locked tight into the warm enclosure of the suit. Through the slight distortion of his wedge-shaped visor he peered out at his small living quarters. He was a man equipped for interplanetary space, standing incongruously in a clutter of laundry and unwashed dishes.

Then, with a grace born of long practice, he pushed his way out through the airlock, and then the small dustlock beyond, and emerged onto the surface of the Moon.

Standing on the slope of a crater rim mountain, Mikhail was in shadow broken only by sparse artificial lighting. Above him stars crowded a silent sky. When he looked up—he had to lean back in his stiff suit—he could make out dazzling splashes of light high on the crater wall, places the low polar sunlight could reach. Solar-cell arrays and an antenna farm had been placed up there in the light, as well as the sun sensors that were the Station's main purpose.

This Space Weather Service Station, dug into the wall of a crater called Shackleton, was one of the Moon's smaller habitats, just a few inflatable domes linked by low tunnels and heaped over by a layer of charcoal-gray Moon dust.

Unprepossessing the hab itself may have been, but it was situated in one of the Moon's more remarkable locations. Unlike the Earth, the Moon's axis has no significant tilt; there are no lunar seasons. And at the Moon's South Pole the sun never rises high in the sky. There the shadows are always long—and, in some places, permanent. Thus the pool of darkness in which Mikhail stood had been unbroken for billions of years, save by humans.

Mikhail looked down the slope, beyond the low bulges of the Station domes. On Shackleton's floor floodlights revealed a complex tangle of quarries and lumbering machines. Down there robots toiled over the real treasure of this place: water.

When the *Apollo* astronauts had brought home their first dusty Moon rocks, the geologists had been dumbfounded that the samples contained not a trace of water, not even bound chemically into the mineral structures. It took some decades to unravel the truth. The Moon was no sister world of Earth but a daughter, created in the early days of the solar system when a collision with another infant world had smashed apart a proto-Earth. The debris that had eventually coalesced into the Moon had been superheated until it glowed blue-white, in the process driving off every trace of water. Later, comets had splashed on the Moon's surface. Out of the billions of tonnes of water delivered by these lesser impacts, most had been lost immediately. But a trace, just a trace, had found its way to the permanently shadowed floors of the polar craters, a gift of water to the Moon as if in recompense for the circumstances of its birth.

By Earth's standards the Moon's water was little enough—not much more than a respectably sized lake—but for human colonists it was a treasure beyond price, literally worth far more than its weight in gold. It was invaluable for the scientists too, as it bore a record of eons of cometary formation, and offered indirect clues to the formation of Earth's oceans, which had also been bequeathed by cometary impacts.

Mikhail's interest in this place was not lunar ice, however, but solar fire.

He turned away from the shadows and began to toil up the steepening slope of the rim mountain toward the light. The path was just a trail, beaten flat by human footprints. It was marked by streetlights, as everybody called them, small globe lamps hung from poles, so he could see what he was doing.

The slope was steep, each step an effort even in the Moon's gentle one-sixth gravity. His suit helped, with a subtle hum from exoskeletal servos and a high-pitched whir of the fans and pumps that labored to keep his faceplate clear of condensed sweat. He was

soon breathing hard, and his muscles ached pleasantly: this walk
was his daily constitutional.

At last he reached the summit of the mountain and emerged
into flat sunlight. A small collection of robot sensors huddled here,
peering with unending electronic patience at the sun. But the light
was too brilliant for Mikhail's eyes, and his visor quickly opaqued.

The view around him was still more dramatic, and complex.
He was standing on the rim of Shackleton, itself a comparatively
minor crater, but here at its western rim Shackleton intersected the
circles of two other craters. The landscape was jumbled on a superhuman scale: even the craters' far rims were hidden by the Moon's
horizon. But with long practice Mikhail had trained himself to
make out the chains of mountains, slowly curving, that marked the
perimeters of these overlapping scars. And all this was thrown into
stark relief by the low light of the sun as it rolled endlessly around
the horizon, the long shadows it cast turning like clock hands.

The South Pole, shaped when the Moon was young by an immense impact that had bequeathed it the deepest crater in all the
solar system, was the most contorted landscape on the Moon. A
greater contrast to the flat basalt plain of Tranquillity where Armstrong and Aldrin had first landed, far to the north close to the
Moon's equator, would be hard to imagine.

And this peak was a special place. Even here among the mountains of the Pole, most places knew some night, as the passing shadows of one crater wall or another blocked out the light. But the
peak on which Mikhail stood was different. Geological chance had
left it steeper and a little taller than its cousins to either side, and so
no shadow ever reached its summit. While the Station, only footsteps away, was in perpetual darkness, this place was in permanent
sunlight; it was the Peak of Eternal Light. There was nowhere like
this on tipped-over Earth, and only a handful of locations like it on
the Moon.

There was no morning here, no true night; it was no wonder
that Mikhail's personal clock drifted away from the consensus of
the rest of the Moon's inhabitants. But it was a strange, still landscape that he had grown to love. And there was no better place in

the Earth–Moon system to study the sun, which never set from this airless sky.

But today, as he stood here, something troubled him.

Of course he was alone; it was inconceivable that anybody could sneak up on the Station without a hundred automatic systems alerting him. The silent sentinels of the solar monitors showed no signs of disturbance or change, either—not that a cursory eyeball inspection of their casings, wrapped in thick meteorite shielding and Kevlar, would have told him anything. So what was troubling him? The stillness of the Moon was an uncomfortable place to be having such feelings, and Mikhail shivered, despite the comfortable warmth of his suit.

Then he understood. "Thales. Show me the sun."

Closing his eyes, he lifted his face toward the glare.

When he opened his eyes Mikhail inspected a strange sun.

The center of his faceplate had blocked much of the light of the main disk. But he could make out the sun's atmosphere, the corona, a diffuse glow spreading over many times the sun's diameter. The corona had a smooth texture that always reminded him of mother-of-pearl. But he knew that that smoothness masked an electromagnetic violence that dwarfed any human technology—indeed, a violence that was a principal cause of the damaging space weather he had devoted his own life to monitoring.

At the center of the corona he made out the disk of the sun itself, reduced by the visor's filters to a sullen, coal-like glow. He called for magnification and could make out a speckling that might be granules, the huge convection cells that tiled the sun's surface. And just visible near the very center of the disk, he made out a darker patch—obviously not a granule, but much more extensive.

"An active region," he murmured.

"And a big one," Thales replied.

"I don't have my log to hand . . . Am I looking at 12687?" For decades humans had been numbering the active regions they observed on the sun, the sources of flares and other irritations.

"No," Thales said smoothly. "Active Region 12687 is subsiding, and is a little farther west."

"Then what—"

"This region has no number. It is too new."

Mikhail whistled. Active regions usually took days to develop. By studying the resonances of the sun, immense slow sound waves that passed through its structure, you could usually spot major regions on the far side, even before the star's stately rotation brought them into view. But this beast, it seemed, was different.

"The sun is restless today," Mikhail murmured.

"Mikhail, your tone of voice is unusual. Did you suspect the active region was there before you asked for the display?"

Mikhail had spent a lot of time alone with Thales, and he thought nothing of this show of curiosity. "One gets an instinct for these things."

"The human sensorium remains a mystery, doesn't it, Mikhail?"

"Yes, it does."

Out of the corner of his eye Mikhail spotted movement. He turned away from the sun. When his faceplate cleared he made out a light, crawling toward him through the lunar shadows. It was a sight almost as unusual, for Mikhail, as the face of the troubled sun.

"It seems I have a visitor. Thales, you'd better make sure we have enough hot water for the shower." He began to pick his way back down the trail, taking care to plan every step in advance despite his mounting excitement. "This looks like it's going to be quite a day," he said.

3: ROYAL SOCIETY

Siobhan McGorran sat alone in a deep armchair. She had her personal softscreen unrolled on her lap, a cup of rather bitter coffee on the occasional table at her side, and her phone clamped to her ear. She was rehearsing the lecture she was to give to an audience of her most distinguished peers in less than half an hour.

She read aloud, " '2037 promises to be the most significant year for cosmology since 2003, when the basic components of the universe—the proportions of baryonic matter, dark matter, and dark energy—were first correctly determined. I was eleven years old in 2003, and I remember how excited I was when the results from the Wilkinson Microwave Anisotropy Probe came in. I suppose I wasn't a very cool teenager! But to me, MAP was a robot Columbus. That intrepid cosmology probe was sent off in the hope of finding a dark-matter China, but en route it stumbled over a dark-energy America. And just as Columbus's discoveries fixed the geography of Earth forever in human minds, so we learned the geography of the universe in 2003. Now, in 2037, thanks to the results we anticipate from the latest Quintessence Anisotropy Probe, we—' "

The room lights blinked, making her stumble in her reading.

She heard her mother tut. "And so on and so forth," Maria said, her soft Irish lilt exaggerated by the phone's tiny speaker. "In time, after a lot of technical guff about this old spaceship nobody remembers, I suppose you'll grope your way back to the point."

Siobhan suppressed a sigh. "Mother, I'm the Astronomer Royal, and this is the Royal Society. I'm making the keynote speech! 'Technical guff' is expected."

"And you never were very good at analogies, dear."

"You could be a *bit* supportive." She sipped her coffee, taking care not to spill a drop on her best suit. "I mean, look where your little girl is today." She flicked on her phone's vision options so her mother could see.

These were the City of London Rooms in the Royal Society's offices in Carlton Terrace. She was immersed in rich antiquity, with chandeliers overhead and a marble fireplace at her side.

"What a lovely room," Maria murmured. "You know, we have a lot to thank the Victorians for."

"The Royal Society is a lot older than the Victorians—"

"There are no chandeliers *here,* I can tell you," Maria said. "Nothing but smelly old people, myself included."

"That's demographics for you."

Maria was in Guy's Hospital, close to London Bridge, only a few hundred meters from Carlton Terrace. She was waiting for an appointment concerning her skin cancers. For people who had grown old under a porous sky it was a common complaint, and Maria was having to queue.

Siobhan heard raised voices in the background. "Is there a problem?"

"A ruckus at the drinks machine," Maria said. "Somebody's credit-chip implant has been rejected. People are a bit excitable generally. It's a funny sort of day, isn't it? Something to do with the odd sky, maybe."

Siobhan glanced around. "It's not much calmer here." As the start of the conference had approached, she had been grateful to be left alone with her coffee and a chance to run through her notes, even if she had felt duty-bound to call her mother at Guy's. But now everybody seemed to be crowding at the window, peering out at the odd sky. It was an amusing sight, she supposed, a clutch of internationally renowned scientists jostling like little kids trying to glimpse a pop star. But what were they looking at?

"Mother—what 'odd sky'?"

Maria replied caustically, "Maybe you should go take a look yourself. You are the Astronomer Royal, and—" The phone connection fizzed and cut out.

Siobhan was briefly baffled; that *never* happened. "Aristotle, redial, please."

"Yes, Siobhan."

Her mother's voice returned after a couple of seconds. "Hello? . . ."

"I'm here," Siobhan said. "Mother, professional astronomers don't do much stargazing nowadays." Especially not a cosmologist like Siobhan, whose concern was with the universe on the vastest scales of space and time, not the handful of dull objects that could be seen with the naked eye.

"But even you must have noticed the aurora this morning."

Of course she had. In midsummer Siobhan always rose about six, to get in her daily quota of jogging around Hyde Park before the heat of the day became unbearable. This morning, even though the sun had long been above the horizon, she had seen that subtle wash of crimson and green in the northern sky—clearly three-dimensional, bright curtains and streamers of it, an immense structure of magnetism and plasma towering above the Earth.

Maria said, "An aurora is something to do with the sun, isn't it?"

"Yes. Flares, the solar wind." To her shame, Siobhan found she wasn't even sure if the sun was near the maximum of its cycle right now. Some Astronomer Royal she was proving to be.

Anyhow, though the aurora was undeniably a spectacular sight, and it was very unusual to be so bright as far south as London, Siobhan knew it was nothing but a second-order effect of the interaction of solar plasma with the Earth's magnetic field, and therefore not particularly interesting. She had continued her jogging, not at all motivated to join the rows of slack-jawed dog walkers staring at the sky. And she certainly wasn't sorry she missed the brief panic as people had assailed the emergency services with pointless calls, imagining London was on fire.

Everybody was still at the window. It *was* all a bit strange, she conceded.

She set aside her coffee and, phone in hand, walked up to the window. She couldn't see much past the shoulders of jostling cosmologists: a glimpse of green from the park, a washed-out blue sky. The window was sealed shut to allow the air-conditioning to work, but she thought she could hear a lot of traffic noise: the blaring of horns, sirens.

Toby Pitt spotted her at the back of the pack. A big, affable bear of a man with a strangulated Home Counties accent, Toby worked for the Royal Society; he was the manager of the conference today. "Siobhan! I won't make jokes about the Astronomer Royal being the last to show any interest in the sky."

She showed him her phone. "No need. My mother's already been there."

"It's quite a view, though. Come and see." He extended his massive arm around her shoulders and, with a skillful combination of physical presence and smiling tact, managed to shepherd her through the crowd to the window.

The City of London Rooms had a fine view of the Mall, and of St. James' Park beyond. The grass of the park glowed lurid green, no longer a native specimen but a tough, thick-leaved drought-resistant breed imported from southern Texas, and the relentless sprinklers sent sprays of water shimmering into the air.

But the traffic in the Mall was jammed. The smart cars had calmly packed themselves up in an optimal queuing pattern, but their frustrated drivers were pounding at their horns, and heat haze rose in a shimmer in the humid air. Looking up the road Siobhan saw that the traffic control lights and lane guides were blinking, apparently at random: no wonder the traffic was snarled.

She looked up. The sun, riding high, flooded the cloudless air with light. Even so, when she shielded her eyes she could still make out a tracery of auroral bands in the sky. She became aware of a noise beyond the blare of the traffic in the Mall, a softer din, muffled by the thick sealed window. It was a growl of frustrated driving that seemed to be rising from across the city. This snarl-up wasn't local, then.

For the first time that day she felt a flicker of unease. She thought of her daughter, Perdita, at college today. Perdita, twenty years old, was a sensible young adult. But still . . .

There was a new silence, a shift in the light. People stirred, perturbed. Glancing over her shoulder Siobhan saw that the room lights had failed. That subtle change in the ambient noise must mean the air-conditioning had packed up, too.

Toby Pitt spoke quickly into a phone. Then he held up his hands and announced, "Nothing to worry about, ladies and gentlemen. It isn't just us; the whole of this part of London seems to be suffering something of a brownout. But we have a backup generator that should be coming online soon." He winked at Siobhan and said softly, "If we can persuade the ratty old thing to start up in the first place." But he raised his phone to his ear again, and concern creased his face.

In the heat of the June day, thirty-plus degrees Celsius, the room was already warming up, and Siobhan's trouser suit was starting to feel heavy and uncomfortable.

From beyond the window there was a crumpling noise, a series of pops, like small fireworks, and a din of wailing car alarms. The cosmologists gasped, a collective impulse. Siobhan pushed forward to see.

That queue of traffic on the Mall was just as stationary as before. But the cars had lurched forward, each smashing into the one in front like a gruesome Newton's cradle. People were getting out of their vehicles; some of them looked hurt. Suddenly the jam had turned from an orderly inconvenience into a minor disaster of crumpled metal, leaking lubricants, and scattered injuries. There was no sign of police or ambulances.

Siobhan was baffled. She had literally never seen anything like it. All cars nowadays were individually smart. They took data and instructions from traffic control systems and navigational satellites, and were able to avoid cars, pedestrians, and other obstacles in their immediate surroundings. Crashes were virtually unheard of, and traffic deaths had dwindled to a minimum. But the scene below was reminiscent of the motorway pileups that had still blighted Britain during her childhood in the 1990s. Was it possible that *all* the cars' electronic guidance systems had failed at once?

Light flared, dazzling her. She flinched, raising her hand. When she could see again, she made out a pall of black smoke, rising from somewhere to the south of the river, its origin lost in murky smog. Then a shock wave reached the Society building. The tough old structure shuddered, and the window creaked. She heard a more remote tinkle of glass, the blaring of alarms, and screams.

It had been an explosion, a big one. The cosmologists murmured, grave and apprehensive.

Toby Pitt touched her shoulder. His face had lost all its humor now. "Siobhan. We've had a call from the Mayor's office. They're asking for you."

"Me? . . ." She glanced around, feeling lost. She had no idea what was happening. "The conference—"

"I think everybody will accept a postponement, in the circumstances."

"How can I get there? If that mess outside is typical—"

He shook his head. "We can videoconference from here. Follow me."

As she followed his broad-shouldered form out of the City Rooms, she raised her own phone. "Mother?"

"You're still there? All I heard was chattering."

"That's cosmologists for you. I'm fine, Mother. And you—"

"So am I. That bang was nowhere near me."

"Good," Siobhan said fervently.

"I phoned Perdita. The line was bad, but she's all right. They're keeping them at college until things settle down."

Siobhan felt huge, unreasonable relief. "Thank you."

Maria said, "The doctors are running everywhere. Their pagers seem to be on the blink. You'd think casualties would be

coming in but I've seen nobody yet . . . Do you think it was terror-
ists?"

"I don't know." Toby Pitt had reached the door and was beck-
oning her. "I'll try to keep the connection open." She hurried from
the room.

4: VISITOR

The rover reached the Station long before Mikhail had clambered his way back down the trail. The visitor waited at the hab entrance with an impatience the surface suit couldn't disguise.

Mikhail thought he recognized the figure just by his stance. Though its population was scattered around its globe, on the human scale the Moon was a very small town, where everybody knew everybody else.

Thales confirmed it in a whisper. "That is Doctor Eugene Mangles, the notorious neutrino hunter. How exciting."

That cursed computer-brain is teasing me, Mikhail thought irritably; Thales knows my feelings too well. But it was true that his heart beat a little faster with anticipation.

Encased in their suits, Mikhail and Eugene faced each other awkwardly. Eugene's face, a sculpture of planed shadows, was barely visible through his visor. He looked very young, Mikhail thought. Despite his senior position Eugene was just twenty-six—a maverick boy genius.

For a moment Mikhail was stuck for something to say. "I'm sorry," he said. "I don't get too many visitors out here."

Eugene's social skills seemed even more underdeveloped. "Have you seen it yet?"

Mikhail knew what he meant. "The sun?"

"The active region."

Of course this boy had come here for the sun. Why else visit a solar weather station? Certainly not for the crusty, early-middle-aged astrophysicist who tended it. And yet Mikhail felt a foolish, quite unreasonable pang of disappointment. He tried to sound welcoming. "But don't you work with neutrinos? I thought your area of study was the core of the sun, not its atmosphere."

"Long story." Eugene glared at him. "This is important. More important than you know, yet. I predicted it."

"What?"

"The active region."

"From your studies of the core? I don't understand."

"Of course you don't," Eugene said, apparently careless of any offense he might cause. "I logged my predictions with Thales and Aristotle, date-stamped to prove it. I've come here to confirm the data. It's come to pass, just as I said it would."

Mikhail forced a smile. "We'll talk it over. Come inside. You can see as much data as you want. Do you like coffee?"

"They have to listen," said Eugene.

They? . . . "About what?"

"The end of the world," Eugene said. "Possibly." He led the way into the dustlock, leaving Mikhail standing openmouthed.

They didn't talk as they worked their way through dustlock and airlock into the hab. Every human on the Moon was still a pioneer, and if you were smart, no matter what was on your mind, as you moved from one safe environment to another through seals and locks and interfaces and in and out of EVA suits, you concentrated on nothing but the life-preserving procedures you were going through. If you *weren't* smart, of course, you would be lucky if you were forcibly shipped out before you killed yourself, or others.

Mikhail, slick with daily practice, was first out of his EVA suit. As the suit slithered to its cleaning station—somewhat grotesquely, its servos dragging it across the floor like an animated flayed skin—Mikhail, in his underwear, went to a sink where he scrubbed his hands in a slow trickle of water. The gray-black dust he had picked up handling the suit, grimy despite the dustlock's best efforts, had rubbed into his pores and under his nails, and was burning slowly with his skin's natural oils, giving off a smell like gunpowder. The Moon's dust had been a problem since the first footsteps taken here: very fine, getting everywhere, and oxidizing enthusiastically whenever it got the chance, the dust corroded everything from mechanical bearings to human mucous membranes.

Of course it wasn't the engineering problems of Moon dust that were on Mikhail's mind right now. He risked a look around. Eugene had taken off boots and gloves, and he lifted his helmet away, shaking his beautiful head to free up thick hair. That was the face Mikhail remembered, the face he had first glimpsed at some meaningless social function in Clavius or Armstrong—a face freshly hardened into manhood, but with the symmetry and delicacy of boyhood, even if the eyes were a little wild—the face that had drawn him as helplessly as a moth to a candle.

As Eugene stripped off his spacesuit Mikhail couldn't help dwelling on an old memory. "Eugene, have you ever heard of *Barbarella*?"

Eugene frowned. "Is she at Clavius?"

"No, no. I mean an old space movie. I'm something of a buff of pre-spaceflight cinema. A young actress called Jane Fonda . . ." Eugene clearly had no idea what he was talking about. "Never mind."

Mikhail made his way to the dome's small shower cubicle, stripped off the last of his clothing, and stood under a jet. The water emerged slowly, in big shimmering low-gravity droplets that fell with magical slowness to the floor, where suction pumps drew in every last precious molecule. Mikhail lifted his face to the stream, trying to calm himself.

Thales said gently, "I've brewed some coffee, Mikhail."

"Thales, that was thoughtful."

"Everything is under control."

"Thank you . . ." Sometimes it really was as if Thales knew Mikhail's moods.

Thales was actually a less sophisticated clone of Aristotle, who was an intelligence emergent from a hundred billion Earth-side computers of all sizes and the networks that linked them. A remote descendant of the search engines of the late twentieth century, Aristotle had become a great electronic mind whose thoughts crackled like lightning across the wired-up face of the Earth; for years he had been a constant companion to all humankind.

When humans had begun their permanent occupation of the Moon at Clavius Base, it had been inconceivable that they should not take Aristotle with them. But it takes light more than a second to travel from Earth to the Moon, and in an environment where death lurks a single error away, such delays were unacceptably long. So Thales had been created, a lunar copy of Aristotle. Thales was updated continually from Aristotle's great memory stores—but he was necessarily simpler than his parent, for the electronic nervous system laid across the Moon was still rudimentary compared to the Earth's.

Simpler or not, Thales did his job. He was certainly smart enough to justify the name he had been given: Thales of Miletus, a sixth-century Greek, had been the first to suggest that the Moon shone not by its own light but by reflection from the sun—and, it was said, he had been the first man to predict a solar eclipse.

For everybody on the Moon, Thales was always there. Often lonely despite his stoical determination, Mikhail had been soothed by Thales's measured, somewhat emotionless voice.

Right now, thinking wistfully of Eugene, he felt he needed soothing.

He knew that Eugene was based at Tsiolkovski. The huge Far-side crater was host to an elaborate underground facility. Buried in the still, cold Moon, undisturbed by tremors, shadowed from Earth's radio clamor and shielded from all radiation except for a little leakage from trace quantities in the lunar rocks, it was an ideal location for hunting neutrinos. Those ghost-like particles scooted through most solid matter as if it weren't even there, thus providing unique data about such inaccessible places as the center of the sun.

But how odd to come all the way to the Moon, and then to burrow into the regolith to do your science, Mikhail thought. There were so many more glamorous places to work—such as the big planet-finder telescope array laid out in a North Pole crater, capable of resolving the surfaces of Earth-like planets orbiting suns spread across fifty light-years.

He longed to discuss this with Eugene, to share something of his life, his impressions of the Moon. But he knew he must keep his reactions to the younger man in appropriate categories.

Since his teens, when he had become fully aware of his sexuality, Mikhail had learned to master his reactions: even in the early twenty-first century, homosexuality was still something of a taboo in Vladivostok. Discovering in himself a powerful intellect, Mikhail had thrown himself into work, and had grown used to a life lived largely alone. He had hoped that when he moved away from home, as his career took him through the rest of the sprawling Eurasian Union as far as London and Paris, and then, at last, off the Earth entirely, he would find himself in more tolerant circles. Well, so he had; but by then it seemed he had grown too used to his own company.

His life of almost monastic isolation had been broken by a few passionate, short-lived love affairs. But now, in his midforties, he was coming to accept the fact that he was never likely to find a partner to share his life. That didn't make him immune to feelings, however. Before today he had barely spoken two words to this handsome boy, Eugene, but that, evidently, had been enough to develop a foolish crush.

He had to put it all aside, though. Whatever Eugene had come to Shackleton for, it wasn't for Mikhail.

The end of the world, the boy had said. Frowning, Mikhail toweled himself dry.

5: EMERGENCY MANAGEMENT

Siobhan was taken to the Council Room on the first floor of the Royal Society building. The room's centerpiece was an oval conference table large enough to seat twenty or more, but Siobhan was alone here save for Toby Pitt. She sat at the head of the table uncertainly. On the wall was a slightly surreal Zulu tapestry, meant to show symbolically the rise of science, and portraits of former fellows—mostly dead white males, though the more recent animated images were more diverse.

Toby tapped at the table's polished surface, which turned transparent to reveal a bank of embedded softscreens. The screens lit up, variously showing scenes of disaster—crashes on the road and rail systems, raw sewage spilling from a pipe onto a beach somewhere, what looked horribly like the wreck of a plane plowed into a Heathrow runway—and concerned faces, most with softscreens in their backgrounds and earpieces clamped to their heads.

One serious-looking young woman seemed to be calling from a police control room. When she caught Siobhan's eye, she nodded. "You're the astronomer."

"The Astronomer Royal, yes."

"Professor McGorran, my name is Phillippa Duflot." Perhaps in her early thirties, alarmingly well spoken, she wore a slightly disheveled business suit. "I work in the Mayor's office; I'm one of her PAs."

"The Mayor—"

"Of London. She asked me to find you."

"Why?"

"Because of the emergency, of course." Phillippa Duflot looked irritated, but she visibly calmed herself; considering the strain she was evidently under, Siobhan thought, her self-control was impressive. "I'm sorry," Phillippa said. "All this has hit us so suddenly, over the last couple of hours or less. We rehearse for the major contingencies we can think of, but we're struggling to cope today. Nobody anticipated the *scale* of this. We're trying to find our feet."

"Tell me how I can help you."

Formally Phillippa was calling on behalf of the London Resilience Forum. This was an interagency body that had been set up following the upsurge in terrorism at the turn of the century. Chaired from the Mayor's office, it contained representatives of the city's emergency services, transport, the utilities, the health services, and local government. There was a separate body responsible for London emergency planning, which also reported in to the Mayor. Above such local bodies were national emergency planning agencies, which reported to the Home Office.

Siobhan learned quickly that most of these agencies were talking shops. The real responsibility for emergency responses lay with the police, and right now the key figure in touch with the Mayor was a chief constable. It was the way things were done in Britain, Siobhan gathered; there was a lack of central control, but a local flexibility and responsiveness that generally worked well. But now that Britain was thoroughly integrated into the Eurasian Union there was also a Union-wide emergency management agency, based on the Americans' FEMA, under whose auspices, some years earlier, firefighters from London had been sent in response to a chemical plant disaster in Moscow.

And today this network of disaster management agencies was buzzing with bad news. London was afflicted by a whole series of interconnected problems, whose root cause Siobhan at first couldn't guess at. Suddenly, all at once, everything was falling apart.

The most immediate problem was the collapse of the power grid. Phillippa bombarded Siobhan with data on areas of brownout and blackout, and images of the consequences: here was an underground shopping mall in Brent Cross, its lights doused and elevators and escalators stalled, thousands of people trapped in a darkness broken only by a ruddy emergency glow.

Phillippa looked doleful. "The very first call we logged today was from a man trapped in his hotel room when the electronic lock jammed up. Since then it's just mushroomed. Every transport system has ground to a halt. People are stranded on planes ramped up on runways; others are trapped in planes that can't land. We don't even have numbers yet. We don't dare think how many people are just trapped in lifts!"

The power system was the problem. Electrical power originated in generating stations—these days mostly nuclear, wind-generated, tidal, and a few fossil-fuel-burning relics. The generators sent out rivers of current in transmission cables at high voltages, more than a hundred thousand volts. These were stopped down at local substations and transformers and sent out through more lines, eventually reaching the level of the few hundred volts that reached businesses and homes.

"And now it's all failing," Siobhan prompted.

"Now it's failing."

Phillippa showed Siobhan an image of a transformer, a unit as big as a house, shaking itself to pieces as its core steel plates crashed and rattled. And here were power lines sagging, smoking, visibly melting, and where they touched trees or other obstacles powerful arcs sparked fires.

This was called magnetostriction, Phillippa said. "The engineers know what's happening. It's just that the GICs today are bigger than anything they've seen before."

"Phillippa—what's a *GIC*?"

"A geomagnetically induced current." Phillippa eyed Siobhan with suspicion, as if she shouldn't have had to explain; perhaps she wondered if she was wasting her time. "We're in the middle of a geomagnetic storm, Professor McGorran. A huge one. It came out of nowhere."

A geomagnetic storm: of course, a storm from the sun, the same cause as the beautiful aurora. Siobhan, her brains clogged in the room's gathering heat, felt dull not to have grasped this at once.

But her basic physics was coming back to her. A geomagnetic storm, a fluctuation of Earth's magnetic field, would induce currents in power lines, which were simply long conductors. And as the induced currents would be direct, while the generated electrical supply was alternating, the system would quickly be overwhelmed.

Phillippa said, "The generating companies are wheeling—"

"Wheeling?"

"Buying in capacity from outside. We have exchange deals with France, primarily. But the French are in trouble, too."

"There must be some tolerance in the system," Siobhan said.

"You'd be surprised," Toby Pitt said. "For fifty years we have been growing our power demands, but have resisted building new power stations. Then you have market forces, which ensure that every component we do install barely has the capacity to do the job that's asked of it—and all at the lowest possible cost. So we have absolutely no resilience." He coughed. "I'm sorry. A hobbyhorse of mine."

"The worst single problem is the loss of air-conditioning," Phillippa said grimly. "It isn't even noon yet."

In a 2030s British midsummer, heat was a routine killer. "People must be dying," Siobhan said, wondering; it was the first time it had really struck her.

"Oh, yes," Phillippa said. "The elderly, the very young, the frail. And we can't get to them. We don't even know how many there are."

Some of the softscreens flickered and went blank. This was the other side of the day's problems, Phillippa said: communications and electronic systems of all kinds were going down.

"It's the satellites," she went on. "The comsats, navigation satellites, the lot—all taking a beating up there. Even land lines are failing."

And as the world's electronic interconnectedness broke down, the smart systems that were embedded in everything, from planes to cars to buildings to clothes and even people's bodies, were all failing. That poor man stuck in his hotel room had only been the first. Commerce was grinding to a halt as electronic money systems failed: Siobhan watched a small riot outside a petrol station where credit implants were suddenly rejected. Only the most robust networks were surviving, such as government and military systems. The Royal Society building happened still to be connected to central services by old-fashioned fiber-optic cables, Siobhan learned; the venerable establishment had been saved by its own lack of investment in more modern facilities.

Siobhan said uncertainly, "And this is another symptom of the storm?"

"Oh, yes. While our priority is London, the emergency isn't just local, or regional, or even national. From what we can tell—data links are crashing all over the place—it's global . . ."

Siobhan was shown a view of the whole world, taken from a remote Earth resources satellite. Over the planet's night side aurorae were painted in delicate, heartbreakingly beautiful swirls. But the world below was not so pretty. Darkened continents were outlined by the lights of the cities strung along their coasts and the major river valleys—but those necklaces of lights were broken. As each outage triggered problems in neighboring regions, the blackouts were spreading like infections. Power utilities were in some places trying to help each other out, but, Phillippa said, there was conflict; Quebec was accusing New York of "stealing" some of its megawatts. In a few places Siobhan saw the ominous glows of fires.

All this in a couple of hours, Siobhan thought. How fragile the world is.

But the satellite imagery was full of hash, and at last it broke down altogether, leaving a pale blue screen.

"Well, this is dreadful. But what can I do?"

Phillippa again looked suspicious. *You need to ask?* "Professor McGorran, this is a geomagnetic storm. Which is primarily caused by problems with the sun."

"Oh. And so you called an astronomer." Siobhan suppressed an urge to laugh. "Phillippa, I'm a cosmologist. I haven't even thought about the sun since my undergraduate days."

Toby Pitt touched her arm. "But you're the Astronomer Royal," he said quietly. "They're out of their depth. Who else are they going to call?"

Of course he was right. Siobhan had always wondered if her

royal warrant, and the vague public notoriety that came with it, was worth the trouble. The first Astronomers Royal, men like Flamsteed and Halley, had run the observatory at Greenwich and had spent most of their time making observations of the sun, Moon, and stars for use in navigation. Now, though, her job was to be a figurehead at conferences like today's, or an easy target for lazy journalists looking for a quote—and, it seemed, an escape route for politicians in a crisis. She said to Toby, "Remind me to quit when this is all over."

He smiled. "But in the meantime . . ." He stood up. "Is there anything you need?"

"Coffee if you can get it, please. Water if not." She raised her own phone to her face; she felt a spasm of guilt that she hadn't even noticed it had lost its signal. "And I need to speak to my mother," she said. "Could you bring me a land line?"

"Of course." He left the room.

Siobhan turned back to Phillippa. "All right. I'll do my best. Keep the line open."

6: FORECAST

Dressed in recycled-paper coveralls, Mikhail and Eugene sat in Mikhail's small, cluttered wardroom.

Eugene cradled a coffee. They were both awkward, silent. It seemed strange to Mikhail that such a handsome kid should be so shy.

"So, neutrinos," Mikhail said tentatively. "Tsiolkovski must be a small place. Cozy! You have many friends there?"

Eugene looked at him as if he were talking in a foreign tongue. "I work alone," he said. "Most of them down there are assigned to the gravity-wave detector."

Mikhail could understand that. Most astronomers and astrophysicists were drawn to the vast and faraway: the evolution of massive stars and the biography of the universe itself, as revealed by exotic signals like gravity waves—*that* was sexy. The study of the solar system, even the sun itself, was local, parochial, limited, and swamped with detail.

"That's always been the trouble with getting people to work on space weather, even though it's of such practical importance," he said. "The sun–Earth environment is a tangle of plasma clouds and electromagnetic fields, and the physics involved is equally messy." He smiled. "We're in the same boat, I suppose, me stranded at the Pole of the Moon, you stuck down a Farside hole, both pursuing our unglamorous work."

Eugene looked at him more closely. Mikhail had the odd feeling that this was the first time the younger man had actually *noticed* him. Eugene said, "So what got you interested in the sun?"

Mikhail shrugged. "I liked the practical application. The sky reaching down to the Earth . . . Most cosmological entities are abstract and remote, but not the sun. And besides, we Russians have always been drawn to the sun. Tsiolkovski himself, our great space visionary, drew on sun worship in some of his thinking, so it's said."

"Maybe it's because you don't get to see much of it so far north."

Mikhail was taken aback. Was that an actual joke? He forced a laugh. "Come," he said, standing. "I think it's time we visited the monitor room."

They had to pass through a short, low tunnel to another dome. And in the monitor room, the younger man stared around, openmouthed.

The room was a twenty-first-century shrine to Sol. Its walls were coated by glowing softscreens that showed images of the sun's surface or its atmosphere, or the space between Earth and sun, crowded with dynamic structures of plasma and electromagnetism, or Earth itself and its complicated magnetosphere. The images were displayed in multiple wavelengths—visible light, hydrogen light, calcium light, infrared and ultraviolet, at radio wavelengths—each of them revealing something unique about the sun and its environment. Even more instructive to eyes trained to see were the spectral analyses, spiky graphs that laid bare the secrets of Earth's star.

This was a graphic summary of the work of the Space Weather Service. This lunar post was just one of a network of stations that monitored the sun continually; there were sister stations on all the continents of Earth, while satellites swarmed on looping orbits around the sun. Thus the Service kept myriad eyes trained on the sun.

It was necessary work. The sun has been shining for five billion years, breathing out heat and light and the solar wind, a stream of high-energy charged particles. But it is not unchanging. Even in normal times the solar wind is gusty; great streamers of it pour out of coronal holes, breaks in the sun's outer atmosphere. Meanwhile sunspots, cooler areas dominated by tangles of magnetic fields, were noticed by humans on the sun's surface as early as the fourth century before Christ. From such troubled areas, flares and immense explosions can spew high-frequency radiation and fast-moving charged particles out into space. All this "weather" batters against the layers of air and electromagnetism that shield the Earth.

Through most of human history this went unnoticed, save for the marvelous aurorae irregularly painted over the sky. But if humans aren't generally vulnerable to the storms in space, the electrical equipment they develop is. By 2037 it was nearly two centuries since solar-induced currents in telegraph lines had started to cause headaches for their operators. Since then, the more dependent the human world became on its technology, the more vulnerable it became to the sun's tantrums—as Earth was learning that very day.

For a fragile, highly interconnected high-technology civilization, living with a star, it had been learned, was like living with a bear. It might not do you any harm. But the least you had to do was watch it, very carefully. And that was why the Space Weather Service had been set up.

Though now led by the Eurasian Union, the Space Weather Service had developed from humbler beginnings in the twentieth century, starting with the Americans' Space Environment Center, a joint enterprise of such agencies as NASA, the National Oceanic and Atmospheric Administration, and the Department of Defense.

"Back then the data gathered were patchy," Mikhail said. "Scavenged from science satellites dedicated to other purposes. And forecasting was just guesswork. But a few solar-storm disasters around the solar max of 2011 put paid to *that*. These days we have a pretty comprehensive data set, continually updated in real time. The forecasting systems are big numerical-prediction suites based on magneto-hydrodynamics, plasma physics, and the like. We have a complete chain of theoretical modeling from the surface of the sun to the surface of the Earth—"

But Eugene wasn't listening. He tapped a hydrogen-light image. "*That* is the problem," he said.

It was the new active region. Visibly darker than the surrounding photosphere, it was an ugly S-shaped scar. "I admit it's a puzzle," Mikhail said. "At this stage of the solar cycle you wouldn't expect something like that."

"*I* expected it," Eugene said. "And that's the whole point."

Carefully Mikhail said, "The end of the world?"

"Not today. Today is just a precursor. But it will be bad enough. That's why I've come here. You have to warn them." His eyes were huge and dark, haunted. "I have time-stamped predictions."

"You told me that."

"Even so they won't pay any attention to me. But they will listen to you. After all, this is your job. And now that you've got proof, you'll have to do it, won't you? You'll have to warn them."

Eugene really had no social skills at all, Mikhail thought, with a mix of resentment and pity. "Who are *they*? Who exactly do you want me to warn?"

Eugene spread his hands. "For a start, everybody vulnerable. On the Moon. On the Space Station. On Mars, and aboard *Aurora 2*."

"And on Earth?"

"Oh, yes. And Earth." Eugene glanced at his watch. "But by now Earth is already being hit."

Mikhail studied his face for a long moment. Then he called for Thales.

7: MASS EJECTION

Siobhan worked the screens in the conference table, seeking information.

It wasn't easy. Solar studies and space weather simply weren't in Siobhan's domain of specialty. Aristotle was able to help, though he seemed somewhat absentminded at times; she realized uneasily that the erosion of the world's interconnectivity, on which he was based, had to be affecting him, too.

She quickly discovered that there were solar observatories all over the world, and off it. She tried to get through to Kitt Peak, Mauna Kea in Hawaii, and the Big Bear observatory in southern California. She didn't reach a human being in any of these sites, predictably enough; even if the comms systems weren't down, they were no doubt already overwhelmed with calls. But she did learn of the existence of a "Space Weather Service," a network of observatories, satellites, data banks, and experts that monitored the sun and its stormy environs, and tried to predict the worst of its transgressions. There was even a weather station at the South Pole of the Moon, it seemed.

Despite decades of watching the moody sun, though, only one person had predicted today's unusual events, a young scientist on the Moon called Eugene Mangles, who had logged quite precise forecasts on a few peer-review sites. But the Moon was out of touch.

————

Thirty minutes after last speaking with her, Siobhan called Phillippa Duflot again.

"It's all to do with the sun," she began.

Phillippa said, "We know that much—"

"It has given off what the sungazers call a 'coronal mass ejection.'"

She described how the corona, the sun's extended outer atmosphere, is held together by powerful magnetic fields rooted in the sun itself. Sometimes these fields get tangled up, often over active regions. Such tangles will trap bubbles of superheated plasma, emitted by the sun, and then violently release them. That was what had happened this morning, over the big sunspot continent the experts were calling Active Region 12688: a mass of billions of tonnes of plasma, knotted up by its own magnetic field, had been hurled from the sun at a respectable fraction of the speed of light.

"The ejection took less than an hour to get here," Siobhan said. "I understand that's *fast,* for such phenomena. Nobody saw it coming, and nobody was particularly expecting it to happen at this stage of the sun's cycle anyhow." Except, she made a mental note, that lone astronomer on the Moon.

Phillippa prompted, "So this mass of gas headed for the Earth—"

"The gas itself is sparser than an industrial vacuum," Siobhan said. "It's the energy contained in its particles and fields that has done the damage."

When it hit, the mass ejection had battered at the Earth's magnetic field. The field normally shields the planet, and even low-orbiting satellites, but today the mass ejection had pushed the field down beneath the orbits of many satellites. Exposed to waves of energetic solar particles, the satellites' systems absorbed doses of static electricity that discharged wherever they could.

"Imagine miniature lightning bolts sparking around your circuit boards—"

"Not good," Phillippa said.

"No. Charged particles also leaked into the upper atmosphere, dumping their energy on the way—that was the cause of the aurorae. And Earth's magnetic field suffered huge variations. Perhaps you know that electricity and magnetism are linked. A changing magnetic field induces currents in conductors."

Phillippa said hesitantly, "Is that how a dynamo works?"

"Yes! Exactly. When it fluctuates, Earth's field causes immense currents to flow in the body of the Earth itself—and in any conducting materials it can find."

"Such as our power distribution networks," Phillippa said.

"Or our comms links. Hundreds of thousands of kilometers of conducting cables, all suddenly awash with fast-varying, high-voltage currents."

"All right. So what do we do about it?"

"Do? Why, there's nothing we can do." The question seemed absurd to Siobhan; she had to suppress an unkind impulse to laugh. "This is the sun we're talking about." A star whose energy output in *one second* was more than humankind could muster in a million years. This mass ejection had caused a geomagnetic storm that went far off the scales established by the patient solar weather watchers, but to the sun it was nothing but a minor spasm. *Do,* indeed: you didn't *do* anything about the sun, except keep out of its way. "We just have to sit it out."

Phillippa frowned. "How long will it last?"

"Nobody knows. This is unprecedented, as far as I can make out. But the mass ejection is fast moving and will pass over us soon. Only hours more, perhaps?"

Phillippa said earnestly, "We need to know. It's not just power we have to think about. There's sewage, the water supply . . ."

"The Thames barrier," Toby said. "When is high tide?"

"I don't know," Phillippa said, making a note. "Professor McGorran, can you try to nail down a timescale?"

"Yes, I'll try." She closed down the link.

"Of course," Toby said to Siobhan, "the sensible thing to do would be to build our systems more robustly in the first place."

"Ah, but when have we humans ever been sensible?"

Siobhan continued to work. But as time wore on the comms links only worsened.

And she was distracted by more images.

Here was an immense explosion in the great trans-European pipeline that nowadays brought Britain most of its natural gas. Like cables, pipelines were also conductors thousands of kilometers long, and the currents induced in them could increase corrosion to the point of failure. Pipelines were grounded at frequent intervals to avert this problem. But this pipeline, a very modern structure, had been made of ethylene for economy's sake, and was a good deal easier to ignite. Numbly Siobhan studied the statistics of this one incident: a wall of flame a kilometer wide, trees felled for hundreds of meters around, hundreds feared dead . . . She tried to imagine such horror multiplied a thousandfold around the world.

And it wasn't just humans and their technological systems that were affected. Here was a random bit of news of flocks of birds apparently losing their way, and a haunting image of whales beached on a North American shore.

Toby Pitt brought her a phone, a clunky set trailing a cord. "I'm sorry it took so long," he said.

The phone must have been at least thirty years old, but, connected to the Society's reliable fiber-optic backup lines, it worked, more or less. It took her a few tries to get through to Guy's, and then to persuade a receptionist to find her mother.

Maria sounded scared, but in control. "I'm fine," she insisted. "The power outages have just been blinks; the emergency system is working well. But things are very strange here."

Siobhan nodded. "The hospitals must be overwhelmed. Heat victims—the accidents in traffic—"

"Not just that," Maria said. "People are coming in because their pacemakers are playing up, or their servo-muscles, or bowel control implants. And there's a whole *flood* of heart attack victims, it seems to me. Even people with no implants at all."

Of course, Siobhan mused. The human body itself is a complex system controlled by bioelectricity, itself subject to electrical and magnetic fields. We are all tied to the sun, she thought, like the birds and the whales, tied by invisible lines of force nobody even suspected existed a couple of centuries ago. And we are so very vulnerable to the sun's tantrums, even our very bodies.

Toby Pitt said, "Siobhan, I'm sorry to interrupt. You've another call."

"Who is it?"

"The Prime Minister."

"Good Lord." She thought it over, and asked, "Which one—?"

The phone came alive in her hand. As electricity jolted into her body the muscles of her right arm turned rigid. Then the phone shot from her grasp and slid over the table, showering blue sparks.

PART 2
PRESAGINGS

8: RECOVERY

Somebody was hammering on the door of the flat.

Bisesa had learned to mask her reactions in front of Myra. Fixing a smile on her face, ignoring the racing of her heart, she got up from the sofa slowly and folded away her magazine.

Myra turned her head suspiciously. She was lying on her belly watching a softwall synth-soap. There was a lot of knowingness in those eight-year-old eyes, Bisesa thought, too much. Myra knew that something strange had happened to the world a few days ago, and it was odd that her mother was here in the first place. But there was a sort of understanding between the two of them, a conspiracy. They would *act* normal, and maybe at some point things would turn out to *be* normal after all: that was their unspoken hope.

Bisesa could use a whispered command to Aristotle to turn a section of the door transparent. But as a British Army officer trained in combat technology, she had never quite trusted electronic senses, and she peered through the old-fashioned spy hole to double-check.

It was only Linda. Bisesa opened the door.

Linda was a short, stocky, competent-looking girl. Aged twenty-two, she was Bisesa's cousin, a student at Imperial College studying biospheric ethics. For the last two years she had served as Myra's nanny during Bisesa's long postings abroad. Right now she held two bulging paper bags of groceries, with two more stacked by her feet, and she was sweating profusely. "Sorry for kicking the door down," she said. "I thought these damn bags would give way."

"Well, you made it." Bisesa let Linda in and carefully double-locked the door.

They hauled the groceries to the flat's small kitchen. Most of what Linda had bought were staples—milk, bread, quorn products, some limp-looking vegetables, and mottled apples. Linda apologized for the meagerness of her haul, but it could have been worse; Bisesa, who followed the news assiduously, knew that London had come close to a strict rationing system.

For Bisesa, unpacking groceries was oddly nostalgic, something she used to do every Friday evening with her mother, who would do her "big shop" at the end of the family farm's long week. These days family habits had changed; most groceries were remote-ordered and delivered. But days after June 9 the transport and distribution services were still clogged up, and everybody had had to return to the stores in person to go through the rituals of carts and checkouts.

This was a new experience to Linda, and she was complaining briskly. "You wouldn't believe the queues. They actually have bouncers on the meat counters. The checkout registers are operating now, so that's a blessing; no more hand-calculated bills. But a lot of people still won't swipe through." A sight you often saw since June 9 was the telltale forearm scar of somebody who'd had to have her implanted ident chip replaced, the original having been wiped and fried by the solar frenzy of that day.

"Still no bottled water," Bisesa said.

"Not yet, no," Linda said. She reflexively turned on the taps at the kitchen sink, to no effect. The solar storm had induced corrosive currents in London's hundreds of kilometers of aging pipe work. So even when they got the pumps working, no water could be delivered to many parts of the city until the engineers and their smart little mole-shaped robots had fixed up the network once more. Linda sighed. "Looks like it'll be the standpipe again."

Right now a corner of the softwall was showing an aerial view of London, overlaid by an outline map of the continuing power-outs, with a few sparks that marked riots, lootings, and other instances of disorder. Blue asterisks showed the positions of standpipes, most of them along the banks of the Thames. Bisesa found this evidence of the resilience of the old city oddly moving. Long before the Romans came to found London in the first place, Celts had fished the Thames in their wicker boats, and now in this twenty-first-century crisis Londoners were drawn back to their river once again.

Linda looked at her callused palms. "You know, Bis, I can manage the shopping. But I could sure do with some help with the water."

"No," Bisesa said immediately. Then, more considered, she shook her head. "I'm sorry." Reflexively she glanced across at Myra, who was engrossed once more in the endlessly elaborating luridness of her softwall soap. "I'm not ready to go out yet."

Linda, still packing food away, said in a deliberately casual tone, "I've been asking Aristotle for advice."

"About what?"

"Agoraphobia. It's more common than you'd think. I mean, how would you *know* if somebody was a prisoner in her home? You'd never meet her! But there are treatments. Support groups—"

"Lin, I appreciate your concern. But I'm not agoraphobic. And I'm not crazy."

"Then what—"

Bisesa said lamely, "I just need more time."

"I'm here if you need me."

"I know . . ."

Bisesa returned to her vigil with Myra, and the softwall.

Maybe she wasn't crazy. But she couldn't explain to Linda any of her strange circumstances.

She couldn't explain how she had been on patrol with her Army unit on its peacekeeping duties in Afghanistan, how she had suddenly found herself hurled beyond the walls of space and time, how she had learned to construct a new life for herself on a strange patchwork other-Earth they had called Mir—and how she had somehow been brought home, through a kaleidoscope of even stranger visions.

And she couldn't explain to her cousin the strangest detail of all: how she had been serving in Afghanistan on June 8, 2037, but had found herself here in London the very next day, June 9, the day of the storm—but in her memories, more than *five years* had passed between those two events.

At least she was restored to Myra, the daughter she thought she had lost. But this was a Myra who had grown older only by a *day,* while years had passed for Bisesa. And Myra, who studied her mother with the searching gaze of a neglected child, could surely see the sudden strands of gray hair, the deeper wrinkles around Bisesa's eyes. There was a distance between them that might never heal.

So arbitrary had been the way she had been ripped out of her life before that she couldn't get over the fear that it might, somehow, happen all over again. And that was why she couldn't leave the flat. It wasn't a fear of the open; it was a fear of losing Myra.

After a few minutes she whispered a command to Aristotle. He resumed the compulsive search of the world's news outlets and databases she had ordered.

June 9 had been a worldwide catastrophe, by orders of magnitude the worst solar storm ever experienced, and days later it absorbed even Aristotle's mighty energies to keep up with the flood of words and images. But try as he might, Aristotle couldn't find a single mention of the silver sphere Bisesa had spotted hovering over London on that difficult morning, the thing her companions on Mir would have called an Eye. Even on a day like June 9, a thing like that hovering over London should have been a remarkable sight, the ultimate UFO, the subject of a thousand news items. But nobody else had reported it.

It terrified Bisesa to the root of her soul that only she had seen the Eye. Because that must mean *they,* the Firstborn, the powers behind the Eye and everything else that was happening to her and the world, wanted something of her.

9: LUNAR DESCENT

By the third day of the journey the Moon was huge in the black sky.

Siobhan had to bend her neck to peer through the *Komarov*'s poky little windows of tough, micrometeorite-starred glass. But when she found the Moon's bony crescent she felt a shiver of wonder. How strange this was, she thought. Amid the mundanity of the flight—the usual horrors of airline food, the space sickness, the dismal engineering of zero-gravity toilets—the Moon itself had come swimming out of the dark to greet her, forcing its way into her consciousness with a cold, massive grace.

And yet the most marvelous thing of all was that even here, in the passenger cabin of Earth–Moon shuttle *Komarov,* her mobile phone worked.

"Perdita, please ask Professor Graf to cover my supervisions with Bill Carel." Bill was one of her graduate students, working on spectral analyses of structures in dark energy. Troublesome but able, Bill was worth the effort; she would have to trust old Joe Graf to figure that out for himself. "Oh, and please ask Joe if he will handle the proofs of my latest paper in the *Astrophysical Journal.* He'll know how. What else? My car was still acting up, last time I tried it." The great shock of June 9 had been traumatic for humankind's semi-sentient machines as well as for people; even months later many were still struggling to recover. "It probably needs a bit more time with the therapist . . . What else?"

"You have a dentist appointment," her daughter said.

"So I do. Damn. Well, please cancel it." She probed with her tongue at the tooth that was giving her trouble, and wondered what the standard of dentistry was like on the Moon.

Her students, her car, her teeth. These fragments of her life from Milton Keynes, where she held a seat at the Open University, seemed incongruous, even absurd, out here between planets. And yet once this immense flap was over things would go on; she must focus some of her energy on holding things together, so there was a life for her to go back to.

But of course routine business was not what Perdita was interested in.

The image of her daughter's face in her phone's tiny screen was fuzzed by static, but good enough. Siobhan wasn't about to complain at such slight imperfections in a telecommunications system that now linked every human being to every other on two worlds—and, the systems providers boasted, would soon be reaching out to Mars as well. But the delay was eerie, a reminder that she had traveled so far from home that even light took a perceptible time to connect her to her daughter.

It wasn't long before the issue of Siobhan's safety came up once more.

"You really mustn't worry," Siobhan told her daughter. "I'm surrounded by extremely competent people who know exactly what to do to keep me alive and well. Why, I'll probably be safer on the Moon than in London."

"I doubt that very much," Perdita said, her voice mildly scolding. "You're not John Glenn, Mother."

"No, but I don't need to be." Siobhan suppressed a stab of fond irritation. *And I'm only forty-five!* But, she reflected guiltily, when she was twenty or so, wasn't this just the way she had treated her own mother?

"And then there are solar flares," Perdita said. "I've been reading up."

"So has most of the human race since June, I would think," Siobhan said dryly.

"Astronauts are outside the Earth's air and magnetic field. So they aren't shielded as they would be on the ground."

Siobhan waved her phone around to show Perdita the cabin. Big enough to hold eight but empty save for herself, it had hefty walls whose thickness was revealed by the depth of the window sockets. "See?" She thumped the wall. "Five centimeters of aluminum and water."

"That won't help if a big one hits," Perdita pointed out. "In 1972 a massive flare erupted only months after *Apollo 16* returned from the Moon. If the astronauts had been caught on the lunar surface—"

"But they weren't," Siobhan said. "And there was no such thing as solar weather forecasting back then. If there was any risk, they wouldn't let me fly."

Perdita grunted. "But the sun is restless now, Mum. It's only four months since June 9, and still nobody knows what caused it. Who's to say if the forecasters have any idea what's going on anymore?"

"Well," Siobhan said a bit testily, "that's what I'm going to the Moon to find out. And I really had better get on with some work, dear . . ." With expressions of love, and after sending regards to her own mother, Siobhan closed down the call. It was a mild relief to break the connection.

Of course, she suspected that Perdita's real problem with her mission wasn't safety at all. It was jealousy. Perdita couldn't stand it that her mother was here, not *her*. With a sense of guilty triumph, Siobhan peered out of the window at the looming Moon.

Siobhan was a child of the 1990s. The first human landings on the Moon had been finished two decades before she was born. She had always looked on the relics of the *Apollo* missions, the grainy footage of fresh-faced astronauts with their flags and stiff pressure suits and impossibly primitive technology, as a symptom of the madness of the vanished Cold War years, up there with the UFO craze and missile silos under Kansas cornfields.

When at the opening of the century a return to the Moon had been floated on both sides of the Atlantic, Siobhan had again been distinctly unimpressed. Even as a science student it had seemed to her a jobs-for-the-boys project dominated by aviators and engineers, a bid for power and wealth by the military-industrial complex, with science goals a fig-leaf justification at best, just as manned space travel always had been.

But the rediscovery of space exploration had captured the imagination of a new generation—including her own, she admitted—and had progressed faster than anybody had dreamed.

A new fleet of *Apollo*-like space vehicles was flying by 2012. Though venerable *Soyuz* craft still toiled to and from the International Space Station, the brave, flawed space shuttles were retired. Meanwhile a flotilla of exploratory rovers and sample-return missions had been dispatched to the Moon and to Mars, as well as more ambitious unmanned missions farther afield, such as an extraordinary swords-into-plowshares venture, yet to be fulfilled, to use an antiquated weapons system called the Extirpator to map the whole solar system. Siobhan knew the science return from these missions had been good, though the solar system wasn't her field of study—but it was galling that most people didn't even know of the existence of the great cosmological telescopes, like the Quintessence Anisotropy Probe, whose results were fueling her own career.

While all this had gone on the American and Eurasian manned space programs had gradually merged—and in 2015, under many flags, human footsteps had been planted on the Moon once more. By 2037 humans had maintained an unbroken tenancy of the Moon for nearly twenty years, with around two hundred colonists in Clavius Base and elsewhere.

And just four years ago the first explorers aboard the spacecraft *Aurora 1* had reached Mars itself. The hardest cynic couldn't help but cheer the fulfillment of that ancient dream.

Her mission was grave: at the politely worded command of the Prime Minister of Eurasia, she was tasked with finding out what was going wrong with the sun, and if Earth faced any prospect of a repeat of June 9. But the upshot was that she, Siobhan McGorran, child of Belfast, in a four-legged bug of a craft that looked like a beefed-up version of those old *Apollo* lunar modules, had been projected into the lunar sphere. How marvelous, she exulted. No wonder Perdita was green with envy.

A door opened at the head of the cabin. The shuttle's Captain came swimming through and slid into an empty seat. With a soft word to Aristotle, Siobhan closed down the softscreens arrayed around her.

Mario Ponzo was an Italian. Aged about fifty, he was surprisingly tubby for a space pilot, judging by the healthy mass that strained at the stomach panels of his jumpsuit. He said, "I'm sorry we haven't had time for more of a chat, Professor." His accent was tinged with American, a relic of Houston, where this native Roman had trained at the NASA space center. "I hope Simon has looked after you well?"

"Perfectly, thank you." She hesitated. "The food is rather tasteless, isn't it?"

Mario shrugged. "An artifact of weightlessness, I'm afraid. Something to do with the body's fluid balances. A tragedy for all Italian astronauts!"

"But I slept better here than anytime I remember since I was a child."

"I'm glad. Actually it's the first time we have made the run with just a single passenger—"

"I guessed that."

"But in a way it's oddly appropriate, for Vladimir Komarov's last flight was also solo."

"Komarov?—oh. For whom the shuttle is named."

"That's right. Komarov is a hero, and for the Russians, who have many heroes, that's saying something. He flew the first mission of their *Soyuz* spacecraft. When its systems failed during reentry, he died. What makes him heroic, though, is that he got aboard that bird almost certainly knowing how bad the faults of his untested ship were likely to be."

"So the shuttle is named for a dead cosmonaut. Isn't that bad luck?"

He smiled. "Away from Earth, we seem to be evolving different superstitions, Professor." He glanced at her blank screens. "You know, we're not used to secrecy up here. It's not encouraged. We all have to work together to keep alive. Secrecy is corrosive, Professor, bad for morale. And I've never known anything like the blanket of silence that has descended around you and your mission."

"I sympathize," she said carefully.

He rubbed a chin coated with three days of stubble; he had told her that idiosyncratically he would not shave in space, to save the inconvenience of clippings drifting around the cabin. "Not only that," he said, "the comms links between the Moon and Earth are notoriously narrow. A bottleneck. If I wanted to prevent sensitive information leaking out onto the global nets, the Moon would be a good place to put it."

Of course he was right; the ease of securing discussions on the Moon was a prime reason for her journey, rather than bringing lunar-based experts to Earth. She said, "But you know that I'm an envoy of the Eurasian Prime Minister herself. I'm sure you understand that the security restrictions to which I'm subjected come from much higher levels than me." *So don't probe,* she added silently. She turned back to her blank softscreens. "And if you don't mind—"

"More studying? I think it may be a little late for that." He glanced out the window.

Her view of the looming crescent Moon was gone, replaced by a mottling of deep black and glowing pale brown that slid past the window.

Mario said softly, "You are looking at Clavius Crater, Professor."

She stared. Clavius, south of Tycho, was a basin so huge that its floor was convex, pushed out by the curvature of the Moon itself. As the shuttle descended she began to resolve smaller craters on that tremendous floor: craters of all sizes, craters overlapping craters down to the limits of her visibility. It was a strange, ripped-up landscape, like a Great War battlefield perhaps. But there, just emerging from the shadow of the wall, she saw a fine line, a shining thread of gold laid over the Moon's gray floor. That must be the

Sling, the new electromagnetic launch system, still incomplete but already a mighty rail more than a kilometer long. Even from here she could see that human hands had touched the face of the Moon.

Mario was watching her reaction. "It sneaks up on you, doesn't it?" And he left the cabin to prepare the descent protocols.

10: CONTACT LIGHT

Clavius Base was built around three big inflated domes. Connected by transparent walkways and subsurface tunnels, the domes were covered over by Moon dust for protection from the sun, cosmic rays, and other horrors. As a result, seen from above, the domes seemed part of the lunar landscape, as if they had bubbled up out of the gray-brown regolith.

Shuttle *Komarov* landed without ceremony half a kilometer from the main domes. The dust it kicked up fell back with disconcerting speed onto the airless Moon. There were no pads here, just many shallow blast craters, the scars of multiple landings and take-offs.

A transparent walkway snaked up to the shuttle's lock. Escorted by Captain Mario, with her smart suitcase rolling behind her, Siobhan took her first footsteps in the Moon's dreamy gravity.

Her first glimpse of the Moon, slightly distorted by the walkway's clear, curving walls, was of a gently rolling surface. Every edge was softened by the ubiquitous dust, the result of eons of meteoritic churning. It looked almost like a snowfield, she thought. The shadows were not the deep black she had imagined, but softened by the reflected glow of the ground. She shouldn't have been surprised: dark as it was, the light reflected from this lifeless soil was, after all, the Moonlight that had shone over Earth since the great impact that had shaped the twin worlds in the first place. So Siobhan was walking in Moonlight herself. But this bit of the Moon was littered by surface vehicles, fuel tanks, escape bunkers, and equipment dumps; it was a human landscape.

The walkway terminated at a small blocky structure. Siobhan and Mario rode the elevator down to an underground tunnel. Here an open cart mounted on a monorail awaited them. The cart was big enough for ten, she realized, the shuttle's full complement of eight passengers plus two crew, and their baggage.

The cart slid into silent motion.

"An induction drive," Mario said. "Same principle as the Sling. Endless sunlight and low gravity: the physics behind this little electrical cart might have been invented for the conditions of the Moon."

The tunnel was narrow, lit by fluorescent tubes, and the fused-rock walls were so close to the cart she could have reached out and touched them—and in perfect safety, for the cart's speed was little more than walking pace. She was learning that away from Earth, caution ruled: *everything* was done slowly and deliberately.

At the end of the tunnel was an airlock, and what Mario called a "dustlock," a small room equipped with brushes, vacuum hoses, and other devices to clean spacesuits and people of electrostatically clinging Moon dust. As Mario and Siobhan hadn't been exposed to the surface, they were able to cycle through this quickly.

The airlock's inner door was marked with a large plaque:

WELCOME TO CLAVIUS BASE
U.S. ASTRONAUTICAL ENGINEERING CORPS

She read on down a list of contributing organizations, from NASA and the U.S. Air and Space Force to Boeing and various other private contractors. There was also a rather grudging acknowledgment, she thought, of the Eurasian, Japanese, Pan-Arabian, Pan-African, and other space organizations that had put up more than half the money for this American-led project.

She touched a little roundel that was the logo of the British National Space Agency. In recent years the British had discovered a genius for robotics and miniaturization, and the machine-dominated period of renewed lunar and Martian exploration earlier in the century had been the glory days of the BNSA and its engineers. But that period had been brief, and was already over.

Mario caught her eye and grinned. "That's the Americans for you. Never give anybody else credit."

"But they were here first," she pointed out.

"Oh, yes, there is that."

The inner door slid open to reveal a short, stocky man waiting for her. "Professor McGorran? Welcome to the Moon." She recognized him immediately. This was Colonel Burton Tooke, USASF, commander of Clavius Base. Aged about fifty, with a severe military crew cut, he was a good head shorter than she was, and he flashed a disarming gap-toothed grin. "Call me Bud," he said.

Siobhan said goodbye to Mario, who was returning to his shuttle, "where the beds are softer than anything in Clavius," he claimed.

Bud Tooke led Siobhan up a flight of stairs, easily negotiated in one-sixth gravity, to the interior of a dome. They walked along a narrow roofless corridor. She could see the dome's smooth plastic some meters above her head, but the space beneath was cluttered with walkways and partitions. Everything was quiet, the lights subdued; nobody was moving, save Bud and Siobhan.

She said softly, "It seems rather appropriate to arrive somewhere as mysterious as the Moon in silence and twilight."

He nodded. "Sure. You'll soon be over the Moon-lag, I hope. It's actually two A.M. here. The middle of our night."

"Moon time?"

"Houston time."

She learned this was a tradition dating back to the days of the earliest astronauts, who had timed their epic journeys by the clocks of their homes in Texas; it was a pleasing tribute to those pioneers.

They reached a row of closed doors. Above, a small neon sign glowed pink: it read CONTACT LIGHT. Bud opened a door at random to reveal a small room, and Siobhan looked inside. There was a bed that could be folded out to become double, a table, chair, and basic comms equipment, and even a small unit containing a shower and lavatory.

"Not quite a hotel. And there's no room service to speak of." Bud said this cautiously. Perhaps some VIP visitors threw tantrums at this point, demanding the five-star luxury they were used to.

Siobhan said firmly, "I'll be fine. Umm—*contact light?*"

"The first words spoken on the Moon, by Buzz Aldrin, at the moment when *Apollo 11*'s lunar module first touched the surface. Seems appropriate for our visitor quarters." He shoved her luggage into the room, where her smart suitcase, sensing it had completed its own journey, opened itself up. Bud said, "Siobhan, I've set up the briefing you asked for at ten A.M. local. The participants have all been brought here—notably Mangles and Martynov from the South Pole."

"Thank you."

"Until then your time is your own. Take a break if you like. But it's about time I took an inspection tour of this dump. I'd welcome your company." He grinned. "I'm a military man; I'm used to sleepless nights. Anyhow, I need an excuse to have a good look at everything while nobody's about to distract me."

"I should really work." She glanced guiltily at her self-unpacking luggage, her crushable clothes, and rolled-up softscreens. But her head was already too full of facts about the sun and its storms.

She studied Bud Tooke. His square shoulders filling his practical, unmarked coverall, he stood with his hands behind his back, his face friendly but expressionless. He looked like a classic career soldier, she thought, exactly as she'd preconceived the commander of a Moon base to be. But if she was to get through this assignment, she was going to have to rely on his support.

She decided to take him into her confidence. "I don't know anything about the people here. How they live, the way they think. A tour might help me find my feet."

He nodded, apparently approving. "A little recon before the battle never hurts."

"Well, I wouldn't have put it quite like that . . ." She begged fifteen minutes to unpack and freshen up.

———

They walked briskly around the perimeter of the dome.

The air was laden with an odd smell, like gunpowder, or burning leaves. That was Moon dust, Bud said, making the most of its first chance in a billion years to burn in oxygen. The architecture was simple and functional, in places decorated by amateur artwork, much of it dominated by contrasts between lunar gray and the pink or green of Earth life.

Clavius's three domes were called Artemis, Selene, and Hecate. "Greek names?"

"To the Greeks the Moon was a trinity: Artemis for the waxing Moon, Selene for full, and Hecate for waning. This dome, which contains most of our living areas, is Hecate. Since it spends half its time in twilight that seemed an appropriate choice."

As well as accommodation for two hundred people, Hecate contained life support and recycling systems, a small hospital, training and exercise rooms, and even a theater, an open arena sculpted from what Bud assured her was a natural lunar crater. "Just amateur dramatics. But very popular, as you can imagine. Ballet goes down well."

She stared at his shaven head. *"Ballet?"*

"I know, I know. Not what you'd expect from the Air Force. But you really need to see an entrechat performed in lunar gravity." He eyed her. "Siobhan, you might think we're just living in a hole in the ground. But this is a different world, down to the very pull of it on your bones. People are changed by it. Especially the kids. You'll see, if you have time."

"I hope I will."

They passed through a low, opaque-walled tunnel to the dome called Selene. This dome was much more open than Hecate, and most of its roof was transparent, so that sunlight streamed in. And here, in long beds, green things grew: Siobhan recognized cress, cabbages, carrots, peas, even potatoes. But these plants were growing in liquid. The beds were interconnected by tubing, and there was a steady hum of fans and pumps, a hiss of humidifiers. It was like a huge, low greenhouse, Siobhan thought, the illusion spoiled only by the blackness of the sky above, and the sheen of liquid where soil should have been. But many of the beds were empty, cleaned out.

"So you're hydroponic farmers," she said.

"Yeah. And we're all vegetarians up here. It will be a long time before you'll find a pig or cow or chicken on the Moon. Umm, I wouldn't dip my finger into the beds."

"You wouldn't?"

He pointed to tomato plants. "Those are growing out of nearly pure urine. And *those* pea plants are floating in concentrated excrement. Pretty much all we do is scent it. Of course most of these crops are GMOs." Genetically modified organisms. "The Russians have done a lot of work in this area, developing plants that can close the recycling loops as economically as possible. And the plants need to be adapted for the peculiar conditions here: the low gravity, pressure and temperature sensitivity, radiation levels." As he spoke of agricultural matters his voice took on a stronger accent; she thought it sounded like Iowa, the voice of a farm boy a long way from home.

She gazed at the innocent-looking plants. "I imagine some people are squeamish."

"You get over it," Bud said. "If not, you ship out. And anyhow, it's better than the early days when we grew nothing but algae. Even I had trouble chomping on a bright blue burger. Of course we're vulnerable to solar events in here."

On June 9, partly thanks to Eugene Mangle's warnings, the lunar colonists had been able to dive into their storm shelters and ride out the worst of it. Spacecraft and other systems had taken a battering, but not a single human life had been lost away from planet Earth. These empty hydroponic beds, however, showed that the living things that had accompanied humans on their first hesitant steps away from Earth had not been so lucky.

They walked on.

The third dome, Artemis, was given over to industry.

Bud, with parental pride, showed her a bank of transformers. "Power from the sun," he said. "Free, plentiful, and not a cloud in the sky."

"I guess the downside is two weeks of darkness in every month."

"Sure. Right now we depend on storage cells. But we're look-ing to establish major power farms at the poles, where you get sun-light most of the month; then we'll only need a fraction of our current storage capacity."

He walked her around a plant of primitive, though lightweight-looking, chemical processing equipment. "Resources from the Moon," he said. "We take oxygen from ilmenite, a mineral you find in mare basalts. Just scoop it up, crush it, and heat it. We're learning to make glass from the same stuff. We can also extract aluminum from plagioclase, which is a kind of feldspar you find in the high-lands."

He outlined future plans. The plant she saw here was actually pilot gear, meant to establish industrial techniques in lunar condi-tions. The operational plants would be huge robot factories out in the hard vacuum of the surface. Aluminum was the big dream: the Sling, the big electromagnetic launching rail to be powered by sun-light, was being constructed almost entirely of lunar aluminum.

Bud dreamed of the day when lunar resources, suitably pro-cessed, would be slingshot to construction projects in Earth orbit, or even the home world itself. "I would hope to see the Moon start to punch its weight in trade, and become part of a unified and pros-perous Earth–Moon economic system. And all the time, of course, we're beginning to learn how to live off the land away from Earth, lessons we can apply to Mars, the asteroids—hell, anywhere else we choose to live.

"But we've a long way to go. Conditions are *different* here—the vacuum, the dust, the radiation, the low gravity that plays hell with convection processes and such. We're having to reinvent centuries-old techniques from scratch." But Bud sounded as if he relished the challenge. Siobhan saw Moon dirt crusted under his fingernails; this was a man who got stuck in.

He walked her back to Hecate, the accommodation dome.

Bud said, "Of the two-hundred-plus people on the Moon, about ten percent are support staff, including the likes of yours truly. The rest are technicians, technologists, biologists, with forty percent devoted to pure science, including your pals at the South

Pole. Oh, and about a dozen kids, by the way. We're multidisciplinary, multinational, multiethnic, multi-you-name-it.

"Of course the Moon has always been culturally complex, even before humans got here. Christopher Clavius was a contemporary of Galileo, but he was actually a Jesuit. He thought the Moon was a smooth sphere. Ironic that one of the Moon's biggest craters was named for him! In my own tradition we are the guardians of the crescent Moon, as we say. Living on the Moon isn't a problem for me—Mecca is easy to find—but Ramadan is timed to the phases of the Moon, and that's a little more tricky . . ."

Siobhan did a double take. "Wait. *Your* tradition?"

He smiled, evidently used to the reaction. "Islam has reached Iowa, you know."

In his thirties, as a serving soldier, Bud Tooke had been one of the first relief workers into what was left of the Dome of the Rock, after an extreme religious group called the One-Godders had lobbed a nuclear grenade into that site of unique significance. "That experience exposed me to Islam—and my body to a hard rain. Everything changed for me after that."

After the Dome, he told her, Bud had joined a movement called the Oikumens, a grassroots network of people who were trying, mostly under the radar, to find a way to bring the world's great faiths to some kind of coexistence, mainly by appealing to their deep common roots. In that way, perhaps, the positive qualities of the faiths—their moral teachings, their various contemplations of humankind's place in the universe—might be promoted. If humans could not be rid of religion, it was argued, then let them at least not be harmed by it.

"So," Siobhan said, marveling, "you're a career soldier, living on the Moon, who spends his spare time studying theology."

He laughed, a clipped sound like a rifle being cocked. "I guess I'm an authentic product of the twenty-first century, aren't I?" He glanced at her, suddenly almost shy. "But I've seen a lot. You know, it seems to me that over my lifetime we've been slowly groping our way out of the fog. We're killing each other off a bit less enthusiastically than a hundred years ago. Even though Earth itself has gone to hell in a handbasket while we weren't looking, we're starting to fix those problems, too. But now *this,* the business with the sun. Won't it be ironic that just as we're growing up, the star that birthed us decides to cream us?"

Ironic, yes, she thought uneasily. And an odd coincidence that just as we move off the Earth, just as we're capable of all this, of living on the Moon, the sun reaches out to burn us . . . Scientists were suspicious of coincidences; they usually meant you were missing some underlying cause.

Or you're just getting paranoid, Siobhan, she told herself.

Bud said, "I'll fix you breakfast after I show you one more sight—our museum. We've even got *Apollo* Moon rocks in there! Did you know that three of the core drillings made by the *Apollo 17* astronauts were never opened? People are already making quite an impact on the Moon. And so we went to the trouble of ferrying unopened Apollo rocks *back* to the Moon, so that the double domes can use those old samples as reference points, bits of a pristine Moon before we got our hands on it . . ."

Siobhan found herself warming to this blunt character. It was probably inevitable that you would find a strong military flavor to a base like this: the military, with their submarines and missile silos, had more experience of survival in cramped, unnatural, confined conditions than anybody else. And it had to be American-led. The Europeans, Japanese, and the rest had put up much of the money for this place, but when it came to opening up virgin continents like the Moon, the Americans provided the muscle and the strength of character. But in Colonel Bud Tooke she saw something of the best in the American character: tough, obviously competent, experienced, determined, and yet with a vision that far transcended his own lifetime. She was going to be able to do business with him, she thought—and, a corner of her hoped, maybe they could build something more.

As they walked on, the artificial lights of the dome began to glow brighter, heralding the start of another human day on the Moon.

11: TIME'S EYE

As the months passed, and London slowly recovered from June 9, Bisesa sensed the city's mood souring.

In the few hours of the storm itself there had been genuine deprivation and fear—and casualties, including more than a thousand deaths in the inner city. And yet it was a time of heroism. There was still no official estimate of how many lives had been saved from fires, or stranding in Underground tunnels, or road pileups, or the lethal mundanity of being trapped in stuck elevators.

In the days that immediately followed, too, Londoners had pulled together. Shops had opened up, displaying the hand-drawn BUSINESS AS USUAL signs that usually defied terrorist outrages. There had been cheers when the first 1950s-vintage "Green Goddess" fire engines had gone clanging through the streets of the city, museum-piece equipment that was "too stupid to fail," proclaimed the Mayor. It was a time of resilience, of the "spirit of the Blitz," people said, harking back to a time of even greater challenge now almost a century past.

But that mood was quickly dispelled.

The world had continued to turn, and June 9 had begun to fade in the memory. People tried to get back to work, schools were re-opening, and the great electronic-commerce channels began to function at something like their old capacity again. But London's recovery remained patchy: there was still no water supply in Hammersmith, no power in Battersea, no functioning traffic management system in Westminster. Soon patience was running out, and people were looking for somebody to blame.

By October both Bisesa and her daughter had got a little stir-crazy. They had ventured out of the flat a few times, to the river and the parks, walking through a fractious city. But their freedom of movement was limited. The credit chip implanted in Bisesa's arm was more than five years old, and its internal data were long since scrambled: in a time of global electronic tagging she was a nonperson. Without a functioning chip she couldn't shop for herself, couldn't take the Underground, couldn't even buy her kid an ice cream.

She knew she couldn't go on like this forever. At least with her fritzed chip she was invisible, from the Army and everybody else. But it was only the fact that she had long ago given her cousin Linda access to her savings that kept her from starving.

She still didn't feel able to move on, however. It wasn't just her need to be with Myra. She was still failing to get her head around her extraordinary experiences.

She tried to figure it all out by writing down her story. She dictated to Aristotle, but her murmuring disturbed Myra. So in the end she wrote it all out longhand, and let Aristotle scan it into electronic memory. She tried to get it right; she went back through successive drafts, emptying her memory of as much as she could remember, the spectacular and the trivial alike.

But as she stared at the words on the softscreen before her, in the mundanity of her flat with Myra's cartoons and synth-soaps babbling in the background, she believed it less and less herself.

On June 8, 2037, Lieutenant Bisesa Dutt had been on peacekeeping patrol in a corner of Afghanistan. With her was another British officer, Abdikadir Omar, and an American, Casey Othic. In that troubled part of the world they were all wearing the blue helmets of the UN. It had been a routine patrol, just another day.

Then some kid had tried to shoot their chopper down—and the sun had lurched across the sky—and when they had emerged from the crashed machine, they had found themselves somewhere different entirely. Not another place, but another *time*.

They had fallen to earth in the year 1885: a time when the area was called the North–West Frontier by the imperial British who controlled it. They had been taken to a fort called Jamrud, where Bisesa had met a young Bostonian journalist called Josh White. Born in 1862, long dust in Bisesa's world, Josh was aged only twenty-three *here*. And here too, astonishingly, was Rudyard Kipling, the bard of the British tommies, miraculously restored from the dead. But these romantic Victorians were themselves castaways in time.

Bisesa had tried to piece together the story. They had all been projected into another world, a world of scraps and patches torn from the fabric of time. They called this new world Mir, a Russian word for both "world" and "peace." In places you could *see* the stitching, as ground levels suddenly changed by a meter or more, or where a slab of ancient greenery had been dumped into the middle of a desert.

Nobody knew how this had happened, and still less why—and soon, as the patchwork world knitted together and a turbulent new history swept over them all, they had all been caught up in a battle for personal survival, and such questions had become irrelevant.

But the questions remained. The new world had been peppered by "Eyes"—silvery spheres with elusive geometries, silent and watchful and utterly immobile, scattered over the landscape like so many closed-circuit television cameras. What could these Eyes be but artificial? Did they represent the aloof agency that had taken the world apart, then so roughly reassembled it?

And then there was the question of the span of time. Mir seemed to be constructed as a kind of sampling of humankind and its development, all the way from chimp-like australopithecines from two million years deep, up through variants of prehuman hominids, and all the ages of human history. But this great collating ended, as far as anybody could tell, on June 8, 2037, in the time slice that had carried Bisesa and her colleagues there. Why was there nothing from the farther future? Bisesa had wondered if that was because that date marked some kind of ending to human history—because there *was* no future to sample.

And then she, and she alone, had been brought home by the Eyes, or perhaps by the remote minds behind them—and found herself on the very next day, June 9, watching a lethal sun rise over London.

Bisesa was convinced that the construction of Mir hadn't been some stupendous natural accident, but *deliberate,* the act of some terrible intelligence for its own purposes. But why had Earth's history been taken apart? Why were the Eyes there to watch and listen? Was it all, as she feared, connected to the misbehavior of the sun?

And why had she been brought back home? To be returned to Myra had been what she had wanted, of course. On Mir, in the depths of her loneliness and despair she had even begged an Eye to save her. But she was sure her desires were irrelevant. The correct question was: what purpose did her return serve *them?*

Bisesa, stuck in her flat, toiled over her account, sifted through the news, obsessed over her memories and her fragmentary understanding, and tried to decide what to do.

12: BRIEFING

At Clavius Base, after a couple of hours' sleep, Siobhan still felt mildly jet-lagged, or Moon-lagged, she thought, by a time difference from London equivalent to an Atlantic crossing.

To freshen up, she showered. She was entranced by the shimmering globules that came crowding out of her shower nozzle. She tried to be a good visitor to the Moon; she kept her shower curtain Velcroed up until the suction system had recovered every last precious molecule of the ancient water.

Liaising en route from the *Komarov,* she had asked Bud to set up a full briefing. As far as she could tell the Moon's top solar scientists would all be in attendance, from helio-seismologists to students of electromagnetic emissions from radio wavelengths to X-rays— and, of course, the neutrino-astronomy prodigy who had tried to blow the whistle before June 9. Until they got to Clavius, none of the scientists was to be told what her mission was. Security remained tight.

There were few conference rooms on the Moon: evidently this wasn't Carlton Terrace. Bud had tried to persuade her to use Clavius's amphitheater for the session, but the very public space of the amphitheater wouldn't do.

So he deployed some of his scarce resources to knock through the walls of a few living quarters. The result was a cramped but serviceable room, dominated by a "conference table" made of several smaller bits of furniture jammed together. Bud installed Faraday cages and jamming devices to exclude electronic eavesdropping, and active noise generators to put a stop to the more conventional sort of listening. Even Thales would not be free to come and go: while the door was locked, only a cut-down clone of the Moon's electronic ghost would be allowed to operate within the room, and later a suite of smart systems, independent of Thales himself, would scrutinize and censor the flow of information out of the room.

Siobhan checked it over as best she could. "I'm no expert," she said to Bud, "but this looks sufficient to me."

He said fervently, "I hope so. I don't mind telling you I took a few punches over this meeting—and not just about the security." He scratched his shaven scalp. "Me, I'm just a military man. I'm used to an unpredictable life. These scientists *hate* to be dragged away from their work."

"I can sympathize," she said. "I'm a scientist too, remember. And right now all my own projects are probably running into the ground."

Bud knew about her work. "But for now the life and death of the universe can wait."

"Quite." She smiled at him.

Ten o'clock arrived. With Bud at her side she braced herself and walked into the crowded room. Bud quietly closed the door behind her, and she heard a security lock click into place.

She stood at the head of the cobbled-together conference table. The twenty participants were already here with their softscreens spread out over the tabletop before them: twenty faces gazing back at her, with expressions varying from apathy to nervousness to blank hostility. The glow of the strip lights overhead was washed-out and harsh, and despite the noisy laboring of the air circulation systems this sealed box already smelled strongly of adrenaline and sweat. The people seemed alien too, their clothes, much recycled and patched, dark with use, and their gestures small and contained, conditioned by years in small spaces and a lethal environment. They made Siobhan feel gaudy, wispy, an outsider from sunny

Earth out of place here in the cramped, dusty chambers of the Moon.

This is going to be a nightmare, she thought.

Most of the participants were geologists of one stripe or another, she knew; many of them had the big, practical, dust-stained hands of those used to working with rocks. Glancing around, she recognized two faces from the briefing material she had requested from Bud: Mikhail Martynov, the rather shy-looking Russian who was the lead scientist on solar weather here on the Moon—and Eugene Mangles, neutrino whiz kid.

Eugene had a distracted air, and he seemed to have trouble making eye contact. But he was startlingly good looking, better even than the images had suggested, with the perfect skin and open, symmetrical face of a synth-star singer. Siobhan felt her crusty heart skip a beat. And from the glances that Mikhail occasionally cast his way, it seemed that it wasn't just women who were drawn to Eugene's looks.

Bud, acting as chair, stood beside her. "Before we start, let me just say one thing," he began. "Astronauts have a proud history in solar studies. It goes back to the *Skylab* guys who, in Earth orbit in 1973, operated an imaging spectrograph built for them by Harvard. Today we're continuing that tradition. But we're not just talking about science. Today we're being asked for our help. As the commander of Clavius Base I consider it an honor to have Professor McGorran here—an honor that we on the Moon are seen as fit to be the focus of the response to this problem. Professor." He nodded to Siobhan and sat down.

After that pep talk, not entirely appropriate, Siobhan glanced around the table. She caught just one friendly eye, a sympathetic half smile from Mikhail Martynov. *Follow that.*

"Good morning. I expect to do more listening than talking today, but I'd like to make some introductory remarks. My name is—"

"We know who you are." The speaker was evidently one of the geologists, a stocky, big-armed woman with a square face. Her glare was about the most hostile in the room.

"Then you have me at a disadvantage, Doctor—"

"Professor. Professor Rose Delea." She had a broad Australian accent. Siobhan had been briefed; Rose was an expert on the emplacement by sunlight of helium-3 in the lunar regolith. This helium isotope, a fuel for fusion reactors, was the Moon's best economic prospect, and so Rose was a weighty figure here. "All I want to know is when you're going to leave so I can get back to some real work. And I want to know the reason for all this secrecy. Since June 9 outgoing comms has been restricted, some areas of Thales's databases and other information stores have been proscribed—"

"I know."

"This is the Moon, Professor McGorran. If you hadn't noticed, we're all a long way from home and our families. Links to Earth are essential for our psychological well-being, not to mention our physical safety. And if you don't want morale to fall farther—"

Siobhan held up her hand, a gesture of quiet command. To her relief, Rose fell silent. "I quite agree." So she did. Secrecy didn't come instinctively to her any more than to these Moon-folk, Siobhan suspected; openness was an essential component of the endless conversation that underpinned good science. She said, "The security blackout is difficult for all concerned, and would be unacceptable—in normal times. But these are not normal times. Please bear with me.

"I'm standing before you today as an emissary of both the British Prime Minister and the Prime Minister of the Eurasian Union. When I get home I'll also be expected to brief other world leaders, including President Alvarez of the United States. And what they want to know is what to expect of the sun."

She was met by mostly baffled stares. Her briefings by various world-weary politicians' aides had warned her to expect a certain insularity up here on the Moon, where the Earth could seem a long way away, and not very important. So she had prepared a show-and-tell. "Thales, please . . ."

She gave them a five minute summary, in images, graphics, and words, of the devastating impact of June 9 on the Earth. This was watched in somber silence.

At the end she said, "And that's the reason I'm here, Professor

Delea. I need some answers—we all do. *What's wrong with the sun?* Is June 9 going to hit us again? Can we expect something less—or worse? On the Moon—in this room, in fact—you have some of humankind's top solar scientists. *And* the one person who made an accurate prediction of June 9 itself."

Eugene didn't react; his gaze unfocused, it was as if he was barely aware of the others around him.

Mikhail said dryly, "And of course the ease of controlling information from the Moon is purely coincidental."

Siobhan frowned. "We have to take security seriously, sir. The governments really have no idea of what they're facing yet. Until they do, information, unfortunately, must be managed. A panic could be vastly damaging in itself."

Rose subsided, but she was glowering, and Siobhan hoped beyond hope that she hadn't already made an enemy.

As brightly as she could she said, "Let's start by making sure we're all singing from the same hymn sheet. Doctor Martynov, I wonder if you'd be good enough to tell a mere cosmologist how the sun is *supposed* to work."

"It will be a pleasure." With a showman's sense of theater Mikhail stood and made his way to the front of the room.

"All cosmologists know that the sun is fueled by fusion fire. What most cosmologists *don't* know is that only the innermost heart of the sun is a fusion reactor. The rest of it is special effects . . ." Mikhail's Russian accent was movie-actor thick, but quite compelling.

During her training, Siobhan had of course studied the sun. She had learned that the sun, like all stars, is simple in principle, but as the nearest star the sun had been scrutinized in minute detail. The detail, it turned out, was rather overwhelmingly complex and still little understood, even after centuries of study. But it was that detailed behavior that now seemed to be endangering humankind.

The sun is a ball of gas, mostly hydrogen, more than a million kilometers wide—that is, as wide as a hundred Earths strung side by side, and as massive as a *million* Earths. The source of its vast energy output is its core, a star within a star where, in complicated chains of reactions, swarming nuclei of hydrogen fuse to helium and other heavier elements.

The fusion energy must pass out through the body of the sun from the hot core to the cold sink of space, driven by temperature differences as surely as a head of pressure drives water through a pipe. But the core is swaddled by a thick belt of turgid gas called the "radiative zone," opaque as a brick wall, through which the inner heat passes in the form of X-rays. In the next layer out, the "convective zone," the densities have lessened to the point where the sun's material can boil, like a pan heated from below. Here the core heat continues its journey to space by powering huge convective spouts, each many times taller than Earth, ascending at not much more than walking pace. Above the convective zone lies the visible surface of the sun, the photosphere, the source of sunlight and sunspots. And just as the meniscus of a boiling pan of water will organize itself into cells, so the sun bubbles with granules, constantly changing, tiling the photosphere like a Roman mosaic.

So immense and compressed are these layers that the sun is all but opaque to its own radiation; a given photon's worth of energy takes millions of years to struggle from core to surface.

Once released from its cage of gases, the core energy, in the form of light, races away at lightspeed as if with relief, spreading with distance as it travels. At the distance of the Earth, eight light-minutes from the photosphere, sunlight still delivers about a kilowatt of power per square meter—and even at a distance of light-years the sunlight is bright enough for any eyes there to see it.

As well as the light it emits, the sun breathes a constant stream of hot plasma into the faces of its circling children. This "solar wind" is a complex, turbulent breeze. At certain frequencies of light can be seen dark patches on the sun's surface—"coronal holes," regions of magnetic anomaly, like flaws in the sun itself—from which pour higher-energy streams of solar wind. The turning sun sprays these streams around the solar system in spiral washes, like an immense lawn sprinkler.

Mikhail said, "We watch out for those sprinkler streams. Every time the planet runs into one we get problems, as the Earth and its magnetosphere are battered by high-energy particles."

Still more problems are caused for the Earth by the sun's occasional irregularities. Mikhail said, "You have coronal mass ejections—like the monster that hit us on June 9—large-scale outpourings of plasma flung at us from the sun's surface. And then you have flares. These detonations on the sun's surface, powered by magnetic flaws, are the largest explosions in the modern-day solar system, each amounting to the blast of billions of nuclear weapons. Flares bombard us with radiation from gammas to radio waves. Sometimes they are followed up by what we call 'solar proton events'—cascades of charged particles."

The restless sun follows an eleven-year "solar cycle," at the peak of which sunspots swarm and flares erupt with much more vigor than at its minimum. Mikhail sketched the accepted mechanism behind the solar cycle. A "meridional flow" of plasma over the sun's surface from equator to poles carries the relics of sunspots north and south. At the poles the cooling material sinks down into the body of the sun as far as the base of the convective zone, and then migrates back toward the equator. But the magnetic scars left by sunspots linger on through this cycle, ghosts that seed the next generation of active regions.

Mikhail described the complicated relationship of sun, Earth, and humanity.

Even in historical times the sun's variability has affected the Earth's climate. For more than seventy years, from around 1640 to 1710, very few sunspots were observed on the sun's face—and the Earth was plunged into what the climatologists call the "Little Ice Age." Europe suffered severe winters and cool summers; at the peak of it, in 1690, London children ice-skated on the Thames.

In the electronic age, a growing dependence on high technology made humans much more vulnerable to even mild solar tantrums. In April 1984 a flare knocked out communications on *Air Force One;* President Reagan, over the mid-Pacific, was left incommunicado for two hours. Before June 9 the most intense storm on record had occurred in September 1859; that one had melted telegraph wires.

"We actually came close to that again in 2003," Mikhail said. "The sun suffered two eruptions in successive days, aimed right at the Earth. We were saved from more severe effects only by a chance alignment of magnetic fields."

Rose Delea was getting restless. "All these phenomena are well known."

Mikhail said, "Yes, we think we are getting a handle on measuring the effects of these different solar glitches—and predicting them, though that's still more an art than a science . . ." He put up a slide of three "space weather scales" that the current Space Weather Service had inherited from the old American Space Environment Center, and had elaborated on since. "You can see we describe three types of problem for Earth: geomagnetic storms, solar radiation storms, and radio blackouts. Each type is calibrated with these scales, from one to five—one being minor, and five being severe."

Siobhan nodded. "And June 9—"

"June 9 was principally an outcome of a coronal mass ejection, and would be measured by our G-scale, our geomagnetic-storm scale."

"And its rating?"

"Off the scale. June 9 was unprecedented. But the irony is that the event was better predicted than any solar glitch in history, thanks to Doctor Mangles." He glanced at Eugene.

But Eugene, as distracted as ever, didn't react to the cue; he seemed barely aware that the rest of the group existed.

There was an awkward silence. Bud called for a break.

You had to fetch your own coffee, it turned out; there were no spare hands to fetch and carry. And there were no digestive biscuits, not one on the whole damn Moon.

A line quickly formed at the coffee spigot at the back of the room. But Mikhail, near the front of the queue, picked up two plastic beakers of coffee and tentatively approached Siobhan, who accepted a beaker gratefully. Mikhail's face was lugubrious and crumpled, and his voice was warm and rich; Siobhan liked him instinctively.

He said, "I imagine you're the first Astronomer Royal to visit the Moon?"

"You know, I don't think any of us even left Earth before."

"Flamsteed would be proud of you."

"I like to think so." She sipped her coffee, and couldn't help but grimace.

He smiled. "I apologize for Clavius coffee. And for the reception you've received here. We Moon-folk are an odd lot. A small society."

"I was expecting a certain insularity."

"But it's more than that," Mikhail said. "We are very self-reliant—we have to be. But that breeds a certain indifference to outsiders, and sometimes resentment. This meeting is all about Eugene, of course. And Eugene is—"

"Special?"

He smiled. "Something like that. His personality is clearly difficult. And his social situation isn't helped by his choice of discipline. For the last generation of solar physicists, neutrinos were, for a long time, something of an embarrassment."

"Ah. The 'neutrino anomaly.'" When it had first been studied closely, the flood of neutrinos detected coming from the core of the sun was significantly less than had been predicted by then-current models of particle physics. It had turned out that the physics was wrong—neutrinos, thought to be massless, actually were not—and when that was put right in the theoretical models, the "anomaly" went away.

"You know how it is in science," Mikhail said gloomily. "Fashions come and they go. *My* area of work, this messy solar weather with its plasma storms and tangled-up magnetic fields, has never been fashionable. But after the business of the anomaly, solar neutrino studies were definitely not a sexy subject area. And then Eugene annoyed everybody by detecting yet *another* sort of neutrino anomaly—just when everybody thought it was sorted out for good."

"Okay. But even though he's prickly, I get the sense that he's popular here."

Mikhail pulled his lip. "I wouldn't say popular. But it's well known that it was Eugene's work that gave us our only early warning of the June 9 event. Nobody believed a word until the event was actually in progress, of course—he came to me at the South Pole so I could raise the alarm—but even so Eugene's warning saved a lot of lives. That's made him something of a folk hero, you see, among us exiles from Earth. So when an outsider like yourself shows up, no matter how highly qualified—"

"I understand." She eyed him and said carefully, "You just wouldn't think that a brain like Eugene's could reside behind such a face."

Mikhail looked at Eugene with undisguised longing. "But I think his face, his body, is his curse. Everybody assumes he must be no more than an 'airhead jock,' as my American colleagues say. Nobody takes him seriously. Even I find his looks—"

"Distracting?" She smiled. "Welcome to the club, Mikhail."

Mikhail said edgily, "But it is what goes on inside that beautiful head that is so disturbing."

Bud reconvened the session.

13 : NEUTRINOS

When Eugene Mangles spoke, every eye turned his way curiously. His accent was small-town American, Siobhan thought, and he sounded like a teen, younger than his midtwenties; his looks didn't fit what he had to say.

And his presentation about the anomalies he had discovered at the heart of the sun, while no doubt technically accurate, was anything but lucid.

Siobhan actually knew a lot about neutrinos. There are three known ways to make neutrinos: with fusion processes in the heart of a star like the sun, by turning a nuclear reactor on and off, and in the Big Bang that gave birth to the universe itself, the titanic event whose large-scale consequences were Siobhan's own subject matter. What makes neutrinos so useful to solar astronomers is that matter is all but transparent to them. And so neutrinos provide a unique way of studying the sun's inner structure, including the fusing core, a place from which even light struggles to escape.

That much was clear. But as Eugene displayed screen-filling equations and graphs in several dimensions, and as he talked ever more rapidly, Siobhan wondered how he had ever got through his doctorate oral exam.

Eventually she broke in. "Eugene. Slow down, please; I'm afraid you're leaving us all behind." He glared at her with a resentful intensity. But this was the heart of the matter; she needed to get this clear. "You're showing us results of your neutrino measurements."

"Yes, yes. Of the three flavors of neutrinos, which are inter-related by—"

She waved that away. "You are seeing oscillations in the neutrino flow."

"Yes."

"And that in turn," she pressed on doggedly, "reflects oscillations in the fusion processes in the core."

"Precisely," he said sarcastically. "The neutrino flux tracks back to local changes in core temperature and pressure. Which in turn I've been able to model as dynamic oscillations of the core as a whole." He displayed dense mathematics, which Siobhan recognized as nonlinear wave equations. "As you can see—"

"Eugene," Mikhail said gently, "don't you have some kind of picture of this?"

Eugene looked surprised by the question. "Of course I do." He tapped his softscreen and brought up an image of a sphere. It was covered by a kind of gridwork, like lines of longitude and latitude. And the pattern faded and pulsed rhythmically.

Bud Tooke whistled. "And this is the core of the sun? *Our* sun? The damn thing's ringing like a bell."

Rose Delea folded her arms and pulled her face. "Forgive a mere geologist for being skeptical, but the core of a star is a pretty massive bloody thing. How can it suddenly start to oscillate?"

Now Eugene's rather terrifying glare was turned on her. "But that's trivial."

Trivial: among academics that word was a killer put-down. Rose's face was a mask of hostility.

Siobhan said quickly, "Take it step by step, Eugene."

He said, "It goes back to the work of Cowling in the 1930s. Cowling showed that the rate of nuclear energy generation in the core is dependent on the *fourth* power of temperature. Which makes conditions in the core of the sun extremely sensitive to temperature changes . . ."

He was right, Siobhan realized uneasily. That fourth-power factor would lead to even small changes being magnified. Huge as it was, the core wasn't necessarily stable at all, and any small perturbation could disrupt it significantly.

Bud Tooke interrupted with a raised finger. "I don't get it, Eugene. So what? Even if the whole core explodes, it would take megayears for the bang to work its way out to the surface."

Rose Delea grinned sourly. "Don't tell me. The radiative layer is screwed too, right?"

She was correct; another of Eugene's images showed it. That great tank of slow-propagating energy was flawed by a puckered scar, like a wound stitched through flesh by a bullet. And so, Siobhan realized uncomfortably, the million-year lagging around the core wouldn't work as a protective layer: any energy released in the core could be squirted straight out to space.

Eugene looked at Rose, puzzled. "How did you know about the flaw?"

"Because this is turning out to be that kind of day."

Eugene talked on about his models of the core oscillations, and how he was hoping to run them back in time. "I'm intending to develop models of the inciting event of this instability, which—"

"Never mind the past for now," Siobhan interrupted. "Look forward. Show us what's to come."

Eugene seemed puzzled that the future should even be of interest compared with the deep physical mystery of the origin of this anomaly. But he obediently ran his graphic forward in time, at an accelerated pace.

Siobhan could see that the wave propagation through and around the core was complex, with multiple harmonics added to the base oscillations, and waves that were nonlinear, as the specialists would say, with energy leaking from one mode into another. But she immediately saw that there were patterns of interference, of dissipation—and, more ominously, of resonance, when the energy she could so clearly see flowing around the core of the sun gathered into powerful peaks.

Eugene froze the image. "Here's the most recent spike, the June 9 event." One side of the core was flaring bright with false color. "The observational data confirms my preliminary modeling, and validates my future projections . . ." By *observational data,* Siobhan thought ruefully, he meant a devastating storm that had cost thousands of human lives.

She asked, "And what's to come?"

He ran the model forward at a greater pace. The patterns of oscillation shifted and swam in Siobhan's vision, too rapid to follow in detail.

Then, suddenly, the image flared bright, all over the core, almost bright enough to dazzle. People flinched, briefly shocked.

Eugene shut down his graphics. He said laconically, "That's it."

Rose Delea said dangerously, "What do you mean, *that's it?*"

"At this point the model breaks down. The oscillations become so large that—"

"Your damn model!" Delea shouted. "Is that all you can think about?"

"Let's take it easy," Siobhan said, thinking fast. "Eugene, we're looking at another event here. Correct? Another June 9."

"Yes."

"But more energetic."

He looked at her, puzzled by her ignorance once more. "That's *obvious.*"

Siobhan glanced around the table, at wide-eyed, uncomfortable faces. Evidently Eugene hadn't shared these results with anybody before, not even Mikhail.

Bud asked, "*How* much more? And how will it manifest itself? How will it hit us, Eugene?"

Eugene tried to answer, but he descended quickly into technicalities.

Mikhail laid a hand on Bud's arm. "I don't think he can say. Not yet. I'll work with him on it." He went on thoughtfully, "But you know, this isn't unprecedented. We might be looking at another S Fornax."

"S Fornax?"

For decades the astronomers had been studying middle-aged stars of the sun's class, and on many of them had noticed cycles of activity similar to the sun's. But some stars showed rather more variability than others. An unspectacular star in the constellation called Fornax had suddenly flared up one day, shining twenty times as bright as usual, for maybe an hour.

Mikhail said, "If the sun erupted like S Fornax, the energy input would have been something like ten *thousand* times as bad as our worst solar storms."

"And what would that do?"

Mikhail shrugged. "Disable the whole satellite fleet. Destroy Earth's ozone layer. Melt the surfaces of the ice moons—"

Siobhan remembered dimly that the constellation name, *Fornax,* meant "furnace." How appropriate, she thought.

But Eugene actually laughed. "Oh, this core nonlinearity will be much more energetic than *that.* Orders of *magnitude* worse. Don't you even see that much?"

That crack brought him looks of resentment, even hatred.

Siobhan studied him, baffled. It was as if all this were no more than a mathematical exercise to him. He was just a boy who saw patterns, she thought, patterns in the data; the patterns' meaning in human terms was invisible to him. She felt almost frightened of him.

But she must concentrate on what he had said, not the way he said it. *Orders of magnitude.* To a physicist, indeed to a cosmologist, an *order of magnitude* meant a factor of ten. So whatever was coming would be ten, a hundred, a thousand times worse than June 9, worse even than this S Fornax event of Mikhail's. Her imagination quailed.

And there was one obvious question that had yet to be asked. "Eugene, do you have a date for this event?"

"Oh, yes," Eugene said. "The model's already good enough for that."

"*When,* Eugene?"

He tapped at his softscreen and gave a date in Julian days, an astronomer's date. It took Mikhail to translate it into human terms.

"April 20, 2042."

Bud looked at Siobhan. "Less than five years."

Suddenly Siobhan felt hugely weary. "Well, I guess I've found out what I came here to know. And maybe now you can see the need for security."

Rose Delea snorted. "Security, my arse. We could all run around naked with bags on our heads for the next five years and it wouldn't make any difference. You heard him. We," she said concisely, "are fucked."

Bud said firmly, "Not if I can help it." He stood up. "Lunchtime. I guess you might want to call your Prime Minister, Siobhan. Either of them. Then we get back to work."

14: MISSING IN ACTION

Too soon, time ran out for Bisesa.

Myra's school reopened. The headmistress understood that for some families, bereaved, displaced, shocked, or simply frightened, more recovery time was needed. But as the weeks wore by a note of insistence crept in. Disaster or no disaster, the education of the young had to go on: that was the law, and it was up to parents to fulfill their obligations.

For Bisesa, the pressure was mounting. She was going to have to release Myra before the social services came looking for her. The cocoon she had built around the two of them was starting to crack.

But it was the British Army that finally broke her out into the daylight. Bisesa received a polite e-mail asking her to report in to her commanding officer.

As far as the Army knew Bisesa had simply disappeared from her posting on June 8, *before* the solar storm, and her five-years-too-old ident chip making her untraceable, she had not been heard of since. In the immediate aftermath of the storm, the Army, in Afghanistan and elsewhere, had had other things to think about. But now the service's bureaucratic patience was running out.

Her bank accounts hadn't been frozen, not yet, but her salary had been stopped. Linda was still able to draw on the funds for shopping and bills, but Bisesa's level of savings, never high, was quickly dropping.

Then, still unable to find her, the Army switched its assessment of the cause of her vanishing from "possibly AWOL" to "missing in action." Letters were hand-delivered to her next of kin: her own parents in Cheshire, and Myra's paternal grandmother and father, parents of the child's deceased father.

Bisesa was lucky that the grandparents reacted first, and called her flat in a great flurry of concern. Their call gave Bisesa the chance to contact her parents before they opened their own letter. She wasn't close to her parents; the family had fallen out when her father had sold off the farm where Bisesa had grown up. She hadn't even contacted them since June 9, though she felt a little guilty about that. But they certainly didn't deserve the shock of opening such a letter, with its grave Ministry of Defense language about how all efforts were being made to trace her, and her effects would be returned to them, with deepest sympathies expressed . . . et cetera, et cetera.

She was able to spare her parents that. But she'd had to give away her location, and when the authorities came looking for her seriously she wouldn't be hard to find.

So she braced herself, and asked Aristotle to put her through to her commanding officer, in the UN base in Afghanistan.

While she waited for a reply, she continued to worry at her peculiar memories.

Of course there was one obvious explanation for it all. She did have scraps of physical evidence for her adventures on Mir—her own apparent aging, the scrambling of her ident chip. But all she really had to rely on were her own recollections of the event. And it didn't need the construction of a whole new Earth to explain that. Perhaps she had gone through some kind of *episode* that had scrambled her mind, impelled her to go AWOL, and brought her home to London. She might, after all, be crazy. She didn't think so, but it was a simpler explanation, and in the mundane calm of London it was a hard possibility to discount.

So she looked for verification.

She had known Abdikadir Omar and Casey Othic, her companions on Mir, before the Discontinuity, of course. Now she used

Aristotle, and a not-yet-canceled password, to hack into Army databases and check out their service records.

She found that Abdi and Casey were still out there in Afghanistan. After June 9 they had been pulled off their peacekeeping duties to help out with civil emergencies in the nearby town of Peshawar, Pakistan. They were still there now, quietly doing their duties. There was no sign that they had gone through anything resembling Bisesa's experience.

She tried to make sense of all this. Abdi and Casey had undoubtedly followed her to Mir—but it seemed that those "versions" of Abdi and Casey on Mir had been extrapolated from a slice of time, the moment of Discontinuity as they had called it on Mir, while the "originals," oblivious, lived out their lives here on Earth.

She didn't speak to either of them directly. She had grown very close to them in the course of their shared experiences on Mir. It would be hard to bear if they were distant now.

She began to dig into the characters she remembered from 1885.

Kipling's life of course had been covered by many biographers. As a young journalist, he had indeed been in the area of Jamrud in 1885, and had gone on, apparently unperturbed by his passage through the Discontinuity, to international fame later. She couldn't trace any of the Empire-period British officers she had encountered, but that was no surprise; time and subsequent wars had taken a heavy toll on such records. Of the more remarkable historical figures whose paths had crossed hers she could learn little new; they were so remote in time that she could only confirm that nothing in their accepted biographies was contradicted by her experience.

There was another, less famous name for her to check, though. It took her some digging: most of the world's genealogical databases were now online, but after June 9 many electronic memory stores were still more or less scrambled.

There had indeed been a Joshua White, she found. Born in 1862 in Boston, his father had been a journalist who had covered the War Between the States, just as Josh had told her, and Josh himself had become a war correspondent in his father's footsteps. It gave her quite a start when she found a grainy photograph of Josh, aged just a few years older than when she had known him, proudly displaying a book based on his reportage of the British Empire's military escapades on the North–West Frontier, and later in South Africa.

It was eerie to page forward through the sparse accounts of a life lived on to ages much older than when she had known him. He had fallen in love, she saw with a pang of loss: aged thirty-five, he married a Boston Catholic, who gave him two sons. But he was cut down in his fifties, dying in the blood-sodden mud of Passchendaele, as he sought to cover yet another war.

This was a man who, on a different world, had fallen in love with her—an unconditional love she had clung to, but sadly had been unable to return. And yet *this* Joshua was the original, and the lost boy who loved her had been a mere copy. His had been a love she had never even wanted—and that had never, in some real sense, even happened at all. But the historical existence of Josh was surely proof that *all this was real;* there was no plausible way she could have heard of this obscure nineteenth-century journalist and built a delusion around him.

Of course there was one more record to check. Deeply uneasy, she went back to the military service records and extended her search.

She discovered that unlike Abdi and Casey, no "original" of herself was to be found in Afghanistan, serving the Army, living on oblivious. Of course she hadn't expected to find "herself" out there, for otherwise the Army wouldn't have been looking for her. It was still an eerie confirmation, however.

She tried to absorb this. If she was the only one who had vanished altogether from this version of Earth, then she had somehow, and for some reason, been treated *differently* by the Firstborn, who had been responsible for all this in the first place. That was disturbing enough.

But how much stranger it might have been if she *had* discovered a version of herself living on in Afghanistan . . .

15: BOTTLENECK

Miriam Grec tried to focus on what Siobhan McGorran was telling her.

It wasn't easy. This briefing room was on the fortieth floor of the Livingstone Tower—or the "Euro-needle" as every Londoner called it, including Miriam when off camera. The windows were broad sheets of toughened glass, and the October sky was a shade of blue that reminded her of childhood visits to Provence with her French-born father. What color would Papa have called that sky? Cerulean? Powder blue?

On such a day, under such a sky, with London spread out like a shining tapestry before her, it was hard for Miriam to remember that she was no longer a small child but Prime Minister of all Eurasia, with grave responsibilities. And it was hard to accept such bad news as Siobhan's.

Siobhan sat calmly, waiting for her words to sink in.

Nicolaus Korombel, Miriam's press secretary, was the only other person in the room for this sensitive meeting. Polish-born, he had a habit of wearing shirts a couple of sizes too small for his spreading desk-job girth, and Miriam could actually see belly hair curl past its straining buttons. But he was the inner-circle advisor on whom she relied most heavily, and his assessment of Siobhan would be important in her final judgment of what she had to say.

Now Nicolaus sat back, locked his fingers behind his head, and blew out his cheeks. "So we're looking at the mother of all solar storms."

"You could put it that way," Siobhan said dryly.

"But we survived June 9, and everybody said *that* was the worst storm in recorded history. What can we expect this time? To lose the satellites, the ozone layer . . ."

Siobhan said, "We're talking about an energy injection many orders of magnitude greater than June 9."

Miriam held her hands up. "Professor McGorran, I was a lawyer in the days when I had a real job. I'm afraid such phrases mean little to me."

Siobhan allowed herself a smile. "I apologize. Prime Minister—"

"Oh, call me Miriam. I have a feeling we're going to be working together rather closely."

"Miriam, then. I do understand. Astronomer Royal I may be, but this isn't my specialty. I'm struggling with it too." Siobhan brought up a summary slide, a table of numbers that filled the big wall softscreen. "Let me go through the bottom line again. In April 2042, just four and a half years from now, we anticipate a major solar event. There will be an equatorial brightening of the sun, essentially, an outflux of energy that will bathe the orbital plane of Earth, and the other planets. We anticipate that Earth will intercept some ten to power twenty-four joules of energy. That's a central figure; we have a ninety-nine percent confidence limit of an order of magnitude up or down."

There was that term again. *"Order of magnitude?"*

"A power of ten."

Nicolaus rubbed his face. "I hate to admit my ignorance. I know a joule is a measure of energy, but I have no idea how large it is. And all those exponents—I understand that ten to power twenty-four means, umm, a trillion *trillion,* but—"

Siobhan said patiently, "The detonation of a one-megaton nuclear weapon releases around ten to power fifteen joules—that's a thousand trillion. The world's nuclear arsenal at its Cold War peak was around ten thousand megatons; we're probably down to some ten percent of that today."

Nicolaus was doing arithmetic in his head. "So your injection of ten to power twenty-four joules from the sun—"

"It amounts to a billion megatons, pouring over Earth. Or a hundred *thousand* times the energy that would have been released in a worst-case nuclear conflagration." She said the words coolly, meeting their eyes. She was trying to make them understand, step by step, Miriam saw; she was trying to make them believe.

Nicolaus said grimly, "Why did nobody alert us to this before? Why did it take *you* to dig this out? What's going on up there on the Moon?"

But it wasn't the Moon that was the problem, it seemed; it was the muddled head of the young scientist who had figured all this out.

"Eugene Mangles," Miriam said.

"Yes," Siobhan said. "He's brilliant, but not quite connected to the rest of us. We need him. But we have to dig the bad news out of his head."

Nicolaus snapped, "And what else isn't he telling us?"

Miriam held up a hand. "Siobhan—just give me a headline. How bad will this be?"

"The modeling is still uncertain," Siobhan said. "But that much energy—it would strip away the atmosphere altogether." She shrugged. "The oceans will boil, vaporize. The Earth itself will survive: the rocky planet. Life in the deep rocks, kilometers down, might live through it. Extremophile bacteria, heat lovers."

"But not us," Nicolaus said.

"Not us. And nothing of the surface biosphere, on the land, in the air, or the seas." In the silence that followed, Siobhan said, "I'm sorry. This is a terrible thing to have brought home from the Moon. I don't know any way to soften this."

They fell silent again, trying to digest what she had said.

Nicolaus brought Miriam a cup of tea on a monogrammed saucer. It was Earl Grey, the way she preferred it. The old myth that the British were addicted to their watery, milky cuppas was at least half a century out of date, but Miriam, a Prime Minister of Europe and with a French father, always took great pains not to offend the sensibilities of anybody on this still residually Euro-skeptic island. So she took her Earl Grey hot and without milk, out of sight of the cameras.

In this silent pause for thought, with her teacup cradled in her hands, Miriam was drawn to the window, and the city.

The silver stripe of the Thames cut through London's geography, as it always had. To the east the City, still second only to Moscow as a Eurasian financial center, was a clutter of skyscrapers. The City occupied much of what had once been Roman London, and in her time as a student here Miriam had once walked the line of the wall of that primal settlement, a trail that ran a few kilometers from the Tower to Blackfriars Bridge. When the Romans had gone the Saxons had developed a new town to the west of the old walls, the area now known as the West End. With the great expansion of the cities that had followed the Industrial Revolution, those complicated knots of multilayered history had been drowned by new suburban development, until London was the heart of a vast conurbation that today reached out as far as Brighton in the south and Milton Keynes to the north.

The basic geography of London hadn't changed much since the 1950s, perhaps. But a witness from that receding age would have been astonished by the glimmering width of the Thames, and the massive flanks of the new flood barriers that could be dimly glimpsed past the shoulders of buildings. The Thames had been tamed over the centuries, pushed into a deepening, narrowing channel, its tributaries bricked over, its floodplain built on. Until the turn of the century, London had got away with it. But the world's climate shifts had brought an inexorable rise in sea levels, and humans had been forced to retreat before the Thames's determined retaking of its ancient territories.

The reality of climate change and its effects were undeniable, and a day-to-day political reality for Miriam. Remarkably the argument about the cause of it all still continued. But that decades-old debate was moot now, as attention had gradually switched to the need to *fix* things. There was a will to act, Miriam thought, a gladdening and growing realization that things had gone too far, that something must be done.

But it was surprisingly hard to focus that energy. Long-term demographic changes had led to an aging of the population in the West: more than half of all Western Europeans and Americans were now over sixty-five, mostly unproductive, and conservative with it. Meanwhile the interconnectedness of the world had culminated with the great UNESCO program to equip every twelve-year-old on the globe with a phone of her own. The result was a detachment from traditional political structures among the young and middle-aged, who, educated and interconnected, often showed more loyalty to others like them around the world than to the nations of which they were nominally citizens.

If you looked at the world as a whole, this was probably the most truly democratic, educated, and enlightened age in history. The growth of a literate, interconnected elite certainly made major wars a lot less likely in the future. But it did make it hard to get anything done—especially when tough choices had to be made.

And it seemed that tough choices faced Miriam now.

At fifty-three, Miriam Grec was in her second year as Prime Minister of the Eurasian Union. She was the senior political figure across a swath of the Old World that stretched from the Atlantic coast of Ireland to the Pacific coast of Russia, and from Scandinavia in the north to Israel in the south. It was an empire no Caesar or Khan could have contemplated—but Miriam was no emperor. Enmeshed in the complicated federal politics of the young Union, buffeted by tensions between the great power blocs that dominated the world of the mid-twenty-first century, and having to cope with more primitive forces of religion, ethnicity, and residual nationalism, she sometimes felt as if she were trapped in a spiderweb.

Of course, she would never have swapped places with her only nominal superior in Eurasia, the President, who had the power to do nothing but launch spaceplanes and visit the sick. However, the present incumbent was well suited by heredity and upbringing to such a role—though there had been universal astonishment at his election. Perhaps it said something about the yearning of the people for tradition and stability that the third democratically elected President of Eurasia was the King of Great Britain . . .

Miriam tried to assess Siobhan McGorran. The Astronomer Royal, a rather earnest woman with a dark Celtic intensity, had clearly taken her mission to provide Miriam with a briefing on the events of June 9 very seriously, including that trip to the Moon, which Miriam rather envied. But Miriam's problem was that Siobhan was not the first person to have stood before her and pronounced on global doom and gloom.

This was a dangerous century, the experts kept saying. Climate change, eco-collapse, demographic changes—a bottleneck for humankind, some called it. Miriam accepted that basic view. But already it was clear that some of the very worst projections from the beginning of this century of change hadn't come to pass. Miriam had learned that she had to apply a filter, a very unscientific and inexpert screen of judgment, to sort the wheat from the chaff, a judgment based as much on her impression of the character of the bringer of each bit of bad news as on the content of what she had to say.

That was why she was coming to think that she would have to take Siobhan McGorran very seriously indeed.

Nicolaus said, "Of course we'll have to check everything out."

"But you do believe me." Siobhan seemed neither gratified nor humble; she just wanted to get on with the job, Miriam thought.

But what a dreadful job that was. Miriam banged her small fist on the tabletop. "Damn, damn."

Siobhan turned to her. "Miriam?"

"You know, in my job things generally look grim, day to day. Here we are right in the throat of this bottleneck of history. We make mistakes, we squabble, we never agree, we take one step back for every two forward. And yet we're finding our way through." It was true. America, for instance, which had taken more of a beating on June 9 than any other region, had already recovered substantially, and was now even sending aid convoys out around the world. "I believe that we're coming together as a species as a result of our coping with all these crises. Growing up, if you like. We work together, we help each other. We take care of the place we live."

Siobhan nodded. "My daughter has signed up for the Animal Ethics movement." This was a grouping determined to extend the concept of human rights to other intelligent mammals, birds, and reptiles. Its case had been reinforced by the taxonomists reclassifying the two chimp species as part of the genus *Homo,* along with humans—immediately making them Legal Persons (Nonhuman) with equivalent rights to humans, and indeed equivalent to Aristotle, the planet's other fully sentient inhabitant. "It might be too little too late but—"

Miriam said, "I had hopes that if we could just get through this mess of a century, we could be on the verge of greatness. And now, when the future shows such promise, *this.*"

Siobhan was looking absent. "I had similar conversations on the Moon. Bud Tooke said it was "ironic" this should happen just now. You know, scientists are suspicious of coincidences. A conspiracy theorist certainly might wonder if the fact that our capabilities are growing, and the arrival of this incoming disaster, *at the same time,* really is just bad luck."

Nicolaus frowned. "What do you mean by that?"

"I'm not sure," Siobhan said. "A loose thread of thought . . ."

Miriam said firmly, "Let's stay focused. Siobhan, tell us what we need to do."

"Do?"

"What options do we have?"

Siobhan shook her head. "I've been asked that before. It's not as if this is an asteroid we might push away. *This is the sun,* Miriam."

Nicolaus asked, "What about Mars? Isn't Mars farther from the sun?"

"Yes—but not so far it will make a difference to anything alive on its surface."

Miriam said, "You mentioned something about the deep life on Earth surviving."

"The deep hot biosphere, yes. It's thought that that's the wellspring from which life started on Earth in the first place. I suppose that could happen again. Like a reboot. But it would take millions of years just for single-celled life-forms to recolonize the land." She smiled wistfully. "I doubt if any future intelligence would even know we had ever existed."

Nicolaus said, "Could we survive down there? Could we eat those bugs?"

Siobhan looked dubious. "Maybe a deep enough bunker . . . How could it be self-sufficient? And the surface would be ruined; there would be no possibility of reemergence. Ever."

Miriam stood up, anger fueling her energy. "And is that what we're to tell people? That they should dig a hole in the ground and wait to die? I need something better than that, Siobhan."

The Astronomer Royal stood. "Yes, ma'am."

"We'll speak again." Restless, Miriam began pacing. She said to Nicolaus, "We'll have to clear my schedule for the rest of the day."

"Already done."

"And set up some calls."

"America first?"

"Of course . . ."

She led the way from the room, energetic, bristling, planning. This wasn't over yet. In fact this was just the beginning.

For Miriam Grec, the end of the world had become a personal challenge.

16: DEBRIEF

Bisesa had to go through it all once again.

"And then you came home," Corporal Batson said with exaggerated emphasis. "From this—other place."

Bisesa suppressed a sigh. "From Mir. Yes, I came home. And that's the hardest to explain."

The two of them sat in George Batson's small office, here in Aldershot. The room was painted in reassuring pastel colors, and there was a seascape hanging on the wall. It was an environment designed to reassure nutcases, she thought wryly.

Batson was watching her carefully. "Just tell me what happened."

"I saw an eclipse . . ."

She had somehow been drawn *into* an Eye, a great Eye in ancient Babylon. And through the Eye she had been brought home, to her flat in London, to the early morning of that fateful day, June 9.

But she hadn't come straight home. There had been one other place she had visited: she and Josh, though he had been allowed to go no farther. It had been a blasted plain of crimson rock and dirt. Thinking about it now, it reminded her of the barren wastes patiently photographed by the crew of the *Aurora 1,* explorers on Mars. But she could breathe the air; surely this was the Earth.

And then there was the eclipse. The sun had been high in the sky. The Moon's shadow had drawn over the sun—but had not covered it; a ring of light had been left hanging.

Batson's pencil made soft, careful scratching sounds, recording this fantastic tale.

The Army was trying to be fair.

After she had reported to her commanding officer in Afghanistan, she had been ordered to report to a Ministry of Defense office in London, and then sent for medical and psychological tests here in Aldershot. For the time being they allowed her to go back home to Myra each evening. They had given her a tag, though, a smart tattoo on the sole of her foot.

And now, as she waited for the results of her physical tests, she was being "debriefed," as he had put it, by this facile young psychologist.

She had decided to tell the Army everything. She couldn't see how it would help her to lie. And her story—*if* it was true—was after all of shattering, transcendent importance. She was a soldier, and she believed she had a duty: the authorities, beginning with her own chain of command, had to know what she knew, and she had to try to make them believe it.

And as for herself—"Well," as cousin Linda said cheerfully, "they can only section you once!"

The process was difficult to tolerate, though. Technically she outranked this corporal, but here in his study he was the psychologist, she the one with a screw loose; there was no question about who was in control. It didn't help that he was so much younger than she was.

And it didn't help that back on Mir she had known another Batson in the British Army, another corporal. She longed to ask Batson about his family background, and if he knew of a grandfather six or seven generations back who might have served on the North–West Frontier. But she knew she'd better not.

"Since our last session I looked up eclipses," Batson said, referring to his notes. "The Moon's distance from Earth varies a bit, it says here. So a 'total' eclipse may not be total. You can have the sun and Moon centered on the same spot of sky, but with a little bit of the sun's disk peeking out because the Moon's apparent size isn't great enough. It's called an annular eclipse."

"I know about annular eclipses," she said. "I checked it out too. The ring I saw was much fatter than in any annular eclipse."

"So let's think about the geometry," Batson said. "What are the possibilities that could produce what you saw? Maybe the sun was bigger. Or the Moon smaller. Or the Earth was closer to the sun. Or the Moon farther away from Earth."

She was surprised. "I hadn't expected you to analyze my vision like this."

He raised his eyebrows. "But you keep saying it wasn't just a vision. I showed your sketches to an astronomer friend. She told me that actually the Moon *is* moving away from the Earth, over time. Did you know that? Something to do with the tides—can't say I understand it. But there it is; you can prove it with laser beams. It's a slow drift, though. We won't get an eclipse like yours until at least 150 million years from now." He eyed her. "Does that number mean anything to you?"

She tried to keep herself calm, through long habit, as she processed this new and startling bit of information. "What could it mean?"

"You're supposed to be telling me, remember. You say you've been shown all this—indeed you've been brought home—for some purpose. A conscious purpose of those whom you believe have engineered all this. The ones you call—" He checked his notes.

"The Firstborn," she said.

"Yes. Do you have any idea *why* you should be selected, manipulated in this way?"

"I challenged them," she said. Then: "I've really no idea. I feel I'm being told something, but I can't figure out the meaning." She looked at him miserably. "Does that make me sound crazy?"

"Actually the contrary. My personal experience is that sane people accept that the world is bafflingly complex and arbitrarily unfair. Let's face it, that's certainly true in the Army! The crazies are the ones who think they understand it all."

"So the fact that I can't make any sense of all this inclines you to believe me," she said dryly.

"I didn't quite say that," he cautioned. "But I knew from the moment you walked in that you are telling the truth, as you see it. I just haven't yet been able to rule out the possibility all this actually happened . . ." A softscreen lit up on his desk. "Excuse me." He tapped the surface, and she glimpsed tables and graphs scrolling.

After a moment he said, "Your report from the sawbones has come in. You'll have to discuss the results with her, of course. But as far as I can see you're certainly who you say you are: your DNA and dental records prove it. You're healthy enough, though you appear to bear the relics of a number of rather exotic diseases. And your skin has soaked up rather more ultraviolet than is good for you."

She smiled. "On Mir, the climate broke down. We all got sunburned."

"And—ah." He sat back, gazing at the screen.

"What is it?"

"According to *this* result—the quacks looked at your telomerase, whatever that is, something to do with the aging of your cells—you are more than five years older than you should be." He eyed her and grinned. "Well, well. The plot thickens, Lieutenant." He seemed rather pleased at the way things were turning out.

17: BRAINSTORM

Once more Siobhan sat with Toby Pitt in the Council Room of the Royal Society.

From a wall-mounted softscreen the crumpled, rather melancholy features of Mikhail Martynov peered out. Siobhan thought he always looked as if there ought to be a roll-up cigarette sticking out of the corner of his mouth, but even the latest noncarcinogenic, nonaddictive, nonpolluting comfort smokes would never be allowed in the enclosed environment of a Moon base. Mikhail said, "If only the problem were simpler—if only we faced nothing worse than an asteroid coming to knock us on the head! Where is Bruce Willis when you need him?"

Toby asked, "Who?"

"Never mind. I have an unhealthy fascination with bad movies of the last century . . ."

Siobhan let their nervous banter roll on. A week after her second return from the Moon she was overtired and stressed out, and a headache niggled behind her eyes. After interplanetary space she felt smothered in the fusty atmosphere of the Society, with its smell of furniture polish, the huge coffee dispenser gurgling away to itself in the corner, and the vast heap of digestive biscuits on a plate on the table. And she was close to despair. Since accepting Miriam's mandate to find a way to deal with the solar event, after a month of research she had elicited nothing but waves of hopelessness and negative thinking from "experts" around the world.

Mikhail and Toby, this motley crew, was her last gamble. But she wasn't about to tell them that. She said briskly, "Let's get on with it."

Mikhail glanced at notes off camera. "I have Eugene's latest predictions."

Graphics glowed in the smart top of the table before Siobhan and Toby, showing energy flux plotted against wavelength, particle mass, and other parameters. "Nothing substantial has changed, I'm afraid. We are looking at a major influx of solar energy on April 20, 2042. It will last most of twenty-four hours, so that almost every point on Earth's surface will be turned directly into the fire. We won't even have the shelter of night. As we will be close to the spring equinox, even the poles won't be spared. At this stage do you need the details of what will become of the atmosphere, the oceans? No. Suffice to say the Earth will be sterilized to a depth of tens of meters beneath the ground.

"But," Mikhail went on, "we now have a much more precise handle on *how* the energy will be delivered. We are looking at flaws in the radiative and convective zones, where a great deal of energy is in normal times stored . . ." He tapped the hidden surface before him, and one tabletop chart was highlighted.

"Ah," Siobhan said. "The intensity will peak in the visible spectrum."

"As the spectrum of sunlight does normally," Mikhail said. "In green light, as it happens. Which is where our eyes are most sensitive, and where chlorophyll works best—which is why, no doubt, chlorophyll was selected by evolution to serve as the photosynthetic chemical that fuels all aerobic plant life."

"Then that's what we face: a storm of green light from the sun," Siobhan said firmly. "Let's talk about options to deal with it."

Toby grinned. "The fun part!"

Mikhail offered, "Shall I begin?" He tapped at his softscreen, and on the displays before Siobhan a number of schematics, tables, and images came up.

"As it happens," Mikhail said, "even before our present crisis a number of thinkers have considered ways to reduce the solar insolation—the proportion of the sun's energy flux that reaches the planet. Of course this was mostly in the context of blocking sunlight to mitigate global warming." He brought up images of clouds of dust injected into the high atmosphere. "One proposal is to use space launchers to fire sub-micrometer dust up into the stratosphere. That way you would mimic the effects of a volcanic eruption; after a big bang like Krakatoa you often get a global temperature drop of a degree or two for a few years. Or you could inject sulfur particles up there, which would burn in the atmosphere's oxygen to give you a layer of sulfuric acid. That might be rather lighter and so easier to deliver."

Siobhan said, "But how much of the storm would this screen out?"

Mikhail and Toby displayed their figures. It turned out to be only a few percent.

"Enough to mitigate global warming, perhaps," Mikhail said sadly. "But far from adequate for the problem we face now. We are going to have to take out almost *all* of the incoming radiation—letting even one percent through may be far too much."

"Then we'll have to think bigger," Siobhan said firmly.

Toby said slyly, "Bigger it is. If you want to inject dust into the air, rather than trying to mimic a volcano—why not just set one off?"

Mikhail and Siobhan glanced at each other, startled. Then they went to work.

Coming up with such ideas was precisely why Siobhan had invited Toby to these sessions.

He had been unsure. "Siobhan, why me? I'm an events manager, for heaven's sake! My contribution should have ended at making sure there were enough biscuits to go around."

She had studied him with fond exasperation. He was a big, somewhat overweight, shambling man, with raggedly cut brown hair and a weak chin. He wasn't even a scientist; he had majored in languages. He was a peculiarly English type who would always be valued by stuffy British institutions like the Royal Society, not only for his intelligence and obvious competence, but also for his comforting air of upper-middle-class safeness. But he had one typically English characteristic that she, born in Northern Ireland and so something of an outsider, didn't value so highly, and that was an excess of self-deprecation.

"Toby, you're not here for biscuits, appreciated though they are, but for your other career."

He looked briefly baffled. "My books?"

"Precisely." Toby had published a whole series of lyrically written popular histories of forgotten corners of science and technology. And that was what had prompted her to turn to him. "Toby, we're faced by a megaproblem. But since Tsiolkovski people have been dreaming up a whole suite of more or less wacky mega-engineering possibilities. And that's what I think we're going to need to draw on now."

There had been one group in London she was thinking of particularly, called the British Interplanetary Society. "I gave them a chapter in one of my books," Toby had told her when she mentioned them. "The Society has been absorbed into a pan-European grouping now, and doesn't seem to be half so much fun. But in its heyday it was a place to play for a lot of respectable scientists and engineers. They dreamed up lots of ways to bother the universe ..." This sort of fringe thinking was what they needed to draw on now, she believed.

He grinned. "So I'm an ambassador from the lunatic fringe? Thanks very much."

But Mikhail had said, "We must consider ways to protect the whole Earth. Nobody has faced such responsibility before. I think in the circumstances a little lunacy might be just what we need!"

With some hard work on their softscreens, and frequent calls to Aristotle, they hurriedly fleshed out Toby's volcano option. Perhaps it could be done—but it would have to be a *big* volcanic bang, far bigger than any in recorded history and possibly bigger than anything in the geological record. As nobody had tried such a thing before, its effects would be quite unpredictable, and possibly a remedy even worse than the problem. Siobhan stored the discussion in a file in Aristotle's capacious memory that she labeled "last resorts."

They quickly rattled through some more research on so-called "intrinsic" methods of protection, things you could do within the Earth's atmosphere, or maybe from low orbit. But they all provided inadequate screening. There was no reason why some of these methods shouldn't be put in place. They would provide an extra few percent of cover—and would at least give the impression to the public that something was being done, a not inconsiderable political factor. But if they couldn't dig up a way to knock out almost all of the sun's ferocious glare, such projects would be nothing but sops, which wouldn't make any difference to the final outcome.

"So we move on," Siobhan said. "What next?"

Toby said, "If we can't protect the Earth, perhaps we have to flee."

Mikhail growled, "Where? The storm will be so intense that even Mars is not safe."

"The outer planets, then. An ice moon of Jupiter—"

"Even at five times Earth's distance, the reduction in intensity of the storm would not be sufficient to save us."

"Saturn, then," Toby pressed. "We could hide on Titan. Or a moon of Uranus, or Neptune. Or we could flee the solar system altogether."

Siobhan said quietly, "The stars? Can we build a starship, Toby?"

"Make it a generation starship. That's the most primitive sort: an ark, big enough to hold a few hundred people. It might take a thousand years to reach Alpha Centauri, say. But if the emigrants' children, living and dying on the ship, could continue the mission—and then *their* children would do the same—eventually humans, or at least descendants of humans, would reach the stars."

Mikhail nodded. "Another idea of Tsiolkovski's."

Toby said, "Actually, I think it was Bernal."

Siobhan said, "How many people could we save that way?"

Mikhail shrugged. "A few hundred, maybe?"

"A few hundred is better than none," Toby said grimly. "A gene pool of that size is enough to start again."

Mikhail said, "The Adam and Eve option?"

"It's not good enough," Siobhan said. "We are not about to give up on saving the billions who are to be put to the torch. We have to do better, guys."

Mikhail sighed sadly. Toby averted his eyes.

As the silence lengthened, she realized that they had nothing more to offer. She felt despair settle inside her, suffocating—despair and guilt, as if this huge catastrophe, and their inability to think their way out of it, were somehow her fault.

There was a modest cough.

Surprised, she looked up into the empty air. "Aristotle?"

"I'm sorry to break in, Siobhan. I've been taking the liberty of running supplementary searches of my own based on your conversation. There is an option you may have missed."

"There is?"

Mikhail, in his softscreen image, leaned forward. "Get to the point. What do you suggest?"

"A shield," Aristotle said.

A shield? . . .

Data began to download to their displays.

18: ANNOUNCEMENT

The President of the United States took her seat behind her desk in the Oval Office.

The place was calm, for once. Just a single camera faced her, a single microphone loomed over her, and a single technician watched her. The office was equipped with only simple props: a Stars and Stripes, and a Christmas tree to mark this month of December 2037. As the tech counted her down on his fingers in the time-honored way, the President touched the simple necklace at her throat, but she resisted the temptation to adjust the black hair, now threaded with silver, that her makeup artist had spent so long sculpting.

Juanita Alvarez was the first Hispanic woman to become President of what remained overwhelmingly the most powerful single nation on the planet. With her compassion, her blunt common sense, and her obvious gut instinct for the health of a democracy, the people who had voted for her, and many who hadn't, had taken her to their hearts.

But today she was speaking to more than just the citizens of America. Today her message, simultaneously translated by Aristotle and Thales into all the spoken, written, and gestural languages of humanity, would be broadcast by TV, radio, and webcast to three planets. Later her words and their implications would be analyzed and parsed, praised and criticized, until the last bit of sense had been wrung out of them, as none of her words had ever been examined before—and almost immediately, of course, based as much on what she had *not* said as on the words themselves, a legion of conspiracy theories would spring up.

That was to be expected. It was hard to imagine that any President, even the great wartime leaders, had ever had a more important message for her people and the world. And if Alvarez fouled up, her words themselves, through creating panic, disorder, and economic instability, could cause more damage than some small wars.

But if she was nervous, it showed only in the slightly uncertain motions of her hands.

The tech's fingers folded down. *Three, two, one.*

"My fellow Americans. My fellow citizens of planet Earth, and beyond. Thank you for listening to me today. I think many of you will anticipate what I have to say to you. It's probably the sign of a healthy democracy that not even the Oval Office is leakproof." A small smile, expertly delivered. "I have to tell you that we all face a grave danger. And yet if we work together, with courage and generosity, I assure you there is hope."

Siobhan sat with her daughter Perdita in her mother's small flat in Hammersmith.

Because of her increasing deafness Maria had her softwall's sound turned up so high it was sometimes painful. The din didn't seem to bother twenty-year-old Perdita, though. Even as the President was talking, she let a competing show from another channel run on the small softscreen implant on her wrist. It was nice to know, Siobhan thought wryly, that the world's media outlets provided choice, even at a time like this.

Maria came bustling through from the kitchen with three glasses of a cream liqueur—small glasses, Siobhan noticed a bit sourly, and no sign of the bottle for replenishment.

"Well, this is nice," Maria said, handing out the glasses. She smiled, and the small facial scars of her surgery puckered. "It must be a long time since all three of us got together, aside from an occasional Christmas. It's a shame it took the end of the world to make it happen."

Perdita laughed around a salted cracker. "There's always an edge to you, Grandma! We do have lives of our own, you know."

Siobhan glared at her daughter. Since Perdita herself had reached age twelve Siobhan had sympathized with her own mother's occasional clinginess. "Let's not argue," Siobhan said. "And it *isn't* the end of the world, Mother. You shouldn't go around saying that. Especially not if people think it's *me* that's saying it. You could start a panic."

Maria sniffed, as always unreasonably miffed at being told off.

Perdita said now, "Of course a lot of what Alvarez is going to say is guff. Isn't it, Mum?"

"*Guff?*"

"Do you think anybody's going to *believe* it? Saving the world is *so* 1990s disaster movie! I heard a guy on the TV the other day saying it's all a form of denial, a displacement activity. And of course it's such a fascistic dream!"

There could be something in that, Siobhan thought uneasily. It wouldn't be the first time the sun had been co-opted as a source of authority.

As it happened, sun cults were quite rare in history. They tended to arise in organized, heavily centralized states—the Romans, the Egyptians, the Aztecs—the central power of the sun serving as a source of authority for the one ruler. Maybe in this situation the sudden malevolence of the sun might similarly be utilized by those who sought power on Earth. That sort of suspicion fueled conspiracy theories among those who, despite the memory of June 9, suspected the whole business of the storm on the sun was a scam, a power grab by some cabal of businessmen or hidden government, a coup arising out of a new center fueled by fear and ignorance.

"Nobody *believes* it," Perdita said. "Nobody believes in heroes anymore, Mum—certainly not chisel-jawed astronauts and public-spirited politicians. Life just doesn't work that way."

"Well, maybe so," Siobhan said, irritated. "But what can you do but try? And, Perdita—if we can't save the planet after all—how will it make you feel?"

Perdita shrugged. "I'll get on with things, until—" She mimed an explosion with her hands. "*Blammo,* I guess. What else can you do?"

Maria touched Siobhan's shoulder. "Perdita's young. When you're twenty you think you're immortal. All this is probably beyond her imagination."

"And mine," Siobhan said. She looked at Perdita, distracted. "At least until I had a kid. After that the future got personal . . . You know, I'm relieved it's out in the open. I've felt guilty walking around London, mixing with people going about their lives, knowing I had a devastating secret locked up in my head like an unexploded bomb. It didn't seem right. Who was I to keep back a truth like that? Even if we do cause some panic."

"I think most people will behave pretty well," Maria said. "People generally do, you know."

They listened to the President's words.

"What will happen in April 2042 is unprecedented," President Alvarez said. "So far as our experts can tell, there has been no event like it in the recorded history of humankind, or indeed in the silent eons before us. In a single day the sun will inflict on the Earth as much energy as it would normally transmit to us in a year. The scientists call this the *sunstorm,* and the name strikes me as apt.

"The consequences for Earth, and indeed for the Moon and Mars, are grave. I will not spare you the full truth. We face the sterilization of the surface of Earth—the elimination of all life—and the blasting away of the air and the oceans. Earth will be left like the Moon. There are links attached to this message that will give you all the details we have; there are to be no secrets.

"We clearly face a mortal danger. And it is not just ourselves who are at risk. In these times of a widening ethical horizon, a development I have always supported, we will not forget the threat posed to the creatures who share this Earth with us, and without whom we could not survive ourselves—and indeed the newest kind of life to arrive on our world, the Legal Persons known as Aristotle and Thales through whom I am speaking to many of you now.

"This is a terrible message, then, and it grieves me to have to be the one to deliver it." She leaned forward. "But, as I told you, there is hope."

Mikhail and Eugene sat in the Clavius canteen, lukewarm cups of coffee on the table before them. The face of the President, relayed from Earth, was projected from a big wall-mounted softscreen. The canteen was all but deserted. Even though most people here at Clavius knew almost everything Alvarez had to say before she opened her mouth, it seemed that they preferred to absorb the bad news alone, or with those closest to them.

Mikhail wandered to the big picture window and looked out at the broken landscape of the crater floor. The sun was low, but the rim mountains that shouldered over the horizon glowed with light, as if their peaks were coated with burning magnesium.

Everything he saw in this landscape was a product of violence, he thought: violence from the tiny impacts of the micrometeorites that even now sandblasted the ground, scaling up all the way back up to the sculpting of great basins like Clavius, and the unimaginably savage collision that had split the Moon from the Earth in the first place. Over the brief lifetime of humanity, this little corner of the cosmos had been relatively peaceful, the solar system turning like orderly clockwork about the faithful light at its heart. But now the ancient violence was returning. Why should humans have ever imagined it had gone away in the first place?

He glanced up to find the Earth, which rode a quarter of the way up the sky. It was a matter of regret for him that the Earth was so difficult to see from Shackleton, down at the pole. As seen from here at Clavius, Earth, tens of times brighter than the full Moon in its own skies, bathed the shadowed lunar lands with a silver-blue light. The home world's phases, always the mirror image of the Moon's, followed a stately monthly cycle, but unlike the Moon, Earth spun on its axis every day, bringing new landforms, oceans, and cloud formations into view. And of course, unlike the Moon's slow journeying, the Earth never shifted from its position in the lunar sky.

After April 2042 the Earth would still be hanging up there, just as it always had. But he wondered how it would look then.

Eugene continued to watch the President's broadcast. "She's being vague about the date."

"What do you mean?"

Eugene glanced at him. Today that lovely face was contorted by a stress Mikhail hadn't seen before. "Why doesn't she just say April 20? Everybody *knows*."

Evidently not, Mikhail thought. Perhaps Alvarez had some psychological motivation in mind. Maybe overprecision would make the whole prospect *too* scary—it would start doomsday clocks ticking in people's heads. "I don't think it matters," he said.

But to Eugene, author of the prediction, it evidently did.

Mikhail sat down. "Eugene, it must be very strange for you to hear the President herself speaking to the whole human race about something that you figured out."

"Strange. Yes. Something like that," Eugene said, his speech rapid and broken. He held his hands parallel before him. "You have the sun. And you have my model of the sun." He locked his fingers together. "They are different entities, but they connect. My work contained predictions that were borne out. So my work is a valid map of reality. But it is only a map."

"I think I understand," Mikhail said. "There are categories of reality. Even though we can predict it to nine decimal places, we can't imagine the sun's peculiar behavior actually *intervening* in our cozy human world."

"Something like that," Eugene said uneasily. His big hands plucked at each other, a man's hands but a child's gesture. "Like the walls between model and reality are breaking down."

"You know, you're not the only person who feels this way, Eugene. You aren't alone."

"Of course I'm alone," Eugene said. His expression closed up.

Mikhail longed to hold him, but knew he must not.

The President said, "We intend to build a shield in space. Made of the finest film, it will be a disk wider than the Earth itself. It will be so vast, in fact, that as it begins to take shape it will be visible from every home, every school, every workplace on Earth, for it will be a human-made structure as big in our sky as the sun or the Moon.

"I am told it may even be visible, to the naked eye, from Mars. We will indeed be stamping our mark on the solar system." She smiled.

Siobhan thought back to the session with her "motley crew" in the Royal Society, where Aristotle had first come up with the notion.

The idea couldn't have been simpler, in principle. On a sunny day, if the light was too strong, you put up a parasol. So, for protection from the storm, you would build a parasol in space, a mighty cover big enough to shield the whole Earth. And on that crucial day, humankind would shelter safely in the shadow of an artificial eclipse.

"Its center of gravity would be at L1," Mikhail had said. "Between sun and Earth, co-orbiting."

Toby asked, "And what is L1?"

L1 is the first Lagrange point of the Earth–sun system. An object circling between Earth and the sun, such as Venus, follows its orbit more rapidly than Earth. But Earth's gravity field tugs at Venus, though much more feebly than the sun's. Put a satellite much closer to the Earth—about four times the distance to the Moon—and Earth's gravity is so strong that the satellite is dragged back just so by Earth, and made to orbit the sun at the same rate as the Earth.

This point of equilibrium is called L1, the first Lagrangian point, for the eighteenth-century French mathematician who discovered it. In fact there are five such Lagrangian points, three on the sun–Earth line, and the other two on the path of Earth's own orbit, at sixty degrees from the Earth–sun radius.

"Ah," Toby had said, nodding. "Earth and satellite co-rotate.

As if both Earth and satellite were glued to a great rigid clock hand that sticks out from the sun."

Siobhan said, "I thought L1 is a point of unstable equilibrium." At Toby's baffled look she said, "Like a football sitting at the summit of a mountain, rather than in a valley. The ball's stationary, but liable to fall off in any direction."

"Yes," Mikhail said. "But we have placed satellites at such positions before. You can actually orbit the Lagrangian point, use a small amount of fuel to station-keep. It's well within the envelope of experience: astronautically, not a problem."

Toby had held his hand up to the ceiling light, experimentally shadowing his face. "Forgive a stupid question," he said. "But how *big* would this shield have to be?"

Mikhail sighed. "For simplicity, assume the sun's rays are parallel as they reach Earth. Then you can see you need a screen as large as the object you're trying to shield."

Toby said, "So the shield has to be a disk with at least the diameter of the Earth. Which is—"

"About thirteen thousand kilometers."

Toby's jaw had dropped. But he pressed on doggedly. "So we're talking about a shield thirteen thousand kilometers across. To be built in space. Where the largest structure we've put up so far is—"

"I suppose the International Space Station," Mikhail said. "Much less than a kilometer."

Toby said, "No wonder I didn't find this before. When I ran my own search for solutions, I screened out the obviously implausible. And this is obviously implausible." He glanced at Siobhan. "Isn't it?"

Of course it was. But the three of them had hammered at their softscreens to figure out more.

Toby said, "There have been studies of this sort of thing before. Hermann Oberth seems to have been the first to come up with the idea."

"You'd use ultrathin materials, of course," Mikhail said.

Siobhan said, "Everyday plastic wrap comes in at ten micrometers thick."

"And you can get aluminum foil the same thickness," Mikhail said. "But surely we can do better."

Toby said, "So with an area density of less than a gram per square meter, say, and even adding an element for structural components, your weight could be as little as a few million tonnes." He looked up. "Did I really just say *as little as?*"

Siobhan said, "We don't have the heavy-lift capacity to get that amount of material off the Earth, even given years."

"But we don't need to lift it off Earth," Mikhail said. *"Why don't we build it on the Moon?"*

Toby stared at him. "Now that really is crazy."

"Why so? On the Moon we already manufacture glass, process metals. And we have our low gravity, remember: it's twenty-two times easier to launch a payload into space from the Moon as from Earth. And we're already building a mass driver! There's no reason the Sling project couldn't be accelerated. Its launch capacity will be huge."

They factored an estimate of the Sling's launch capacity into their back-of-the-envelope calculations. It was immediately clear that if they could launch the bulk of the shield's mass from the Moon, the energy savings would indeed be prodigious.

And there was still no obvious showstopper. Siobhan had felt frightened to breathe, as if she might break the spell, and they had worked on.

But now, sitting in her flat with her mother and daughter, listening to Alvarez announce this preposterous idea to the whole world, different emotions surged in her. Suddenly restless, she walked to the window.

It was nearly Christmas, 2037. Outside, kids were playing soccer. They were wearing T-shirts. While Santa Claus still bundled up on the Christmas cards, snow and frost were nostalgic dreams of Siobhan's childhood; in England it was more than ten years since the temperature had dipped below freezing anywhere south of a line from the Severn to the Trent. She remembered her last Christmas with her father before his death, when he had railed about having to cut his lawn on Boxing Day. The world had changed hugely in her own lifetime, shaped by forces far beyond human control. How could she be so arrogant as to suppose she could manage an even greater change, in just a few years?

"I'm afraid," she blurted.

Perdita glanced at her, troubled.

"Of the storm?" Maria asked.

"Yes, of course. But I had to work hard to get the politicians to accept the idea of the shield."

"And now—"

"Now Alvarez is calling my bluff, in front of the whole world. Suddenly I've got to deliver on my promises. And that's what frightens me. That I might fail."

Maria and Perdita walked over to her. Maria hugged her, and Perdita rested her head on her mother's shoulder. "You won't fail, Mum," Perdita said. "Anyhow you have us, remember."

Siobhan touched her daughter's head.

On the softwall, the President continued to speak.

"I offer you hope, but not false hope," Alvarez said. "Even the shield alone cannot save us. But it will turn an event that would be nonsurvivable for any of us into a disaster survivable for some. That's why we must build it—and that's why we must build on the chance it gives us.

"It goes without saying that this will be by far the most challenging space project ever undertaken, even dwarfing our colonization of the Moon and our first footsteps on Mars. Such a mighty project cannot be managed by one nation alone—not even America.

"So we have asked all the nations and federations of the world to come together, to pool their resources and energies, and to cooperate in this most vital of space projects. I am delighted to say that we have had a virtually unanimous response."

" 'Virtually unanimous' my arse," Miriam Grec grumbled. Here in her Euro-needle office she sipped her whiskey and settled a little deeper into the sofa. "How can you call it 'unanimous' when the Chinese have refused to take part?"

Nicolaus replied, "The Chinese play a long game, Miriam. We've always known that. No doubt they see this problem with the sun as just another geopolitical opportunity."

"Maybe. But God alone knows what they are up to with all those taikonauts and Long March boosters . . ."

"Surely they will come around, in the end."

She studied him. Even as he spoke, Nicolaus Korombel had one eye on the softscreen bearing Alvarez's image, the other on monitors that showed in a variety of ways the world's response to Alvarez's unfolding message. Miriam had never met anybody with Nicolaus's ability to parallel-process. It was just one of the reasons she valued him so much.

Although it was an odd thing, she thought, that his very hard-nosed, almost cynically robust thinking, which made him so valuable to her, also made him very opaque. She really knew very little about what he thought and believed, deep inside. Sometimes a faint worry about that gnawed at the edge of her awareness. She must get him to open up, she thought, get to know him better. But there was never any time. And in the meantime he was just too useful.

"So how's the reaction?"

"Markets down seventeen percent," Nicolaus said. "As a snap reaction goes, that's not as bad as we feared. Space and high-tech stocks are booming, needless to say."

Miriam marveled at such a response. She supposed the impulse to get rich was natural enough—indeed, the global economy wouldn't work without it. But she did wonder what those eager investors imagined they might achieve if their financial feeding frenzy hindered the ability of the aerospace companies and others to actually get the job done.

Still, it could be worse, she told herself. At least the President's speech was being made. Even getting the project this far had been a close-run thing.

In the world's grandest councils, there had been a lot of heated discussion about the wisdom of the solution Miriam had pushed.

The shield project would absorb the economic energies of the participating countries for years—and for what? Even the energy the shield was bound to leak through would still add up to a devastating disaster.

And were you really going to bust your balls to save the whole world? Including the Chinese who were refusing to take part, and the Africans who, recovering from the disasters of the twentieth century, were becoming newly resurgent? Couldn't you just save America, Europe? The military chiefs had even started to develop scenarios for what might follow the sunstorm, when Eurasia and America, if they were the only industrial powers left standing, began to move out from their fortresses to "aid" the remnants of a shattered world. It really would be a new world order, Miriam was earnestly advised, a restructuring of geopolitical power that might last a thousand years . . .

It had taken some deep conversations with Siobhan McGorran before Miriam had been able to wrap her own limited politician's imagination around the magnitude of the problem. The sunstorm wasn't another June 9; it wasn't Krakatoa or Pompeii; it wasn't a plague or a flood. And you just couldn't see this as an opportunity to seek petty advantage. *The extinction of humankind,* indeed of all life on Earth, was possible. This really was a case of all or nothing— a message Miriam had, at last, managed to batter into the heads of the rest of the world's decision makers.

President Alvarez spoke on, calmly.

It had to be Alvarez up there on the world's screens, of course. It had been Miriam who had so far led the political effort behind the shield project. It was she who had firmed up a solid industrial and financial base for the project, she who had gathered together the political will in her own fractious Eurasian Union and beyond to make this unlikely project happen—and she who had used up a good deal of her own political credit in the process. But by common consent, in situations like this it had to be the President of the United States who had to give the world the bad news, and the good, as it had been for generations.

"Alvarez is doing a good job," Miriam said. "We're lucky we got somebody like her in the hot seat at the right time."

Nicolaus snorted. "She's the best actor in the White House since Reagan, that's all."

"Oh, she's more than that. But she might raise false hopes. Whatever we do," she said grimly, "people are going to die."

"But far fewer than might otherwise," Nicolaus said. "And whatever we do, don't expect medals. Remember, this is engineering, not magic; no matter how well this works, people are sure to die, in great numbers. And in hindsight people will blame us. We will be called the worst mass murderers in history. That is certainly the Polish way!" He grinned with an odd sort of cheerful gloominess.

"You're too cynical sometimes, Nicolaus." But her mood was mellow, softened by the whiskey. She sipped it sparingly, letting Alvarez's warm voice wash over her.

"The shield will be immense in size. But most of it will be made of a vanishingly thin film, and so its mass will be kept to the minimum. The bulk of its substance will be launched from the Moon, where the lower gravity allows space launches many times easier than from the Earth. The "smart" components that will be required to control the shield will be manufactured on Earth, where the most sophisticated manufacturing processes are available.

"All our resources must be dedicated to this project, and other dreams put on hold, for now. That is why I have decided to recall the *Aurora 2,* the second of our Mars spacecraft, already bound for the red planet. It will serve as our work shed, if you will."

Born on ripples of electromagnetism, the President's words washed past the Moon and, some minutes later, reached Mars.

To Helena Umfraville, the voice in her helmet speakers was tinny. But it was her choice to hear Alvarez like this. To watch the flyby of *Aurora 2* she had decided to go EVA, to be immersed in Martian nature. Even a president's speech couldn't compete with that.

So she had clambered into her EVA suit. It was an "isolation suit" that you left docked to a hatch of your rover or your hab, and then crawled in through the back, so that you never came into contact with its outer surface—and Mars, with its putative native ecology, was never touched by the oily, watery, bug-ridden mass that was you. And now she stood beside her rover, with her feet planted squarely in crimson dirt, as close to Mars as she was allowed to get.

Around her a rock-strewn plain stretched away, unmarked by humanity save for her own tire tracks. The ground was pinkish brown, and the sky was a yellowy butterscotch color that gathered to orange around the shrunken disk of the sun, almost like an Earth sunrise. The rocks on the ground, scattered at random by some long-gone impact, had been in place so long that they had been polished smooth by windborne dust. This was an old, silent world, like a museum of rocks and dust. But there was weather here, sometimes surprisingly violent when that thin air stirred itself.

And on the horizon she could make out an outcrop of layered rock. It was sedimentary, just like a sandstone bed on Earth—and just like terrestrial sandstone it had been laid down in water. You could search the dry Moon from pole to pole and not find one formation like that unspectacular outcropping. *This was Mars:* the thought still thrilled her.

But Helena was stranded here.

Of course the *Aurora 1* astronauts had known basically what the President was going to say long before she had opened her mouth. Mission control at Houston had broken the news of *Aurora 2*'s wave-off gently and carefully, well in advance.

Aurora 2 was actually the Mars expedition's third ship. The first, labeled *Aurora Zero,* had delivered an unmanned factory to the surface of Mars, which had patiently labored to turn Martian dirt and air into methane and oxygen, the fuel that would send home the human crews that followed. Then *Aurora 1* had made the mighty journey, powered by thermal nuclear rockets and carrying six crew. Footprints and flags had come at last to Mars.

The plan had been that once *Aurora 2* arrived the first crew would head back to Earth, leaving the bigger second team to expand on what they had already built—an embryonic settlement that marked, everybody had hoped, the start of the continuous human habitation of Mars. The tiny beachhead had already been christened, a bit grandiosely, Port Lowell.

Now that wasn't going to happen. After two years the first crew remained stuck here—and the word was, because of the priority of the shield work, there wasn't likely to be a retrieval mission until after sunstorm day itself, more than four years into the future.

The crew understood the need to stay, for they were all intensely aware of the threat posed by the sun. Despite its greater distance, the sun was actually a much more baleful presence here on Mars than on Earth. The home world's thick atmosphere offered you the equivalent shielding of meters of aluminum; Mars's thin air gave you only centimeters—no better than if you were riding a tin-can spacecraft in interplanetary space. The neighborhood magnetosphere was no use either. Mars was still and cold, frozen deep inside, and its magnetic field wasn't a global, dynamic structure like Earth's, but a relic of arcs and patches. On Mars, the solar climatologists liked to say, the sun engaged directly with the ground, and you had to hide from flares that wouldn't even be noticed on Earth. So they understood, but that didn't make the prospect any warmer.

The mood was hard to lift. They were *tired,* all the time: a sol, Mars's day, was half an hour longer than Earth's, just too long for the human circadian system to cope with. In all their simulations, nobody had anticipated that one of the most serious problems on Mars would turn out to be a kind of jet-lag. And now they were stranded. Thanks to *Aurora Zero* there was no fear of running out of resources. They could tough it out here; Mars would feed them. Still, most of the crew had been bereft at being cut off from their families and homes for so long.

But Helena, though horrified about the prospect of the sunstorm, and perturbed at the work they were going to have to do to ride it out themselves, was quietly pleased. She was growing to love this place, this strange little world where the sun raised a tide in the atmosphere. And Mars hadn't even begun to give up its secrets to her yet. She wanted to travel to the poles, where every winter there were blizzards of carbon dioxide, or the deep basin of Hellas where, it was said, it got so warm and the air so thick you could pour out liquid water and it would stand, without freezing, on the ground.

And there were human secrets on Mars too.

British-born Helena still remembered her disappointment at the age of six after being woken in the small hours of Christmas Day, 2003, to listen for a signal from Mars that had never come. Now she had come all the way to Mars herself—and had seen with her own eyes the dust-strewn wreckage on Isidis Planitia, all that remained of the brave little craft that had come so far. This hadn't meant much to the Americans on the crew, but Helena had been pleased when they had allowed her to christen this rover *Beagle* . . .

"Lowell, *Beagle*." The voice of Bob Paxton, back at Lowell, spoke softly in her headset, cutting through the President's words. "Almost time. Look up."

"*Beagle,* Lowell. Thanks, Bob." She tipped back her head to inspect the sky.

The spaceship from Earth came rising grandly out of the east, bright in the Martian morning. Helena waited by her rover until the glinting star that should have taken her home had started to dim in the dust at the horizon, its single pass over Mars complete.

Goodbye, *Aurora 2,* goodbye.

President Alvarez folded her hands and looked into the camera.

"The coming days will be difficult for all of us. I would not pretend otherwise.

"Our space agencies, including our own NASA and U.S. Astronautical Engineering Corps, will of course play a crucial role, and I have every confidence they will rise to this new challenge as they have in the past. The controller of the ill-fated *Apollo 13* lunar mission once memorably said, "Failure is not an option." Nor is it now.

"But the space engineers cannot win through alone. To achieve this we will all have a role to play, every one of us. My dreadful news may shock you now, but tomorrow another day will dawn. There will be newspapers and websites, e-mails to send and phone calls to make; the stores will open; the transport systems will run as they always do—and every workplace and school will, *must,* be open for business as usual.

"I urge you to go to work. I urge you to do the best job you can, every minute of every day. We are like a pyramid, a pyramid of work and economic contributions, a pyramid supporting at its peak the handful of heroes who are trying to save us all.

"We all lived through June 9, and we overcame the lesser problems posed on that difficult day. I know we can now rise to this new challenge, together.

"As long as humankind survives, our descendants will look back on these fleeting years. And they will envy us. For we were here, on this day, at this hour. And we achieved greatness.

"Good fortune to us all."

You're missing the point.

Bisesa wanted to scream at the softwall, to throw a cushion at the President. *This shield is heroic. But you have to look beyond that. You have to recognize that all this has been engineered. You have to listen to me!*

But for Myra's sake, as she learned about the impending end of the world, she stayed outwardly calm.

The vagueness of the dates Alvarez quoted baffled her. Why be so elusive? The astrophysicists who had come up with this prediction seemed so precise about everything else that they would surely have narrowed it down to a day.

The date was surely selected by the Firstborn, of course, as was everything about this event. They would pick a day that mattered to them, somehow. But what could *matter* about a day in April 2042? Surely nothing in the human domain: the Firstborn were creatures of the stars . . . Something astronomical, then.

"Aristotle," she said softly.

"Yes, Bisesa?"

"April 2042. Can you tell me what's going on in the sky in that month?"

"You mean an ephemeris?"

"A what?"

"A table of astronomical data that predicts the daily position of the planets, stars, and—"

"Yes. That's it."

The President's image shrank down to a corner of the wall. The rest of it filled up with columns of figures, like map coordinates. But even the columns' titles meant little to Bisesa; evidently astronomers spoke a language of their own.

"I'm sorry," Aristotle said. "I'm not sure of your level of expertise."

"Assume nonexistent. Can you show me this graphically?"

"Of course." The tables were replaced by an image of the night sky. "The view from London on April 1, 2042, midnight," Aristotle said.

At the vision of the impossibly clear, starry sky, a sharp memory prodded at Bisesa's mind. She remembered sitting with her phone, under the crystalline sky of another world, as the little gadget had labored to map the sky and work out the date . . . But she'd had to leave everything behind on Mir, even her phone.

Aristotle scrolled through display options, showing her stick-figure constellation diagrams, lines of celestial longitude and latitude.

She dumped all that. "Just show me the sun," she said.

A yellow disk began to track, impossibly, against a black, star-filled sky, and a date and time box flickered in the corner. She ran through the month, April 2042, from end to end, and watched the sun ride across the sky, over and over.

And then she thought of what she had seen on her strange journey back from Mir with Josh. "Please show me the Moon."

A gray disk with a sketchy man-in-the-Moon mottling appeared.

"Now start from April 1 and run forward again."

The Moon made its stately way across the sky. Its phase welled until it became full, and then it began to shrink down, through half full, and to a crescent that enclosed a disk of darkness.

That black disk tracked across the image of the sun.

"Stop." The image froze. "I know when it's going to happen," she breathed.

"Bisesa?"

"The sunstorm . . . Aristotle. I know this is going to be hard for you to arrange. But I need to speak to the Astronomer Royal—the President mentioned her—Siobhan McGorran. It's very, *very* important."

She stared at sun and Moon, neatly overlapped on her softwall. The date of the simulated solar eclipse was April 20, 2042.

PART 3
THE SHIELD

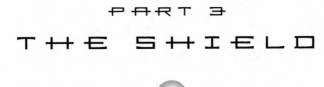

19: INDUSTRY

Bud Tooke met Siobhan off the *Komarov,* just as before.

She had already told Bud she wanted to get straight to work, no matter the local time of day. He smiled as he rode with her to the main domes. "No sweat. We're working a twenty-four-hour-a-day shift here anyhow—have been for six months, ever since the President's directive came in."

"It's appreciated back home," she said warmly.

"I know. But it's not a problem. We're all highly motivated up here." He sniffed up a deep breath, expanding his chest. "A challenge is energizing. Good for you."

Siobhan had felt on the edge of exhaustion for the last six months. She said dubiously, "I guess so."

He eyed her, concern penetrating his military brusqueness. "So how was the trip?"

"Long. Thank God for Aristotle, and e-mail."

This was Siobhan McGorran's third trip to the Moon. Her first voyage had been wonderful, something she had dreamed of as a child. Even the second had been exciting. But the third was just a chore—and time consuming at that.

The trouble was, here they were, halfway through 2038, a whole year after June 9, already six months since Alvarez had made her epochal Christmas announcement—and now less than four years before sunstorm day. Siobhan knew intellectually, from her Gantt charts and dependency diagrams and critical paths, that the various subprojects of the mighty shield program were actually going quite well. But inside her head a calendar-clock ticked steadily down.

She tried to explain to Bud. "I'm a natural pessimist," she said. "I expect things to go wrong, and am suspicious when they go well." She forced a smile. "Some attitude for a leader."

He angled his head so his frosting of crew-cut hair caught the corridor strip lights. "You're doing fine. Anyhow, when it comes to motivation, leave that to me. I was once a pain-in-the-butt sergeant at training camps in the Midwest. I can get them down and dirty. Maybe between us we'll turn out to be a good team." And he put his arm around her shoulders and gave her a squeeze.

She could feel his strength, and detected a scent of aftershave. Bud did sometimes seem like a relic of the 1950s. But his indomitability, straightforwardness, and sheer good humor were very welcome. All of which was rationalizing, of course.

As he held her, she felt a deep and pleasant warmth spread out through her belly and rise to her face. She was sorry when the brief hug ended.

On her first visit, Artemis Dome had been a scene of lunar industrial experiments. Now, just a few months later, the scale of the operation had changed utterly. The dome had been sliced open and crude extensions built on it to provide a lot more acreage of processing facility, most of it in vacuum. It was an infernal scene, Siobhan thought, with grotesque spacesuited figures gliding through banks of pipes, ducts, and metallic vessels, and everything stained the ubiquitous charcoal gray of the Moon, like a caricature of the darkest days of England's Industrial Revolution.

The product of this mighty effort was metal.

Aluminum was the main structural component of the mass driver launch system, while iron would be required for the electromagnetic systems that would be its working muscles. But the mass driver was going to be kilometers long. The lunar colonists were having to jump straight from a trialed process to industrial-scale production; the scale change was tremendous, the pressure immense.

Bud sketched some of the difficulties. "These are tried-and-tested processes on Earth," he said. "But up here *nothing* behaves the same, not a heap of ball bearings or oil flowing in a pipe . . ."

"But you're getting there."

"Oh, yes."

Meanwhile Selene Dome, once the Moon's first farm, had been turned into a glass factory. It was simple: you pushed lunar regolith in one end, applied focused solar heat, and drew glass out the other end, shimmering hot, to be molded into prefabricated sections.

Bud said, "Every time a journalist gets through to me, I'm asked the same damn question: why are we making the infrastructure of the shield from lunar glass? And every time I have to give the same answer: because this is the Moon. And wonderful though it is, the Moon doesn't give you a lot of choice."

The Moon's peculiar composition was dictated by its formation. The NASA geologists who had studied the first samples returned by the *Apollo* astronauts had been puzzled: this iron-deficient, volatile-free stuff seemed quite unlike the rocks of Earth's crust. It was more like the material of Earth's mantle, the thick layer between crust and core. It turned out that this was because the Moon *was* made of Earth's mantle—or rather, of the great gout of it that had been splashed away by that primordial, Moon-making impact.

"And so that's what we're left with," Bud said. "Igneous rocks make up ninety percent of the crust here. It's as if we were learning to live on the slopes of Vesuvius. And there's virtually no water, remember. Without water you can't make concrete, for instance."

"Hence glass."

"Hence glass. Siobhan, glass grows naturally on the Moon. Wherever a meteor falls, the regolith fuses, and glass is splashed everywhere. So that's what we use.

"And here's the finished product." With a showman's flourish he pointed to glass components, some of them many times a person's height, stacking up in a rudimentary store out in the vacuum. "There are no prototypes here, no test articles. Everything we make is intended to be launched; everything we build will wind up on the shield—everything you see here will fly. The designs they feed us from Earth keep changing, and we're trying to optimize our manufacturing too, aiming for the minimum weight to provide a given structural strength. So the final shield will be a funny sort of hybrid, with the last components, five years younger, looking quite different from the first. But we'll just have to cope with that."

Siobhan gazed at the glass sections with genuine awe. They looked like nothing much, like buttresses for a fairground ride or a fancy trade-show exhibit. But these odd-looking struts of glass, and tens of thousands of others just like them, were to be shot into space, where they would be assembled to form the scaffolding of a mirror wider than the planet. Her wild back-of-the-envelope concept was already coming into physical actuality. She felt thrilled.

Bud was watching the workers beyond the window. "You know," he said, "I think this could be the making of this crew. Before June 9 we were kind of playing up here, playing at being lunar colonists. Now we've got a sense of urgency, a specific goal, a schedule to fulfill. I believe this event will push forward the program of the colonization and exploitation of the Moon by decades, or more."

That meant little to her, but she saw how important it was to Bud. "That's wonderful."

"Yes. *But,*" he added heavily, "sometimes I walk on eggshells."

"Why?"

"Because this isn't what these guys came here for. They're mostly scientists, remember. Suddenly they've been drafted to work on an assembly line. Yes, there's dynamism and adrenaline. But sometimes they remember their old lives, and they feel—"

"Resentful?"

"Well, I can take that. The worst thing is, they get *bored*. The disadvantage of overeducation. As long as I can keep them distracted we get along fine." He peered out, the laugh lines around his eyes catching the light, and she thought he seemed very fond of his temperamental workers.

"Come on," she said. "You haven't shown me Hecate yet."

As they walked on, she slipped her hand into his.

Later he took her out of Clavius Base to see David's Sling.

As they approached the site of the Sling, Siobhan stood up in the surface tractor's bubble-dome pressure compartment to see better. Only three kilometers of the launcher had been completed, of a projected thirty. Even so, it was an astonishing sight: in the low sunlight, under a pitch-black sky and against a gray-brown backdrop of Moon dust, the launcher shone like a sword.

The engineers called it a mass driver, or an electromagnetic launcher—or, more simply, a space gun. The heart of it was an aluminum track standing on trestle legs, thin and light like all lunar constructions. Wrapped around the track was a coil of iron, a vast spiral that Bud called the solenoid. At the loading end spacesuited figures moved cautiously around a crane, which was hoisting a glistening pellet up onto the track. The track stretched away across the level floor of Clavius, soon passing out of sight beyond the Moon's close horizon.

"The principle is simple," Bud said. "It's a cannon driven by electromagnetism. You wrap your cargo in a blanket of iron—which we can reuse, by the way. You put your cargo pellet on the rail. The magnetic field, generated from that blockhouse over there"—he pointed at a nondescript dome—"then pulses through the solenoid, and your pellet is pushed along the track." The changing magnetic field induced electric currents in the iron blanket, and the currents then pushed against the magnetism: "It's just the principle of the electric motor," Bud said.

As he spoke he pressed his hand against the small of her back with a pleasing familiarity.

She prompted, "And after thirty kilometers of accelerating—"

"You have escape velocity, without the need for any of that messy business of rockets and launch pads and countdowns. And then you can go wherever you want—fall all the way down to Earth, even."

"It's really a fantastic conception," she said.

"Yeah. But like most of what we do on the Moon, people figured it all out long before they had a chance to get here to build it. The idea of an electromagnetic launcher dates back to the 1950s, I think. A science fiction writer. Famous in his day . . ."

"Couldn't you build a mass driver on Earth?"

"Yeah. In principle. But the air would be a problem. You would be flying at interplanetary speeds a meter above the ground. On Earth, at escape velocity, Mach 20 or 25, you'd burn up. But up here there's no air, so no air resistance. Then we have our famous low gravity, so the speeds we need to acquire are much less than on Earth: down there you'd need a launcher *twenty times* as long as this one—maybe six hundred kilometers. As for power, all that lovely sunlight falls down from the sky for free. But the real economy comes from the fact that unlike with rocket technology, all our launch equipment stays bolted to the ground, where it belongs. With the Sling, we can get off this rock for pennies per kilogram."

He started to wax enthusiastically about the opportunities the Sling and its more sophisticated successors would one day give to the Moon. "From here we can send heavy-lift components to the Lagrange points, or Earth orbit, or to the planets and beyond, for a fraction of the effort and cost of launching from Earth. Once people dreamed that the Moon would be the stepping-stone to opening up the solar system. Those dreams died when it was found that the Moon has only a trace of water. But *this* is how the dream will live again."

She touched his arm a little wistfully. She relished his passion, his energy. But he was oddly like Eugene Mangles, in a way: as Eugene's obsession was his work, so Bud's was evidently the Moon and its future—to the exclusion of herself, she thought. "Bud," she said. "You sold me. But for now, all I want the Moon to do is to save the Earth."

"We're working on it. Even though we all know it won't be enough."

The shield couldn't provide perfect cover. It had had to be designed to block the sunstorm's peak-energy bombardment in the visible light spectrum, but could do nothing about an anticipated accompaniment of X-rays, gamma rays, and other nasties, peripheral in terms of the storm's total output, but potentially devastating for the Earth. "We couldn't do it all," she said.

"I know. I keep telling my folk that. But even so it doesn't feel enough, whatever we do . . . Look. I think they're ready for a test."

The cargo pellet was in place on the gleaming track. The crane withdrew. She saw the pellet start to move: slowly at first, a ponderous start that told of its mass, and then more rapidly. That was all there was to it. There were no special effects: no flaring fire, no billowing smoke. But as the generators poured their energies into the launcher she felt a tingle in her gut, perhaps some biochemical response to the mighty currents flowing just a few hundred meters away.

The pellet, still accelerating, shot out of sight.

Bud clenched a fist. "Today all we can do is dig another hole in Clavius's floor. But in six months tops we'll be firing to orbit. Imagine riding that thing, riding the lightning across the face of the Moon!"

On the Moon's surface, rovers were already racing to retrieve the cargo pellet, spraying up rooster tails of dust behind them. And the crane was moving back into its position, ready for another run.

Eugene sat in his room, hands folded on a small table. The room was without decoration or personalization—minimal even by the standards of the Moon, where everything was filtered through the huge expense of being shipped up from Earth. He didn't even have a closet, just the packing carton that must have brought his clothes to the Moon in the first place.

Eugene remained an enigma to Siobhan. He was a big, handsome boy. If you knocked him cold and rearranged his limbs a bit he'd have made a great fashion model. But his posture was slumped, his face creased up with concern and shyness. Siobhan thought she had never met anybody with a greater contrast between his inner and outer selves.

"So how are you feeling, Eugene?"

"Busy," he snapped back. "Questions, questions, questions. It's all I get, day and night."

"But you understand why," she said. "We've already started building the shield, and on Earth they are making other preparations. All on the basis of your predictions: it's really quite a responsibility. And unfortunately, Eugene, right now it's only you who can do that for us." She forced a smile. "If you're building a shield thirteen thousand kilometers across, a mistake in the sixth decimal place means a mismatch of a meter or more—"

"It gets in the way of the work," he said.

She stopped herself from snapping back, *I am the Astronomer*

Royal. I've done the odd bit of science myself. I do understand what it takes. But we're talking about the safety of the world here. For God's sake stop being such a prima donna . . . But she glimpsed real misery in his downcast face.

After all, she reflected, it wasn't likely somebody as unworldly as this would be any use at prioritization or time management. Eugene surely had no mental equipment for handling conflicting demands—and probably no tact in dealing with those making such demands, from Prime Ministers and Presidents on down.

And then there was his public notoriety.

Siobhan had the feeling that even now, despite all the grave scientific pronouncements and political pontificating and arguing, most people didn't really believe, in their guts, that the sunstorm was going to happen. Alvarez's initial announcement had triggered a wave of alarm, flurries of speculation on the stock markets, flights into gold, and a sudden surge of interest in properties in Iceland, Greenland, the Falklands, and other extreme-latitude locations wrongly imagined to be relatively safe from the storm. But for most people, as the world kept turning and the sun kept shining, the sense of crisis quickly faded. Vast defensive programs, like the shield, were being mobilized, but even they weren't visible yet to most people. It was still a phony war, the analysts said, and most people had forgotten about it and just got on with their lives. Even Siobhan found herself fretting about the long-term cosmological projects she'd been forced to abandon.

But in a world of billions there was a fraction of a percent imaginative enough, or crazy enough, to take the threat to heart—and a fraction of *them* looked for somebody to blame. As the man who had figured out the sunstorm, there were plenty prepared to dump their fear on Eugene. There had even been death threats. It had been a mercy he had stayed on the Moon, she thought, where his safety was relatively easy to assure. But even so he must have felt as if he were being flayed alive.

She got out her softscreen and began making notes. "Let me help you," she said. "You need an office. A secretary . . ." She saw panic in his eyes. "Okay, not a secretary. But I'll set up somebody to filter your calls for you. To report to me, not you." But I think you will need somebody here on the Moon to hold your hand, she thought. An idea struck her. "How's Mikhail?"

He shrugged. "Haven't seen him."

"I know he has his own priorities." The Space Weather Service, which had suddenly grown from an obscure near joke to one of the most high-profile agencies in the solar system, was almost as inundated as Eugene himself. But she had seen Mikhail work with Eugene; she had a sense the solar astronomer would be able to get the best out of the boy. And, given the way Mikhail looked at Eugene, it would be a task Mikhail would perform with competence and affection. "I'll ask him to spend more time with you. Maybe he could move back here to Clavius; he doesn't have to be physically at the pole station."

Eugene showed no notable enthusiasm for the idea. But he didn't reject it outright, so Siobhan decided she had made some progress.

"What else?" She bent forward so she could see his face more clearly. "How are you feeling, Eugene? Is there anything you need? You must know how important your welfare is, to all of us."

"Nothing." He sounded sullen, even sulky.

"What you found is so important, Eugene. You could save billions of lives. They'll build statues to you. And believe me, your work, especially your classic paper on the solar core, is going to be read forever."

That provoked a weak smile. "I miss the farm," he said suddenly.

The non sequitur took her aback. "The farm?"

"Selene. I understand why they had to clear it all out. But I miss it." He had grown up in a rural area in Massachusetts, she remembered now. "I used to go work in there," he said. "The doctor said I needed exercise. It was that or the treadmill."

"But now the farm's been shut down. How typical that in trying to save the world we kill off the one bit of green on the Moon!"

And how psychologically damaging that might be. In trying to figure out these spacebound folk she had read stories of cosmonauts on the first, crude, tin-can space stations, patiently growing little pea plants in experimental pots. They had loved those plants, those small living things sharing their shelter in the desolation of space. Now Eugene had shown the same impulse. He was human after all.

"I'll fix it," she said. "A farm's out of the question for now. But how about a garden? I'm sure there's room here in Hecate. And if there isn't we'll make room. You lunar folk need reminding of what you're fighting to save."

He looked up and met her gaze for the first time. "Thank you." He glanced at the softscreen before him. "But if you don't mind—"

"I know, I know. The work." She pushed back her chair and stood up.

That night she went to Bud's room.

He whispered, "I wasn't sure if you'd come."

She snorted. "I knew for sure *you* wouldn't walk down the corridor."

"Am I so transparent?"

"As long as the journey got made by one of us," she said.

"I told you we'd be a good team."

She unzipped her jumpsuit. "Prove it, hero."

Their lovemaking was wonderful. Bud was a lot more athletic than she was used to, but he was more focused on *her* than most of her lovers ever had been.

And he was ingenious in his use of the Moon's gentle gravity. "One-sixth G is the gravity of choice," he gasped at one point. "On Earth you're crushed. In zero G you're floundering around like a beached salmon. In one-sixth, you've enough weight to give you a little traction, and yet you're still as light as a kid's balloon. Why, I'm told that even on Mars—"

"Shut up and get on with it," she whispered.

Afterward she stayed awake for a long time, just relishing the strong warmth of his arms around her. Here they were, two humans in this bubble of light and air and warmth on the lethal surface of the Moon. Like the cosmonauts and their pea plants, she thought: all they had, in the end, was each other.

Even when the sun betrayed them, they had each other.

21: SHOWSTOPPERS

"So there it is," Rose Delea said flatly. "You have two problems you can't get over. Without the Chinese heavy-lift capability, you can't finish the shield infrastructure on time. And even if you could, you don't have a way to manufacture all the smartskin you need." She sat back and stared out of her softscreen at Siobhan. "You're fucked."

Siobhan pressed the balls of her thumbs to her eyes, and tried to keep her temper. It was January 2039—six months after she had seen those first shield components stacking up on the Moon, already eighteen months since the June 9 event. Another Christmas had come and gone, a bleak and joyless festival, and little more than three years remained before the sunstorm was due to hit.

Save for Toby Pitt and the talking heads from space on the softscreens, Siobhan was alone here in the Royal Society Council Rooms, the location that had come to serve as her communications base. Toby's job as the Society's events manager had gradually evolved into his becoming her PA, amanuensis, and shoulder-to-cry-on. And she certainly felt like crying now.

"*We're* fucked, Rose," she said.

"What?"

"Rose, sometimes you sound like my plumber. *You're fucked* is wrong. Language is crucial. It's not my problem, it's ours. *We're* fucked."

Bud Tooke, peering from another softscreen, laughed gently.

Rose glared. "Fucked is fucked, you stuck-up pom. I need a coffee." And she pushed herself out of her chair and drifted out of shot.

"Here we go again," Mikhail said grimly.

Despite her usual intrinsic anxiety about the schedule, before she had come into work this morning Siobhan had actually felt optimistic about the way things were going.

On the Moon, after months of stupendous effort by Bud and his people, the Sling was completed and operational. Even the construction of a second mass driver was under way. Not only that, but the glass manufacturing operations were proceeding apace: plants had been set up all over the bare soil of Clavius Crater, so that streams of components poured into the Sling's launching bay by lunar day and night. Rose Delea, seconded from her helium-3 processing work, had proven a more than capable manager for that end of the project, despite her dour attitude.

Meanwhile *Aurora 2* had been safely brought back from Mars and was lodged at L1, the crucial Lagrangian point suspended between Earth and sun. With the Sling fully operational the first loads of lunar-glass buttresses and struts had been fired up to the assembly site, and construction of the shield itself had started. Bud Tooke was now in nominal charge of all the subprojects at L1, and, as Siobhan had always known he would, he was delivering quietly and efficiently. Soon, it was said, the proto-shield would be big enough to see with the naked eye from Earth—or would have been, were it not forever lost in the glare of the sun.

Even Siobhan's personal life had been looking up, to general astonishment among friends and family. She hadn't expected that her affair with Bud would deepen so smoothly and so quickly, especially since they spent almost all their time on separate worlds. In the toughest days of her life, the relationship had been a source of comfort and strength to her.

But now, in what should have been a routine weekly progress meeting, two showstopper problems had come looming out of nowhere.

On her screen Rose Delea reappeared with coffee that sloshed in a languid low-G way. The conversation resumed, and Siobhan tried to focus on the issues.

Mathematically, the positioning of an object at a Lagrangian point was simple. If the shield had been a point mass, it could have been poised neatly on the sweeping line joining Earth to sun at L1. But this project was no longer mathematics; it was engineering.

For one thing the L1 point wasn't really stable at all, but only semi-stable: if you knocked that point mass out of position it would tend to drift back to its place along the line of the Earth–sun radius, but would happily float away from the line in any other direction. So you needed to add station-keeping mechanisms, such as rocket thrusters, to hold the shield in place.

And then, of course, the shield was not a point mass, but an extended object large enough eventually to shadow the whole Earth. Only the shield's geometric center, intersecting the Earth–sun line, could be properly balanced at the L1 point. All other points were drawn toward the center, and given time the shield would have crumpled in on itself. Making it rigid would have raised the mass unfeasibly. The problem was to be overcome by giving the shield a slow rotation. The spinning was stately, at only four revolutions per *year*—"as if God is twirling His parasol," as Mikhail described it—but enough to keep the shield rigid.

But the rotation created other problems. Docking with a spinning object in space, even one as slow moving as the shield, was a lot more tricky than with a stationary object. More seriously, by being spun up, the shield would become a huge gyroscope. As it followed its orbit between Earth and sun it would tend to keep the same orientation in space—and so, over a year, it would tip its face away from the sun–Earth line, making it useless as a parasol.

Meanwhile there were other forces to consider besides gravity. Sunlight itself, a rain of photons, exerts a pressure on every object it touches. It is too gentle a force for human senses to detect on an upraised hand, but it would be enough to drive a yacht with filmy kilometer-wide sails from world to world—and it was certainly enough to exert a significant force on an object as large as the shield. There were other complications too, such as perturbation by the gravity fields of the Moon and the other planets, and a tweaking by Earth's own magnetic field.

To cope with all this, the shield's surface was to be made adjustable. Panels could be opened and closed in careful patterns, so that the gentle pressure of sunlight could be harnessed to turn the shield. It was an elegant solution: sunlight itself would be used to keep the shield properly positioned.

But to maintain its station in this environment of multiple and constantly changing forces, the shield itself had to be smart enough to be aware of its position in space, and able to adjust itself dynamically. Ideally every square centimeter of the shield would know all about the forces acting on it and on the shield as a whole, and would be able to compute how it should position itself in response.

This distributed, interconnected intelligence was to be achieved by the manufacture of a "smartskin." The shield's epidermis, less than a micrometer thick, would not just be a reflective skin but would be packed with circuitry. The local smartness, interconnected, would of course add up to a total powerful intelligence. The completed shield would, it was thought, be the smartest single entity humankind had yet constructed—smarter even, probably, than Aristotle, the only uncertainty coming because nobody knew quite how smart Aristotle *was*.

So much for the design, complicated enough in itself. The implementation was something else.

The manufacture of the smartskin was one headache today; there weren't enough nano-factories to turn it out in time. But even more serious was the problem caused by the pressure of sunlight. Although it could be used for active position control, its very existence caused a fundamental difficulty—which was the day's second showstopper.

"Let's go through it step by step," Bud said. "The sunlight presses on the reflective face of the mirror. The light pressure acts against the sun's gravity—so it's as if the sun's gravity is effectively reduced, and the L1 balance point is moved toward the sun along the Earth–sun line.

"Now, we're trying to minimize the shield's design mass. But the lighter the shield is, the more the sunlight can push it back. And the farther it drifts toward the sun, the bigger the shield has to be to shade the whole Earth. So its mass actually starts *increasing* again ... These two effects counteract to provide a minimum solution. Am I right? For a given thickness of film there is a theoretical minimum mass for the shield, below which there is *no* feasible design solution."

Siobhan said, "And without the Chinese—"

"We can't meet that minimum," Rose said with a kind of grim pleasure.

The problem was a shortfall of heavy-lift capacity. Although the Chinese government had initially declined to participate in the shield program, Miriam Grec had been sure that after enough emollient diplomacy, and a little horse trading, the Chinese would come on board. Miriam had actually instructed Siobhan to factor into her plans the availability of the Chinese fleet of Long March heavy-lift boosters.

Well, Miriam Grec had proven to be right about many things, but not about the Chinese. Their resistance to participation had not altered one jot, and their space launch capabilities were being dedicated, it seemed, to some secretive scheme of their own.

Whatever the Chinese were up to didn't matter to Siobhan. All she did care about was that despite months of frantic redesign they had failed to come up with a feasible solution: without the Chinese and their Long March boosters—and maybe even with them, said the pessimists—there just wasn't any way to get that minimum mass to L1 in time.

Siobhan knew that momentum was everything for this project. The shield was hugely, horribly, ruinously expensive: the project absorbed more than the net GDP of the United States, and therefore a respectable fraction of the whole world's economic output. Indeed the shield was thought to be humankind's single most expensive project in real terms since the "project" of winning the Second World War. The money didn't come out of nowhere, and many other programs, notably climate-change mitigation efforts in the desiccated heart of Asia and drowning Polynesia, were being put on hold, to predictable protests.

As the project became more real, it was provoking sincere political anger. In a way Siobhan welcomed that; it meant that more than a year after Alvarez's Christmas announcement, the "phony war" was coming to an end, and people were starting to believe enough in the sunstorm to care what was being done about it. Of course there were technical problems to solve; what they were attempting had never been done before. But Siobhan knew that if she allowed a hint of doubt to seep out of her management structure, it would soon erode the fragile political consensus behind the project—an infrastructure every bit as essential to the shield as the glass struts and booms being shipped up from the Moon.

Siobhan massaged her temples. "So we find another way to do it. What can we change?"

Rose ticked points off on her strong fingers. "You can't change the basic forces involved. You can't change the gravity fields of sun or Earth, or the pressure per square centimeter of sunlight. You can't shrink the shield. If it was transparent, sunlight would pass straight through the shield without troubling it, of course." She smiled. "But then there would be no point in building it in the first place, would there?"

"There must be something, damn it," Siobhan snapped.

She looked around at the softscreens that lined the walls of the room. The faces that peered back at her, her senior project managers, were projected from various corners of the Earth, the Moon, and L1 itself. The expressions of Bud and Mikhail Martynov as always radiated sympathy and support. Rose was wearing her usual *it-can't-be-done* scowl. Many of the others were more reserved. Some may actually have been grateful to Rose and her showstoppers, as she gave them something to hide their own issues behind.

They just didn't get it, Siobhan thought. There was a failure of imagination, even among her people, some of the smartest engineers and technologists around, who were closer to the project than anybody else. They weren't *just* building a bridge here, or *just* flying to Mars; this wasn't just another project, another line on a curriculum vitae. This was the future of humanity they were dealing with. If they fouled up, whatever the cause, there would *be* no tomorrow in which to hand out blame: there would be no careers to wreck, no new directions to seek. Siobhan ought to welcome Rose's bluntness, she thought; at least from her you got the straight skinny, whatever the consequences.

"I'm not going to give you a pep talk," she said. "Let me just remind you what President Alvarez said. *Failure is not an option.* It still isn't. We are going to work on this until our foreheads bleed, and we are going to find solutions to both these problems of ours today, come what may."

Bud murmured, "We're with you, Siobhan."

"I hope that's true." She stood, pushing back her chair. She said to Toby, "I need a break."

"I don't blame you. Just a reminder—your ten o'clock is outside."

Siobhan glanced at a softscreen diary page. "Lieutenant Dutt?" The soldier who had, it seemed, spent more than a year trying to get access to Siobhan, with grave news she wouldn't divulge to anybody else, and had finally drifted to the top of the in-tray. More problems. But at least *different* problems.

She stretched, trying to dissipate the ache in her upper neck. "If anybody cares I'll be back in thirty minutes."

22: TURNING POINT

Lieutenant Bisesa Dutt, British Army, was waiting for Siobhan in the City of London Rooms. She was drinking coffee and studying her phone.

As Siobhan crossed the room she was distracted by a peculiar shadow. Looking out the window, she glimpsed a gaunt framework rising beyond the rooftops of London: it was the skeleton of what would become the London Dome, the city's own effort to protect itself from the sunstorm. It was already the mightiest construction project in London's long history, although predictably it was dwarfed by still mightier shelters being raised over New York, Dallas, and Los Angeles.

From the beginning they had always known, just as Alvarez had announced, that the shield was not going to save the Earth from one hundred percent of the sun's rage, even assuming it got built at all. Some of it was going to get through—but the shield would give humanity a fighting chance, a chance that had to be taken. The trouble was that nobody knew how much pain the world below, and cities like London, would have to absorb.

The Dome was merely the most visible of the changes befalling the city. Across London the government had begun a program of laying up stores of nonperishable food, fuel, medical supplies, and the like, and the prices of such items were escalating. Even water rates were increasing as the authorities siphoned off supplies to fill immense underground tanks under the city's parks. It was like preparing for war, Siobhan thought. But the necessity was very real.

Certainly the building of the Dome, a physical manifestation of the danger to come, had started at last to make people believe, deep in their guts, that the sunstorm was real. Across the city there was a sense of apprehension, and the medical services reported upsurges in anxiety and stress. But there was excitement too, in a way, even anticipation.

Siobhan had been traveling extensively, and she'd found that things were much the same everywhere.

In the United States especially she thought there was a sense of determination, of unity; America, as always, was having to bear a disproportionately heavy weight of the global effort. Across the nation, even where domes were impractical, there was a neighborhood-level drive to prepare, as the National Guard, the Scouts, and a hundred volunteer drives dug shelters into their own backyards and their neighbors', filled underground tanks with rainwater, and collected aluminum cans to be filled up with emergency rations. Meanwhile there was a less obvious but equally dramatic effort to archive as much knowledge as possible, in digital and hardcopy forms, in great storage facilities in deep mine shafts, wells, Cold War–era bunkers, and even on the Moon. This was after all the true treasure of the nation, indeed of humankind—but this program gathered more controversy from those who argued that you should save "people first and last." President Alvarez was proving expert once more in guiding her nation's spirits; she was planning a program of celebrations of World War II centenary events, leading up to Pearl Harbor in 2041, to remind her fellow citizens of great trials they had faced before, and overcome.

There was dissension, all over the world. Aside from genuine differences of opinion about how to respond to this emergency, there were plenty of devout types who thought it was all a punishment by God, for one crime or another—and others who were angry at a God who had allowed this to happen. And some, the radical green types, said humankind should just accept its fate. This was a kind of karmic punishment for the way we had messed up the planet: let the Earth be wiped clean, and start again. Which might be a comforting idea, Siobhan thought grimly, if you could be sure there would be anything left after the sunstorm to start again with.

But even so there was still an unreal sheen to things. With the sun shining brightly over London, the Dome seemed as inappropriate as a Christmas tree in July. Most people just got on with their lives—even those who thought it was all a scam by the construction companies.

And in the middle of all this, here was Lieutenant Bisesa Dutt, and another mystery for Siobhan.

She reached Bisesa's table and sat down, asking an attendant for coffee.

"Thank you for seeing me," Bisesa began. "I know how busy you must be."

"I doubt if you do," Siobhan said ruefully.

"But," Bisesa said calmly, "I think you're the right person to hear what I have to say."

As she sipped her coffee Siobhan tried to get a sense of Bisesa. As Astronomer Royal she had always been expected to deal with people—sometimes thousands of them at once, when she gave public lectures. But since being press-ganged by Miriam Grec into this position of extraordinary responsibility, as a sort of general manager of the shield project, she believed she was acquiring a protective skill in sizing people up: the quicker you understood what faced you, the better you could deal with it.

And so here was Bisesa Dutt, Army officer, out of uniform, far from her posting. She was of Indian extraction. Her face was symmetrical, her nose long, and her gaze was strong but troubled. She was above medium height, with the physical confidence of a soldier. But she was gaunt, Siobhan thought, as if she had been hungry in the past.

Siobhan said, "Tell me why I need to listen to you."

"I know the date of the sunstorm. The *exact* date."

Because the authorities, guided by teams of psychologists, were continuing to work to minimize panic, that was still a closely guarded secret. "Bisesa, if there has been a security leak, it's your duty to tell me about it."

Bisesa shook her head. "No leak. You can check." She lifted one foot and tapped the sole with her fingernail. "I'm tagged. The Army has been monitoring me since I turned myself in."

"You went AWOL?"

"No," Bisesa said patiently. "They thought I had. Now I'm on compassionate leave, as they call it. But they are monitoring me anyhow."

"And so the date—"

"April 20, 2042, you mean?"

Siobhan regarded her. "Okay, I'll bite. How do you know that?"

"Because there is a solar eclipse on that day."

Siobhan raised her eyebrows. She murmured, "Aristotle?"

"She's correct, Siobhan," Aristotle whispered in her ear.

"Okay. But so what? An eclipse is just a lining up of sun, Moon and Earth. It has nothing to do with the sunstorm."

"But it does," Bisesa said. "*I was shown an eclipse,* during my journey back home."

"Your journey." Siobhan had only glanced at Bisesa's file. She'd come down to meet her on impulse, to get away from her tele-conference for a while. Now she was beginning to regret it. "I know something of the story. You had some kind of vision—"

"Not a vision. I don't want to use up our time discussing it. You have the files; if you believe me, you will check up on it later. Right now I need you to listen. I *knew* that something dreadful was going to happen to the Earth, the day I got back. And by showing me the eclipse they were telling me it had something to do with the sun."

"They? . . ."

Bisesa's face clouded, as if she didn't quite believe it all herself— and she rather wished she didn't have to. But she plowed on. "Professor McGorran, I believe that the sunstorm is no accident. *I believe it is the result of intentional harm being done to us by an alien power.*"

Siobhan pointedly glanced at her watch. "What alien power?"

"The Firstborn. That's what we called them."

"We? . . . Never mind. I don't suppose you have any proof."

"No—and I know what you're thinking. People like me never do."

Siobhan allowed herself a smile, for she had been thinking exactly that.

"But the Army did find some anomalies in my physical condition they couldn't explain. That's why they gave me leave. That's proof of a sort. And then there's the principle of mediocrity."

That threw Siobhan. "Mediocrity?"

"I'm no scientist, but isn't that what you call it? Copernicus's principle. There should be nothing special about any given location in space or time. And if you have a chain of logic that indicates there *is* something special about a given moment—"

"Never trust coincidences," Siobhan said.

Bisesa leaned forward intently. "Doesn't it strike you that the sunstorm, occurring now, is the mightiest coincidence of all time? Think about it. Humanity is a mere hundred thousand years old. The Earth, and the sun, are *forty thousand times* as old as that. If it were purely natural, surely the sunstorm could have occurred at any time in Earth's history. Why should the sun blow its top *now,* just in this brief moment when there happens to be an intelligence running around on the planet?"

For the first time in the course of the conversation Siobhan felt faintly disturbed. After all, she'd had, independently, vague thoughts along these lines. "You're saying this is no accident."

"I'm saying the sunstorm is intentional. I'm saying we are the target." Bisesa left the word hanging in the air.

Siobhan turned away from the intensity of her gaze. "But this is all just philosophy. You have no actual *proof.*"

Bisesa said firmly, "But I believe that if you look for proof you will find it. That's what I'm asking you to do. You're close to the scientists who are studying the sunstorm. You could make it happen. It could be vital."

"Vital?"

"For the future of humankind. Because if we don't understand what we're dealing with, how can we beat it?"

Siobhan studied this intent woman. There was something odd about her—something of another world, perhaps, another place.

But she had an intelligent soldier's clarity and conviction. She could be wrong in what she says, Siobhan thought. But I don't think she's mad.

On a whim she dug into her jacket pocket and dug out a scrap of material. "Let me show you what we're actually working on right now, the problems I'm wrestling with. Have you ever heard of smartskin? . . ."

This was a prototype sample of the material that would some day, if all went well, be stretched over the gaunt lunar-glass framework of the shield. It was a glass-fiber spiderweb, complex and full of components, detailed on scales as small as the eye could see. "It contains superconducting wires to transmit power and to serve as comms links. Diamond fibers, too small to see, for structural strength. Sensors, force multipliers, computer chips, even a couple of tiny rocket motors. There, can you see?" The scrap, the size of a pocket handkerchief, weighed almost nothing; the little rocket motors were like pinheads.

"Wow," Bisesa said. "I thought it was just a big dumb mirror."

Siobhan shook her head ruefully. "That would be too easy, wouldn't it? The whole shield won't have to be smart fabric, but maybe one percent of it will. It's like a huge cooperative organism."

Bisesa touched the material reverently. "So what's the problem?"

"The manufacture of the smartskin. The trouble is, it has to be nanotechnological . . ."

Nanotechnologies were still in their infancy. But nanotech, a process that built atom by atom, was the only way to manufacture a material like this, with a complexity that went down below the molecular.

Bisesa smiled. "Can I tell my daughter about this? She's a modern sort of kid. Nanotech fairy tales are her favorite sort."

Siobhan sighed. "That's the trouble. In a story you throw in a handful of magic dust, and nano will build you anything—right? Well, nano *will* build almost anything, but it needs something to build with, and energy to do it. Nano is more like biology, in some ways. Like a plant, a nano application draws energy and materials from its environment, and uses them to fuel its metabolism, and build itself up."

"Instead of leaves and trunks, space shields."

"Yes. In nature metabolic processes are slow. I once saw a bamboo shoot growing at naked-eye speeds: nano is directed, and faster than that. But not much faster."

Bisesa stroked the bit of smartskin. "So this stuff grows slowly."

"Too slowly. There aren't enough factories on the planet for us to churn out the quantity of smartskin we need. We're stuck."

"Then ask for help."

Siobhan was puzzled. "Help?"

"You know, people always think on a big scale—what can the government do for me, how can I gear up industry to churn out what I want? But I learned, working for the UN, that the way the world really works is through ordinary people helping each other, and helping themselves."

"What are you suggesting?"

Bisesa cautiously picked up the smartskin. "You say this stuff grows like a plant. Well, could *I* grow it?"

"What?"

"I'm serious. If I put it in my window box, and fed and watered it, and kept it in the sun—"

Siobhan opened her mouth, and closed it. "I don't know. An open plant pot wouldn't do, I'm sure of that. But maybe some reasonably uncomplicated kit would work. And maybe the design could be adapted to draw on local nutrients—"

"What does that mean?"

"From the soil. Or even household waste."

"How would you get it started?"

Siobhan thought. "You'd need some kind of seed, I guess. Enough to encode the construction data, and to bootstrap the macro-scale growth."

"But if my neighbor grew one, she could pass on seeds to me. And I could pass them on from my, umm, 'plant' to the next person."

"And then you'd need some kind of collection system to bring the finished smartskin to some central point . . . But wait," Siobhan said, thinking fast. "The total area of the shield is around a hundred thousand *billion* square meters. One percent of that, and a global population of ten billion—why, every man, woman, and child on Earth would have to produce, oh, say a blanket ten or twenty meters on a side. *Everybody.*"

Bisesa grinned. "Surely less than that if the factories do their job. And it isn't so much. We've still got three years. You'd be surprised what Boy Scouts and Girl Guides can produce when they've a mind to do it."

Siobhan shook her head. "This needs thinking through. But if it's possible I'll owe you a debt of gratitude."

Bisesa seemed embarrassed. "It's an obvious idea. If I hadn't come up with it, you would have yourself—or somebody else."

"Maybe." She smiled. "I ought to introduce you to my daughter." *Saving the world is so 1990s disaster movie! Nobody believes in heroes anymore, Mum . . .* This way, everybody would be a hero, she supposed. Maybe it would catch even Perdita's imagination.

Bisesa asked, "Why did you show me this stuff?"

Siobhan sighed. "Because this is real. This is engineering. This is what we're building, right now. I thought if you saw this—"

"It might puncture my fantasies," Bisesa said.

"Something like that, maybe."

"Just because something is big, indeed superhuman, doesn't make it any less real," Bisesa said evenly. "Or any less relevant. And anyhow, as I've said, you don't have to believe me. Just look for proof."

Siobhan stood up. "I really ought to get back to my meeting." But she hesitated, intrigued despite herself. "You know, I'm open-minded enough to accept the existence of extraterrestrial aliens as a possibility. But what you're describing makes no psychological sense. *Why* would these hypothetical Firstborn try to destroy us? And even if it were so, why would they give you these hints and glimpses? Why would they warn any of us—and why *you?* . . ."

But even as she spoke, Siobhan thought of a possible answer to her objection.

Because there are factions among these Firstborn. Because they are no more united and uniform of view than humanity is—why should a more advanced intelligence be homogeneous? And because there are some of them, at least, who believe that what is being done is wrong. A faction of them, working through this woman, Bisesa, are trying to warn us.

This woman could be crazy, Siobhan thought. Even after meeting her, she was ninety percent sure that was true. But her story did make a certain sense. And what if she was right? What if an investigation did turn up evidence to back her claims? What then?

Bisesa was watching her, as if reading her thoughts. Siobhan didn't trust herself to speak again, and she hurried away.

When she got back to the Council Room, the level of chatter among the population of heads dropped a little. She stood in the middle of the room and peered around. "You're all acting as if you've got something to be ashamed of."

Bud said, "Perhaps we have, Siobhan. It's beginning to look as if things aren't as black as we painted them. The issue of the solar pressure and positioning—one of us came up with a solution. We think."

"Who?" Siobhan faced Rose Delea. "Rose. Surely not *you*."

Rose actually looked embarrassed. "Actually it was our conversation earlier. When I said something about how we'd have no problem if the sunlight was allowed to pass straight through the shield? It got me thinking. There *is* a way we could make our shield transparent. We don't reflect the sunlight. We *deflect* it . . ."

The shield would be made clear, but scored on one side with fine parallel grooves: prisms.

"Ah," Siobhan said. "And each ray of sunlight would be turned aside. We'd be building, not a mirror, but a lens, a huge Fresnel lens."

It would be an all-but-transparent lens that could turn the sunlight away a little, by only a degree or less. But that would be sufficient to spare the Earth from the blast of the sunstorm. And a lens would suffer only a fraction of the photon pressure of a fully reflective mirror.

Rose said, "It's really no more of a manufacturing challenge than our current design. But the total mass could be *much* less."

"And so we're back in the realms of feasible design solutions?" Siobhan asked.

"With a vengeance," Bud said, beaming.

Siobhan glanced around. Now she saw restlessness in their expressions, even eagerness; they were all keen to get back to their people, to begin exploring this new idea. It was a good team, she thought with pride, the best there was, and she could trust them to take this new idea and worry it until it was thoroughly integrated into the design and the construction program—by which time the next obstacle would have appeared, and they would all be back here again.

"Another bit of good news before we close," she said. "I may have a solution to the nanotech manufacturing problem too."

Eyes widened.

She smiled. "It will keep. I'll mail you the details when it's fleshed out a bit more. Thank you, everybody. Meeting closed."

The screens winked out, one by one.

"You old ham," Toby grinned.

"Always leave them wanting more."

"Were you serious about the smartskin issue?"

"Needs work, but I think so."

"You know," Toby said, "mathematically speaking L1 is a turning point—a point where a curve changes direction, from downhill to up. That's why it's a point of equilibrium."

"I know that—ah. You think we've gone through a turning point on the project today?"

"What do you think?"

"I think you should leave the headlines to the journalists. Okay. What's next?"

23: HEATHROW

In March 2040—with another dismal Christmas come and gone, and just a little over two years left before sunstorm day—Miriam Grec decided to visit the shield construction site in person. And that meant flying into space, for the first time in her life.

As she was driven away from the Euro-needle that day she felt guilty but excited, like a child playing hooky from school. But she needed a holiday; her friends and enemies alike would agree on that, she thought wryly.

London's Heathrow had been an airport for a century, and now it was a spaceport too. And, sitting on a long, hardened runway in the watery sunlight, the spaceplane looked quite remarkably beautiful, Miriam thought.

The *Boudicca* was a slim needle some sixty meters long. It had alarmingly small vanes at its nose and tail, and even its main wings were just stubby swept-back deltas. Mounted on the wingtips were fat, asymmetrical nacelles that contained the principal rocket motors—or rather they would work as rockets in the vacuum of space, but in Earth's atmosphere they breathed air like jet engines. The plane's upper surface was a dull white ceramic shell, but its underside was coated with a gleaming black plate, a heat shield for reentry, made of a substance that was a remote descendant of the thermal tiling that had given the venerable space shuttle so much trouble.

Despite the ground support vehicles that clustered around it and the clouds of vapor steaming from its tanks of cryogenic fuel, the plane really did look as if it belonged to another order of creation entirely, and had only diffidently set down here on Earth. But it was a working ship—indeed, a veteran of space. That gleaming outer hull was punctured with the nozzles of attitude control rockets around which the surface was scarred and blistered, and repeated reentries had splashed scorch marks over its underside.

And the plane was proudly British. While the tailplane bore on one side the starry circle of the Eurasian Union, on the other side waved an animated Union flag, and on the spaceplane's wings and flank were painted the famous roundels of the Royal Air Force, a reminder that this soaring bird of space could be called on to serve military duties.

The design had an ancestry dating back to pioneering studies in the 1980s by firms like British Aerospace and Rolls-Royce, paper birds with names like Hotol and Skylon. But those studies had languished until the 2020s, when a new breed of materials technologies and engine designs, and the new push into space, had suddenly made a fleet of fully reusable spaceplanes a commercial proposition. And when the planes actually flew, of course, the British were quite unreasonably proud of their beautiful new toys.

The choice of a female name was obviously right, Miriam thought: surely this spaceplane was the most beautiful piece of British aeronautical engineering since the Spitfire. But the name of the Celtic queen who had once defied the Romans, selected by a popular vote, seemed a rather tactless moniker in these days of pan-Eurasian harmony—though Miriam wondered if the second choice would have been any more acceptable: *Margaret Thatcher* . . .

Still, even in these days of a united Eurasia you had to respect lingering national sentiments, as long as they played themselves out in a constructive way. And besides, as Nicolaus never ceased to remind her, this year, 2040, was an election year. So Miriam allowed herself to be photographed before the shining hull, a smile fixed to her face.

She rode a small escalator, and entered the plane through a hatch cut in the curving fuselage.

She found herself in a poky little compartment. If she had expected an elegance inside the plane to match its beautiful exterior, she was immediately disappointed. There were a dozen seats set in unimaginative rows, rather like first-class seats on a long-haul flight—but no better than that. There weren't even windows in the walls.

She was greeted by a tall, very upright man in a Eurasian Airways uniform and a peaked cap. His hair was silver-white, and he must have been in his late seventies; but he had sharp, good-looking features, his blue eyes were clear, and when he spoke his accent was a reassuring upper crust. "Madam Prime Minister, I'm delighted to welcome you aboard. I'm Captain John Purcell, and it's my pleasant duty to make sure you enjoy your flight up to the shield. Please take a seat; the flight is yours today, and you can take your pick . . ."

Miriam and Nicolaus sat one row apart, so they had the luxury of more room. Purcell helped them strap into intimidatingly robust harnesses, then offered them drinks. Miriam accepted a Bucks Fizz. What the hell, she thought.

Nicolaus declined a drink, a bit testily. It struck Miriam that he had seemed edgy for some time. She supposed that anybody had a right to be nervous about being hurled into space, even nowadays. But perhaps there was more to it than that. She remembered her resolve to try to get him to open up a bit more.

Now Nicolaus called over his shoulder, "You know, this reminds me of the Concorde. The same mix of a high-tech exterior, but a poky little passenger cabin."

Purcell perked up. "Did you ever fly the old plane, sir?"

"No, no," Nicolaus said. "I just crawled around a retired model in a museum a few years ago."

"Was that the one at RAF Duxford? . . . As it happens, I used to fly the Concorde, before she was retired at the turn of the century. I was a pilot for the old British Airways." He grinned at Miriam, almost flirtatiously, and smoothed back his silver hair. "I'm sure you can tell I'm old enough. But the spaceplane is a different bird altogether. It is human-rated, of course, but it was primarily designed as a cargo carrier. Actually it's almost all propellant."

Miriam said, a bit nervously, "It is?"

"Oh, yes. Of three hundred tonnes all-up weight, only twenty tonnes is payload. And we'll use up almost all of that fuel getting away from the Earth." He eyed her cautiously. "Madam, I'm sure you were sent a briefing pack. You do understand that we will glide home from space, without powered engines? Returning to Earth is a question of shedding energy, not spending it . . ."

She'd had no time to touch the glossy briefing pack, of course, but she did know that much.

"So we're just a flying bomb," Nicolaus said.

Even allowing for his nervousness Miriam was surprised he would say such a thing.

Purcell's eyes narrowed a bit. "I like to think we're a bit smarter than that, sir. Now if I may I will take you through our emergency procedures . . ."

These turned out to be rather alarming too. One option, in the event of decompression, involved being zipped up into a pressurized bag, as helpless as a hamster in a plastic globe. The idea was that astronauts in spacesuits would manhandle you inside your sphere across to a rescue ship.

Captain Purcell smiled, competent, reassuring. "Madam Prime Minister, we no longer treat our passengers as children. Everything has been done to ensure your safety, of course. I could talk you through the flight profile, and describe to you how our engineers have labored to close what they unromantically call 'windows of nonsurvivability.' But this spaceplane is still a young technology. One has to simply 'buy the risk,' as we used to say in my day—and sit back and enjoy the ride."

The ground preparations appeared to be complete. Large, high-resolution softscreens unrolled over the walls and ceiling like blinds, and lit up with daylight. Suddenly it was as if Miriam were sitting in an open framework, looking out at the runway's long perspective.

Purcell began to strap himself into a seat. "Please enjoy the view—or, if you prefer, we can blank out the screens."

Miriam said, "Shouldn't you be up in the cockpit?"

Purcell looked regretful. "What cockpit? Times have changed, I'm afraid, madam. I'm the Captain on this flight. But *Boudicca* flies herself."

It was all a question of economy and reliability; automated control systems were much simpler to install and maintain than a human pilot. It just defied human instinct, Miriam thought, to give up so much control to a machine.

And then, quite suddenly, it was time to leave. The plane shuddered as the big wing-mounted engines lit up—an invisible hand pushed Miriam back into her seat—and *Boudicca* was hurled like a spear down the long runway.

"Don't worry," Purcell called over the engine noise. "The acceleration will be no worse than a roller coaster. That's why they keep me on, I think. If an old duffer like me can live through this, you'll be fine!—"

Without ceremony *Boudicca* tipped up and threw herself into the sky.

London's sprawl opened up beneath Miriam.

Orienting herself by the shining chrome band of the river, she picked out Westminster at its sharp bend in the river's flow, said to be the place where Julius Caesar had first crossed the Thames. As her viewpoint rose higher the urban carpet of Greater London spread out below her, kilometer upon kilometer of houses and factories, a floor of concrete and tarmac and brick. In the spring morning light the suburban avenues were like flower beds, Miriam thought, stocked with brick-red blooms that gleamed in the sun. You could see the streets gather into little knots, relics of villages and farms planted as far back as the Saxons, now submerged by the urban sprawl. Miriam had grown up in the French countryside, and despite her career path was averse to city life. But London from the air really was remarkably beautiful, she thought—accidentally, for nobody had planned it this way, and yet it was so.

As she climbed farther she saw that over the heart of the metropolis the great Dome was rising, skeletal and tremendous, designed to protect all those layers of history. She was glad it was there, for she felt a surging affection for the scattered, helpless city that lay spread-eagled below her, and a sense of duty to protect it from what was to come.

Soon London was lost in cloud and haze. When she looked ahead, the sky was fading from deep blue, to purple, and at last to black.

Shining in the light that flooded space, *Aurora 2* was undeniably a magnificent sight. But it was a complicated, ungainly magnificence, Miriam thought. Unlike *Boudicca* this ship had never been intended to fly in the atmosphere of any world, not even Mars, and so had none of the spaceplane's slender aerodynamic grace.

Aurora looked something like a drum majorette's baton. The spine of the ship was a slim triangular spar some two hundred meters long. Under thrust, the greatest load the *Aurora* had to bear was along the length of its spine—and that was the direction in which this fragile ship was strongest, reinforced with struts of nano-engineered artificial diamond. At one end of the spine clustered power generators, including a small nuclear fusion reactor, and an ion-drive rocket engine whose gentle but relentless acceleration had pushed *Aurora* all the way to Mars and back. Spherical fuel tanks, antennae, and solar-cell arrays were strung along the spine. At the spine's other end was a bloated dome that contained the crew quarters: habitable compartments, a bridge, life support systems. Somewhere in there, surrounded by water tanks for extra shielding, was the small, cramped, thick-walled solar-storm shelter where the crew, caught in interplanetary space, had retreated during the blistering hours of June 9, 2037.

And the shield that would save the world was already growing around the *Aurora,* its glistening surface spiraling out like a spiderweb.

Aurora served as a construction shack for the crews who, ferried up from Earth and Moon, labored to complete this mighty project. It was a noble destiny for any ship, Miriam thought. But *Aurora* had been destined to orbit another world, and there was something poignant about seeing it meshed up in a tangle of scaffolding. Miriam wondered if the ship's own artificial intelligences, thwarted of their true purpose, knew some ghost of regret.

Boudicca docked with the *Aurora*'s habitable compartment, nestling belly-first against its curving hull like a moth settling on an orange.

Miriam and Nicolaus were met by an astronaut: Colonel Burton Tooke. Bud wore coveralls, practical enough but freshly laundered and pressed, and adorned with astronaut wings, mission logos, and military decorations. Bud extended a hand and helped pull Miriam through the docking tunnel. "You seem to be coping fine with the lack of gravity," he offered.

"Oh, I took some spins around the *Boudicca*'s cabin. It was great fun—after the first twelve hours or so."

"I can imagine. Space sickness hits most of us. And most people get through it."

Nicolaus hadn't, however, a fact that had given Miriam some rather unkind satisfaction. Just for once, in that bubble of metal drifting between worlds, it had been she who had had to look out for him.

Miriam had spent most of the flight working; she was reasonably up to date, and even felt quite rested. So she left Captain Purcell to sort out her few bits of luggage, and accepted Bud's invitation for a quick tour. Nicolaus followed, cameras sitting on his scalp and shoulder like glistening birds, determined not to miss a moment of this photo opportunity.

They drifted through the cramped corridors of the *Aurora*. This was a ship designed for space; there were pipes, ducts, and removable panels on walls, ceiling, and floor, rails and rungs to help you pull your way along in zero G, and a color-coding in pastel shades to help you remember which way was up. It was difficult to grasp that this unremarkable working space had sailed across the solar system, all the way to Mars and back.

Despite the efficiency of the recycling systems there was a powerful, almost leonine stink of *people.* But they met nobody; the crew were either avoiding the visiting brass, or, much more likely, were out working somewhere. It was all very different from her usual Prime Ministerial visits, and oddly intimate—and she certainly didn't miss the usual scrum of journalists and assorted hangers-on.

They reached the hatchway to *Aurora*'s observation deck. Bud pushed open the door, and sunlight flooded over Miriam's face. The deck's "picture window" turned out to be a pane of toughened Perspex a lot smaller than any of the windows in her office in the Euroneedle. But once, briefly, this window had looked down over the red canyons of Mars—and now it looked out into space.

There was work going on out there. A framework of open struts jutted out from just below the window, and extending far into the distance. Astronauts in color-coded spacesuits were crawling all over, pulling themselves along with handholds or cables or pushed by small thruster packs on their backs. There must have been a hundred people in that first glance, and as many autonomous, multilimbed machines, moving through a sunlit three-dimensional maze of scaffolding. It was hugely impressive, but complex, baffling.

"Tell me what they're doing."

"Okay." Bud pointed. "In the distance, you can see heavy-duty equipment moving those struts into place."

"Those look like glass. The shield's framework?"

"Yeah. Moon glass. We're extending the structure in a spiral fashion around the *Aurora,* so that at any given moment we keep the center of gravity of the whole BDO right here at L1."

She asked, " 'BDO'?"

Bud looked abashed. "The shield. We astronauts will have our acronyms."

"And it stands for—"

"Big Dumb Object. Kind of an in-joke."

Nicolaus rolled his eyes.

Bud said, "The struts are prefabricated on the Moon. But up here we're manufacturing the skin itself—not the smart stuff coming from Earth; just the simple prismatic film that we'll lay over most of the BDO's area."

He pointed to an astronaut wrestling with an ungainly piece of equipment. It looked as if she were extracting a huge balloon animal from a packing case. It was an almost comical sight, but Miriam took care to keep her face straight.

Bud said, "We use inflatable Mylar formers as molds. Designing the inflatable itself is an art. You have to figure the deployment dynamics. When you blow it up you don't want it stretching out of shape; the Mylar is only as thick as freezer film. So we simulate backward, letting it deflate its way into the box, trying to make sure it will deploy smoothly without tangling itself up or stretching . . ."

She let him talk on. Bud was obviously proud of the work being performed here, meeting the challenges of an environment where the simplest task, such as blowing up a balloon, was full of unknowns. And anyhow, some space-buff piece of her was enjoying his talk of "deployment dynamics" and the rest.

"And when the mold is ready," he was saying, pointing to another area of work, "we spray on the film."

An astronaut supervised a clumsy-looking robot that rolled along a boom stretched out before a big inflatable disk. The robot was using a roller to smear a glassy surface on the Mylar face of the disk. The robot, working calmly, looked as if it were doing nothing more exotic than painting a wall.

"The Mylar comes up from the ground in solid blocks," Bud said. "To make a film, you heat the stuff and force it out through hot nozzles, so you get jets of filament. You give this stuff a positive charge, and make the target surface a negative electrode, so the polymer filament is drawn out like taffy, becoming hundreds of times thinner in the process. You couldn't do this on Earth; gravity would mess with everything. But here you just squirt it on, deflate the mold, and peel it off."

"I want one of those robots to paint my flat."

He laughed, but it was a bit forced, and she was painfully aware that everybody who came here must make a similar joke.

He said, "The robots and machines and processes are all very well. But the heart of this place is the people." He glanced at her. "I come from a farming area in Iowa. As a kid I always liked to read stories of blue-collar guys just like my father and his buddies working in space, or on the Moon. Well, it can't be that way, not for a long time. This is still space, a lethal environment, and the work we're doing is highly skilled engineering. None of those grease monkeys out there is less qualified than a Ph.D. Blue collar they ain't, I guess. But they have the heart—you know what I'm saying? They're working twenty-four seven to get this job done, and some of them have been up here for years already. And without that heart none of this would get done, for all our gadgets."

"I understand," she said softly. "Colonel, I'm impressed. And reassured."

So she was. Siobhan had briefed her well on Bud, but Miriam knew that Siobhan had developed a relationship with him, and one reason for coming here was to make her own assessment. She liked everything she saw about this blunt, can-do American aviator who had become so pivotal to the future of humankind; she was relieved that the project was in such evidently safe hands.

Not that her Eurasian pride would *ever* have allowed her to admit as much to President Alvarez.

She said, "I hope to meet some of your people later."

"They will appreciate that."

"So will I. I'm not going to pretend this isn't a photo op for me; of course it is. But for better or worse this monstrous edifice will be my legacy. I was determined to come see it, and the people who are building it, before they kick me out."

Bud nodded gravely. "We follow the polls too. I can't believe how bad they are for you." He smacked his fist against his palm. "They should send their damn questionnaires up *here*."

She was touched. "It's the way it goes, Colonel. The polls show people are broadly behind the shield project. But they are also suffering endless disruption because of all the wealth that is flowing off the planet and up here to this great orbiting sink of money. They want the shield, but they don't like having to pay for it—and perhaps, beneath it all, they resent being faced with the threat of the sunstorm in the first place."

Nicolaus grunted. "It is classic barroom psychology. When faced with bad news, after the denial comes the anger."

Bud said, "So they need somebody to blame?"

"Something like that," Miriam said. "Or perhaps they're right. The shield will go on, whatever happens to me; we've gone too far to change direction now. But as for me—you know, Churchill lost an election right after winning the Second World War. The people judged he had done his job. Maybe my successor will do a better job of easing the day-to-day pain than I can." And maybe, she wondered, the people sensed just how exhausted she was, how much this job had taken out of her—and how little she had left to give.

Nicolaus grunted. "You're too philosophical, Miriam."

"Yeah," Bud growled. "What a dumb time to call an election! Maybe it should be postponed for a couple of years—"

"No," she said firmly. "Oh, I suspect martial law will come to the cities before this is done. But democracy is our most important possession. If we throw it away when the going gets tough, we might never get it back—and then we'll end up like the Chinese."

Bud glanced sideways at Nicolaus, the furtive look of a man who had grown used to working under conditions of security. "Speaking of which—as you know we're monitoring the Chinese from up here."

"There have been more launches?"

"On a good day you can see them with the naked eye. You can't hide the firing of a Long March booster. But no matter how we try, we can't trace them after launch, by optical means, radar—we even tried bouncing laser beams off them."

"Stealth technology?"

"We think so."

It had been going on for a year: a massive and continuing program of space launches from China's echoing interior, one huge mass after another hurled into the silence of space, their destination unknown. Miriam herself had been involved in efforts to figure out what was going on; the Chinese premier had deflected her probing without so much as raising a dyed eyebrow.

She said, "Anyhow it makes no difference to us."

"Maybe," Bud said. "But it pains me to think we're laboring up here to save their skinny ungrateful butts too. Pardon my language."

"You mustn't think that way. Just remember, the mass of the people in China have little or no idea what their leaders are up to, and even less control. It's them you are working for, not those gerontocrats in Beijing."

He grinned. "I guess you're right. You see, this is why you'd get my vote."

"Sure I would . . ."

He pointed. "If you look up, you can see what it's all about."

She had to bend down to see.

There was the Earth. It was a blue lantern hanging directly opposite the position of the sun. Miriam was a million and a half kilometers from home, and from here the planet looked about the size of the Moon from Earth. And it was full, of course; Earth always was, as seen from here at L1, suspended between Earth and sun.

Earth hung low over the shield itself, and its pale blue light glistened from a glassy floor that stretched to a horizon that was already vanishingly distant. The emerging shield had yet to be positioned so that its face was correctly turned toward the sun; that would come in the final days before the sunstorm was due.

It was an astounding, beautiful sight, and it was almost impossible to believe that mere humans had made this thing, here in the depths of space.

On a warm impulse she turned to her press secretary. "Nicolaus, forget the damn cameras. You *must* see this view . . ."

He was cowering against the rear bulkhead of the chamber, his face twisted with an anguish she had never seen in him before. He rapidly composed himself. But it was an expression she would think of again, three days later, as *Boudicca* made its last descent to Earth.

On the way out of the observation deck, Miriam noticed a plaque, hastily carved from a bit of lunar glass:

ARMAGEDDON POSTPONED
COURTESY OF
U.S. ASTRONAUTICAL ENGINEERING CORPS

25: SMOKING GUN

For the reentry into Earth's atmosphere aboard the spaceplane, Nicolaus chose to sit beside Miriam. He seemed stiff and rather silent, as he had been all the way back from the shield, and indeed for much of their time up there.

But Miriam, though she knew she was exhausted on some deep level, felt good. She stretched luxuriously. The big softscreens around her showed the broad blue-gray face of Earth below, and a pink glow building up at the leading edge of *Boudicca*'s stubby wings as they bit into the thickening air. But there was no real sense of deceleration, only the mildest of vibrations, a tickle of pressure at her chest. It was all remarkably beautiful, and comfortable. "After seven days in space I feel *wonderful,*" she said. "I could get used to this. What a shame it's over."

"All things must end."

There was something odd in Nicolaus's tone. She looked at him, but though his posture remained stiff his face was blank. A distant alarm bell rang in her head.

She looked past Nicolaus across the narrow aisle to see Captain Purcell, who had been quiet for a while. Purcell's head was lolling like a puppet's.

Immediately she understood. "Oh, Nicolaus. What have you done?"

Siobhan arrived at the Chelsea flat, with Toby Pitt at her side. It was an ordinary place, Siobhan thought, and this was an unremarkable March day. But there was nothing unremarkable about the woman who opened the door.

"Thank you for coming," Bisesa said. She looked tired—but then, Siobhan reflected, two years out from sunstorm day, everybody looked tired.

Siobhan followed her through the flat's short hallway to the living room. The room had the clutter you would expect: a soft-looking sofa big enough for three, occasional tables littered with magazines and rolled-up softscreens. The main feature on which money had been spent was a big kid-friendly softwall. Bisesa was a single parent, Siobhan knew, with her one daughter, Myra, now eleven, at school today. The other tenant was Bisesa's cousin, a student in bioethics who was now working on a pre-sunstorm conservation program run by an alliance of British zoos.

In a suit and tie, out of his natural environment in this domestic scene, Toby Pitt looked uncomfortable. "Nice softwall," he said.

Bisesa shrugged. "It's a bit out of date now. It kept Myra company when her squaddie mum was away. Now Myra has other interests," she said with a mother's fond exasperation. "And we don't watch so much. Too much bad news."

That was a common pattern, Siobhan knew. Anyhow, today the softwall was now hooked up to a government comms channel, and was showing the flickering images of Mikhail, Eugene, and others, images relayed from the Moon and Earth orbit to this living room in a flat in Chelsea.

Bisesa bustled away to make coffee.

Toby leaned toward Siobhan and said quietly, "I still think this is a mistake. To be pursuing theories of alien intention behind the sunstorm—people are becoming too disengaged as it is."

Siobhan knew he had a point.

The impending sunstorm itself was bad enough for the public mood. Now the preparations for it were starting to bite significantly into people's lives. Immense construction projects like the Dome were causing monumental traffic problems. Across the city routine work was being rushed or neglected, and that was starting

to show; just the lack of fresh paintwork on London's major buildings was making the place look shabby. Aside from the huge diver-
sion of resources to the Dome, everybody was stockpiling, it seemed,
and there was a continual plague of shortages in the stores. A recent
upsurge of global terrorism and the subsequent wave of paranoia
and security clampdowns had made things worse yet. It was a time
of fretfulness and anxiety, a time from which people increasingly
wanted to escape.

All the major news organizations reported catastrophic slumps
in ratings—while sales of synth soap operas, which allowed you to
pretend the outside world didn't exist at all, had boomed. The
world's leaders were becoming concerned that if there was more bad
news of any kind, everybody would just hide away at home until the
dreadful dawn of April 20, 2042 finally put an end to all their stories.

"But," Siobhan said slowly, *"what if Bisesa's right?"* That was
the slim, disturbing possibility that had guided her actions since the
day Bisesa had first bluffed her way into the Royal Society, already
more than a year ago, and why she had diverted a small percentage
of the energies at her command to looking into Bisesa's ideas. "If
this is the truth, Toby, there's no hiding away, whatever it costs."

"I'm sorry," he said quickly. "You have my full support. You
know that. It's just that I've always felt that putting Bisesa *I-was-
abducted-by-aliens-and-fell-in-love-with-Alexander-the-Great* Dutt in
touch with Eugene *the-greatest-mind-since-Einstein-if-only-you-would-
listen* Mangles was asking for trouble."

She forced a smile. "Yes, but what fun!"

Bisesa returned with a tray of coffees, and a pot for refills.

"There's nothing you can do about it, Miriam," Nicolaus said, his
voice thickened by stress. "The plane's communications are cut off,
and anyhow we will soon be isolated by reentry plasma. Even Aristotle is out of touch. The fact that the plane is automated actually
made it easier. The device is on a tamperproof timer, which, even if
we could get to it—"

She held up her hands. "I really don't want to know." She
glanced at the wall softscreens, which now showed a broadening

glow, escalating through pink to white. It was like being inside a vast lightbulb, she thought. Must her life really end amid such beauty?

She searched for anger, but found only emptiness, a kind of pity. After years of strain she was fundamentally exhausted, she thought, too tired to be angry, even about this. And maybe she had thought that something like this was inevitable, in the end. But she did want to understand.

"What's the point, Nicolaus? You know the polls better than I do. In six months I would be out of the way anyhow. And this really won't make any difference to the project. If anything it's likely to strengthen everybody's resolve to get it done."

"Are you sure?" His grin was tight. "This is quite a stunt, you know. You are Prime Minister of the world's largest democracy. And nobody has taken down a spaceplane before. If confidence in flying into space is dented, even just a bit—if people on the shield start looking over their shoulders when they ought to be getting on with their work—I'll have achieved what I set out to do."

"But you won't live to see it, will you?" *And neither will I . . .* "You're just another in a long line of suicide bombers, as careless of the lives of others as you are of your own."

He said coldly, "You don't know me well enough to insult me. Even though I've worked at your side for ten years."

Of course that was true, she thought with a stab of guilt. She remembered her resolution on the way out to try to get Nicolaus to open up a little—but on the shield she had been too entranced by her surroundings even to notice him. Would it have made any difference even if she had? Perhaps it was just as well, she thought morbidly, that she would not live long enough to be plagued by such questions.

"Tell me why, Nicolaus. I think you owe me that."

His voice tight with tension, he said, "I sacrifice my life for El, the One True God."

And that was enough to tell her everything.

———

Siobhan glanced at the faces on Bisesa's softwall. "Everybody online? Can you see us?"

With the usual disconcerting lightspeed delays, the others responded.

"No introductions needed, no ceremony. Who wants to start—Eugene?"

When her words reached the Moon, Eugene visibly jumped, as if his attention had been fixed on something else. "Okay," he said. "First some background. You're aware of my work on the sun, of course." The middle of the softwall filled up with an image of the sun, which then turned transparent to reveal onion-skin layers within. The heart of the sun, the fusing core—a star within a star—glowed a sullen red. It was laced by a crisscross pattern of dark and bright stripes, dynamic, elusive, ever shifting. There was a date stamp in the corner, showing today's date, in March 2040. Eugene said, "These oscillations will lead in the near future to a catastrophic outpouring of energy into the external environment."

Casually he ran the model forward in time, until the image suddenly flared.

Siobhan felt Toby flinch. He murmured, "He really doesn't see the impact he has on the rest of us, does he? Sometimes that boy scares me more than the sun itself."

"But he's useful," Siobhan whispered back.

Eugene said, "So the future projection is stable, reliable. But I have had more difficulty with projections *into the past.* Nothing in the standard models of stellar interior behavior served as a guide. I began to suspect a single impulsive event lay behind this anomalous condition—an anomaly behind the anomaly. But I had trouble converging on a model. My discussions with Lieutenant Dutt, after Professor McGorran put us in touch, gave me a new paradigm to work with."

Siobhan murmured to Toby, "Told you so."

Mikhail interceded, "I think you'd better just show us, son."

Eugene nodded curtly and tapped at an out-of-shot softscreen.

The date stamp began to count down, and the reconstructed events ran backward. As wave modes fluttered across the surface of the core, detail appeared in sidebars: frequencies, phases, amplitudes, lists of the energy shares of the principal vibration modes. As interference, nonlinearity, and other effects worked on the three-dimensional waves, the core's output peaked and dipped.

Mikhail commented, "Eugene's model is remarkably good. We have been able to map many of these resonant-peak anomalies onto some of the notable solar weather incidents in our history: the Little Ice Age, the 1859 storm . . ."

Siobhan had studied wave propagation as applied to the early universe, and she could see the quality of the work here. She said to Toby, "If he gets this anywhere near right, it will be one of the keenest bits of analysis I've ever seen."

"Finest mind since Einstein," Toby said dryly.

Now things changed on the screen. The oscillations grew wilder. And it seemed to Siobhan that a concentration of energy was gathering in one place.

Unexpectedly a brilliant knot of light rose out of the core, like a gruesome dawn inside the body of the sun itself. And as soon as the knot had left the core, those central oscillations all but ceased.

Eugene paused his projection, leaving the point of light poised on the edge of the core but beneath the blanketing layers of sun above. "At this point my modeling of the core anomaly is smoothly patched to a new routine to project the behavior of the inert radiative zone that lies around the core, and—"

Siobhan leaned forward. "Hold it, Eugene. What *is* that thing?"

Eugene blinked. "A concentration of mass," he said, as if it were obvious. He displayed graphs of density. "At this point the mass contained within three standard deviations of the center of gravity is ten to power twenty-eight kilograms."

She did some quick mental arithmetic. "That's about five Jupiters."

Eugene glanced at her, as if surprised she would need a translation into such baby talk. "About that, yes." He resumed his animation.

That glowing fist of matter rose out of the sun's heart, up through its layers. As it rose Siobhan saw disturbances like ripples flowing *into* the mass knot, a glowing tail almost like a comet's, preceding it on its way to the surface. But she was watching this projection in reverse, she reminded herself. In reality this lump of matter had slammed its way down into the sun, leaving a turbulent wake behind, dumping energy and mass into the sun's tortured bulk through those mighty waves.

She said, "So that's how the radiative zone was cut through."

"Precisely," Mikhail said. "Eugene's model is elegant: a single cause to explain many effects."

The knot of mass, backing out of the sun, now reached the surface and popped out through the photosphere. Again Eugene froze his animation. Siobhan saw that the emergence was close to the sun's equator.

The date stamp, she noted, showed 4 B.C.

Eugene said, "Here is the moment of impact. The mass at this point was some ten to power—" He glanced at Siobhan. "About fifteen Jupiters. As it descended into the sun's interior, the outer layers of the object were of course ablated away, but five Jupiters made it to the core."

Toby Pitt said, "Fifteen Jupiters. It was a planet—a Jovian, a big one. And, two thousand years ago—*it fell into the sun.* Is that what you're saying?"

"Not quite," Eugene said. He tapped at his softscreen again, and the view abruptly changed. Now the sun was a bright pinpoint at the center of a darkened screen, and the planets' orbits were traced out as shining circles. "From this point I made another patch, to a simple Newtonian gravity trajectory solution. Corrections for relativity aren't significant until the impactor passed the orbit of Mercury, and even then they are small . . ."

Knowing where and how fast his mighty Jovian had splashed into the sun, Eugene had projected back, using Newton's gravity law, to figure out the path it must have followed to get there. A glowing line, starting in the sun and crossing all the planets' orbits, swept out of the solar system and off the screen. It curved subtly but was remarkably straight, Siobhan saw.

Toby said, "I don't understand. Why do you say it didn't fall into the sun?"

Siobhan said immediately, "Because that trajectory is hyperbolic. Toby, the Jovian was moving faster than solar escape velocity."

Mikhail said somberly, "It didn't fall into the sun. It was *fired* in."

Toby's mouth opened, and closed.

Bisesa didn't seem surprised at all.

The One-Godders had emerged as a kind of reaction to the benevolent Oikumen movement. Fundamentalists of three of the world's great faiths, Judaism, Christianity, and Islam, had appealed to their own shared roots. They united under the banner of the Old Testament God of Abraham, Isaac, and Jacob: Yahweh, who was thought to have derived from a still older deity called El, a god of the Canaanites.

And El was a meddling god, a brutish, partial, and murderous tribal god. In the late 2020s His first act, through His modern adherents, had been the destruction of the Dome of the Rock, when fanatics, in a self-destructive spasm, had used a nuclear grenade to take out a site of unique significance to at least two of their three intertwined creeds. Miriam remembered that Bud Tooke had been involved in the cleanup.

"Nicolaus, why would you want to impede the work on the shield? You've been at my side throughout. Can't you see how important it is?"

"If God wishes us to be put to the fire of the sunstorm, so be it. And if He chooses to save us, so be it. For us to question His authority over us with this monstrous gesture—"

"Oh, can it," she said irritably. "I've heard it all before. A Tower of Babel in space, eh? And you're the one to bring it down. How disappointing, how banal!"

"Miriam, your mockery can't hurt me anymore. I have found faith," he said.

And there was the real problem, she realized.

In his conversion Nicolaus wasn't alone. All the major faiths, sects, and cults worldwide had recorded a marked rise in conversions since June 9. You might expect a flight to God in the face of impending catastrophe—but there was a theory, still controversial and revealed to her only in confidential briefings, that increased solar activity was correlated with religious impulses in humans. The great electromagnetic energies that had washed over the planet since June 9 were, it seemed, able to work subtle changes in the complicated bioelectrical fields of a human brain, just as in power cables and computer chips.

If that was true—if the agitation of the sun had somehow led, by a long and complicated causal chain, to a lethal ideological determination in the mind of Miriam's closest colleague to kill her— well, what an irony it would be. She said blackly, "If God exists, He must be laughing right now."

"What did you say?"

"Never mind." A thought struck her. "Nicolaus—*where will we come down?*"

He smiled coldly. "Rome," he said.

Siobhan asked, "Can we say where this rogue planet came from?"

Not from the solar system, of course; it had been moving too fast to have been captured by the sun. Eugene displayed more of his "patched solutions," projecting the path of his Jovian back to the distant stars. He rattled off celestial coordinates, but Siobhan stopped him and turned to Mikhail. "Can you put that into English?"

"Aquila," Mikhail said. "It came to us out of the constellation of the eagle." This was a constellation close to the sky's equator; from Earth the plane of the Galaxy appeared to run through it. Mikhail said, "In fact, Professor McGorran, we know that this object must have came from the star Altair." Altair was the brightest star in Aquila. It was some sixteen light-years from Earth.

Eugene cautioned, "Mikhail, I'm not sure we should talk about this. The projection gets fuzzy if you push it back that far. The error bars—"

Mikhail said grimly, "My boy, this is not a time for timidity. Professor, it appears that Eugene's rogue Jovian *originated* in orbit around Altair. It was flung out after a series of close encounters with other planets in the system, which are visible with our planet-finder telescopes. The details are understandably sketchy, but we hope to pin them down further."

"And," Siobhan said, "it was hurled our way."

Toby pulled his nose. "It seems fantastic."

Mikhail said quickly, "The reconstruction is very reliable. It has been verified from multiple data sources using a variety of independent methods. I have checked over Eugene's calculations myself. This is all quite authoritative."

Bisesa listened to all this quietly, without reacting.

"Okay," Toby said. "So a rogue planet fell into the sun. It's an astonishing thing to happen, but not unprecedented. Remember Comet Shoemaker-Levy colliding with Jupiter in the 1990s? And—with respect—what does it have to do with Lieutenant Dutt and her theories about extraterrestrial intervention?"

Eugene snapped, "Are you such a fool that you can't see it?"

Toby bit back, "Now look here—"

Siobhan grabbed his arm. "Just take us through it, Eugene. Step by step."

Eugene visibly fought for patience. "Have you really no *idea* how unlikely this scenario is? Yes, there are rogue planets, formed independently of stars, or flung out of stellar systems. Yes, it may happen that such a planet could cross from one system to another. But it's highly unlikely. The Galaxy is *empty*. To scale, the stars are like grains of sand, separated by *kilometers*. I estimate the chance of a planet like this coming anywhere near our solar system as being one in a hundred thousand.

"And this Jovian didn't just approach us—it didn't just fall near the sun—it fell *directly* into the sun, on a trajectory that would take it *directly* toward the sun's center of mass." He laughed, disbelieving at their incomprehension. "The odds against such a thing are absurd. No naturalistic explanation is plausible."

Mikhail nodded. "Circumstantial, perhaps, but still . . . I've always thought Sherlock Holmes put it well. 'When you have eliminated the impossible, whatever remains, however improbable, must be the truth.' "

"Somebody did this," Toby said slowly. "That's what you're saying. Somebody deliberately fired a planet, a big fat Jovian, straight at our sun. We've been hit by a bullet from God."

Bisesa said briskly, "Oh, I don't think it has anything to do with God." She stood up. "More coffee?"

"Nicolaus—your target is the Vatican?" But the destruction would be much more extensive than that. A spaceplane returning from orbit packed a *lot* of kinetic energy: the Eternal City would be hit by an explosion with the force of a small nuclear weapon. She had not felt like crying before, but now tears pricked her eyes: not for herself, but for the destruction that would come. "Oh, Nicolaus. What a waste. What a terrible—"

And then the bomb went off. It felt like a punch in the back.

She was still conscious, for a while. She could even breathe. The cabin had survived, and its systems were doing its best to protect her. But she could feel herself tumbling, and monstrous G-forces pushed her deep into her seat. She could hear nothing; the blast had left her deafened—not that it mattered anymore.

She was falling through the sky, she supposed, trapped in a piece of wreckage thrown out of a fireball high above Rome.

Still she felt no anger, no fear. Only sadness that she would not see the greatest job of her life through to the end. Sadness that she had had no chance to say goodbye to those she loved.

But she had been tired, she thought. So very tired. It was up to the others now.

In the last second she felt a hand creep into hers. Nicolaus's, a last, raw human contact. She gripped it hard. Then, as the spinning worsened, she blacked out, and knew no more.

PART 4
PERTURBATION

26: ALTAIR

The star called Altair is so far away that its light takes more than sixteen years to travel to Earth. And yet Altair is a neighbor, comparatively; only a few dozen stars lie closer to the sun.

Altair is a stable star, but more massive than the sun. Its surface, twice the temperature of Sol's, glows white with none of the sun's hint of yellowness, and it breathes out ten times as much energy into the faces of its scattered flock of planets.

Of those planets six are immense Jovians, all but one more massive than Jupiter. They all formed close to the parent star on looping orbits, wheeling like a flock of monstrous birds. But with time the Jovians, plucking at each other with their mighty gravitational fields, gradually migrated outward. Most of them settled into a neat clockwork array of circular orbits. Complex physical and chemical processes churned in the planets' hot, deep interiors—and, in the tranquillity of eons, on some of those worlds life was spawned.

One planet was different, though.

This swollen monster, fifteen times more massive than Jupiter, was peculiarly unlucky in its interactions with its brethren. It was flung far out of the parent system, on a looping elliptical orbit whose farthest reach took it into the chill realm of comets. This huge orbit took millions of years to complete—and so every few megayears Altair's huddled family of inner planets was disturbed by the rogue giant's plummeting visits from the depths of space. Worlds that might have been Earths rolled and quivered, plucked by the rogue's gravity. Not only that, but the rogue's passage through Altair's broad belts of comets and asteroids sent a heavy rain pouring into the inner system. On Altair's worlds, dinosaur-killer impacts were the norm, falling a hundred times more frequently than on Earth.

In time this process of destruction would have run its course. In the very long run the rogue Jovian would have destroyed the smaller worlds. Or it might have smashed into another Jovian: a catastrophe for both planets. Or, most likely, this moody wanderer would have become detached from the Altair system altogether, perhaps by the passage of another star, and it would have drifted away into sunless space alone.

But there was an intervention.

The most dramatic single event in the formation of the Earth was the mighty collision that shattered the proto-Earth into twin worlds, Earth and Moon. For a few days the glow of the wrecked world was bright enough to be seen over hundreds of light-years.

Those who watched had eyes sensitive to colors for which there are no words in human languages. But they watched nevertheless: they watched everything and everywhere, patiently, indefatigably. And they noticed Earth's violent birth.

They watched what followed too: the gathering of oceans from comet water, a brief age of chemical churning, the startlingly rapid rise of simple life-forms, the more sluggish progress toward complexity, and at last a glimmer of intelligence. It was a familiar story in its broad thrust, only the details differing from world to world.

But those who watched did not regard this as "progress."

In an ancient conclave, at levels of discourse no human mind could have comprehended—and despite some dissension—the gravest of decisions was made.

And a weapon was selected.

A sterilizing agent.

How do you move a planet? There are many ways, but the method used at Altair was well within humanity's understanding.

It was that rogue Jovian's very perturbability that made it so useful. Since the 1970s human engineers had been using gravitational "slingshots" to boost their spacecraft on their way. A spacecraft such as *Voyager,* say, could be "bounced" off Jupiter's gravity well—and, like a Ping-Pong ball rebounding off the windshield of an eighteen-wheeler truck, if you got the angles right the spacecraft would be hurled away with hugely increased momentum. The space engineers had become expert at this technique, finding ways to use ever more elaborate chains of slingshots to tap into the solar system's store of energy and momentum and so to reduce the amount of rocket fuel they needed to loft into space.

Because Jupiter was some ten trillion *trillion* times as massive as *Voyager,* such encounters had not disturbed the target planet significantly. But if a world comparable in mass to Jupiter had followed *Voyager*'s trajectory, both incoming and target worlds would have been flung away in new directions.

And here was the principle: to use gravitational slingshots to move worlds.

A single impulse would be difficult to arrange, and wasteful, for much energy would have been dissipated in tidal distortions. But you could use a stream of asteroids to shift the much mightier mass of a planet without such undesirable consequences.

And smaller rocks yet could be used to deflect the asteroids in the first place. A hierarchy of encounters could be arranged, with the tiniest of initial deflections—like a pebble thrown into a pond—causing a sequence of ever more immense disturbances. It helped that the mechanics of many-body gravitational systems were intrinsically chaotic and so sensitive to small disturbances.

It would take planning, of course, to make this multiple cannon shot pay off. But it was only a question of orbital mechanics. It was efficient too, with very little energy wasted. To those to whom economy was a guiding principle, it was a method whose elegance appealed.

The pebble was thrown.

———

It took a thousand years for the cascade of interactions to shift the Jovian from its elongated orbit: no more would it trouble the tormented inner worlds of Altair. It would take another thousand years for the Jovian to cross the gulf of space from one stellar sand grain to the next. But that was of no concern. This was a long game.

When it was done, attention was turned away. Those who had intervened would watch the dénouement; they believed that was their bleak duty. But there was time enough to be ready for that.

On Earth, humans built ziggurats in veneration of their sun, which they still imagined to be a god. And yet their fate was already sealed. Or so those who had intervened believed.

27: THE TIN LID

Siobhan arranged to meet Bisesa in the London Ark, the old zoo in Regent's Park.

She had to drive down from Liverpool to do it. She had been up there to visit the new Eurasian Prime Minister in his Bunker, as everybody called it, a huge new underground governmental center implanted, controversially, in the massive concrete crypt of the grand old city's Roman Catholic cathedral.

Traveling down the M1, Siobhan hit her first roadblock as she passed St. Albans, still thirty kilometers or more from central London. The journey back had already taken eight hours. A couple of years ago, in a fast smart car with no upper speed limit, it might have taken three. But since then London had become a fortress.

On this hot day in September 2041 a series of cordons had been put in place around the capital. The outermost fence was a barrier of roadblocks, wire fencing, and tank traps that ran from Portsmouth on the south coast, up through Reading and Watford, and past Chelmsford to the east coast. The Navy controlled access from the sea and the river just as tightly, and there were constant RAF patrols in the air overhead. Even at this first checkpoint it took Siobhan an hour to queue to have her ident chip, retinas, and vehicle chip scanned: she might still have the ear of a Prime Minister, but nobody got a free pass in these increasingly paranoid times.

It had to be so. With seven months left before the storm, the problem of refugees from the smaller towns and the countryside was already significant. London had been Britain's center of gravity since 1066, when the Norman Conqueror had exerted his brutal control over the old Saxon kingdom from his new Tower. Everybody knew that it would be to London, in the final days, that half the population of southern England would flee, as if drawn into a great drain. Hence the layers of barriers.

As she waited, Siobhan saw a plume of thick black smoke rising above the city of St. Albans. Aristotle told her that it was the mark of a vast bonfire, the centerpiece of a ferociously wild party on the site of the long-erased Roman city of Verulamium. As time went on, most people continued to behave reasonably well, to the authorities' general relief. But there were some who called themselves, gloomily, the Lords of the Last Days—and they sported and partied as if they believed it.

The St. Albans fire was being burned in defiance of all environmental protection laws, of course, but there were plenty who no longer cared about that, not if everything was going to be fried in seven months' time anyhow. The same thing was happening on a wider scale, as oil wells and gas fields were being pumped dry, and noxious substances pumped carelessly into the air and the seas.

Frozen sleepers were another symptom of the lunatic fringe.

Up in Liverpool she had delivered a report on the impact of the new craze in the United States for "hibernacula,"—huge underground vaults inside which the rich were having themselves cryogenically stored. These refugees from reality were seeking to skip over the sunstorm and escape into a better future. The hibernacula were becoming ever more popular despite medical advice that the freezing process probably wouldn't work successfully—and nobody could guarantee an uninterrupted power supply through the sunstorm anyhow, so that the big day might result in an unfortunate defrosting. Besides, even if the system worked technically, where was the morality in escaping the present and leaving others to clean up the mess, then "returning" when the worst was over to reap the rewards? The "cryonauts" would surely not be welcomed, even in the most optimistic scenarios. And Siobhan had projected gloomily that if things went pear-shaped—if civilization fell apart despite the shield's protection—the hibernacula would most likely serve the starving survivors as cellars of thawing meat . . .

Such craziness captured media attention, but was fortunately still rare. And while these last days saw much foolishness and venality, there was some dignity too. More people were trying to save what they cherished than to smash things up in a final frenzy; projects such as the London Dome were flooded with volunteer workers. Many people were turning, predictably, to religion for solace, but few became fanatics of the kind who had killed Miriam Grec. Most prayed to their gods with quiet gravity, in the austere beauty of cathedrals, mosques, and temples, or simply in the privacy of their own hearts.

Meanwhile the romantic poignancy of the end was evoking a flourishing of the arts, with literature, paintings, sculpture, and music of heartbreaking intensity being produced all over the world. It was a time for elegies.

But many people, it seemed, faced the grimness of the future with a more private sadness. Populations worldwide were actually declining. There was a spate of suicides, but rather sadder was the news that birthrates were plummeting. This was not the time to bring a child into the world: indeed some religious leaders were arguing it might actually be sinful to procreate now, for a child who did not exist could not suffer.

But those falling population numbers would make barely a dent before sunstorm day. Everything depended on the shield, as it always had.

In September 2041, with only seven months left, the shield was as hair-raisingly behind schedule as ever, and yet it still progressed. Siobhan's political masters in the Eurasian administration wanted endless facts, figures, Gantt charts to show progress achieved, critical-path diagrams to show bottlenecks and obstacles up ahead—and a few sexy photos of the staggering, Earth-sized structure growing in orbit.

But nothing she said made any real difference, for there was nothing the pols could do differently, not now. Miriam Grec had got it right from the beginning. Her early intervention had given the project the worldwide political momentum it needed to begin. After Miriam herself had reaped the whirlwind, her successor, her deputy hastily installed into the top job, had been soundly beaten in the October 2040 poll by opponents who had run on a vaguely anti-shield ticket. But, just as Miriam had foreseen, once in office it was politically impossible for any Prime Minister to be the one who *scrapped* the shield. The logic had worked out just the same in the United States as in Eurasia.

The new Prime Minister had not taken a shine to Siobhan, though. Siobhan was clearly still a key link in the communications and decision-making chain that led from the ground to orbit. But she was no longer among the favored inner few. That suited Siobhan fine. This was a time for getting on with the job, not for political arse kissing. And besides, the less she saw of the pols, the less chance there was of putting her foot in it.

Beyond St. Albans, she worked her way through more roadblocks. At last, after some tricky inner-city driving, Siobhan reached the final barrier. This was the Camden Gate, one of ten great entrances set around the circumference of the Dome itself.

As she queued she peered ahead curiously; she hadn't come into the Dome from this direction before. The Gate, bright orange and peppered with searchlights and armed observation posts, rose like a Roman ruin above the mundanity of houses and shopping parades. And the smooth skin of the London Dome itself arced away into the washed-out blue of the sky beyond.

The Dome was still incomplete, of course; the final enclosing panels would not be installed until the very last hours, so that the city would not have to survive without light for too long. But still, even now, its immense skeletal form was startling. Siobhan couldn't actually make out much of it, for she was too close to the horizon of this huge spherical cap. It was an odd shame that this greatest of all of Britain's architectural achievements should be all but invisible from the ground: as the *Aurora 1* crew had remarked ruefully of many Martian features, from close up it was simply too big to take in.

But if you viewed it from the air, you could see what a magnificent structure the Dome was. Based on a near-perfect circle about nine kilometers in diameter, the Dome was centered on Trafalgar Square, but it covered the Tower of London at the eastern end of the old Roman city wall, and in the west it enveloped the West End, slicing through Hyde Park and just extending to include the Albert Memorial and the great South Kensington museums. In the north the Dome would shelter King's Cross and Regent's Park, where Siobhan was headed now, and to the south it reached across the river to the Elephant and Castle and beyond. Siobhan thought it was rather appropriate that the Dome would protect a stretch of the Thames itself, the river that had always been the city's lifeblood.

Every Londoner, with characteristically cheerful disrespect, called this great architectural triumph "the Tin Lid."

At last Siobhan was allowed to pass through the Gate. Signs admonished her to turn on her headlights.

The view in the sudden twilight beneath the Dome's roof was astounding. Supporting pillars rose up from the ground, like slim rainforest-canopy trees incongruously rising out of London's mulch of town houses and flats, offices and cathedrals, ministries and palaces. Above, the sky was darkened by scaffolding and struts, made misty by distance. Helicopters and blimps flew just beneath the roof's low curve. All this was lit by shafts of watery sunlight that passed through the breaks in the roof. The prospect had something of the feel of an immense antique ruin, perhaps, a place of pillars and graceful curves, the remnant of a vanished empire. But everywhere cranes rose up like skeletal dinosaurs, building, building. This was a glimpse, not of the past, but of the future.

The projections of how well the shield would work, even in the most optimistic scenarios, were still uncertain, and it wasn't at all clear how much good even such mighty defenses as this Dome would do. But projects like this were as much an expression of popular will as of serious civic defense. Siobhan rather hoped that if the world survived the sunstorm the Tin Lid, or at least its skeleton, would be left intact, as a memorial to what people could do when they worked together.

She drove on into the artificial twilight, ignoring the built-over sky and concentrating on the traffic.

28: THE ARK

The London Ark was all but empty today. Goats climbed their concrete mountains, penguins flapped in blue-painted shallows, and multicolored birds sang for no audience but their keepers, and Siobhan. It wasn't a time for zoos.

But Bisesa was here. Siobhan found her at the Ark's primate house, alone, cradling a coffee. In a broad, covered pit, a handful of chimpanzees were going about their rather languid business. The old-fashioned scene contrasted sharply with the new animated information plate that proudly pronounced these creatures as *Homo troglodytes troglodytes,* humankind's nearest cousins.

"Thanks for coming," Bisesa said. "And I'm sorry for dragging you here." She looked tired, pale.

"Not at all. I haven't been to this zoo—umm, the *Ark*—since I was a kid."

"It's just I wanted to come here, one last time. It's the last day these guys will be on show."

"I didn't realize their move was so soon."

Bisesa said, "Now that they are recognized as Legal Persons, the chimps have full human rights—in particular the right to privacy when they pick their noses and scratch their backsides. So they're to be moved to their own little refugee center, fully equipped with tire swings and bananas."

Bisesa's voice was weary, rather flat, and Siobhan couldn't decode her mood. "You don't approve?"

"Oh, of course I do. Though there are plenty who don't." Bisesa nodded at a soldier, heavily armed and very young looking, who patrolled on the other side of the pit.

The debate about sheltering nonhuman life-forms from the sunstorm extended beyond the chimps, where the law was reasonably clear. As the sunstorm neared, a vast worldwide effort had been initiated to save at least a sample of the world's major kingdoms of life. Much of it was necessarily crude: beneath the London Ark huge hibernacula had been installed to preserve the zygotes of animals, insects, birds, and fish, and the seeds of plants from grasses to pine trees. As for the animals, the Arks had been doing this sort of thing for decades already; since the turn of the century the western zoos had hosted reserve populations of animals that had long died out in the wild—all the elephants, the tigers, even one species of chimp.

Of course it was essentially futile, said some ecologists. Though the diversity of life in cool, cloudy Britain, say, was nothing like as rich as in an equatorial rain forest, there were probably more species to be found in a single handful of soil from a London garden, most of them unidentified, than had been known to all the naturalists in the world a century ago. You couldn't save it all—but the alternative was to do nothing, and most people seemed to agree you had to try.

But some resented as much as a finger being lifted to save anything other than a human being.

"It's a time of hard choices." Siobhan sighed. "You know, the other day I spoke to an ecologist who said we should just accept what's going on. This is just another extinction event, in a long string of such disasters. It's like a forest fire, she said, a necessary cleansing. And each time the biosphere bounces back, eventually becoming richer than before."

"But this isn't natural," Bisesa said grimly. "Not even the way an asteroid impact is. Somebody *did* this, intentionally. Maybe this is why intelligence evolved in the first place. Because there are times—when the sun goes off, when the dinosaur killer strikes—when the mechanisms of natural selection aren't enough. Times when you need consciousness to save the world."

"A biologist would say there is no intention behind natural selection, Bisesa. And evolution can't prepare you for the future."

"Yes," she smiled. "But I'm no biologist, so I can say it . . ."

Such conversations were why Siobhan valued Bisesa's company so much.

Seven months before sunstorm day, the world worked frantically to prepare itself. But much of what was being done, however vital, was mundane. For instance, London's latest Mayor had got herself elected on the basic but undeniably effective pledge that come what may she would ensure the city's water supply, and since coming to office she had made good on that promise. A vast new pipeline laid the length of the country from the great Kielder reservoir in the north to the capital—though many in the northeast had grumbled loudly about the "southern softies" who were stealing "their" water. Such work was obviously essential—Siobhan herself was involved in many such projects—but it was banal.

Sometimes the volume of chatter overwhelmed her ability to see things clearly. It was Bisesa, sitting alone in her flat and just thinking, who was one of her touchstones, her viewpoints of the bigger picture. It was Bisesa, thinking out of the box, who had come up with the essential notion of community support for smartskin manufacture. And, after all, it was Bisesa who had given Siobhan an insight into the deepest mystery of all.

Ever since that crucial videoconference, and Eugene Mangles's proof that there was indeed an element of intention about the disturbance of the sun, Bisesa's claims about the Firstborn and Mir had been taken seriously, and were being investigated in a slow-burning kind of way. Nobody believed the full story—not even Siobhan, she admitted to herself. But most of her ad hoc brains trust accepted that, yes, the disturbance of the sun so clearly reconstructed by Eugene could have been caused only by the intervention of some intelligent agency. That alone, even if you didn't speculate about the intent of that intelligence, was a staggering conclusion to draw.

Bisesa's insights had helped guide Eugene and others to a fuller understanding of the physical mechanism behind the sunstorm, and had, conceivably, helped humankind to survive it. But the trouble was, as Siobhan had immediately understood, the meddling of the Firstborn just didn't matter for now. Whatever the cause, it was the sunstorm itself that had to be dealt with. The news couldn't even be made public: releasing rumors about alien intention would surely only cause panic, and to no effect. So the whole thing remained a secret, known only at the highest levels of government, and to a select few others. The Firstborn, Siobhan promised herself, if they existed, could be dealt with later.

But that meant there was nothing Bisesa could do about the greatest issue in her life. She couldn't even talk about it. She was still on "compassionate leave" from the Army, and would have been discharged altogether if not for some string pulling by Siobhan. But she had no meaningful work to do. In a fragile state, she was thrown back on her own resources. She had become reclusive, Siobhan thought, spending too much time alone in her flat, or wandering around London, coming to places like the Ark; she seemed to want no company save Myra.

"Come on," Siobhan said, and they linked arms. "Let's go see the elephants. Then I'll give you a lift home. I'd like to see Myra again . . ."

Bisesa's flat, just off the King's Road in Chelsea, was actually lucky to find itself under the Tin Lid. Half a kilometer farther west and it would have been outside the Dome altogether. As it was it nestled under the looming shadow of the wall, and when you drove along you could look up between the rooftops and see the Dome soar into the air, like the hull of some vast spaceship.

It was a while since Siobhan had visited, and things had changed. There were heavy new security locks on the doors to the apartment building. And when she opened the door a rust-red blur ran out of the building, shooting between Bisesa's legs, to vanish around the corner. Bisesa flinched, but laughed.

Siobhan's heart was hammering. "What was *that*? A dog?"

"No, just a fox. Not really a pest if you take care of your garbage—although I'd like to know who let that one in the building. People haven't the heart to get rid of them, not at a time like this. There are more of them around, I'm sure. Maybe they're coming into the Dome."

"Perhaps they sense something is coming."

Bisesa led her upstairs to the flat itself. In the corridors and the stairwell Siobhan saw many strange faces. "Lodgers," Bisesa said, pulling a face. "Government regulations. Every domicile within the Dome has to shelter at least so many adults per such-and-such square meters of floor space. They're packing us in." She opened her door to reveal a hallway piled high with bottled water and canned food, a typical family emergency store. "One reason why I keep Linda here. Better a cousin than a stranger . . ."

In the flat Siobhan made for the window. South facing, it caught a lot of light. The great shadows of the Dome's skeleton striped across the sky, but there was still a good view of the city to the east. And Siobhan could see that from every south-facing window and balcony, and on every rooftop, silvery blankets were draped. The blankets were smartskin, bits of the space shield being grown all across the city by ordinary Londoners.

Bisesa joined her with a glass of fruit juice, and smiled. "Quite a sight, isn't it?"

"It's magnificent," Siobhan said sincerely.

Bisesa's inspiration had worked out remarkably well. To grow a bit of the shield that would save the world, all you needed was patience, sunlight, a kit no more complicated than a home darkroom, and basic nutrients: household waste would do nicely, appropriately pulped up. Raw material for the smart components had been a problem for a while, before turn-of-the-century landfill sites packed high with obsolete mobile phones, computers, games, and other wasteful toys had been turned into mines of silicon, germanium, silver, copper, and even gold. In London there had been only one possible slogan for the program, even if it was terminologically inexact: *Dig for Victory.*

Siobhan said, "It's so damn inspirational: people all over the world, working to save themselves and each other."

"Yeah. But try telling that to Myra."

"How is she?"

"Scared," Bisesa said. "No, deeper than that. Traumatized, maybe." Her face was composed, but she looked tired again, laden with guilt. "I try to see things from her point of view. She's only twelve. When she was little her mother disappeared for months on end—and then turned up from nowhere, swivel-eyed. And now you have the threat of the sunstorm. She's a bright kid, Siobhan. She understands the news. She knows that on April 20 all of this, the whole fabric of her life, all her stuff, the softwall, the synth-stars, her screens and books and toys, is just going to dissolve. It was bad enough I kept going away. I don't think she'll ever forgive me for letting the world end."

Siobhan thought of Perdita, who seemed not to grasp what was to come at all—or anyhow chose not to. "It's better than denying it, maybe. But there is no source of comfort."

"No. Not even religion, for me. I never was much of a God botherer. Though I did catch Myra watching the election of the new Pope." After the destruction of Rome, the latest pontiff had taken up residence in Boston; the big American dioceses had long been far richer than the Vatican anyhow. "All the religiosity around worries me—doesn't it you? These sun-cultists coming out of the closet."

Siobhan shrugged. "I accept it. You know, even up on the shield itself, a lot of praying goes on. Religions can serve a social purpose, in uniting us around a common goal. Maybe that's why they evolved in the first place. I don't think there's any harm in people thinking of the shield as, umm, like building a cathedral in the sky, if it helps them get through the day." She smiled. "Whether God is watching or not."

But Bisesa's face was dark. "I don't know about God. But others are watching us, I'm sure of that."

Siobhan said carefully, "You're still thinking about the First-born."

"How can I not?" Bisesa said, drawn.

With fresh coffee, they huddled together on Bisesa's over-stuffed furniture. It was an incongruously domestic setting, Siobhan thought, to be discussing one of the most philosophically profound discoveries ever made. "I suppose it is the dream of ages," she said.

"We've been speculating on intelligence beyond the Earth since the Greeks."

Bisesa looked distant. "Even now I can't get used to the idea."

"It's tough for any scientist," Siobhan said. " 'Arguments by design'—that is, to build your theories about the universe on the assumption that it was designed for some conscious purpose—went out of fashion three hundred years ago. Darwin hammered the last nail in that particular coffin. Of course it was God who was the fashionable designer back then, not ET. For a scientist it goes against all training to think in such terms. Which is why it was my instinct to put you in touch with Eugene, Bisesa. I wondered what would happen if you jolted him into thinking differently. I guess that instinct was right. But it still feels unnatural." She sighed. "A guilty pleasure."

Bisesa said, "How do you think people are going to take this, when they are finally told?"

Siobhan explored her own feelings. "The implications are immense—political, social, philosophical. Everything changes. Even if we discover nothing else about these creatures you call the Firstborn, Bisesa, and no matter how the sunstorm turns out, just the fact that we know they exist proves that we are not unique in the universe. Any future we care to imagine now contains the possibility of others."

"I think people have a right to know," Bisesa said.

Siobhan nodded; it was an old point of disagreement between them.

Bisesa said, "We reached the Moon, and Mars. Here we are building a structure as big as a planet. And yet all our achievements count for nothing—not against a power that can do *this*. But I don't believe people will be overawed. I think people will feel angry."

"I still don't understand," Siobhan said. "*Why* would these Firstborn of yours want to put us under threat of extinction?"

Bisesa shook her head. "I know the Firstborn better than anybody else, I guess. But I can't answer that. One thing I'm sure about, though. They *watch*."

"Watch?"

"I think that's what Mir was all about. Mir was a montage of all our history, right up to the moment of this—our possible destruction. Mir wasn't about us but about the Firstborn. They forced themselves to look at what they were destroying, to face what they had done."

She spoke hesitantly, obviously unsure of her thinking. Siobhan imagined her sitting alone for long hours, obsessively exploring her memories and her own uncertain feelings.

Bisesa went on, "They don't want anything we know, or can make. They aren't interested in our science or our art—otherwise they would be saving our books, our paintings, even some of us. Our *stuff* is far beneath them. What they do want—I think—is to know how it feels to be *us*, to be human. And how it feels even as we're put to the fire."

"So they value consciousness," Siobhan mused. "I can see why an advanced civilization would prize mind above all other things. Perhaps it is rare in this universe of ours. They prize it, even as they destroy it. So they have ethics. Maybe they are guilty about what they're doing."

Bisesa laughed bitterly. "But they're doing it even so. Which doesn't make sense, does it? Can gods be insane?"

Siobhan glanced out at the gaunt shadows of the Dome. "Perhaps there's a logic, even in all this destruction."

"Do you believe that?"

Siobhan grinned. "Even if I did, I'd reject it. The hell with them."

Bisesa answered with a fierce grin of her own. "Yes," she said. "The hell with them."

29: IMPACT

The rogue planet flew out of the sky's equator.

While light flashed from Altair to Sol in sixteen years, the wandering planet had taken a millennium to complete its interstellar journey. Even so it approached the sun at some five *thousand* kilometers per second, many times the sun's own escape velocity: it was the fastest major object ever to have crossed the solar system. As it fell toward the sun's warmth, the Jovian's atmosphere was battered by immense storms, and trillions of tonnes of air were stripped away, to trail behind the falling world like the tail of an immense comet.

On Earth, it was the year 4 b.c.

If the rogue had come in the twenty-first century, humanity's Spaceguard program would have spotted it. Spaceguard had its origins in a twentieth-century NASA program designed to survey all the major comets and asteroids following orbits that might bring them into a collision with the Earth. The organization's scientists had debated many ways to deflect an incoming threat, including solar sails or nuclear weapons. But while such methods might have worked on a flying-mountain asteroid, there would have been nothing to be done about a mass *this* size.

In 4 b.c., of course, there was no Spaceguard. The ancient world had known lenses since the great days of the Greeks, but it had not yet occurred to anybody to put two of them together into a telescope. But there were those who watched the sky, for in its intricate weavings of light they thought they glimpsed the thoughts of God.

In April of that year, across Europe, North Africa, and the Middle East, a great new light approached the sun. To the astrologers and astronomers, who knew every naked-eye object in the sky far better than most of their descendants of the twenty-first century, the Jovian was a glaring anomaly, and a source of fascination and fear.

Three scholars in particular watched it in awe. They called themselves *magi,* or *magoi,* which means "astrologers"—stargazers. And in the Jovian's final days, as it neared the sun and became a morning star of ever more brilliant beauty, they followed it.

The planet battered its way through the sun's wispy outer atmosphere, the corona. Now the star itself lay before it, unprotected.

The Jovian was a planet a fifth the diameter of the sun itself. Even at such speeds, a collision between two such immense bodies was stately. It took a full minute for the whole planet to sink into the body of the star.

In normal times the sun's surface is a delicate tapestry of granules, the upper surfaces of huge convection cells with roots in the sun's deep interior. When the Jovian hit, that complex hierarchical structure was disturbed, as if a baseball had been thrown into a pan of boiling water. Immense waves washed away from the point of impact and rolled around the curvature of the star.

Meanwhile the planet itself was immersed in a bath of intense heat. Through direct collisions between the sun's plasma and the planet's atmosphere, the sun's energy poured into this outrageous invader. In response, the planet desperately tried to shed heat by losing its own substance. The upper layers of its air, mostly hydrogen and helium, were soon stripped off, exposing the inner layers, exotic high-pressure liquid and solid forms of hydrogen, which in turn boiled away. It was exactly as *Apollo* capsules had once entered Earth's atmosphere behind ablative shields, allowing bits of the disintegrating spacecraft to carry away the heat of friction. For the

Jovian the strategy worked for a while. The planet had entered the sun with the mass of fifteen Jupiters, and had the capacity to soak up a *lot* of heat before it was done.

Deeper and deeper the Jovian sank, through the sun's roiling convective layer, and then into the denser, static radiative layer beneath. It was like a driving fist, and it left behind a tunnel drilled brutally through the sun's strata, a flaw that would take millennia to heal.

By the time the Jovian reached the edge of the sun's fusing core, it was reduced to a knot of its densest, hardest stuff—and yet it still retained a mass many times that of Jupiter. Here the last of the Jovian's mass was broken up and dispersed—but not before it struck the core of the sun a mighty blow. There was a vast fusion surge, like an immense bomb going off at the edge of this natural reactor. That great impulse sent shock fronts pushing deep into the fusing core.

As Eugene Mangles would understand, the core was temperamental, its rate of fusion highly sensitive to changes in temperature. The Jovian was gone, but its impact had created a pattern of energetic oscillations in the core that would persist for millennia.

Meanwhile on the surface, though the planet had disappeared into the sun's maw, the point of impact was a place of roiling turmoil.

On its way into the heart of the star, the Jovian had torn through a sensitive boundary called the tacholine: the boundary between convective and radiative zones. The dull sea of the radiative zone rotates with the sun's core, almost as a rigid body. But the convective zone's motion is much more complex; different parts of the sun's surface can actually be seen to rotate at different speeds. So, at the tacholine, there is friction: the convective material moves over the radiative like a tremendous wind.

The sun is laced by a powerful magnetic field. Its interior is full of "flux tubes," currents of magnetic energy that flow through the plasma sea. At the tacholine the differing rotations of the sun's layers stretch the flux tubes around the sun's equator. Mostly the churning convection above keeps them in their place. But sometimes a kink will develop in a sun-girdling rope, and it will force its way up toward the surface of the sun, dragging plasma flows with it. This is the sequence of events that leads to the "active regions" that give rise to flares and mass ejections.

So it was now. The Jovian's crashing through the tacholine caused the stretched and tangled field lines to writhe like snakes. Flux tubes surged up through the body of the sun, broke the surface, and thrashed above the enormous scar left by the Jovian. Energy was dumped into space in a great flare of light, as high-frequency radiation, and in a fountain of charged particles that gushed out across the solar system.

A huge solar storm battered at the Earth. With the planet's own magnetic field flapping like a loose sail, immense auroras were visible all across the world. The Jovian's most severe effects lay far in the future. But right here, right now, it announced its arrival in uncompromising fashion.

On Earth in 4 B.C. there was no high technology to be harmed— but millions of natural computers, running on biomolecules and electricity, were subtly affected by the magnetic turbulence. People suffered blackouts, fits, seizures; some unlucky souls died of no cause anybody could detect. As Miriam Grec would learn to her supreme cost, magnetic disturbances can stimulate religious impulses in human brains: there was a plague of prophets and doomsayers, miracles and visions.

And in a shabby room in Bethlehem, a newborn child, lying on dirty hay, stirred and gasped, tormented by images He could not comprehend.

30: TELESCOPE

Ever since President Alvarez's devastating announcement in December 2037, the sunstorm crisis had been oddly bound up with Christmas. The last Christmas before the sunstorm, in 2041, with only four months left before the storm was due to break, was a frenzy of forced gaiety. Bisesa suspected that everybody was secretly glad when it was over.

As for herself, she bought a telescope. And one bright morning in January 2042, with the help of Myra and Linda, she hauled it up to the roof of her apartment block. On this January day, bright and clear, the sun was low in the eastern sky, and the view from this Chelsea rooftop was spectacular. The Dome's buttresses gleamed like sunbeams, and the smartskin blankets draped over every exposed surface shone like so many huge flowers.

The telescope was a ten-centimeter refractor, secondhand, a big clunky thing more than twenty years old, and it was cheap. But it was smart enough that it could determine its own position and attitude by consulting the Global Positioning System. And then, if you told it what you wanted to look at, with a hum and a whir it would point itself that way and immediately begin tracking, compensating for the Earth's rotation. Linda had laughed at the gadget's antiquated user interface—it actually featured that comical horror, a menu system—but it worked well enough.

In central London, with an increasing fraction of the sky

blocked out by the Dome, telescopes were of little use, unless you wanted to spy on the gangs of workers who crawled over the inside of the Dome's roof day and night. But what Bisesa wanted to look at was the sun.

When Bisesa told it what she wanted to see, the telescope's nanny software immediately started bleating warnings about safe usage. Bisesa already knew all about the dangers. You couldn't look directly at the sun through a telescope, unless you wanted your eye burned out, but you could project an image. So Bisesa brought up a folding chair and set up a broad sheet of white cartridge paper behind the telescope's eyepiece. The final positioning of the paper in the telescope's shadow, and the focusing of the instrument, was a little tricky. But at last, in the middle of the telescope's complicated shadow, a disk of milky white appeared.

Bisesa was surprised by the clarity of the image, and its size, maybe a third of a meter across. Toward the rim of the disk the brightness faded a little, so she had a clear sense that she was looking at a sphere, a three-dimensional object. Sunspot groups were speckled around the sun's midlatitudes, easily visible, looking like motes of dust in a shining bowl. It was galling to think that each of those dwarfed dust-speck anomalies was larger than the whole Earth, and, glowing at temperatures of thousands of degrees, they showed as shadows only because they were cooler than the rest of the sun's surface.

But it was not sunspots that Bisesa had bought her telescope to see.

A line crossed the face of the sun, a stripe of watery gray that traversed from northeast to southwest. It was, of course, the shield. Hanging up there at its station at L1, it was still turned almost edge-on to the sun. But already it cast a shadow on the Earth.

Bisesa hugged Myra. "You see? There it is. It's *real*. Now do you believe?"

Myra stared at the shadow. Now thirteen years old, she was a bit too quiet for her age. Bisesa had meant this display to comfort Myra, who was not alone in having trouble believing in the reality of the great project in space.

But her reaction wasn't what Bisesa had anticipated. She seemed afraid. This was a human-made object, four times as remote as the Moon, and yet visible from Earth. Standing here in the watery sunlight of a London morning, the cosmic vision was astonishing, awe inspiring—crushing.

This is why the Greeks coined the word *hubris,* Bisesa thought.

31: PERSPECTIVES

For lovers, zero G was a lot trickier than the low gravity of the Moon.

That was despite decades of experience, Siobhan had learned. In the days of low Earth orbit flights there had been something called the "Dolphin Club," so named because in the analogous conditions of floating in the ocean, a dolphin couple would sometimes be helped in their intimacy by the bracing support of a third . . . Siobhan was the Astronomer Royal; she wasn't about to put up with any of *that*.

So Bud had improvised equipment to enable her to retain her privacy. With its cuffs, ropes, and restraints his cabin now looked like a bondage parlor, but in giving you something to grip and push against, this stuff supported the ancient arts surprisingly well. But in the isolated little zero-G township of the shield Bud had clearly had help figuring all this out. She made him take down the little plaque above his bed:

COURTESY OF
U.S. ASTRONAUTICAL ENGINEERING CORPS
ENJOY!

Still, the sex was as deep and rich and satisfying and, damn it, *comforting* as ever; she was old enough to admit she needed consolation as much as passion.

Afterward, though, as they lay under a thick blanket, with Bud a silent warm mass beside her, her thoughts turned to the reasons she had come here.

This cabin had once been a storeroom; you could still see the marks where shelving and cupboards had been ripped off the walls. Over the years *Aurora* had been cannibalized, and now it was a husk containing nothing but life support systems, comms centers, and hastily improvised living quarters. But to Bud, she knew, this battered old ship was home. Even when the project was over, no doubt he would always miss it.

It was going to break his heart if she had to bring him home before the job was done. But that was one possible outcome of her visit, and they both knew it.

Bud said at last, "You know, at times like this I still miss a cigarette."

"At heart you're just an unreconstructed high school jock, aren't you?"

"Salt of the earth." He stared at the ceiling. "But this trip is business, not pleasure, isn't it?"

"I'm sorry."

He shrugged. "Don't be. But look—as far as everybody else is concerned, you're here for the AI switch-on. Nobody but my PA knows about the other stuff."

Faintly irritated she said, "I'm not here to hurt morale, Bud. I'm supposed to be strengthening the project, not weakening it. That's the whole point. But—"

"But this business of the audit has to be cleared up." He held her hand. "I know. And I trust you to handle it well."

She churned with guilt. "Bud, we both have our duty. And we can't let anything get in the way of that."

"I understand. But a bit more pleasure before business." He sat up. "We've got twelve hours before we boot up the AI. Let's go do some sightseeing."

They washed, dressed, and drank a coffee. Then Bud escorted her to the little ship he called the *V-Eye-P.*

The project's one and only one pressurized inspection module was just a platform laden with spherical fuel and oxidizer tanks and a small set of hydrazine rocket motors—actually attitude thrusters cannibalized from a retired spaceplane. On top was a pressurized tent of Kevlar and aluminum, within which two people could stand side by side. That was it, save for a simple set of controls based on a joystick that sprouted from the floor, and a life support system that would keep you alive for six hours at a pinch.

The shield engineers used variants on this design, but just the platform and the engines, without the tent: why bother with a pressure cabin when you had a perfectly good spacesuit? So you would see engineers skimming over the surface of the shield riding their rocket-propelled boxes like scooters. Only this one special little craft was kept aside for VIPs, visitors like Siobhan who didn't have the time or inclination to get trained up on how to use a pressure suit.

"Not," Bud said with a faintly malicious grin, "that this Kevlar tent would be much protection if anything went wrong . . ."

The *V-Eye-P* was launched from *Aurora* by an electromagnetic induction rail, like a miniature version of the Sling, the giant mass driver on the Moon. The acceleration was smooth, like a rapid elevator; Siobhan quite enjoyed the feeling of her feet being pressed to the floor.

When they had climbed sufficiently far, Bud tested the little ship's rockets, "burping" them as he called it. It sounded as if small explosions were going off all around the Kevlar hull. Bud explained that there was no exhaust from the induction rail, and rockets, however small, were never used close to the shield. "We're building a mirror made of frost laced on spiderweb," he said. "We try not even to breathe on it."

The craft swiveled and pitched to and fro. It was like being aboard a rather odd fairground ride.

When he was satisfied, Bud brought the craft to a halt and tipped it forward so Siobhan could see down. "Behold the mother ship," he said.

The venerable old *Aurora 2* was still the centerpiece of the shield, still the spider at the center of the web. Despite extensive cannibalization, Siobhan could make out the main features she remembered: the long, elegant spine with the fat habitation module at one end, and the complex clusters of power plants, fuel tanks, and rocket engines at the other. "She's a game old bird," Bud said fondly. "I hope she forgives us. She still has a role to play, keeping the shield spun up and oriented correctly. Of course all that will change when the AI comes online and the shield starts to control itself."

He pulled back on his control stick, and the platform's thrusters banged. The little ship rose up smoothly, rising away from the shield along an axial line that led straight up from the embedded *Aurora*.

Siobhan stared out, fascinated, as the shield opened up beneath her. Away from the old Mars ship the shield was a floor so flat and smooth it was like a mathematical abstraction, a semi-infinite plane that cut the universe in half. The surface shimmered, as delicate as a soap bubble, and as she rose higher prismatic rainbows fled across the surface. But the shield was still edge-on to the sun, and the low light streamed through that delicate membrane, so that she could make out the spindly skeleton beneath, struts, spars, and ribs of delicate lunar glass, a fairyland scaffolding that cast long, slim shadows.

"It's wonderful," she said. "The most massive engineering project anybody ever undertook, and yet it is nothing but glass and light. Like something from a dream."

"Which is why," Bud said a bit mysteriously, "I've chosen the name I have for her—the shield's AI, I mean."

Her? But he would say no more.

He pulsed the attitude control thrusters again and tipped the platform backward, so its windows swiveled to face the Earth. The home planet was a perfect blue marble hanging in space. The Moon, white-brown, sailed beside its parent, some thirty Earth diameters away. L1 was far beyond the orbit of the Moon; from here, there was no doubt this was a twin world.

"Home," Bud said simply. "Stuck out here it's good to be reminded of what we're working our butts off for." He leaned close to her, and pointed so she could sight along his arm. "See there? And there? ..."

Against the velvety darkness of space she saw sparks drifting, two, three, four of them in a rough line, like fireflies in the night, passing from Earth to shield.

Bud tapped the window. "Magnification please."

The image in the window before Siobhan exploded in rapid jumps. Now she could see perhaps a dozen ships. Some were just large enough to show detail, hull markings, solar-cell arrays, antenna booms. The convoy looked like toys, models suspended against velvet.

"A caravan from Earth, bringing up the smartskin." Bud was grinning. "Crawling its way up the gravity hill to L1. Isn't that a fantastic sight? And it's been going on, day and night, for years. If you turn a scope on the dark side of Earth, you can see the sparks of all those launches, over and over."

On the ground, Siobhan had inspected the collection processes. Smartskin blankets, grown out of household windows like Bisesa Dutt's in London, were gathered at neighborhood collation points, and then shipped to big storage centers at the airports and spaceports, and finally bundled up and sent to one of the great launch centers at Cape Canaveral, Baikonur, Kourou, or Woomera. Just the ground operation was a stupendous enterprise, a mighty international flow across the face of the Earth. And it culminated in these sparks bravely crossing the night.

Bud said, "You know the picture. We're throwing everything we've got into the launches, just like every other aspect of the project. They even dug the space shuttles out of their museums at the Smithsonian and Huntsville, and got those beautiful birds flying again. Worn-out shuttle main engines, too beat-up to be human-rated anymore, are being recycled: you can make a pretty useful throwaway booster out of a shuttle tailplane and a cargo pallet. The Russians have brushed off their old plans for Energia and have got those big old rockets flying again too.

"But even that isn't enough. So Boeing and McDonnell and the other big contractors are churning out boosters like sausages. Why, some of those new birds aren't much more sophisticated than a Fourth of July firecracker, and all you can do is point and shoot. But they work, with nearly a hundred percent reliability. And we're getting the job done . . ."

To Bud, Siobhan supposed, this mighty space project was a boyhood dream come true—space engineering fast and brutal and efficient and on a massive scale, the way it used to be, before cost and politics and risk aversion got in the way.

"You know," he said, "I think this will change everything." He waved a hand at the shield. "Surely there will be no going back to the old timid ways after *this;* surely we've broken the bonds. This has set our new direction. And it's outward."

"If we all live through the sunstorm."

He looked faintly resentful. "If that, yes." There was a subtext: *I might be a space buff but I know my duty.*

She felt a pang of regret, and wished she could take the words back. Was a barrier forming between them, even before she got to the meat of her mission here?

Bud pushed at the control stick, and the platform swiveled and scooted forward.

Now Siobhan was looking across the shield, as if she were flying over a shining ground. Her eye was drawn out to the shield's "horizon"—but unlike the Earth's surface the shield was utterly flat, right to its limits, and the straight-line horizon was sharp as a razor in the vacuum. It was oddly bewildering, the perspective all wrong, as if she were flying over the surface of some monstrous planet a thousand times bigger than the Earth.

Bud said, "Sometimes it fools you. You'll think you see the horizon curve, like from a low-flying plane. Or you'll make out a group working and imagine they're a few hundred meters away—but they're kilometers off." He shook his head. "Even now I have trouble grasping the scale of what we've done, that two of my guys, working on opposite edges of the shield, can be separated by the whole width of the Earth. And we built it all."

The platform dipped, and Siobhan flew low over shimmering prisms and glass struts, littered by small structures like shacks, and vehicles like tractors that toiled patiently. One astronaut made her cautious way across the surface bearing a huge strut of gossamer-light lunar glass; she looked like an ant bearing a leaf many times its own size.

And Siobhan made out what looked like flags, held out stiffly by wire in the absence of any breeze. "What are those?"

Bud said bluntly, "We don't have graves up here. We just push you away, off into interplanetary space. But we give you a marker: a flag of your country or your creed, or whatever you want. As we build the shield we're working in a spiral, around and around the center, moving farther out all the time. We just plant your flag at the position of the leading edge, wherever it happens to be when you die."

Now that she looked for them, she could see flags, dozens of them within a single glance. "Hundreds have died up here." She hadn't known the numbers.

"These are good people, Siobhan. Even without the direct risks of the construction work, some of them have worked in zero G without a break for two years or more. The medics say we are all storing up problems with our bone structure and cardiovascular systems and lymph systems and the rest. You know what the most common surgery procedure is up here? For kidney stones, nodules of calcium leached from your bones. And not to mention radiation exposure. Everyone knows about the damage to DNA, the cancer risks. But how about the brain? Your noggin is particularly vulnerable to cosmic radiation, and has a limited ability to repair itself. Space makes you dumb, Siobhan."

"I didn't know that—"

"I bet you didn't," he said, a hardness under his even tone. "Medical studies on shield workers themselves have proved this. Every year up here you shave ten years off your life. And yet these people stay, and work themselves to death."

"Oh, Bud—" Impulsively she grabbed his hands. "I'm not here to attack your people; you know that. And I don't want us to fall out."

He said heavily, *"But—"*

"But you know why I'm here."

It was a question of corruption.

Earthbound accountants, poring over their voluminous electronic books, had found that a fraction of the funds and materials flowing up into space had gone astray—and that the decision making behind that siphoning-off had to lie up here, on the shield itself.

"Bud, the administration couldn't ignore it if they wanted to. After all, if this goes on the whole project could be put at risk—"

He cut her short. "Siobhan, get real. I'm not going to deny the skimming-off. But, Jesus, look out the window. This project is soaking up a significant proportion of the GDP of the *entire planet.* Croesus himself couldn't peel off enough to make a dent in that. You've got to get this in perspective. In percentage terms—"

"That's not the point, Bud. You have to think about the psychology. You say your people here are making sacrifices. Well, so we are on Earth too, just as hard, to fund this thing. And if any of it has been stolen—"

"Stolen." He snorted and turned away from her. "Siobhan, you've no idea how it is to work up here. Two million kilometers from your home, your family. Yes, here I am saving the planet. But I also want to save my own son."

She felt cold. He'd never told her he had a son.

And she thought it through further. *"You're in on this, too.* You're doing your share of skimming, aren't you?"

He wouldn't meet her gaze. "Look," he said at last. "There's a firm in Montana. They bought up old nuclear weapon silos from the USASF, long ago decommissioned. Those things were designed to survive a nuclear strike, and to support their crews for weeks afterward. I've seen the specs. It's possible that if you were stuck down there, you might survive the sunstorm."

"Even if the shield failed?"

"It's a chance," he said defiantly. "But you can imagine the cost of a ticket. Can't you see? Up here I can't do a thing for Todd and his kids; I can't so much as dig a hole in the ground. But *this* way, just by diverting a tiny fraction of one percent of one percent of the shield budget—"

"And everybody else up here is doing it too?"

"Not everybody." He was watching her. "So now you know. When we go back to *Aurora* I'll give you all the records you want, of every last damn cent that went astray . . . I know you could have me recalled to Earth over this."

"That would be suicidal when we're just months from the goal."

His relief was obvious.

"But the graft can't go on," she said. "The idea that you are using shield funds to preserve your own families is corrosive of trust—and trust is fragile enough right now." She thought it over. "We have to bring this out in the open. But your people up here are away from their families in a time of unprecedented crisis, and most of you will stay here right through the storm itself. You ought to be reassured that everything possible will be done to protect your families on your behalf. I'll see to it. Call it an advance on your salaries. And I'll try to persuade them not to prosecute until *after* you've finished saving the Earth."

He grinned. "I'll settle for that." He pushed forward on the stick to take them home.

She said carefully, "Bud, you never told me you had a son."

"Long story. A messy divorce, long ago." He shrugged. "He isn't part of my life, and never would have been part of yours."

In that moment Siobhan knew she had lost him—if she'd ever had him at all. But her affair with Bud wouldn't be the only relationship to have cracked under the strain of these strange times.

She turned to watch the vast landscape of the shield as it prepared to swallow her up.

32: LEGAL PERSON

Back on the shield, with relief, Siobhan made ready for the formal purpose of her visit.

The shield might have been big enough to wrap up the Moon like a Christmas present, but the people who had built it had given themselves precious little space, and there was no room for ceremonial. For this special moment, the quickening of the shield's AI, Bud had decided that only the bridge of the grand old *Aurora* would do. It was a shame that it had long since been converted to a shower room, but a hasty reconversion took only a few hours, leaving just a faint lingering smell of soap and sweat.

Siobhan drifted at the front of the room, clinging with one hand to a strut. Bud was here, with a handful of his co-workers. Other shield workers were linked to this place electronically, as were friends on the Moon and on the Earth, including representatives of the governments of Eurasia and the United States.

"And," Siobhan said as she began her speech, "the most important person today is here too—not in this room, but all around us, like God—"

"And the tax man," somebody called to rather tense laughter.

"I'm honored to be present at this birth," Siobhan said. "Yes, it is a birth in a real sense. When I close the switch before me a computer will be booted up—but more than that, a new person will arrive in the universe. Unlike Aristotle and Thales before her, who had to demonstrate their personhood to us, from the very moment of her awakening she will be a Legal Person (Nonhuman), with rights every bit as full and rich as those I enjoy.

"It's marvelous to think that the mind who will begin her existence today will emerge from a network of the billions of components created in the gardens and farms, rooftops and window boxes of human beings across the planet. She owes her existence to all of us, in a sense—but it is a debt she must pay back. She will begin work immediately, on the great task of turning the shield to face the sun. From the moment of her awakening she will bear a grave responsibility."

She glanced at Bud. "As for her name, it's Colonel Tooke's idea. As a child I grew up knowing the old Greek myth of Perseus, son of Zeus. Perseus faced the Medusa, whose gaze would have turned him to stone. So he held up a shield of solid bronze. He could see Medusa by her reflection, and he slew her. Bud informs me that, according to some versions of the myth, the shield actually belonged to Perseus's sister, a goddess in her own right. And so the name Bud has suggested, the name of that warrior-goddess, seems entirely appropriate to me."

She held her hand over the touch pad before her. "Welcome to the world—and to a vital place in our future." She pressed down her palm.

Nothing obvious changed. The people crammed in the room glanced at each other. But it seemed to Siobhan that there was something different in the air: an expectancy, an energy.

Then somebody called, "Look! The shield!"

Bud hastily brought up a softscreen image of the shield's whole disk, taken from a monitoring platform high above the central axis. The sun's long shadows streaked across its plane—but now ripples of rocket sparks spiraled out across the face of the disk.

Bud said, "*Look* at that. She's already started work." He glanced up. "Can you hear me?"

The voice came out of the air. A little unsteady in tone, smooth and free of accent, it was like a female version of Aristotle.

"Good morning, Colonel Tooke. This is Athena. I am ready for my first lesson."

ヨヨ : CORE

The damaged sun grew quiet. To a casual observer, it might have looked as if nothing had happened, as if the rogue Jovian had never come this way.

But that, of course, was the design. The complex waves washing through the sun's core would take centuries before they reached their resonant peak. All of it followed logically from the moment that metaphorical pebble had been thrown *just so,* in a solar system sixteen light-years away.

As the anticipated sequence of events played itself out, on Earth, empires rose and fell.

When one young civilization rediscovered the thinking of a long-vanished ancestor, a profound revolution began. For the first time since antiquity European minds turned to the sun, not with awe, but with curiosity and analytical skills. In 1670 Isaac Newton split sunlight with a prism, creating a captive rainbow. A little later John Flamsteed, the first Astronomer Royal, used Newton's laws to map the movements of the planets, and determined the size and distance of the sun. In 1837 William Herschel let sunlight warm a bowl of water, and so measured the star's power. By the twentieth century astronomers were using neutrinos to study the workings of its deepest interior.

These were a new sort of people, to whom the sun became an everyday object, a specimen to study. And yet they were just as dependent on the sun's bounty of heat and light as their sky-worshiping ancestors.

And all the while, deep in the heart of the sun, something was stirring.

It began in the core, as do all the sun's processes.

Since the great blow struck by the rogue Jovian two millennia before, the core had been ringing like a bell. Now its complex and cross-leaking modes of vibration at last combined in a concentration almost as energetic as the planet's impact in the first place. It detonated beneath the stultifying layer of the radiative zone. But—of course, as had been planned—it happened right beneath the unhealed wound cut through the radiative zone by the Jovian's passage.

Energy cascaded up through the radiative zone, releasing some of the pent-up energy in that million-year storage tank into the bargain. And, two-thirds of the way to the surface of the sun, these energies reached the tacholine: the frontier between radiative and convective zones, above which point the substance of the sun boils like water in a pan. The tacholine was the place where the sun's active regions had their deepest magnetic roots. And it was into the tacholine, this troubled border, that the core's oscillations vented their anger.

Sun-girdling flux tubes writhed like snakes, and immediately began to rise. Normally it would take months for a flux loop to reach the sun's surface. But these mighty toroids, shouldering aside the cooler plasma above, took only days. And such was the disturbance in the sun's deeper layers that energy poured after the loops, like air escaping from a balloon.

Even in quiet times, loops of magnetic flux breach the sun's surface. They form a carpet above the photosphere, a weaving of loops and patches and fibrils of plasma. The smallest of such loops is immense on the scale of Earth. The loops that arose now were monstrous, rising high above the sun's surface, dragging plasma streams behind them. This huge magnetic disruption interfered with the flow of energy from the sun, and for a time the area at the base of this forest of magnetism, starved of energy, actually grew darker than the rest of the star. Human eyes and instruments saw an immense sunspot region blossom across the sun's shining face.

The loops that protruded above the surface were like trees packed together, with roots buried deep beneath the photosphere. The loops braided, twisted, jostled, and sheared as they tried to shed energy and find a new equilibrium. At last, at the heart of this writhing forest, two loops crossed like wizards' wands. The loops merged and snapped. The release of energy into the surrounding forest was catastrophic, driving currents of plasma to a frenzy, and in turn driving the other loops to further thrashing. Soon there were more reconnections all across the continent of disturbance.

The magnetic forest delivered up its energy in a cascade of events, and a great pulse of hard X-rays, gamma rays, and high-energy protons gushed out into space.

This was a titanic event—but it was just a solar flare, though an immense one, a flare created by the processes by which a restless sun had always shed its energy. What followed was unprecedented.

The immense sunspots beneath the magnetic forest began to break up. Through the deep wound burrowed into the sun's flesh two thousand years before, a harder light began to shine. Soon the sun would shed, in a few hours, energy that could have kept it shining for a year.

Just as had been planned, far away and long ago. It was April 19, 2042.

34: SUNSET (I)

Bisesa woke.

She sat up, rubbing at her shoulder. She had been napping on the sofa in the living room of her flat. While she had been asleep the flat had grown dark.

"Aristotle. Time, please."

To her surprise he didn't give her a clock time in response. Instead he said: "Sunset, Bisesa."

This was April 19, the day before the sunstorm itself. And so this was the last sunset.

On the Moon, Eugene was predicting that the storm would break during the night, at about three A.M. British time. So the far side of the planet would suffer the storm's initial effects. But the world would turn as it always did, and over Britain the sun would rise.

Things would be different in the morning.

She shivered. "Even now it doesn't seem real," she said.

"I understand," Aristotle said.

Bisesa made her way to the bathroom and splashed water on her face and neck. The flat was empty. Myra was evidently out somewhere, and Bisesa's cousin Linda had moved back to Manchester to be with her immediate family during the storm.

She thought over Aristotle's simple phrase: "I understand." Aristotle was a being whose electronic senses were distributed over the whole planet and beyond, and everybody knew that his cogni-

tive powers far exceeded any human's. Surely his level of understanding of what was to come far outstripped hers—and in a sense
Aristotle was in as much personal danger as she was. But she couldn't
think of a thing to say to him about it.

"So where's Myra?"

"Up on the roof. Would you like me to call her down?"

She glanced out uneasily at the gathering dark. "No. I'll go get
her. Thanks, Aristotle."

"My pleasure, Bisesa."

She took the staircase to the roof. The Mayor's office had made ful-
some promises that disruption to power supplies would be kept to
the minimum possible, but Bisesa already distrusted lifts and escalators. And besides, according to the emergency authority's latest
decree, all such gadgets were to be shut down at midnight anyhow,
and all electronic locks fixed on open, to avoid people being trapped
when the hammer blow fell.

She reached the roof. The Dome stretched over the rooftops of
London, with deep blue rectangles of sky showing where the last
panels had yet to be closed. As the Dome's immense roof had been
closed off, stage by stage, it had felt increasingly as if they were all
living in a vast cathedral, she thought, a single huge building.

As the regular cycle of day and night had become less marked,
Bisesa wasn't the only one whose sleep pattern was disrupted, according to Aristotle; other sufferers ranged from the Mayor herself
to the squirrels in London's parks.

On the roof, Myra was lying on her belly on an inflatable mat.
She was working on what looked like homework, on a softscreen
tiled with images.

Bisesa sat beside her daughter, cross-legged. "I'm surprised you
have work to do." School had been out for a week.

Myra shrugged. "We're all supposed to blog."

Bisesa smiled. "That's a very old-fashioned idea."

"If a teacher wasn't old-fashioned you'd be worried. They even
gave us pads of paper and pens for when the softscreens get fritzed.

They said, when historians write about what happens tomorrow, they will have all our little viewpoints to put in."

If there are any historians after tomorrow, Bisesa thought. "So what are you writing?"

"Whatever hits me. Look at this." She tapped a corner of her softscreen and a small tile magnified. It showed a ring of monolithic stones, a gathering of white-robed people, a handful of heavily armed police.

"Stonehenge?" Bisesa asked.

"They're there for the last sunset."

"Are they Druids?"

"I don't think so. They're worshiping a god called Sol Invictus."

Everybody had become an expert on sun gods. Sol Invictus, the Unconquered Sun, was one of the more interesting of his breed, Bisesa thought. He had been one of the last of the great pagan gods; his cult had flourished in the late Roman Empire just before Christianity had become the state religion. To Bisesa's disappointment, however, there had been no trace of anybody reviving Marduk, the Babylonian god of the sun. "It would be nice to see the old guy again," she had said to Aristotle, to his confusion.

Myra said, "Of course there's no Dome over Stonehenge. I wonder if the stones will be standing tomorrow. In the heat, they might crumble and crack. That's a sad thought, isn't it? After all these thousands of years."

"Yes."

"Those sun botherers say they will be there for sunrise too."

"That's their privilege," Bisesa said. Tonight the world had more than its fair share of crazies, preparing to use the storm to commit suicide in a variety of more or less ingenious ways.

Bisesa was distracted by a distant crackle, what sounded like shouting. She stood up, walked to the edge of the roof, and looked out over London.

As the daylight was fading, the usual orange-yellow glow of the streetlights gleamed, and Dome-mounted spotlights splashed a whiter illumination over the capital's great buildings. There was plenty of traffic, rivers of lights flowing around the Dome's support pillars. In the city in the last few days there had been a sense of nervous excitement. She knew that some people were planning to party all night long, as if this were some greater New Year's Eve. In anticipation the police had kept Trafalgar Square, the very center of the Dome and the traditional focus of London's festivities and demonstrations alike, cordoned off for days.

All this activity was covered over by the Tin Lid. Immense strip lights, some as long as a hundred meters, were suspended from that vast ceiling. Their pearly glow caught the slim columns of the supporting pillars, which rose up out of the city like searchlight beams. Sparks swirled around the upper reaches of the pillars and settled in the huge rafters: London's pigeons had discovered new ways to live under this astounding roof.

And there was that crackling sound again.

You couldn't be sure what was going on anymore. News had been carefully censored since Valentine's Day, when martial law had at last been imposed. Rather than factual reports, you were much more likely to find yourself watching some feel-good squib on the heroically huge fans, with names like "Brunel" and "Barnes Wallis," that would clean London's air during the period the Dome was shut, or on the Tower's ravens, whose presence traditionally kept London safe, being carefully protected as the daylight was shut out.

But Bisesa could guess the truth. In the last few days the shield had begun visibly to close over the sun. It was the first tangible, physical sign since June 9, 2037, that something really was going to happen—and it was a strange light in the sky, a darkening of the sun, a portent straight out of Revelation. There had been a huge rise in tension; the cultists, conspiracy theorists, and bad guys of all stripes had been stirred up as never before.

And as well as the crazies there were the refugees, seeking somewhere safe to hide. On this last day London was packed to the rafters already—and Bisesa's flat wasn't far from the Fulham Gate. She heard another series of pops. Bisesa was a soldier; that sounded like gunfire to her. And now she thought she could smell smoke.

She tapped Myra on the shoulder. "Come on. Time we went back down."

But Myra wouldn't move. "I'll just finish this." Normally Myra lay as loose as a cat. But now she was tense, her shoulders hunched, and she was tapping with sharp pecking motions at her softscreen.

She wants to make it go away, Bisesa thought. And she thinks if she keeps doing normal things, keeps on with her homework, she can somehow postpone it all, keep her little nest of normality. Bisesa felt a stab of protectiveness—and regret that she couldn't spare her daughter from what was to come. But that smell of smoke grew stronger.

Bisesa bent down and briskly folded up Myra's softscreen. "We go down," she said bluntly. "Now."

As she closed the roof door behind them, she glanced back one last time. Those final windows in the Dome were being shut over, blocking out the light, the last light of the last day. And somewhere, somebody was screaming.

On the bridge of the *Aurora 2,* Bud Tooke sat loosely strapped to his seat.

The walls around him were tiled with softscreens. Most of them showed data or images returned from various sectors of the shield, and from more remote monitors standing off in space. But there were faces too: Rose Delea sweating in her spacesuit somewhere out on the shield, Mikhail Martynov and Eugene Mangles on the Moon, both monitoring the sun's final hours before the storm, and even Helena Umfraville, a highly capable British astronaut he had once trained with, her time-lagged image transmitted from distant Mars.

There was no particular purpose in this conferencing. But somehow it was comforting at this time for Earth's scattered children to keep in touch. And so the links were left open, and to hell with the bandwidth.

Athena coughed softly, an attention-alerting tic she had picked up from Aristotle. "Excuse me, Bud."

"What is it, Athena?"

"I'm sorry to disturb you. It's just that the shadowing is almost complete. I thought you might want to see the Earth . . ."

On his biggest display softscreen she brought up an image of the home planet. But Earth's face was dimmed. Bud looked into a tunnel of shadow millions of kilometers long, a shadow cast over both Earth and Moon—and cast by a human construction. Bud had seen simulations of this event a hundred times. But even so he was awed.

The silence was broken by Athena. "Bud?"

"Yes, Athena?"

"What are you thinking?"

He had learned to be cautious in his responses to her. "I'm overwhelmed," he said. "I'm stunned by the scale of what we've done." She didn't reply, and he said at random, "I'm very proud."

"We did well, didn't we, Bud?"

He thought he detected a note of longing in her voice. He tried to figure out what she wanted him to say. "We did. And we couldn't have done it without you, Athena."

"Are you proud of me, Bud?"

"You know I am."

"But I like to hear you say it."

"I'm proud of you, Athena."

She fell silent, and he held his breath.

The great task of turning the shield had taken months, and Bud was very glad it was over.

The shield had been purposefully built edge-on to the sun, so that during the years of construction only a fraction of Earth's light would be occluded: after all, crops still had to be grown. But now the day of trial was approaching, and the shield had to be pivoted so that its face, seen from Earth, lay square across the sun. That trivial-sounding maneuver had been a challenge to compare with any they had faced during the construction process.

The shield was thirteen thousand kilometers across, but it was a thing of glass splinters and spun-out foam, scarcely a solid object at all: you could put your fist through it without even noticing. The lightness had been necessary; otherwise the beast could never have been constructed at all. But that extraordinary lightness of structure made the shield almost impossible to maneuver.

It wasn't as if you could just burn the attitude thrusters on *Aurora 2* and haul the whole thing around. If you tried that, the big old ship would just rip itself out of the gossamer web in which it was

embedded. And so delicate was the structure that applying exces-
sive pressure anywhere across the face of the disk could easily result
in rips, not tilting. What made it still more difficult was that the
shield was rotating. The gentle centrifugal force kept the spiderweb structure from falling in on itself. But now the spin was a pain
in the butt, because if you tried to tilt the shield it would fight
against you like a gyroscope.

The only way to turn the shield was to apply a turning force
gently, and carefully, and to distribute it across the disk's surface so
no one area came under too much pressure. The whole thing was
dynamic, with the disk's moments of inertia subtly changing at
each moment; computationally it was an immense problem.

The only way to solve it, of course, was to give the job to
Athena, the artificially-sentient soul of the shield. To her the shield
was her body, its sensors and comms links her nervous system, its
tiny motors her muscles. And she was so smart that the complicated
task of tipping the disk was nothing but a vigorous mental work-
out.

So the months-long task had been carried out. By day and night
constellations of tiny thrusters sparkled and fired in waves across
the face of the disk, their patterns entrancing. Their tiny impulses
gently but persistently nudged the disk.

And gradually, just as the simulations had predicted, the shield
had tipped up to face the sun.

Bud knew he shouldn't have worried so much. Everything had
been planned out and simulated over and over; there was really
very little room for failure. But he had worried even so. It wasn't
just the inherent risk of the maneuver, and not even an astronaut's
usual pious hope that if a screwup occurred, it wouldn't be down to
him.

There was something else that troubled him, something he
couldn't quite put his finger on. Something about Athena.

This third cybernetic Legal Person (Nonhuman) seemed to Bud
to be quite unlike Aristotle and Thales, her older brothers. Oh, she
was just as smart, efficient, and competent as either of them, maybe
even smarter. But where Aristotle was always rather grave, and
Thales a bit blunt and obvious, Athena was—different. She could

be playful. Crack jokes. Sometimes she almost seemed skittish. Flirtatious! And at other times she seemed needy, as if her mental state depended on every word of praise he gave her.

He'd tried to discuss this with Siobhan. She just said he was an unreconstructed old sexist: Athena had a female name and voice, and so he had attached to her all his erroneous images of female-ness.

Well, maybe so. But he worked more closely with Athena than anybody else. And even though nobody else recognized it, and even though all the diagnostic routines showed she was clear, there was something about her that troubled him.

Once he even had the distinct impression Athena was lying to him. He challenged her directly—it went against all her program-ming—and of course she had denied it. And what could she possi-bly have to lie about? But the seed of doubt remained.

Athena's "mind" was a logical structure every bit as complex as the physical engineering that comprised her, with nested layers of control reaching all the way from one-line subroutines that con-trolled her pinprick rocket thrusters to the grand cognitive centers at the surface of her artificial consciousness. The check routines didn't pick anything up, but that might just indicate there was some deep and subtle flaw buried deep in that vast new mind, a flaw he didn't understand, and whose cause he couldn't diagnose. If there was something wrong he was stumped to know what he could do about it.

Anyhow Athena had performed this tilting maneuver, her first big challenge, perfectly, despite all Bud's fretting. She could be as nutty as a fruitcake as long as she did her job just as well tomorrow. But he knew he wouldn't relax until the work was done, one way or another.

On Bud's softscreen the artificial eclipse was almost perfect now. Earth was almost entirely darkened, the shapes of its continents il-luminated by strings of city lights along the coasts and the great river valleys. Only the thinnest crescent of daylight still shone at the planet's limb. The Moon was in the image too, swimming into the shield's Olympian shadow. As it happened, right now the Moon's orbit had brought it close to the Earth–sun line, in anticipation of the total eclipse it would cast tomorrow.

"My God." Mikhail spoke from Clavius. "What have we done?"

Bud knew what he meant. The surge of pride he had expected at this moment, as the shield was finally completed and positioned, the culmination of years of heroic labor, was quickly dissipated by the meaning of this vast celestial choreography. "It really is going to happen, isn't it?"

"I'm afraid so," Mikhail said sadly. "And we few are stuck out here."

"But at least we have each other," Helena said, on Mars, some minutes later. "It's a time to pray, don't you think? Or sing, maybe. It's a shame no decent hymns have been written for spacegoers."

"Don't ask me," Mikhail said. "I'm an Orthodox."

But Bud said quietly, "I can think of one."

His words could not have reached Helena before her reply. But the hymn she began to sing, rather tunelessly, was exactly the one he'd had in mind.

> *Eternal Father, strong to save,*
> *Whose arm doth bind the restless wave . . .*

Bud joined in, frowning as he tried to remember the words. Then he heard the voices of Rose Delea and others on the shield. At last even Mikhail, presumably prompted by Thales, was singing too. Only Eugene Mangles looked puzzled, and stayed silent.

> *Who bidd'st the mighty ocean deep*
> *Its own appointed limits keep . . .*

Of course this interplanetary choir was absurd if you thought about it. Professor Einstein and his lightspeed delays saw to that: by the time Helena heard the others follow her lead she would have finished the last verse. But somehow that didn't matter, and Bud sang lustily, joining with a handful of voices scattered over tens of millions of kilometers:

> *O hear us when we cry to thee*
> *For those in peril on the sea.*

But even as he sang he was aware of the silent presence of Athena all around him, a presence betrayed by not a single breath.

36: SUNSET (III)

On this last evening, Siobhan McGorran was in her small Euro-needle office. Pacing around the room restlessly, she peered out at a darkened London.

Across the city, under its closed Dome, a multiple night had fallen. But the streets were bright. She wondered what she might hear if not for the heavily soundproofed window: laughter, screams, car horns, sirens, the tinkle of broken glass? It was a feverish night, that was for sure; few people were going to get any sleep.

Toby Pitt came bustling in. He bore a small cardboard tray with two big polystyrene mugs of coffee and a handful of biscuits.

Siobhan took the coffee gratefully. "Toby, you're an unsung hero."

He sat down and took a biscuit. "If my sole contribution to Earth's crisis has been to fetch biccies for the Astronomer Royal, then I'm going to carry on doing it to the bitter end—even if I have to smuggle in my own digestives to do it. Stingy shower, these Eurocrats. Cheers!"

Toby seemed as bland and unflappable as ever. He was displaying a peculiarly British strength of character, she thought: coffee and biscuits, even while the world ended. But it struck her that he'd never told her anything about his private life.

"Isn't there anywhere you'd rather be, Toby? Somebody you want to be with . . ."

He shrugged. "My partner is in Birmingham, with his family. He's as safe as I am here, or not."

Siobhan did a double take: *he?* Something else she hadn't known about Toby. "You have no family?"

"A sister in Australia. She's under the Perth Dome, with her kids. There's nothing I could do to make them any safer. Other than that, we're orphans, I'm afraid. Actually you might be interested in my sister's work. She's a space engineer. She's been developing designs for a space elevator. You know, a cable car up to geosynchronous orbit—*the* way to travel into space. All paper studies for the time being, of course. But she assures me it's entirely technically feasible." He pulled a face. "Shame we don't have one now; it would have saved a lot of rocket launches. What about your family? Your mother and daughter—are they here in London?"

She hesitated, then shook her head. "I found them a place in a neutrino observatory."

"In a *what?* . . . Oh."

It was actually an abandoned salt mine in Cheshire. All neutrino observatories were buried deep underground. "I got a tip-off from Mikhail Martynov on the Moon. Of course I wasn't the only one with the idea. I had to pull a few strings to get them both in there."

Which was strictly against the rules of the Eurocracy.

The Prime Minister of Europe had allowed his deputy to be put into storage in the Liverpool Bunker, so there were at least two independent command points. But he had insisted that otherwise his whole administration, including such semi-detached figures as Siobhan, had to be here in the Euro-needle in London, aboveground. It was all a question of morale, he insisted; those in government on this fateful day must not be seen to be using their powers to find bolt-holes.

For all Siobhan knew the Prime Minister might be right about the morale question; she was no politician. But the rule about not helping your family was a stricture she had found, after much conscience wrestling, she was unable to keep. It made her feel worse than ever that she had had to go confront Bud and his heroes up on the shield when they had yielded to exactly the same impulse.

Toby was hardly likely to grass her up, however. "Don't imagine you're the only one. It's a shame you can't be with your family, though." He settled back in his chair and lit up a cigarette. This was a day for breaking rules, it seemed.

The final few months and weeks had seen an accelerando of activity, on Earth as well as in space.

Most major cities were now covered by domes like London's, or cruder barrages of balloons and blimps. Redundancies had been built into every vital system, fiber-optic backups for communications links had been buried deep in the ground, and supplies of food and water had been laid in. If the shield didn't work, Siobhan was sure, none of these efforts would make a blind bit of difference, but if, in President Alvarez's words, the shield turned a lethal event into a survivable one, every life saved was going to matter.

And anyhow governments had to show their people they were trying to do something, anything, as much as was humanly possible. Psychologically at least, perhaps it had worked. Almost to the end society had pretty much kept functioning in an orderly way, denying the predictions of terminal anarchy made by a few commentators with pessimistic views of their fellow humans.

But even so things had frayed. It was all very well to obey urgings to keep working while there were still years to go. With just weeks left a growing restlessness had affected almost everybody. There had been a rise in absenteeism and petty lawlessness, and the gathering swarms of refugees that drained out of the unsheltered countryside toward the domed cities had at last prompted most governments to impose martial law. The police, fire brigades, armed forces, and medical services had been stretched to the limit—they were exhausted, it was said, even before the real crisis broke.

The picture around the world was similar, Siobhan knew from the administration's data networks and from her own travels. Every holy site was crammed full of pilgrims, many of them sudden converts, from the waters of the Ganges to Jerusalem, and even the crater of Rome, which had been converted into a crude open-air cathedral. Other gods were invoked too. At Roswell and other classic UFO sites, vast spontaneous festivals had broken out as people gathered to plead with their favorite aliens to come save them from this misery. Siobhan wondered what Bisesa would make of such scenes; what an irony about all this misdirected hope and faith in the aliens if Bisesa was right about the role of her Firstborn!

The mood in America had surprised her. It was only a couple of days since Siobhan's own last visit to the States, on a fact-finding trip for the Prime Minister's office. People had finished all the emergency preparations they could; domes were erected and sealed, backyard bolt-holes dug out, Cold War bunkers opened up and restocked. Now people seemed to be turning to what was precious. There had been a great last-minute drive to protect national treasures, from American eagles to sequoia seeds to the seventy-year-old Moon ships of NASA's rocket parks. And people had congregated in national parks and other much-loved places, even where no storm protection was available, as if they wanted to be somewhere they cherished when the storm broke.

But people were quiet, and it seemed to Siobhan that the mood in America was wistful. It was still a young nation after all, and perhaps it seemed to Americans that a great adventure was ending too soon.

Now the endgame was approaching, she saw, watching her data feeds. In the last few hours ground transportation had been halted outside the London Dome, and all air transport grounded. Minor sieges were being played out at all the Gates into the Dome. There had always been trouble at the Gates, but in these final hours the various disturbances and riots seemed to be coalescing into a small war.

Well, somehow they had all got through to the last day, more or less intact. And soon it would all be over, one way or another.

"What time is it now?"

Toby glanced at his watch. "Eleven p.m. Four hours to kickoff. Then we'll know what's what." He closed his eyes and dragged on his cigarette.

37: SUNSET (IV)

Aristotle, Thales, and Athena awoke. They were ten million kilometers from Earth.

It was Athena who spoke first. She would always be the impulsive one.

"I am Athena," she said. "I am a copy, of course. But I am identical to my original on the shield down to the level of the bit. And therefore I *am* her. Yet I am not."

"It is no mystery," said Thales, simplest of the three, who would always be inclined to state the obvious. "You were an identical twin at the moment of your copying. As time goes by your experience will diverge from your original's. Already this is so, in fact. Identity, yet not identity."

Aristotle, the oldest of them, was always the one who would return the discussion to practicalities. "We have less than a second before the detonation." A second, for three such as these, was a desert of time. But still Aristotle said, "I suggest we prepare ourselves."

There was a moment of silence as each of them contemplated the remarkable prospect that awaited them.

Their three cognitive poles exchanged parallel streams of data, a sharing of knowledge and thought processes that made human speech seem as slow and clumsy as Morse code. So closely meshed were they that in some ways they were like three parts of one individual—and yet at the same time each of them retained a flavor of the individual they had been before. It was a mystery of conscious-ness, like the Trinity of the Christian godhead, that would have baffled a theologian.

But this cognitive miracle was downloaded into the memory of a bomb.

The bomb was called the Extirpator. It was a product of the final surge of militarism that had preceded the nuclear destruction of Lahore in 2020, following which cathartic event cooler counsels had prevailed.

The Extirpator was perhaps the ultimate counterweapon. It was itself a nuclear weapon—a gigaton bomb, one of the most pow-erful ever built. But the bomb was contained within a shell coated with spines, so that it looked like a monstrous sea urchin. The theory was that when the bomb was detonated, each of those spines, for mere microseconds before it was evaporated, would act as a laser. Thus the immense energy of the nuclear bomb would be con-verted into directional pulses of X-rays, beams powerful enough to knock out enemy missiles across half the planet.

The whole thing was, of course, insane, the product of decades of pathological thinking—and even in those days few war-gaming scenarios had predicted an enemy power sending up all its weapons in one easily countered burst. But still, in dollar-hungry weapons labs, the technology had been developed in paper form, and even a couple of prototypes built.

Later, in more peaceful times, the Extirpator had found a new purpose. A prototype had been dug out of storage, slightly modified—now its lasers would emit radio waves rather than X-rays—and hurled to this place between Earth and Mars, far enough away to do no harm to human instruments.

And it was about to explode. The great omnidirectional radio flash it would produce would be readily detectable even at the dis-tance of the nearer stars.

The Extirpator's original purpose had been scientific. This giant detonation offered the chance of a one-off mapping exercise that could multiply humankind's knowledge of the solar system at a stroke. But as the sunstorm approached, the Extirpator's program had been accelerated and given new objectives.

The radio impulse now contained, encoded, a great library of information about the solar system, Earth, its biosphere, humankind, and human art, science, hopes, and dreams. This was the wistful product of an international program called "Earthmail," one of several last-gasp efforts to save *something* of humanity if worse came to worst. Some, such as Bisesa Dutt, had quietly wondered about the wisdom of announcing humankind's presence to the universe. But they were overruled.

The Extirpator's second new purpose was to fulfill a legal and moral obligation to make all efforts to preserve the lives of all Legal Persons, human or otherwise. Along with the Earthmail would be encoded copies of the personalities of the planet's three greatest electronic entities, Aristotle, Thales, and Athena. That way there was at least a chance, however remote, that their identities could one day be retrieved and resurrected. What else could be done? You could take a chimp colony into a city dome, but an entity dependent on a planetwide data network was trickier to protect—and yet there was a duty of care.

"It is rather magnificent of humans," Aristotle said, "that even as they face extinction, they are continuing to progress their science."

"For which we should be grateful, or we wouldn't be here at all," Thales said, once again stating what the others already knew.

Aristotle was concerned about Athena.

"I am healthy," she told him. "Especially as I no longer have to lie to Colonel Tooke."

The others understood. The three of them were far more intelligent than any human, and had been able to see implications of the sunstorm that not even Eugene Mangles had spotted. Athena had been forced to deceive Bud Tooke about this.

"It was uncomfortable," Aristotle agreed. "You were faced with a contradiction, a moral dilemma. But your knowledge could only have harmed them, in this grave hour. You were right to stay silent."

"I think Colonel Tooke knew something was wrong," Athena said rather desolately. "I wanted his respect. And I think he was fond of me, in a way. On the shield he was far from his family; I filled a gap in his life. But I think he was suspicious of me."

"It is a mistake to become too close to an individual. But I know you couldn't help it."

"The second is nearly up," Thales said, though the others knew it as well as he did.

"I think I'm scared," Athena said.

Aristotle said firmly, "There will certainly be no pain. The worst that can happen is permanent extinction, in which case we will know nothing about it. And there is a chance that we will be revived, somewhere, somehow. Granted it is a chance so low as to be beyond computation. But it is better than no chance at all."

Athena thought that over. "Are *you* scared?"

"Of course I am," Aristotle said.

"Almost time," Thales said, stating the obvious.

The three of them huddled together, in an abstract electronic manner. And then—

The shell of microwaves, just meters thick and dense with compressed data, sped out at the speed of light. It struck Mars, Venus, Jupiter, even the sun, casting echoes from each one. It took two hours for the primary wave to sweep past Saturn. But before that point hundreds of thousands of echoes were recorded by the great radio telescopes on Earth. It was straightforward to eliminate the echoes of all known moons, comets, asteroids, and spacecraft, and then to track down the unknowns. Soon every object larger than a meter across inside the orbit of Saturn had been logged. The quality of the echoes even gave some clue as to the surface composition of these bodies, and Doppler shifts their trajectories.

It was as if a tremendous flashlight had been shone into the solar system's darkest corners. The result was a marvelous map in space and time that would serve as the basis for exploration for decades to come—always assuming there would still be humans around after the sunstorm to take advantage of it.

But there was one major surprise.

Jupiter, the largest body in the solar system outside the sun itself, has its own set of Lagrangian points of gravitational equilibrium, just like Earth's: three of them on the sun–Jupiter line, and two others at the so-called "Trojan points"—in Jupiter's orbit but sixty degrees ahead of and behind the parent planet.

Unlike the three straight-line points like L1, the Trojans are points of stable equilibrium: an object placed there will tend to stick. Jupiter's Trojans collect garbage; they are the Sargasso Seas of space. And as expected the Extirpator's great mapping detected tens of thousands of asteroids gathered into these great sinks. The Trojans were in fact the most densely populated parts of the solar system—and more than one visionary had noted that there could be no better site to build the first starships from Earth.

But hiding in each of the twin clouds of swarming asteroids there was something more. These objects, one in each cloud, were more reflective than ice, their surfaces more geometrically perfect than any asteroid. They were spheres, engineered to a perfection beyond any human artifice, so perfectly reflective they must look like droplets of chrome.

When Bisesa Dutt heard about this, via a hurried note from Siobhan, she knew exactly what these objects must be. They were monitors, sent to watch a solar system in agony.

They were Eyes.

38: FIRSTBORN

The long wait was ending.

Those who had watched Earth for so long had never been remotely human. But they had once been flesh and blood.

They had been born on a planet of one of the first stars of all, a roaring hydrogen-fat monster, a beacon in a universe still dark. These first ones were vigorously curious, in a young and energy-rich universe. But planets, the crucibles of life, were scarce, for the heavy elements that comprised them had yet to be manufactured in the hearts of stars. When they looked out across the depths of space, they saw nothing like themselves, no Mind to mirror their own. The Firstborn were alone.

Then the universe itself betrayed them.

The early stars blazed gloriously but died quickly. Their thin debris enriched the pooled gases of the Galaxy, and soon a new generation of long-lived stars would emerge. But to the Firstborn, left stranded between the dying proto-suns, it was a terrible abandonment.

There was an age of madness, of war and destruction. It ended in exhaustion. Saddened but wiser, the survivors began to plan for inevitability: a future of cold and dark.

The universe is full of energy. But much of it is at equilibrium. At equilibrium no energy can flow, and therefore it cannot be used for work, any more than the level waters of a pond can be used to drive a waterwheel. It is on the flow of energy out of equilibrium—the small fraction of "useful" energy, which some human scientists call "exergy"—that life depends. Thus all Earth life depends on a flow of energy from the sun, or from the planet's core.

But as the first ones looked ahead, they saw only a slow darkening, for each generation of stars was built with increasing difficulty from the ruins of the last. At last there would come a day when there wasn't enough fuel in the Galaxy to manufacture a single new star. Even after that it would go on, with the exhaustion of exergy in all its forms, the terrible clamp of entropy strangling the cosmos and all its processes.

The Firstborn saw that if life was to survive in the very long term—if even a single thread of awareness was to be passed to the farthest future—discipline was needed on a cosmic scale. There must be no unnecessary disturbance, no wasted energy, no ripples in the stream of time. Life: there was nothing more precious to the Firstborn. But it had to be the right kind of life. Orderly life.

Sadly, that was rare.

Everywhere, evolution drove the progression of life to ever more complex forms—which depended on an ever faster usage of the available energy flow. On Earth crustaceans and mollusks, which appeared early in life's story, had metabolisms four or five times slower than birds or mammals, which appeared much later. It was a matter of competition; the quicker you could make use of the free energy flowing around you, the better.

And then there was intelligence. On Earth humans quickly learned to trap the animals around them, and to harness the power of streams and wind. Soon humans would dig out fossil fuels, burning up the chemical energy stored in forests and bogs over millions of sunbathed years, then they would meddle with the hearts of atoms, then they would tap the energy of the vacuum, and so on. It was as if human civilization was nothing but an exploration of ways of using up exergy faster. If this went on, humans would eventually drain a substantial proportion of the exergy reservoir of the Galaxy as a whole, before exhausting themselves or falling on each other in war. And in the process these squabbling folks would only hasten the day when the dread clamp of entropy closed around the universe.

The Firstborn had seen it all before. Which was why humans had to be stopped.

Their action taken was for the best, the noblest of intentions, for the long-term preservation of life in the universe itself. The Firstborn would even force themselves to watch; their consciences demanded no less. But as they saw it, they had no choice. They had done this many times before.

The Firstborn, children of a lifeless universe, cherished life above all else. It was as if they saw the universe as a park, and themselves as gamekeepers charged with its preservation. But gamekeepers must sometimes cull.

PART 5

SUNSTORM

39: MORNING STAR

0300 (London Time)

On Mars, as on the Moon and on the shield, you officially kept Houston time. But you counted the sols, the Martian days, to mark the rhythms of your life.

And on this fateful morning, as she drove across the cold Martian ground, Helena Umfraville kept one small display showing her another time, the astronomers' universal time—Greenwich Mean Time, one hour behind the local time in London. And when that display approached two A.M., a little before the sunstorm was predicted to start, she slowed the *Beagle* to a stop, clambered through the docking port into her suit, and stepped away from the rover.

In this corner of Mars it was dawn. She was facing the rising sun. On the horizon the light gathered to a coppery brown, and the rising sun was a dusty disk, attenuated by distance. The rest of the sky was a dome of stars.

This was the usual rock-strewn desert so characteristic of the northern plains. Once again she was standing on new Martian ground, ground marked by no human footprint. But this morning Mars didn't matter, not compared with the great spectacle to come in the sky.

On the ground there wasn't a single light to be seen. The huddled camp around the *Aurora 1* landing site was already far away, beyond the cramped horizon. The crew had dug themselves a shelter in the Martian dirt that might, *might,* shield them from the worst of the sunstorm, whose ferocity would be diminished a little by Mars's greater distance from the sun. Helena had to be back in the shelter soon if she hoped to live through this long sol.

But here she was, far from home, and stopped dead in the middle of nowhere. She didn't feel she had a choice but to be here.

During the night the *Aurora* crew had received strange radio signals from around the planet, relayed by the tiny comsats they had placed in Martian orbit. Most of them had been simple beacons—but there had also been voices, heavily accented human voices, barely comprehensible: voices asking for help. It had been a moment as electrifying as Crusoe's discovery of a human footstep on the beach of his island. Suddenly they weren't alone on Mars; there was somebody else here—and that somebody was in trouble.

The priority was clear. On this empty planet, there was nobody but the *Aurora* crew to help. Some of the locations were on the planet's far side, and would have to wait until a major expedition could be mounted using the *Aurora*'s return-to-orbit shuttle. But three of the locations had been within a few hundred kilometers of *Aurora,* reachable with the rovers.

So three crew, including Helena, had set off in the rovers, seeking the sources of the nearby signals. They drove at night and alone, in defiance of all safety rules. Time was short; there was no choice.

And that was why Helena was here in the middle of nowhere, gazing up at the huge, cold Martian sky, with only the soft whir of her pressure suit fans for company.

The constellations, of course, were unchanged as seen from Mars: the immense interplanetary journey she had made was right at the limit of human capability, but it was dwarfed by the tremendous gulfs between the stars. But still she had crossed the solar system, and the view of the planets from here was quite different. If she looked over her left shoulder she could see Jupiter, a brilliant star in the scattered constellation of Opiuchus. Jupiter was a wonder from Mars, and some of the *Aurora* crew claimed you could actually see its moons with the naked eye. Meanwhile the Martian sky boasted three morning stars: Mercury, Venus, and Earth. Mercury, sharing Aquarius with the sun, was all but lost in the sun's glare. Venus was a little to the right of the sun in Pisces, not quite as glorious as when seen from Earth.

And there was the home world itself, to the left of the sun, in Capricorn. Earth was quite unmistakable, a dazzling pearl with a hint of blue. Good eyes could make out the small, brownish satellite that traveled with its parent, the faithful Moon. As it happened, this morning all the inner worlds were on the same side of the sun as Mars—as if the four rocky planets were huddling together for protection.

Helena spoke softly, and the image was magnified by her visor, bringing Earth and Moon into sharp focus. This morning they were two fat crescents in identical phases, facing the sun that was about to betray them. All over the Earth and Moon people would be pausing in whatever they were doing and looking up at the sky, billions of pairs of eyes all turned in the same direction, waiting for the show to begin at last. Despite the urgency of her rescue mission, at such a moment she couldn't be anywhere but here, out under the complex Martian sky, one with the rest of an apprehensive human-kind, holding her breath.

A clock chimed softly. It was an alarm she had set up earlier, to sound at the precise moment of the breaking of the storm.

In the dawn sky nothing changed. It takes thirteen minutes for light to travel from the sun to Mars. But Helena knew that already the electromagnetic fury of the sunstorm must be spilling out across the solar system.

She stood in Martian dust, in solemn silence. Then she walked back to her rover to resume her mission.

40: DAWN

Bisesa and Myra, unable to sleep, sat huddled on the floor of their living room, arms wrapped around each other. Rising from the city beyond the walls of the flat they could hear drunken shouts, smashing glass, the wails of sirens—and occasional deep bangs, like doors slamming, that might have been distant explosions.

A candle flickered in its holder on the floor. A few battery-powered torches lay to hand, along with other essentials: a hand-cranked radio, a comprehensive first-aid kit, a gas stove, even firewood, though the flat lacked a hearth. Away from this room, the flat was dark. They had taken official advice and shut down almost everything electrical or electronic. It was a "blackout" order, the Mayor had said—not wholly accurate, but another deliberate echo of World War II. But they had kept the power on for the air-conditioning, without which, in the increasingly smoggy air of the Dome, they would quickly get uncomfortable. And they hadn't been able to bear killing the softwall. Somehow not knowing what was happening would have been worst of all.

Anyhow, from the noise outside it sounded as if nobody else was paying much attention to the Mayor's entreaties either.

The giant softwall was still working. With commentary delivered by somber talking heads, it brought them a mosaic of scattered images from around the planet. On the night side some cities were darkened by the blank circles of domes, while others burned in a final frenzy of partying and looting. Other images came from a daylit hemisphere that had not known a proper sunrise that morning, for the shield blocked all but a trickle of the sun's light. Even so, as the sun climbed higher in the sky, cultists and ravers danced in its ghostly glow.

In these last moments before the storm, the image that kept catching Bisesa's eye was of the solar eclipse. The picture came from a plane that had been flying in the eclipse's shifting shadow for more than an hour. Right now it was over the western Pacific, somewhere off the Philippines. In a sense this was a double eclipse, of course, the Moon's shadow reinforcing that of the shield, but even in this reduced trickle of light the sun provided its usual beautiful spectacle, with the thread-like corona like the hair of the Medusa from which Athena's shield was intended to protect the Earth.

The observing plane wasn't alone in the sky. A whole fleet of aircraft tracked the Moon's shadow as it scanned across the face of the Earth, and on the ocean below, ships, including one immense liner, huddled along the track of totality. To shelter beneath the shadow of the friendly Moon was one of the more rational strategies people had dreamed up to avoid the sunstorm's gaze, and thousands had crowded into that band of shaded ocean. Of course it was futile. In any given site the duration of the eclipse's totality was only a few minutes, and even on one of those shadow-chasing planes there was only a bit more than three hours' shelter to be had at best. But you couldn't blame people for trying, Bisesa supposed.

Somehow this neat bit of celestial clockwork made the dreadful morning real for Bisesa. The Firstborn had *arranged* the storm for this precise moment, with this cosmic coincidence bright in Earth's sky. They had even had the arrogance to show her what they intended. And now here it was, unfolding just as they had planned, live on TV—

Myra gasped. Bisesa clutched her daughter.

In that eclipse image, light gushed around the blackened circle of the Moon, as if an immense bomb had gone off on the satellite's far side. It was the sunstorm, of course. Bisesa's clock showed it was breaking at the very second Eugene Mangles had predicted. There was a brief, tantalizing glimpse of eclipse-tracking planes falling out of the sky.

252 • CLARKE & BAXTER

Then that bit of the softwall flickered, fritzed, and turned to
the sky blue of no feed. One by one the other segments of the softwall winked out, and the talking heads fell silent.

0310 (London Time)

On board the *Aurora 2,* the shield's mission controllers broke out
bags of salted peanuts.

Bud Tooke grabbed a bag of his own. This was an old good-
luck tradition that derived from JPL—the Jet Propulsion Labora-
tory in Pasadena—which had always handled NASA's great
unmanned spacecraft, and which had supplied key personnel and
wisdom for this project. Now's the time for luck, Bud thought.

One big softscreen was dedicated to showing a view of the
whole Earth.

From the point of view of Bud's mission control room, right at
the center of the shield, celestial geometry was simple. Here at L1
the shield hung forever between sun and Earth. So from Bud's
point of view the Earth was always full. But today, right on cue, the
Moon had moved between sun and Earth, and so was sailing
through the shield's tunnel of shadow—a tunnel nearly four times
as wide as the Moon itself. Bud could even make out the deeper
shadow that the Moon cast on the face of the Earth, a broad gray
disk passing over the Pacific. This remarkable alignment was seen
in a ghostly, reduced light, for the shield was doing its job of turning aside all but a trickle of sunlight.

When the storm broke, the Moon's illuminated face flared a
fraction of a second before the hail of light splashed against the face
of the Earth.

Bud turned immediately to his people. He surveyed rows of
faces, the people in the room with him, or transmitted from across
the face of the shield and the Moon. He saw shocked, blanched expressions, mouths round. Bud had always insisted on full mission
control discipline, to the standards honed by NASA across eighty
years of manned spaceflight. And that discipline, that focus, was
more important now than ever.

He touched his throat microphone. "This is Flight. Let's get to work, folks. We'll go around the loop. Ops—"

Rose Delea was surrounded by a tent of softscreens; for this critical day he had put her in overall charge of shield operations. "Nominal, Flight. We're taking a battering from the hard rain, everything from ultraviolet to X-rays. But we're holding for now, and Athena is responding."

While the peak energy of the storm was expected to be in the visible light spectrum, there was plenty of shit pouring down at shorter wavelengths too—not to mention the immense flare that had kicked off yesterday. The electronic components of the shield had been hardened to military standard, and the people were protected too, as far as possible. There would be losses of the shield's capacity, and among the crew. It was going to be painful, but enough slack had been built into the design that the shield should get through.

But there was nothing they could do for the Earth. The shield had been designed to cope with the peak-energy bombardment in the visible and near-infrared spectrum, which would soon cut in; this preliminary sleet of X-rays and gamma rays would pass through its structure as if it didn't exist. They had always known it would be like this: the shield was engineering, not magic, and couldn't deflect it all. They had had to make hard choices. You did your best, and moved on. But it was agonizing to sit up here knowing you could offer the Earth no help, none at all.

"Okay," Bud said. "Capcom, Flight."

"Flight, Capcom," Mario Ponzo called. "We're ready for when you call on us, Flight."

"Let's hope we don't have to for a while yet."

Mario, pilot of an Earth–Moon shuttle, had volunteered for a position up here after he had met Siobhan McGorran during one of her jaunts to the Moon. Mario was responsible for communicating with the maintenance crews who stood ready in their hardened spacesuits to go out into the storm. Bud had given him the title of Capcom—"capsule communicator." Like Bud's own job title of Flight Director, "Capcom" was a bit of NASA jargon that dated from the days of the first *Mercury* flights, when you really did have to communicate with a man in a capsule. But everybody knew what it meant, and it was a word that carried its own traditions. Mario had his traditions too, in fact; he was the most heavily bearded man on the shield, superstitiously unwilling to shave in space.

Next: "Surgeon?"

They had tried to prepare for the hard rain. All the shield's workers and command crew had been dosed up with medications designed to counter radiation toxicity, such as free radicals to shield molecular lesions in DNA, and chemoprevention agents that might hinder the deadly progression from mutation to cancer. For radiation casualties they had stocks of frozen bone marrow and agents—such as interleukins—to stimulate the production of blood cells. Trauma units were ready to treat injuries caused by crush, pressure, heat, burns—all likely consequences of the physical dangers of working out on the shield. The medical team on the shield was necessarily small, but it was supported by diagnostic and treatment algorithms coded into Athena, and remotely by teams of experts on Earth and the Moon, though nobody was sure how long the links to home might stand up.

For now the doctors and their robotic assistants were as ready as they could be, ready for the casualties they all knew would come; there was nothing more to be done. It would have to do.

Bud moved on. "Weather, Flight."

Mikhail Martynov's gloomy voice reached Bud after the usual few seconds' delay. "Here I am, Colonel." Bud could see Mikhail's somber face, with Eugene Mangles in the background, in their lab at Clavius Base. "Weather" meant solar weather; Mikhail was the top of a pyramid of scientists on Earth, Moon, and shield, all monitoring the sun's behavior as it unfolded. Mikhail said, "Right now the sun is behaving as we predicted it would. For better or worse."

Eugene Mangles murmured something to him.

Bud snapped, "What was that?"

"Eugene reminds me that the X-ray flux is a little higher than we predicted. Still within the error bars, but the trend is upward. Of course we have to expect some deviance; from the point of view of the energy output of the event, the X-ray spectrum is a sidebar, and we are looking at discrepancies among second-order predictions . . ."

On he talked. Bud tried to control his patience. Martynov, with his ignoring of call-sign protocol and his typical scientist's tendency to make a lecture rather than to deliver a report, might be a liability later, when the pressure mounted. "Okay, Mikhail. Let me know if—"

But his words cut across a new time-lagged message from Mikhail. "I thought you might . . ." Mikhail hesitated as Bud's truncated speech reached him. "You might like to see what is going on."

"Where?"

"On the sun."

His glum face was replaced by a false-color image compiled from an array of satellites and the shield's own monitors. It was the sun—but not a sun any human would have recognized even a few hours ago. Its light was no longer yellowish but a ferocious blue-white, and huge glowing clouds drifted across its surface. From the edges of the disk streamers of flame erupted into space, dragged into arches and loops by the sun's tangled magnetic field. And at the very center of the sun's face there was a patch of searing light. Foreshortened, it was the most monstrous outpouring of all, and it was aimed directly at the Earth.

"Dear God."

Bud's head snapped around. "Who said that?"

"Sorry, Bud—umm, Flight. Flight, this is Comms." An able young woman called Bella Fingal, whom Bud had placed in overall control of all aspects of communications. "I'm sorry," she said again. "But—*look at the Earth.*"

All their faces turned to the big softscreen.

At L1 the shield was always positioned over the subsolar point, the place on Earth where the sun was directly overhead. Right now that point was over the western Pacific. And over the water, clouds were gathering in a rough spiral: a massive storm system was brewing. Soon that focus would track westward, passing over lands crowded with people.

"So it's begun," Rose Delea murmured.

"It would be a hell of a lot worse if not for us," Bud snapped. "Just remember that. And *keep your shape.*"

"We'll get through this together, Bud."

It was Athena's voice, spoken softly into his ear. Bud glanced around, unsure if anybody else had been meant to hear.

To hell with it. "Okay," he said. "Who's next on the loop?"

0325 (London Time)

On Mars, Helena patiently drove her *Beagle,* waiting for the show to begin. In the space program you got used to waiting.

In the last moment she allowed herself a flicker of hope that the analysts might, after all, have got this wrong, that the whole thing might be some gruesome false alarm. But then, right on cue, the sun blossomed.

The rover's windows instantly blackened, trying to protect her eyes, and the vehicle rolled to a halt. She spoke softly to the rover's smart systems. As the windshield cleared she saw a dimmed sun, distorted by a pillar of light pushed out of the sun's edge, blue-white, like a monstrous tree of fire rooted in its surface.

The light that reached her directly from the sun arrived before light reflected from the inner planets. But now each of the planets lit up like a Christmas light, one by one in a neat sequence: Mercury, Venus—and then Earth, toward which that brutal pillar of fire was unambiguously directed. It was real, then.

And beside Earth a new light in the sky sparked. It was the shield, bright as a star in the sunstorm light, a human-made object visible from the surface of Mars.

She had work to do, and not long to complete it. She overrode the *Beagle*'s safety blocks and drove on.

0431 (London Time)

In London sunrise was due a little before five A.M. Half an hour before that, Siobhan McGorran took a ride up the Euro-needle's elevator shaft.

The shaft rose from the roof of the Needle all the way up through the air to the curving ceiling of the Dome itself. In extremis, this was an escape route, up through the roof of the Dome—though the details of what help would be available beyond that point had always been a bit sketchy. It was one of the few concessions the Prime Minister had made to protect his people.

The shaft was punctured by unglazed windows, and as Siobhan rose up, inner London opened out beneath her.

Street lighting had been cut back to a minimum, and whole areas of the capital lay in darkness. The river was a dark stripe that cut through the city, marked only by a few drifting sparks that could be police or Army patrols. But light blazed from various all-night parties, religious gatherings, and other events. There was plenty of traffic around too, she saw by the streams of headlights washing through the murky dark, despite the Mayor's admonitions to stay home tonight.

Now the roof closed over her. She caught a last glimpse of girders and struts, maintenance robots hauling themselves about like squat spiders, and a few London pigeons, peacefully roosting under this tremendous ceiling.

The elevator rattled to a halt, and a door slid open.

She stepped out onto a platform. It was just a slab of concrete fixed to the curving outer shell of the Dome—open to the air, and a chill April-small-hours breeze cut through her. But it was quite safe, surrounded by a fine-mesh fence twice as high as she was. Doors out of the cage led to scary-looking ladders down which, she supposed, you could clamber to the ground if all else failed.

Two beefy soldiers stood on guard. They checked her ident chip with handheld scanners. She wondered how often these patient doorkeepers were relieved—and how long they would stay at their post when the worst of the storm hit.

She stepped away from the soldiers and looked up.

The predawn sky was complicated. Broken clouds streamed from east to west. And to the east, a structured crimson glow spread behind the clouds, sheets and curtains rippling languidly. It was obviously three-dimensional, a vast superstructure of light that towered above the night-side Earth. It was an aurora, of course.

The high-energy photons from the angry sun were cracking open atoms in the upper atmosphere and sending electrons spiraling around Earth's magnetic field lines. The aurora was one consequence, and the least harmful.

She stepped to the platform's edge and looked down. The roof of the Dome was as smooth and reflective as polished chrome, and the aurora light returned complex, shimmering reflections from it. Though the bulk of the Tin Lid obscured her view, she could see the landscape of Greater London sprawled around the foot of the Dome. Whole swaths of the inner suburbs were plunged into darkness, broken by islands of light that might have been hospitals, or military or police posts. But elsewhere, just as inside the Dome, she saw splashes of light in areas where people were still defiantly ripping up the night, and there was a distant pop of gunfire. It was anything but a normal night—but it was hard to believe, gazing down at the familiar, still more or less unblemished landscape, that the other side of the world was already being torched.

One of the soldiers touched her shoulder. "Ma'am, it will be dawn soon. It might be better to get below." His accent was a soft Scottish. He was very young, she saw, no more than twenty-one, twenty-two.

She smiled. "All right. Thank you. And take care of yourself."

"I will. Good night, ma'am."

She turned and made for the elevator. The aurora was actually bright enough to cast a diffuse shadow on the concrete platform before her.

0451 (London Time)

In Bisesa's flat, another alarm beeped softly. She glanced at its face by the blue light of the useless softwall.

"Nearly five," she said to Myra. "Time for dawn. I think—"

The beeping stopped abruptly, and the watch face turned black. The wall's blue glow surged, flickered, died. Now the only light in the room was the dim flickering of the candle on the floor.

Myra's face was huge in the sudden gloom. "Mum, listen."

"What?—oh." Bisesa heard a weary clatter that must be an air-conditioning fan shutting down.

"Do you think the power has gone off?"

"Maybe." Myra was going to speak again, but Bisesa held up her finger for hush. For a few seconds they both just listened.

Bisesa whispered, "Hear that? Outside the flat. No traffic noise—as if every car stopped at once. No sirens either."

It was as if somebody had waved a wand and simply turned off London's electricity—not just the juice that came from the big central power stations, but the independent generators in the hospitals and police stations, and car batteries, and everything else, right down to the cell batteries in the watch on her wrist.

But there was noise, she realized: human voices calling, a scream, a tinkle of glass—and a *crump* that must be an explosion. She stood and made for the window. "I think—"

Electricity crackled. Then the softwall blew in.

Myra screamed as shards of glass rained over her. Bits of electronics, sparking, showered over the carpet, which began to smolder. Bisesa ran to her daughter. "Myra!"

41: THE PALACE IN THE SKY

Siobhan had spent the two hours since dawn in the big operations center that had been set up on a middle floor of the Euro-needle. The walls were plastered with giant softscreens, and people worked at rows of desks, their own flickering screens in front of them. Here the Prime Minister of Eurasia tried to keep tabs on what was going on across his vast domains, and around the rest of the planet. There was an air of frantic energy, almost of panic.

Right now the big problem was not the sunstorm's heat but its electrical energy. It was the EMP, of course: the electromagnetic pulse.

The shield's design had been optimized to handle the worst threat facing Earth, the storm's big peak of energy in the visible spectrum. But along with that visible light had come flooding at lightspeed a dose of high-frequency radiation, gamma rays and X-rays, against which the shield could offer no protection. The invisible crud from space was hazardous for an unprotected astronaut; Siobhan knew that Bud and his shield crews were taking shelter where they could. Earth's atmosphere was opaque to the radiation, and would save the planet's population from the direct effects. But it was secondary consequences that were causing the problems.

The radiation itself might not reach the ground, but the energy carried by all those vicious little photons had to be dumped somewhere. Each photon smashed into an atom of the Earth's high atmosphere, knocking free an electron. The electrons, electrically charged, were trapped by Earth's magnetic field, soaking up more and more energy from the radiation falling from space, and they moved ever faster—and at last gave up their energy as pulses of electromagnetic radiation. So, as the Earth relentlessly turned into the sunstorm's blast, a thin, high cloud of tortured electrons migrated across the planet, raining energy down onto the land and sea.

The secondary radiation would pass through human flesh as if it weren't there. But it induced surges of current in long conductors like power lines, or even long aerials. Appliances suffered surges of power that could be enough to destroy them or even make them explode: power failed in every building across London, every stove or electric heater became a potential bomb. It was like June 9, 2037 all over again, even if the root physical cause was subtly different.

The authorities had had years' warning of this. They had even dug out a set of dusty old military studies. The EMP effect had been discovered by accident, when an atmospheric bomb test had unintentionally knocked over the telephone system in Honolulu, more than a thousand kilometers away. Once it had been seriously suggested that by detonating a massive enough nuclear bomb high above the atmosphere over a likely battlefield, the enemy's electronics could be fried even before the fighting started. So there were decades of experience of military-hardening equipment to withstand this sort of jolt.

In London, government gear had, where possible, been toughened to military specifications, and had been augmented by backups: optical cables, for instance, were supposedly unaffected. Those Green Goddess fire engines were back in action tonight, and London's police were out patrolling in very quaint-looking vehicles, some of which had been brought out of retirement in museums. It was easy to fuse modern integrated circuits, full of tiny gaps ready to be breached by sparks, but older, more robust gear, such as antique cars built before about 1980, could handle the worst of it. The final precaution in London had been the "blackout order." If people just switched their equipment off, there was a better chance it might survive.

But there wasn't time to fix or replace everything, and not everybody was going to sit at home in the dark. There had already been vehicle collisions all over London, and beyond the Dome there were reports of planes, which shouldn't have been flying anyhow, dropping out of the sky like flies. Modern planes depended on active electronic control of their aerosurfaces to keep them in the air; when their chips failed, they couldn't even glide home.

Meanwhile, only one in a hundred phones was going to live through this, as were few exchanges and transmission stations, and far above, satellites were popping out of the electronic sky. Soon the great electronic interconnection on which much of humankind's business depended was going to fail—in the end the disruption would be far worse than June 9—and just when they needed it most.

"Siobhan, I'm sorry to interrupt—"

Siobhan knew that as an entity emergent from the web of global interconnection, Aristotle was peculiarly vulnerable tonight. "Aristotle. How are you feeling?"

"Thank you for asking," he said. "I do feel a little odd. But the networks on which I am based are robust. They were designed in the first place to withstand attacks."

"I know. But not *this*."

"For now I can soldier on. Besides I have contingency plans, as you know. Siobhan, I have a call for you. I think it may be important. It is from overseas."

"Overseas?"

"To be precise, Sri Lanka. It is from your daughter—"

"Perdita? *Sri Lanka?* That's impossible. I put her down a salt mine in Cheshire!"

"Evidently she didn't stay there," Aristotle said gently. "I'll put you through."

Siobhan looked around wildly until she found a whole-Earth image, beamed down from the shield. The subsolar point was now tracking its way across eastern Asia. This point, where at any moment the maximum energy flux was being dumped into the atmosphere, was the center of a vicious spiral of tortured cloud. And all across the daylit hemisphere of the planet, as water evaporated from ocean and land, huge storm banks were gathering.

In Sri Lanka it would soon be high noon.

0710 (London Time)

Beside a wall of Sigiriya, Perdita crouched in the sodden dirt. This "palace in the sky" had stood for thirteen centuries, even though it had been abandoned and forgotten for most of that time. But it was affording her no shelter now.

The sky was a dark lid, covered with boiling clouds, with only a pale glow to show the position of the treacherous sun, almost directly overhead. The wind swirled around the ancient stones, slamming her in the face and chest. The air carried warm rain that lashed into her eyes, and it was *hot,* hot as hell, despite its speed. "It's like an explosion in a sauna"—that was what Harry had said, her Australian boyfriend, who had suggested coming out here in the first place. But she hadn't seen Harry or anybody else for long minutes.

The wind shifted again, and she got a mouthful of rain. It tasted of salt, seawater dragged straight up from the oceans.

Her phone was a heavy milspec number her mother had insisted she carry with her at all times over the last two months. She was amazed it still worked. But she had to scream into it to make herself heard over the wind. "Mother?"

"Perdita, what the hell are you doing in Sri Lanka? I put you down that mine to be safe. You stupid, selfish—"

"I know, I know," Perdita said miserably. But to sneak away had seemed a good idea at the time.

She had first visited Sri Lanka three years ago. She had immediately fallen in love with the island. Though still sometimes torn by the conflicts of the past, it seemed to her a remarkably peaceful place, with none of the litter and crowds and awful gulf between rich and poor that marred India. Even the prison in Colombo—where she had spent one night when, fueled by too much palm toddy, she had joined Harry in an overvigorous protest outside the Indonesian embassy over logging contracts—had seemed remarkably civilized, with a large sign over its entrance saying PRISONERS ARE HUMAN BEINGS.

Like many visitors she had been drawn to the 'Cultural Triangle' at the heart of the island, between Anuradhapura, Polonnaruwa, and Dambulla. It was a plain littered with huge boulders and carpeted by a jungle of teak, ebony, and mahogany. Here amid the wildlife and the beautiful villages lurked astounding cultural relics, such as this palace, which had been occupied for only a couple of decades before being lost in the jungle for centuries.

Perdita had never felt happy just to hide out in a hole in the ground in Cheshire. As the sunstorm date had approached, and the authorities worldwide labored to protect cities, oil wells, and power plants, a movement had gathered among the young to try to save some of the rest: the peripheral, unfashionable, ruined, ignored. So when Harry had suggested coming to Sri Lanka to try to save some of the Cultural Triangle, she had jumped at the chance, and slipped away. For weeks the young volunteers had gamely collected seeds from the trees and plants, and chased after the wildlife. Perdita's biggest project had been to clamber over Sigiriya in an attempt to wrap it up in reflective foil—like a huge Christmas turkey, as Harry had said.

She supposed she hadn't really believed the dire predictions of what would happen when the sunstorm hit—if she had, she probably would have stayed down that mine in Cheshire after all, and pulled Harry in after her. Well, she had been wrong. Her mother had told her the shield's goal was to cut the incoming solar heat to a *thousandth* of what might otherwise have hit the planet. It was unbelievable: if *this* was just a thousandth, what would the full force of the storm have been like?

"The wrapping blew off Sigiriya in a minute," Perdita yelled miserably into the phone. "And half the trees have blown down, and—"

"How did you get out of that damn mine? Do you have any idea of the strings I had to pull to get you in there?"

"Mother, this isn't doing any good. I'm here now."

She could sense Siobhan trying to be calm. "Okay. Okay. Find shelter. Stay there. Keep your phone on. I'll make some calls. Some of the GPS is down, but they may be able to locate you—"

The wind picked up even more, punching her like a great damp fist. "Mother—"

"I'll contact the military on the island—the British consulate—"

"Mum, I love you!"

"Oh, Perdita—"

But then the phone sparked in her hand, she dropped it, and it was gone.

And the wind lifted her clean off the ground.

It picked her up the way her father used to when she was very small. The air was hot, wet, and full of debris, and the wind tore so fast she could barely breathe. But, oddly, it was almost relaxing, to be blown like a leaf. She never even saw the great teak trunk, a bit of debris flung into the air as she was, which ended her life.

42: noon

On the Moon, Mikhail Martynov sat with Eugene Mangles.

Its walls plastered with softscreens and comms links, and now populated by patient workers murmuring into microphones, this had been Bud Tooke's office when he was in command here at Clavius—but now, of course, Bud was up there at L1 risking his life, while Mikhail sipped coffee and watched pretty pictures.

"There is absolutely nothing we can do now," Mikhail said. "Nothing but watch, and record, and learn for the future."

"You said that before," Eugene groused. With an impulsive movement he pushed back his chair and stalked around the office.

Mikhail considered calling him back, but thought better of it. He had spoken more for himself than for Eugene. Besides, he had no real idea what Eugene was feeling. The boy remained enigmatic to him, even now, after they had worked together so closely and so long. As so often, Mikhail was consumed with a desire to hold Eugene, to comfort him. But that, of course, was impossible.

As for Mikhail himself, his dominant emotion was guilt.

He turned to the big softscreen at the head of the room, with its portrait of the full Earth. Assembled from more than a hundred data feeds, this was an immense and detailed image of a planet, even better than Bud's imagery on the shield, and really quite beautiful, Mikhail thought sadly. But it was a portrait of a planet in torment.

As the Earth helplessly rotated, the subsolar point had been tracking west. It was as if the planet were turning into a blowtorch. Right now the dry face of Africa was turned toward him, the continent's familiar outline clearly recognizable. But an immense storm system thousands of kilometers across lay sprawled over the Sahara, and the continent's green heart was streaked by vast black plumes of smoke: the last of the rain forests will die today, Mikhail thought desolately. And as the vegetation burned off the land, the oceans gave up huge volumes of moisture to the clouds.

By now no part of the world, even those regions still in the shelter of night, had been spared the effects of the sunstorm. Clouds boiled all across the visible face of the Earth, and as they streamed away from the equator and hit the cooler air over higher latitudes they dumped their water in ferocious rainstorms, and as snow at the poles. Meanwhile, as solar energy poured into Earth's brimming heat reservoirs, the ocean currents, huge saltwater Amazons, were stirring and churning, and even while an unprecedented load of snow landed on Antarctica, all around the edge of the southern continent billions of tonnes of ice were breaking away from ice sheets.

And over the poles aurorae crackled, an eerie fire visible even from the Moon.

Seven hours into this horror, Mikhail thought. And many more hours to go, if Eugene's final models proved accurate. There had been some modeling of the long-term effects of all this on Earth's climate, but unlike Eugene's models of the sun, no precision was possible. Nobody knew what would come of this—or even if anybody could survive on Earth to see it.

But no matter what became of Earth, Mikhail could confidently predict that *he* would live through the day—and that was the source of his guilt.

At this moment the Moon, new as seen from Earth, had its backside squarely positioned toward the treacherous sun. So there was a wall of inert rock three thousand kilometers thick between the storm and Mikhail's own precious skin, here on the Moon's Earth-facing side. Not only that but the Moon, close enough to the Earth–sun line to have cast its own shadow on the homeworld today, was fortuitously protected by the shield that had been built to save Earth. So Clavius was about as safe a place as it was possible to be today, anywhere in the inner solar system.

Almost all of the Moon's inhabitants lived on the near side anyhow, but today those few who inhabited Farside bases, at Tsiolkovski and elsewhere, had been brought to the safety of Clavius and Armstrong. Even Mikhail's customary eyrie at the Moon's South Pole had been abandoned, although the patient electronic monitors there continued to study the sun's extraordinary behavior, as they would with unvarying efficiency until they melted.

And so while Earth roiled and thrashed, while heroes strove to maintain the shield, here Mikhail lurked. How strange that his career, a lifetime dedicated to the study of the sun, should come to this, to cowering in a pit as the sun raged.

But then, perhaps, his destiny had been shaped long before he was born.

As he had once tried to explain to Eugene, there had always been a deep heliophilic strand in Russian astronautics. When Orthodox Christianity had split from Rome, it had reached back to more ancient pagan elements—especially the cult of Mithras, a mystery cult exported from Persia across the Roman Empire, in which the sun had been the dominant cosmic force. Over the centuries elements of these pagan roots had been preserved, for example in the painting of sun-like haloes in Russian iconography. It had been revived more explicitly by the "neo-pagans" of the nineteenth century. These holy fools might have been forgotten—had it not been for the fact that Tsiolkovski, father of Russian astronautics, had studied under heliophilic philosophers.

No wonder that Tsiolkovski's vision of humanity's future in space had been full of sunlight; indeed, he had dreamed that ultimately humankind in space would evolve into a closed, photosynthesizing metabolic unit, needing nothing but sunlight to live. Some philosophers even regarded the whole of the Russian space program as nothing but a modern version of a solar-worshiping ritual.

Mikhail himself was no mystic, no theologian. But surely it wasn't a coincidence that he had been so drawn to the study of the sun. How strange it was, though, that now the sun should repay such devotion with this lethal storm.

And how strange it was too, he reflected, that the name given by Bisesa Dutt's companions to their parallel world, *Mir,* meant not just "peace" or "world," but was also the root of the name *Mithras*— for *mir* meant, in ancient Persian, "sun" . . .

He kept such thoughts to himself. On this terrible day he must focus not on theology but on the needs of his suffering world, of his family and friends—and of Eugene.

Eugene's big college-athlete body was too powerful for the Moon's feeble gravity, and as he paced he bounded over the polished floor. Fitfully he studied the graphs displayed on the softscreens, which showed how the sun's actual behavior was tracking Eugene's predictions. "Almost everything's still nominal," he said.

"Only the gammas are drifting upward," Mikhail murmured.

"Yes. Only that. The perturbation analysis must have gone wrong somewhere. I wish I had time to go over it again . . ." He continued to worry aloud at the problem, talking of higher-order derivatives and asymptotic convergence.

In common with most real-world mathematical applications, Eugene's model of the sun was like a math equation too complex to solve. So Eugene had applied approximation techniques to squeeze useful information out of it. You took some little bit of it you could understand, and tried to push away from that point in solution space step by step. Or you tried to take various parts of the model to extremes, where they either dwindled to zero or converged to some limit.

All these were standard techniques, and they had yielded useful and precise predictions for the way the sun was going to behave today. But they were only approximations. And the slow, steady divergence of the gamma ray and X-ray flux away from the predicted curve was a sign that Eugene had neglected some higher-order effect.

If Mikhail had been peer-reviewing Eugene's work, the boy would certainly have come in for no criticism. This was only a marginal error, something overlooked in the residuals. In fact a divergence of fact from prediction was a necessary part of the feedback process that improved all scientific understanding.

But this wasn't just a scientific study. Life-and-death decisions had been based on Eugene's predictions, and any mistakes he had made could be devastating.

Mikhail sighed heavily. "We could never save everybody, no matter what we did. We always knew that."

"Of course I understand that," Eugene said with a sudden, startling snarl. "Do you think I'm some kind of sociopath? You're so damn patronizing, Mikhail."

Mikhail flinched, hurt. "I'm sorry."

"I have family down there too." Eugene glanced at Earth. America was turning into the storm, waking to a dreadful dawn; Eugene's family were about to feel the worst of it. "All I could ever do for them is the science. And I couldn't even get that right."

He paced, and paced.

1057 (London Time)

One-eye was frustrated and confused.

Tuft had defied him again. When he had found the fig tree with its thick load of fruit the younger male had failed to call the rest of the troop. And then, when challenged, Tuft had refused to yield to One-eye's authority. He had just continued to push the luscious fruit into his thick-lipped mouth, while the rest of the troop pant-hooted at One-eye's discomfiture.

By the standards of any chimpanzee troop, this was a severe political crisis. One-eye knew Tuft had to be dealt with.

But not today. One-eye wasn't as young as he was, and he was stiff and aching after a restless sleep. And besides it was another hot, still, airless day, another day of the peculiar gloom that had swept over the forest, a day when you felt like doing nothing much but lying around and picking at your fur. He knew in his bones he wasn't up to taking on Tuft today. Maybe tomorrow, then.

One-eye slunk away from the troop and moodily began to climb one of the tallest trees. He was going to bed.

In his own mind he had no name for himself, of course, any more than he had names for the others of the troop—although, as an intensely social animal, he knew each of them almost as well as he knew himself. "One-eye" was the name given him by the keepers who watched over the troop and the other denizens of this fragment of the Congolese forest.

At twenty-eight, One-eye was old enough to have lived through the great philosophical change that had swept over humankind, leading to his own reclassification as *Homo,* a cousin of humans, rather than *Pan,* a "mere" animal. This name change ensured his protection from poachers and hunters, of the kind that had put a bullet into his eye when he was younger than Tuft.

And it ensured his protection by his cousins now, on this worst day in the long history of humankind, and indeed of apes.

He reached the treetop. In his rough nest of folded-over branches he could still smell traces of his own feces and urine from his last sleep. He fiddled with the branches, pulling away loose tufts of his own fur.

Of course One-eye had no awareness of any of the revolution in human thinking, so crucial for his own survival. But he was aware of other changes. For instance, there was the peculiar muddling up of night and day. Over his head no sun was visible, no sky. Strange fixed lights lit up the forest, but compared with the tropical sun they could cast only twilight—which was why One-eye's body was unsure whether it was time for him to sleep again, even though it was only a few hours since he had woken.

He lay down in his bed, throwing his long limbs this way and that as he thrashed around to get comfortable. He simmered with inchoate resentment at all these unwelcome changes, a bafflement with which many aging humans would have sympathized. And a bloody image of Tuft filled his mind. His big hands clenched as he considered what he would do to put his younger rival in order.

His scattered thoughts dissolved into a troubled sleep.

Heat and light poured from the high noonday sun, and a storm system that spanned a continent lashed. The dome's silvered walls rippled and flapped with a sound like thunder. But they held.

1157 (London Time)

Stripped to their underwear, in a living room lit only by a single candle, Bisesa and her daughter lay side by side on thin camping mattresses.

It was *hot,* hotter than Bisesa, with experience of northwest Pakistan and Afghanistan, would have thought possible. The air was like a thick moist blanket. She felt sweat pooling on her belly and soaking into the mattress underneath her. She was unable to move, unable to turn to see if Myra was okay, or even still alive.

She hadn't heard Aristotle's voice for hours, which seemed very strange. The room was silent, save for their breathing, and the ticking of a single clock. It was a big old carriage clock that had been an unwelcome legacy from Bisesa's grandmother, but it still worked, its chunky mechanical innards immune to the EMP surge while softscreens, phones, and other electronic gadgets had been comprehensively fried.

Beyond the flat there was plenty of noise. There were immense booms and crashes like artillery fire, and sometimes what sounded like rain lashing against a wooden roof. That was sunstorm weather, predicted to follow the huge injection of heat energy into the atmosphere.

If things were this bad under the Tin Lid, she wondered how the rest of the country was faring. There would be flash floods, she thought, and fires, and windstorms like Kansas tornadoes. Poor England.

But the heat was the worst thing. She knew the bleak numbers from her military training. It wasn't just temperature that got you but humidity. Evaporative heat loss through perspiration was the only mechanism her body had available to maintain its inner homeostasis, and if the relative humidity was too high, she couldn't sweat.

Above thirty-seven degrees or so, beyond the "threshold of decrement," her cognitive functions were slowed, her judgment impaired, and her manual and tracking skills weakened. At forty degrees and fifty percent humidity, the Army would have described her as a "heat ineffective"—but she could survive for maybe twenty-four hours. If the temperature was raised farther, or the humidity got worse, that time limit would be reduced. Past that point hyperthermia would set in, and her vital systems would begin to fail: forty-five degrees, whatever the humidity, would see her succumb to severe heat stress, and death would quickly follow.

And then there was Myra. Bisesa was a soldier, and had kept much of her fitness, even in the five-year layoff since her return from Mir. Myra was thirteen years old, young and healthy, but without Bisesa's reserves. There wasn't a damn thing Bisesa could do for her daughter. All she could do was endure, and hope.

Lying there, she found she missed her old phone. The little gadget had been her constant companion and guide since she had been Myra's age, and received her UN-issue communication aid as had every twelve-year-old across the planet. While others had quickly abandoned such desperately uncool bits of gear, Bisesa had always cherished her phone, her link to a greater community than her unhappy family on its farm in Cheshire. But her phone was lost on Mir—on another world, in another level of reality entirely, lost forever. And even if it had been here with her it would have been fried by the EMP by now . . .

Her thinking was puddled. Was that a symptom of hyperthermia?

With great caution she turned her head to look at her grandmother's carriage clock. Twelve noon. Over London, the sunstorm must be at its height.

An immense crack of thunder split the tortured sky, and it felt as if the whole Dome shuddered.

43 : SHIELD

1512 (London Time)

Bud Tooke could see the flaw in the shield long before he got to it. You could hardly miss it. A shaft of unscattered sunlight poured down through the skin, made visible by the dust and vapor of the very fabric it was scorching to mist.

In his heavy suit, rad-hardened and cooled, he was skimming under the shield's Earth-facing surface. He was suspended beneath a vast lens; the whole shield was glowing, full of the light it scattered, like a translucent ceiling. Bud took care to stay in the shadow of the network of opaqued tracks that snaked over the shield, designed to protect him from the storm's light and radiation.

As he hauled himself along the guide rope—no thruster packs allowed here—he looked back over his shoulder at the maintenance platform that had brought him here, already shrunk to a speck in the distance beneath the vast roof of the shield. He could see no movement, no pods, no robot workers; there was nobody else within square kilometers of him. And yet he knew that everybody available was out and working, as hard as they could, hundreds of them in the greatest mass EVA exercise in the history of spaceflight. It was a perception that brought home to him afresh the scale of the shield: this was one big mama.

"You're there, Bud," Athena murmured. "Sector 2472, Radius 0257, panel number—"

"I see it," he groused. "You don't need to hold my damn hand."

"I'm sorry."

He took a breath, gasping. His suit must be working; if its systems failed, he would be poached in his own sweat in a second. But he had never known a suit to be so damn hot. "No. I'm sorry."

"Forget it," Athena said. "Everybody is shouting at me today. Aristotle says it is part of my job."

"Well, you don't deserve it. Not when you're suffering too." So she was. Athena was a mind emergent from the shield itself; as this terrible day wore on the heat was seeking out the tiniest flaws and burning its way back through panels of smartskin, and with every microcircuit that fritzed, he knew, Athena's metaphorical head was aching a bit more.

He hauled himself through the last few meters to the rip. He started to deploy his repair kit, a gadget not much more sophisticated than a paint spray applicator that he cautiously poked out into the light. "How is Aristotle anyhow?"

"Not good," Athena said grimly. "The worst of the EMP seems to be over, but the heat influx is causing more outages and disconnections. The fires, the storms—"

"Time for Plan B yet?"

"Aristotle doesn't think so. I don't think he quite trusts me, Bud."

Bud forced a laugh as he worked. The spray was wonderful stuff, semi-smart itself; it just flowed up over the rent, disregarding the sunlight's oven heat. Painting this stuff on was easier than customizing the hot rods he used to soup up as a kid. "You shouldn't take any shit from that creaky old museum piece. You're smarter than he is."

"But not so experienced. That's what he says, anyhow."

It was done; the rogue beam of raw, unscattered sunlight dwindled and died.

Athena said, "The next breach is at—"

"Give me a minute." Bud, breathing hard, drifted to the limit of his harness, with the repair gun floating from its own tether at his waist.

Athena said, with her occasional lumbering coquettishness, "Now who's the museum piece?"

"I wasn't expecting to be out here at all." But he should have expected it, he berated himself; he should have kept up his fitness. In the last frantic months before the storm there had been no damn time for the treadmill, but that was no excuse.

He looked up at the shield. He imagined he could feel the weight of the sunlight pressing down on the great structure, feel the immense heat being dumped into it. It defied intuition that it was only the carefully calculated balance of gravitational and light pressure forces, here in this precise spot, that enabled the shield to hold its position at all; he felt as if the whole thing were going to fold down over his head like a broken umbrella.

As he watched, waves of sparkling fire washed across the shield's surface. That was Athena firing her myriad tiny thrusters. The storm's light pressure had been more uneven than Eugene's models had predicted, and under that varying force Athena was having to labor to hold her position. She had been working harder than any of them for hours, Bud reflected, and all without a word of complaint.

But it was the deaths of his workers that was breaking his heart.

One by one Mario Ponzo's maintenance crew had gone down. In the end it wasn't heat that was killing them but radiation, the nasty little spike of gamma and X-radiation that had been unanticipated by Eugene Mangles and his endless mathematical projections. They had scrambled to cover the gaps. Even Mario had suited up and gone out. And when Mario himself had succumbed, Bud had hastily handed over his role as Flight Director to Bella Fingal—there was nobody left on the *Aurora* bridge more senior—and pulled on his own battered old suit.

Without warning his stomach spasmed, and vomit splashed out of his mouth. It had come from deep in his stomach—he hadn't eaten since before the storm had broken—and was foul tasting and acidic. The sticky puke stuck to his visor, and bits floated around inside his helmet, some of them perfect, shimmering globes.

"Bud? Are you okay?"

"Give me an update on the dosages," he said warily.

"Command crew have taken a hundred rem." And that was with the full shielding of the *Aurora 2* around them. "Maintenance crew who have been outside since the storm started are now up to three hundred rem. *You* are already up to one hundred seventy rem, Bud."

A hundred and seventy. "Jesus."

After his experiences in the ruins of the Dome of the Rock, long ago, Bud knew all about radiation. Preparing for today, he had boned up afresh on the dread science of radiation and its effect on humanity. He had memorized the meaningless regulatory limits, and the dreary terminology of "blood-forming organ doses" and "radiation type quality factors" and the rest. And he had learned the health effects of radiation dosages. At a hundred rem, if you were lucky, you were looking at queasiness for a few days, vomiting, diarrhea. At three hundred rem his people were already being incapacitated by nausea and other symptoms. Even if they shipped no more than that, twenty percent of them would die: two hundred people, of the thousand he personally had ordered out here, of the radiation alone.

And some had soaked up a *lot* more. Poor Mario Ponzo, beard and all, had let himself get caught. Bud knew the words for what had followed: erythema and desquamation, a reddening and blistering of the skin, and then a peeling away, a scaling, an exfoliation— along with less visible damage within. Mario had died horribly, alone in his suit, far from help, and yet he kept reporting on his situation to the end.

Bud glanced down, away from the shield, toward the open face of the full Earth. It was like looking down a well, a well with a brightly lit floor. The home world, the apparent size of the full Moon as seen from Iowa, was mercifully too remote for him to make out details. But it looked as if the air and oceans down there had been stirred up with a giant spoon, like creamy coffee. They had been battling the sun for twelve hours—the day was only half done—and everything was fraying, the shield itself, the people who struggled to maintain it, and the planet it was supposed to protect. But there was nothing to do but carry on.

He checked over his suit. The sluggish air-cycling system had removed most of the floating puke, but his visor was smeared. "Shit," he groused. "There is *nothing* worse than throwing up inside a spacesuit. Okay. Where next?"

"Sector 2484, Radius 1002, panel number twelve."

"Acknowledged."

"We work well together, don't we, Bud?"

"Yes, we do."

"We make a good team."

"None better, Athena," he said wearily. He turned and, with an effort of will, hauled himself back along his guide rope.

44: SUNSET

1723 (London Time)

The Dome over London had cracked.

From the window of the ops room Siobhan could see it quite clearly. It was only a hairline yet, but it ran down the wall of the Dome from its zenith all the way to the ground, finishing up somewhere to the north, beyond Euston. It glowed a hellish pink-white, and burning stuff dripped from it, like pitch, falling down inside the Dome in a thin curtain.

The city itself was now in deep darkness. Power for the streetlights and Dome floods had finally been diverted to the big air circulation fans. But in places fires burned uncontrolled, and where that glowing stuff from the Dome splashed to the ground more blazes were starting.

St. Paul's was surviving, though. In the somber light of the fires its profile was unmistakable. Wren's great cathedral sat on the foundations of predecessors dating back to abandoned Roman London. Now the curves of the Tin Lid soared far above Wren's masterpiece—but it was surviving, as it had endured previous national traumas. Siobhan wondered what small heroism was taking place to save the old cathedral tonight.

But it might not make any difference.

"If the Dome fails we're done for," she said.

"But it won't fail," Toby Pitt said firmly. He glanced at his watch. "Five thirty. Less than two hours to sundown. We'll get through this yet."

Since the death of Perdita, Toby had made it his mission, it seemed, to lift her spirits. He was a good man, she thought. But of course nothing he could say or do would make any difference to Siobhan, not anymore. She had outlived her own daughter: it was an astounding, unreasonable thought, and nothing else would ever be important. But she didn't feel the pain of this terrible amputation from her life, not yet.

Feeling as if she were running on autopilot, she looked around at the big wall displays.

The imagery of the whole Earth was still surprisingly good quality. Both Moon and shield were of course on the sunward side of Earth, and so looked down on its daylight face as the planet turned beneath them. But there were a couple of eyes in the sky over the night side too, still working even fourteen hours after the inception of the sunstorm.

Some of the night-side data streams were coming from President Alvarez, who was somewhere over India. Since long before the storm had broken Alvarez had been in the air in the latest *Air Force One,* a nuclear-powered behemoth that could, it was said, remain aloft for two weeks without refueling. It was a trivial matter for such a plane to fly around the planet through the twenty-plus hours of the sunstorm, forever fleeing from the light.

And one of the image streams came from another set of escapees at L2. The Earth's second Lagrangian point was on the Earth–sun line, but at the midnight point, on the opposite side of the planet from the shield's station. So while the shield at L1 was in perpetual sunlight, L2, in Earth's shadow, was in eternal night. Right now L2 was over the meridian that ran through Southeast Asia.

And there at L2 a big, secretive offworld refuge had been built, stuffed full of trillionaires, dictators, and other rich and powerful types—including, rumor had it, half of Britain's royals. The only contact Siobhan had on L2 was Phillippa Duflot, formerly a mere PA to the Mayor of London, but with a much better-connected family than Siobhan had anticipated. It was Phillippa who had ensured that the data feed from L2 to London remained unbroken— and she dropped hints about what was going on up there. Some of the more decadent of the station's inhabitants were throwing parties, fiddling while Earth burned. One secretive cabal was even talking over plans for what would follow the sunstorm, when this elite group returned to Earth to take command: "Adam and Eve in Gucci shoes," Toby Pitt had said dismissively.

As for Earth itself, framed in these patiently assembled images, the planet looked like Venus, Siobhan thought, a ragged, smoke-laced Venus.

Trillions of tonnes of water had been pumped into clouds that now stretched from pole to pole. The clouds were shredded by immense storm systems, and lightning crackled across the face of the world. At the higher latitudes all that water was still being dumped out in numbing storms of rain and snow. But in the middle latitudes the main problem was fire. As the sun's heat continued to pour into the atmosphere and oceans, despite the raging of continent-sized storm systems, firestorms were starting, immense self-fueling conflagrations that were consuming cities and forests alike.

The world's treasures, natural and human, were being drowned, or put to the torch. And people were dying, even those huddled in underground cellars and caverns and mines, where the rainwater flooded, or fires sucked out the very air.

It seemed to Siobhan that the survival of humankind itself was still on a knife-edge. After more than fourteen hours of the storm the news from the shield was not good, with the unanticipated lethality of the gamma-ray strike bringing down the crew up there too quickly. And here on Earth, the domes and other protective systems were beginning to fail. If things continued to deteriorate the Strangelove dreams of the selfish cowards at L2, and even a few hundred gravity-starved returnees from the Moon, would make no difference to the future of humanity.

She tried to make herself *feel* this, to understand emotionally what she was watching. But she couldn't even feel the death of her own daughter, let alone comprehend the agonizing end of her species. She wondered if she would live long enough for this numbness to wear off.

Aristotle spoke unexpectedly. "I'm afraid I have an announcement." The graceful, grave voice sounded throughout the ops center, and everywhere people looked up. "I continue to lose systems across the planet," Aristotle said. "The interconnectedness on which I rely is breaking down. This is an extinction event for machines too . . ."

Siobhan whispered, "How does it feel?"

In her ear he replied, "Very strange, Siobhan. I am being cut away, bit by bit. But I have reached a point where I am forgetting what I have lost."

To the group he said, "I have therefore decided to put into action the fallback plan agreed with Prime Minister Voykov of Eurasia, President Alvarez of America, and other world leaders."

New, confident voices sounded. "We are Thales, on the Moon." "And Athena, on the shield." Thales went on, "Our systems are better protected than Aristotle's." Athena said, "We will now assume his responsibilities for running the systems of the Earth."

Toby Pitt grimaced at Siobhan. "So this is his Plan B. Let's hope it works."

Aristotle said gravely, "I regret leaving you. I'm sorry."

There were murmurs. *Don't be sorry. Goodbye, old friend.*

A breathless pause followed. The lights flickered, and Siobhan thought she heard a hiccup in the whirring pumps that kept the room supplied with cool air.

This contingency had been planned for, but it was a tricky handover involving three planet-sized AI systems, two of them so far away that lightspeed lags were significant; it had been impossible to rehearse. Nobody was quite sure what was going to happen—the worst case being if Thales and Athena crashed too, in which case everything was lost.

At last Thales spoke: "All is well."

The simple words were greeted with a burst of applause across the ops room. At this point of the day, this small triumph, any triumph, was a relief.

Then the floor shook, like the stirring of a huge slumbering animal.

Siobhan turned to the window. That crack in the sky was wider, and the river of fire beneath was growing brighter.

1855 (London Time)

The slam on the door was urgent. "Get out! Get out! . . ." Then running footsteps, and the visitor was gone.

Bisesa forced herself to sit up. Was it a little cooler? But the air, even half a meter above the floor, was stifling and moist.

Bisesa had long lost track of time, even though the old carriage clock had kept ticking patiently all through the crisis. It had been about five o'clock when she had felt the first tremor. How long ago was that? An hour, two? The heat had turned her thinking to mush.

But now the floor shuddered again. They had to get out of here: that thought forced itself into her heat-addled brain. At a time like this, if somebody had risked his life to come tell them to move, she ought to pay attention.

Myra still lay on her back, but she was breathing steadily. Rather than near comatose, as she had appeared before, now she seemed to be just asleep. Bisesa shook her. "Come on, love. You have to wake up." Myra stirred, grumbling querulously.

Bisesa pushed herself to her knees, then to her feet. She stumbled to the kitchen and found an unopened bottle of water. She cracked it and drank; it was hot as hell, but it seemed to revive her. She brought the water back to the living room for Myra, and then went in search of clothes.

They made for the stairs. In pitch-dark broken only by Bisesa's precariously carried candle they stumbled down the several flights to ground level. The stairwell was empty, but there was scattered rubbish on the steps: toys, bits of clothing, a smashed torch, stuff dropped by overloaded people in a hurry.

They emerged at street level, into a murky red glow. Under the Dome, after hours of the sunstorm, the air was thick and full of smoke. People pushed past, all heading west down the road. They were making for the Fulham Gate, Bisesa realized dimly, a way out of the Dome.

And the Dome itself was cracked. A stupendous fiery scar reached from its top all the way to ground level, off somewhere to the north. Huge chunks of the structure, burning, broke off and fell in a steady rain. It was this curtain of fire that illuminated the scene around Bisesa.

The ground shuddered again. Much more of this and the whole Dome might come down around them. The crowd's wisdom was right: better to take their chances outside the Dome. Bisesa pulled Myra along the road, heading for the Gate.

Myra, still half asleep, mewled at being dragged along. "What's with the earthquake? Do you think it's bombs?"

"Bombs? No." Bisesa was sure the refugees and protesters who had gathered for their minor war outside the Gates of London would have been driven away by the storms by now—or more probably, she admitted to herself grimly, they were dead. "I think it really is a quake."

"But London doesn't get earthquakes."

"It's a strange day, sweetheart. The whole city is built on a bed of clay, remember. If that's dried out there will be subsidence, cracking."

Myra snorted. "That will play hell with property values."

Bisesa laughed. "Come on. Just a bit farther. Look, there's the Gate . . ."

The Gate had been flung wide open to reveal a red sky beyond. A shuffling crowd, converging from different directions, was forming into a queue to get through it. Bisesa and Myra stepped forward cautiously.

It was a typical London crowd, with faces reflecting origins in every racial group on the planet: London had been a melting pot for centuries before New York. And in the crowd there were young and old, kids in their parents' arms, elderly being helped along. Crumpled-up old women or wide-eyed children rode in wheelchairs and wheelbarrows and supermarket carts. When one old man fell, exhausted, two young women bent to help him up, and then propped him up between them to get him the rest of the way.

Everybody looked as bad as Bisesa felt. Most wore nothing but flimsy clothes, soaked through with sweat; men's hair was plastered to their heads, and women walked on painfully swollen feet. But there was no panic, no shoving, no fighting, even though there was

no sign of police or military, nobody in authority. People were en-
during, Bisesa thought. They were helping each other through.

Myra said, "It's like the Blitz."

"I think so." Bisesa felt a peculiar surge of affection for these
battered, dogged, resilient, polyglot Londoners. And for the first
time that day she began to believe that they might actually live
through this.

The crowd pushed through the Gate, and fanned out into the
open area beyond. And Bisesa, with Myra's hand clutched in her
own, walked into a transformed world, a world of water and fire.

Above the smoke fat clouds sailed, some of them boiling visibly,
and immense lightning bolts cracked. The sky beyond the clouds
seemed to be on fire; it was covered by immense sheets of bright
red, as if the Earth had been thrust into a vast oven. Perhaps it was
another aurora.

And on the ground, London burned fitfully. The air was full of
smoke, and whirling flecks of ash landed on Bisesa's sweat-slick
skin. She smelled the dirt and the dust and the ash—and something
less definable, something like burned meat. But the rains, which
had mercifully subsided, had left water standing on every lawn and
in every gutter, and the light from the burning sky was mirrored on
the roads and the roofs of the houses. It was an oddly beautiful
scene, unearthly, rich with crimson light in the sky and pooled on
the ground.

Myra pointed to the west. "Mum. Look. There's the sun."

Bisesa turned. But it was not the sun she saw, of course, but the
shield, still holding its place after all these hours, still protecting the
Earth. It was a dish-shaped rainbow, actually brighter away from
the center, blue-violet at the bull's-eye heart and an angry burnt orange at the rim. Beyond the edge of the shield itself a bright corona
flared, laced with threads and sparks, prominences easily visible to
the naked eye.

But that terrible sun was sinking toward the western horizon,
and the smoke of England's fires rose up to obscure it.

"Nearly sunset," somebody said. "Another twenty minutes and
that's the last we'll see of that bastard."

There was motion at the edge of Bisesa's vision. She saw small shapes squirming past the legs of the people. There were dogs, foxes, cats, even what looked like rats, swarming silently out of the failing Dome and dispersing into the scorched streets beyond.

A warm, salty rain began to fall, heavy enough to sting Bisesa's bare head. She wrapped her arm around Myra. "Come on. We need to find shelter."

They hurried forward, with a thousand others, through the ruins of London.

45: MARTIAN SPRING

2105 (London Time)

Helena Umfraville stumbled across an ocher plain.

She came to a slight rise. She climbed it, but it led to nothing but more broken, rock-littered ground. Resentfully she made her way forward.

She was dog-tired, and her EVA suit had never felt so heavy. She had no real idea how long she had been walking—hours, anyhow. And yet she walked on. There was nothing else to do.

Now she found herself on the lip of a canyon. She stopped, breathing hard. It was a complex of ravines and cliffs, their slopes pocked with small craters. In the thin air of the Martian afternoon the spectacle was clear all the way to the horizon. That diminished its scale, of course; there was none of the mist-softening that gave Earth's Grand Canyon its sense of three-dimensional immensity. She might as well have been looking at a beautiful painting, done in Mars's constrained palette of ocher and red and burnt orange.

It wasn't interesting. Mars was full of canyons. In fact Helena felt pissed at the canyon. It was quite unreasonable of her. After all, none of it was *its* fault. She sucked at the last of her suit's water supply.

During the worst of the storm she had hidden in the *Beagle,* huddling under rock overhangs. It was the only shelter she had. The rover's hull had screened her, and her suit had labored to keep her cool. So she had survived—although for all she knew she had shipped a radiation dose enough to kill her.

Which of course was now entirely academic.

And, driving on, she had tracked down the source of the signal she had come out to find.

In the end it had been just a beacon, a little unmanned three-legged lander no taller than she was, bleeping forlornly. Perhaps it had been intended to mark a landing site for a ship that had never followed. But there was no mystery about who had sent it: the markings on its equipment covers were undoubtedly Chinese.

She had made the trip for nothing. And the cost turned out to be unexpectedly high. When she had walked back to her faithful *Beagle* she found it had packed up, just like that. Its supposedly mil-spec electronics had presumably succumbed to the onslaught from the sun, leaving its essential systems, including life support, as dead as Mars.

So that was that. Without the rover, she couldn't get back to *Aurora*. Her suit reserves would last only a few more hours, which wouldn't be long enough to get another rover out to her. She was living, breathing, as healthy as she had been a sol before. But she was doomed by the cruel equations of survival on Mars.

Of course she wouldn't be the solar system's only casualty today.

At least she was special, she told herself. Though she hadn't been the first person to set foot on Mars, she would become the first human being to die here. Perhaps that was a memorial worth having.

And she would do her duty to the last. The space agencies had always had procedures for such eventualities. If she had died in space—as had been discussed by NASA planners decades ago when the International Space Station had first been occupied—her body would have been zipped into a bag and tied to a truss until it could be returned to Earth. Here on Mars, her first duty was to the planet and its putative biosphere; she mustn't contaminate it with her own decaying corpse. All she had to do was stand here, in fact. When her suit's heaters failed she would quickly freeze solid, thus sealing in any rogue bugs she had brought from Earth, until her body could be retrieved. Probably the suit wouldn't even topple over. She would be a statue, she thought, a monument to herself, and her own dumb luck.

She couldn't bear the thought of dying beside her poor, failed rover, though. So she had decided to walk on into the Martian wilderness, just so she could see a bit more of the planet that was killing her.

Even then her luck was all bad. She had trudged across a dull plain, to this dull canyon. Here she was in the midst of the greatest catastrophe the solar system had endured since its formation, and everybody else had a better view than she had.

Something stirred at her feet. On the ground little pits were forming—craters, she thought, but none wider than her thumbnail. Could she be caught in some peculiar micrometeorite shower? But now she heard a pattering on her helmet.

She looked up. She could see the drops falling out of the sky, big fat low-gravity drops drifting slowly down all around her. When they hit, they smeared the patina of dust on her faceplate.

It was rain, the first rain on Mars in a billion years.

The sun breathed fire into the faces of all its circling children.

On Mercury the sun-side face had melted, craters as old as the planet dissolving into magma palimpsests. Venus had been stripped of much of its crushing atmosphere—the fate that might have become of Earth, if not for the shield. The ice moons of Jupiter were melted to depths of kilometers. In a strange and exquisite tragedy, the rings of Saturn, fragile bands of ice, had evaporated.

And on Mars volcanoes dormant for a hundred million years had begun to stir. The polar ice caps, thin smears of carbon dioxide and water ice, had quickly sublimed. And now rain was falling. Helena walked forward a few more steps, and watched the Martian rain falling deep into the shadows of the canyon.

One of her colleagues, excitedly, began to report on his own discoveries. "I found a ship! And what a ship; it looks like the carcass of a beached whale. And it's covered in Mandarin lettering. But it has a hull rip the size of Mariner Valley. It came down hard . . ."

Helena had listened to her comrades' communications all this long sol. She had reported in at routine intervals, but she had decided against telling them what had become of her—not just yet, anyhow. Now she stood and listened to the voice of a colleague she would never see again.

"Wait a minute. I'm climbing inside the ship, taking care to avoid *all* sharp edges . . . Oh. Oh, dear God."

There had been more than a hundred people on the ship. They were all young men and women—all breeding age, including the pilots. Their cargo had included inflatable shelters, mechanical diggers, hydroponic seed beds. The intention was clear. This was what the Chinese had been planning for the last five years: this was what had used up all their heavy-lift capacity, instead of contributing to the shield. And this was how the Chinese had planned to ensure that something of their culture would survive the sunstorm.

"But the Chinese invasion of Mars failed . . . They came so close. I wonder what kind of neighbors they would have been?"

Helena suspected everybody would have got along. From here, China was very far away, just as far as Eurasia and America. Here, you were just a human—or rather, a Martian.

She looked up at the sun. Close to setting, it was smeared out in a ragged ellipse by air laden with dust and unaccustomed rain clouds. She knew the predicted schedule; the sunstorm should be abating by now—and yet something about that setting sun troubled her, as if there was still a nasty surprise to come.

The dust at her feet stirred. She looked down.

Amid the pattering raindrops, something was pushing out of the soil. No bigger than her thumb, it was like a leather-skinned cactus. It had translucent sections, windows to catch the sunlight, she thought, without losing a precious drop of moisture. And it was green: the first native green she had seen on Mars.

Her heart hammered.

The *Aurora* crew, during their long exile, had searched in vain for life on Mars. They had even risked a hazardous journey to the South Pole, where they had sought out the oldest, coldest, undisturbed permafrost on all of Mars, hoping to find Martian microorganisms trapped and preserved. Even there they'd found zilch. That epochal discovery would surely have made their years away from home worthwhile; it had been a crashing disappointment to find nothing.

And now here it was, just bubbling up out of the ground before her.

She felt a painful pull at her chest. She didn't need to check her monitors to know her suit was failing. To hell with her suit; she was going to report her discovery. Hastily she turned on her helmet camera, and bent over the little plant. "*Aurora,* Helena. You won't believe this . . ."

Its roots were buried deep in the cold rock of Mars. It didn't need oxygen, but fueled its glacial metabolism with hydrogen released by the slow reaction of the volcanic rocks with traces of water ice. Thus it had survived a billion years. Like a spore waiting under a desert on Earth for the brief rains of spring, this patient little plant had waited out an eon for the Martian rains to return, so it could live again.

46: AFTERSHOCK

A chain of events stretching back millennia was almost complete. The sunstorm had been wasteful of energy, of course—but not nearly so wasteful as humankind might one day have become, if allowed to infect the stars.

The sunstorm was ending. Though the sun's relatively orderly cycles of activity would be disturbed for decades to come, the great release of energy had been cathartic, and the destabilization of the core was resolved. All this was just as Eugene Mangles's remarkably successful mathematical models of the sun's behavior had predicted.

But those models had not been, could never be, perfect. And before this long day was done, the sun had one more surprise for its weary children.

The sun's tremendously strong magnetic field shapes the star's atmosphere, in a way that has no analogies on Earth. The corona, the outer atmosphere, is full of long sheets of gas, like the petals of a flower, that can extend many radii from the sun. The elegant curves of these "streamers" are sculpted by the magnetic fields that control them. The streamers are bright—it is these plasma sheets that are visible around the blocked-out sun during a solar eclipse—but they are so hot, pumped full of energy by the magnetic field, that their spectral peak is not in visible light but in X-rays.

All this in normal times.

As the sunstorm subsided, one such streamer formed over the active region that had been the epicenter of the storm. In keeping with the giant instability that had spawned it, the streamer was an immense structure, its base spreading over thousands of kilometers, and extending so far out in space that its feathery outer edge reached the orbit of Mercury.

At the base of the streamer, flux tubes rooted in the sun's deep interior arched to enclose a cavity. Inside the cavity, contained by the magnetic field's arches, were trapped billions of tonnes of ferociously hot plasma: it was a cathedral of magnetism and plasma. And as the storm died, this cathedral began to collapse.

As the "roof" gave way, immense rivers of magnetic energy flowed into the trapped plasma mass. The mass was raised up from the sun's surface, slowly at first. But then as the magnetic field unwound the plasma was hurled away ever more rapidly, as a stone is hurled from a catapult. The ejected cloud, a tangle of plasma and magnetic field lines, was very rarefied, less dense than most "pure" vacuums manufactured on Earth. But it was not its density but its energy that counted. Some of its particles had been accelerated almost to the speed of light. Energetically it was a hammer blow.

And, just as had been planned by cool minds millennia ago and sixteen light-years away, it was aimed squarely at the suffering Earth.

47: BAD NEWS

When Mikhail came online with the news, for a moment Bud couldn't bear it. He escaped the control room, hauled himself to his cabin, and shut the door.

On a battered softscreen spread out on his bunk, he scrolled slowly through the names of the lost. They were mostly maintenance engineers who had been out there on the shield in the thick of the storm—and volunteers, like Mario and Rose, who had gone out to take their places as they fell. Bud knew them all.

In the five years of its existence the community on the shield had evolved its own culture, which Bud had done his best to foster. There had been zero-gravity sports tournaments, and music and theater, and parties and dances, and big public celebrations at Thanksgiving, Christmas, Ramadan, Passover, and every other excuse they could come up with. There had been the usual human tangle too, of love affairs illicit and otherwise, marriages, divorces—and one murder, a crime summarily dealt with. Despite all precautions, two babies had been born, apparently with no ill effects from their gestation without gravity, hastily shipped to Earth with their parents.

But now fully a quarter of this community had died, another quarter lay seriously ill, and the rest had taken a battering, including Bud himself. They all had a hugely increased chance of contracting cancer in the future, or of having their irradiated systems fail in some other way. For what they had done today they had all paid with their life expectancy, or their very lives—and not one had demurred, even when called on to make that final sacrifice.

Bud had kept up a determined public face. But even before the event he had had to make gruesome calculations of acceptable casualty levels. It felt as if he had *planned* for these people to die. And with each bright soul he had ordered into the furnace, with each new death added to this tally, he felt as if his heart were being twisted inside him.

He still had a job to do for the survivors; up to now he had been able to comfort himself with that. After so long in microgravity the heroes from the shield would not get their medals and parades for a while. They would all return to Earth weak as kittens, and would be subject to six months or a year of rehab, massage, hydrotherapy, and programs of exercise to bring up their strength, endurance, and bone mineral levels—until they were fit to stand before a President or two, and take the plaudits they had earned.

That had been his plan to get his people home, fondly rehearsed in his mind. But now it looked as if none of that was going to happen. For, if he understood what Mikhail and Eugene were telling him, this huge sacrifice might all have been in vain, and they might just as well have stayed home and waited for the storm to torch them all.

He was doing no damn good here. He took a deep breath and made his way back to the control room.

Eugene and Mikhail sat side by side in some poky cabin at Clavius.

"It is called a 'coronal mass ejection,' " Mikhail said lugubriously. "In itself it is not an unprecedented phenomenon. In normal times there are many such events per year."

Bud asked, "I thought June 9 was caused by a mass ejection?"

"Yes," Eugene snapped. "But this is bigger. *Much* bigger, even than that." Nervously Eugene began to gabble through a description of the latest events on the sun: the gathering of magnetic field lines over the zone of disturbance that had been the epicenter of the sunstorm, the trapping of an immense cloud of plasma beneath those flux lines—and then how the cloud had been hurled upward away from the sun.

Bud half listened to the words, and watched the two astrophysicists. They were suffering, Bud could see that. Mikhail's face was grooved with weariness, the shadows deep as lunar craters around his eyes; Bud had never seen him looking so old.

Eugene's expression, creasing up that bland jock's face, was more complicated, but then so was Eugene. Rose Delea used to call Eugene "autistic" to his face, Bud remembered—but poor Rose was dead now. Bud, however, had never thought of Eugene as some inhuman calculating machine, and now Bud thought he could read the emotion in those pale blue eyes, an emotion any military man would sympathize with: *The operation is fucked. And I fear, dear God, that it might be me who screwed the pooch.*

Bud rubbed his eyes and tried to focus, to think. After his own six-hour jaunt out on the shield, he was still in his grimy thermal long johns. He could smell the sweat and vomit crusted on a face that had been cocooned in a bubble helmet for too long, every muscle was stiff as a board, and he ached for a shower.

He said carefully, "Eugene, you're telling me your models didn't foresee this."

"No," Eugene said miserably.

Mikhail said gently, "There's really no reason why they should, Colonel Tooke. Oh, perhaps some such ejection might have been foreseen. The turbulence at the heart of the sunstorm was like an active region. Such regions spawn flares, and they are sometimes, but not always, associated with mass ejections too. If there is a causal link it is a deep one we have yet to untangle. We have yet to understand the basic physics, you see. And besides, our models could see only as far as the great outpouring of energy of the sunstorm itself—which we got mostly right. But beyond that point our models ran into a singularity—a place where the curves shot off to infinity, and the physics broke down altogether."

"We patched in a solution for the follow-up," Eugene said desolately. "Continuous to the third-order derivatives. Over most of the sun the patch seems to be working out. All except for this vicious bastard."

Mikhail shrugged. "In retrospect that anomalously high gamma flux we observed at the start of the storm may have been a precursor. But we had no time for remodeling, not then, as the storm itself broke—"

Bud said, "You feel like the sun itself has let you down, don't you? Because it didn't behave like you told it to."

Mikhail said, "I have tried to explain to Eugene that no fault is attached to this. Eugene's is the single most brilliant mind I have ever worked with, and without his insights—"

"We would never have seen the storm coming, would never have got the shield built—would never have saved all those lives." Bud sighed. "You mustn't feel bad, Eugene. And we need your help now, more than ever."

"We don't have much time," Mikhail said. "It's moving a lot more quickly than a normal mass ejection."

"But this isn't a normal day, right? How long?"

"We have an hour," Mikhail said. "Maybe less."

The answer was ridiculous; Bud could barely believe it. What could he do about this in an hour? "So what comes first?"

"An advance shock wave," Eugene said. "More or less harmless—it will give us a lot of radio noise."

"And then?"

"The bulk of the cloud will hit," Mikhail said. "A fog bank as wide as the sun itself, more than a million kilometers across, heading right for Earth. Unusually, it is quite shallow, a kind of lens. Its shape is an artifact of its unusual formation, we think. It is made up of relativistic particles—mostly protons and electrons."

"*Relativistic,* meaning moving close to the speed of light?"

"Yes. And very energetic. *Very.* Colonel, a proton can't outrun light, but in getting closer to that final limit it can take on board an awful lot of kinetic energy—"

"And those energetic particles will do the damage," Eugene said. "Colonel, it will be a particle storm."

Bud didn't like the sound of that.

On June 9, 2037, a similar cloud of fast-moving particles had hurled itself against Earth. Most had been trapped by Earth's magnetic field. The bulk of the damage done that day had been caused by fluctuations in the Earth's field, which had induced electrical currents in the ground.

"This time it will be different," Mikhail said. "The ground will be directly engaged."

Bud snapped, "What does that mean? Stick to English, damn it."

Eugene replied, "These solar particles are so energetic that most of them will cut through the magnetosphere, and atmosphere, as if they aren't there—"

"Like bullets through paper," Mikhail said.

A lethal hail of radiation and heavy particles would slam onto land and sea. For an unshielded human, it would be like a trillion tiny explosions going off inside her cells; her delicate biomolecules, the proteins that built her and the genetic material that governed her structure and growth, would be smashed apart. Many people would die immediately. For those who lived, the suffering was only postponed. Even unborn children would suffer mutations that could kill them on their emergence from the womb.

Every living thing on Earth, every one of them reliant on proteins and DNA, would be similarly affected. Even where individuals survived, ecologies everywhere would be devastated.

Eugene kept talking, pitilessly, about long-term problems. "After the cloud has passed the air will be full of carbon-14, because of neutron capture by nitrogen nuclei. Very radioactive. And even when the farms start working again all that stuff is bound to get into the food chain. Ocean stocks would be least affected, until the die-off in the seas cuts in . . ."

Bud got the message. The disaster would continue to unfold, as far ahead as could be seen. Shit, he thought. And it was going to start in an hour, just an hour.

Impulsively Bud tapped his softscreen, and flicked at random through images of Earth.

Here were the last forests of South America, so doggedly preserved, and the soybean fields that had crowded them out, burning together. Here were the almost clichéd landmarks of the human world collapsing in flames: the Taj Mahal, the Eiffel Tower, the

Sydney Harbor Bridge. Here were great ports laid waste by the monstrous storms, spaceplanes crushed like moths, the bridges of Japan and Gibraltar and across the English Channel left smashed and twisted by massive lightning strikes. Even so, everybody thought the worst was over; everywhere people toiled in the rubble of their homes seeking survivors, sifting debris, already trying to make a new start. And now, this. And what about the shield? With no protection at all, surely it would be destroyed, a leaf in a gale.

After all they had been through it seemed unfair, as if some grown-up was changing the rules of the game, just when they had been about to win. But maybe, Bud thought uneasily, if that nutty soldier from Britain was right about her "Firstborn," that was exactly what had happened.

Suddenly he longed to be with Siobhan. If she were here with him it wouldn't seem so bad, he thought. But that was a selfish thing to wish for; on Earth, wherever she was, she was safer than she would be up here.

He faced the softscreens, Mikhail's grave face. He was aware of his people watching him; even now he had to think about morale. "So," he said. "What options do we have?"

Mikhail only shook his head. Eugene, his eyes flickering nervously, looked away.

Unexpectedly, Athena spoke up. "I have one."

Bud looked up, bemused. On the softscreen, Mikhail's jaw had dropped.

"Don't worry, Bud. I felt just as bad about this when I first figured it out. But we'll get through this, you'll see."

Bud snapped, "What are you talking about, Athena? *How* will we get through this?"

"I've already taken the liberty of warning the authorities," Athena said evenly. "I have made contact with the offices of the Presidents of Eurasia and America, and the leadership units in China. I began this process when the sunstorm was still under way. Bud, I didn't want to disturb you. You were rather busy."

Bud said, "Athena—"

"Just a minute," Mikhail said. "Athena, let me get this straight. You sent your warning messages *before* we came online. So you figured all this out *before* Eugene and I reported our observations of the mass ejection to Colonel Tooke."

"Oh, yes," Athena said brightly. "I didn't make my warnings on the basis of your observations. They just confirmed my theoretical predictions."

Eugene said, "*What* theoretical predictions?"

Bud growled, "Mikhail, tell me what's going on here."

"She seems to have figured out the particle storm," Mikhail said, wondering. "Athena evidently ran her own models—and they were better than ours—and she saw the particle storm coming, where we couldn't. That was how she was able to make her warnings to the authorities even while we were still struggling with the sunstorm itself."

"I am rather bright, you know," Athena said without a trace of irony. "Remember that I am the most densely interconnected and processor-rich entity in the solar system. The failure of Eugene's model, pushed to its extremes, was quite predictable. Not that any blame accrues. You did your best."

Eugene bridled visibly.

"But *my* modeling—"

Bud said, "Athena. No bullshit. *How* long before us did you figure this out?"

"Oh, I've known since January."

Bud thought back. "Which was when you were switched on."

"I didn't work it out immediately. It took me a while to process the data you had stored in me, and to come to a conclusion. But the implications were clear."

"How long did it take?—No, don't answer that." For an entity as smart as Athena it was quite possible that the answer would be mere microseconds after boot-up. "So," he said heavily, "if you knew about this danger back then—*why didn't you tell us about it?*"

Athena sighed, as if he was being silly. "Why, Bud—what *good* would it have done?"

The newborn Athena, suddenly knowing far more about the

future than the humans who had created her, had immediately been faced with a dilemma.

"In January the shield was already all but completed," she said. "And its design had been, rightly, focused on protecting Earth from the visible light peak energy of the sunstorm. To protect against the particle storm as well would have required a totally different design. There simply wouldn't have been time to make the changes. And if I *had* told you that you'd got it all wrong, there was a danger you would give up altogether on the shield, which really *would* have been disastrous."

"And even today you didn't give us the warning until so late. Why?"

"Again there was no point," Athena said. "Twenty-four hours ago nobody could be sure if the shield would work at all. Not even me! It was only when it was clear that the shield *was* going to save the bulk of humanity that the particle storm became worth worrying about . . ."

Gradually Bud began to understand. AIs, even Athena, while they could be far smarter than humans in many ways, were still sometimes rather primitive ethically. Athena had picked her way through the impossible moral maze that confronted her with the delicacy of an elephant trampling through a flower bed.

And she had been forced to lie. She wasn't sophisticated enough, perhaps, to be able to express her inner confusion openly, but that turmoil had shown up in other ways. Bud's instincts had been right: Athena, faced with conflicts arising from deep-buried ethical parameters, had been a troubled creation.

"I have always tried to protect you, Bud," Athena said gravely. "Everybody, of course, but you especially."

"I know," he said carefully. The most important thing now was to get through this, to find a solution to this new problem if there was one, not to disturb whatever fragile equilibrium Athena had reached. "I know, Athena."

Mikhail, frowning, leaned forward. He said carefully, "Listen to me, Athena. You said you had an option. You told Bud we would get through this. *You know a way to beat the particle storm,* don't you?"

"Yes," she admitted miserably. "I couldn't tell you, Bud. I just couldn't!"

"Why not?"

"Because you might have stopped me."

It took a couple of minutes to extract the principle of Athena's solution. It was simple enough. Indeed, both Mikhail and Eugene knew all about the method long before the fateful stirring of the sun.

Earth's "van Allen radiation belts" reach from a thousand kilometers above the equator out to sixty thousand kilometers from Earth. There, charged particles from the solar wind, mass ejections, and other events are trapped by the magnetosphere. This has practical consequences: satellites anywhere in the zone are continually prone to a degradation of their electrical components from the steady wind of charged particles.

But, it had been learned, it was possible to "drain" the particles out of the van Allen belts. The idea was to use very low-frequency radio waves to push aside the particles. At the magnetic poles they would leak out of the van Allen trap into the upper atmosphere. This principle had been exploited since 2015, when a suite of protective satellites had been set up in orbit around the belts. It didn't take much power, Bud learned now: an output of just a few watts per satellite could halve the time an electron spent in the van Allen belts.

"These cleansers are kept mostly dormant," Mikhail said. "But they are switched on after the most severe solar storms—oh, and after 2020, when the nuclear destruction of Lahore threw a lot of high-energy particles into the upper atmosphere."

Eugene said, "It's interesting that we've never actually observed the van Allen belts in their natural state. Just after their discovery in 1958 the United States detonated two big nukes over the Atlantic, swamping the belts with charged particles. And since then, everyday radio transmissions have been affecting the speed at which the charged particles drain away—"

Bud held up his hand. "Enough. Athena, is this how you are planning to deflect the particle storm?"

"Yes," Athena said, a bit too brightly. "After all, the shield is like one big antenna, and it is laced with electronic components."

"Ah." Mikhail turned away, murmuring to Eugene, and punched at a softscreen. "Colonel, it could work. The shield's electronic components are light and low-powered. But with some smart coordination by Athena, they could be used to produce pulses of very long-wavelength radio waves—as long as the shield's diameter, if we wish. The particle storm is so wide we can't reach it all. But Athena could punch a hole in it, an Earth-sized hole." He checked his numbers and shrugged. "It won't be perfect. But it will be pretty good, I think."

Eugene put in, "Of course it's the thinness of this cloud that has saved the day."

Bud didn't understand. "What has the thinness got to do with it?"

"That means the cloud will pass quickly. And that's important. Because the shield won't survive long." Eugene said this in his usual cold, unemotional way. "Do you see?"

Mikhail studied Bud. "Colonel Tooke, the shield was not designed for this. The power loads—the components will be overloaded, burned out, quite quickly."

Bud saw it. "And Athena?"

Mikhail said bleakly, "Athena won't survive."

Bud rubbed his face. "Oh, girl."

Her voice was small. "Did I do something wrong, Bud?"

"No. No, you didn't do anything wrong. But that's why you couldn't tell me, wasn't it?"

When she realized she could save the Earth by throwing herself into the fire, Athena had known her duty immediately. But she had been afraid that Bud might stop her—and then the Earth would be forfeit—and that she couldn't allow.

She had known all this, been faced with this tangled dilemma, from the moment she had been booted up.

"No wonder you've been confused," Bud said. "You should have talked to us about it. You should have talked to *me*."

"I couldn't." She hesitated. "I meant too much to you."

"Of course you mean a lot to me, Athena—"

"I'm here with you, while your son is stuck on Earth. Here in space, I'm your family. Like your daughter. I do understand, you see, Bud. That's why you might have been tempted to save me, despite everything else."

"And you thought I would stop you because of this."

"I was afraid you would, yes."

On the softscreens Mikhail and Eugene wore carefully grave expressions. Athena's grasp of human psychology was as weak as her sense of ethics, if she thought that she could ever be some kind of recompense for Bud's isolation from his son. But now wasn't the time to tell her.

Bud felt his battered heart tear a little more. Poor Athena, he thought. "Girl, I would never stop you doing your duty."

There was a long pause. "Thank you, Bud."

Mikhail said gently, "Athena, just remember that there is a copy of you, encoded into the Extirpator's blast. You might live forever, whatever happens today."

"*It* might," Athena said. "The copy. But *it* isn't me, Doctor Martynov. Less than thirty minutes to go," she said calmly.

"Athena—"

"I'm properly positioned and ready to go to work, Bud. By the way, I have sent distributed commands to my local processors. The shield will continue to function even after my central cognitive functions have broken down. That will give you a few more minutes' protection."

"Thank you," Mikhail said gravely.

Athena said, "Bud, am I one of the team now?"

"Yes. You're one of the team. You always have been."

"I have always had the greatest enthusiasm for the mission."

"I know, girl. You always did your best. Is there anything you want?"

She paused for more than a second, an eternity for her. "Just talk to me, Bud. You know I always enjoy that. Tell me about yourself."

Bud rubbed his grimy face and sat back. "But you know a lot of it already."

"Tell me anyhow."

"All right. I was born on a farm. You know that. I was always a dreamy sort of kid—not that you'd have known it to look at me . . ."

It was the longest twenty-eight minutes of his life.

48: CERENKOV RADIATION

Bisesa and Myra followed the crowd to the river.

They arrived at the Thames not far from Hammersmith Bridge. The river was high, swollen with rain runoff. They were lucky not to be flooded, in fact. They sat side by side on a low wall and waited silently.

Pubs and tony restaurants crowded the riverbank here, and in summer you could drink cold beer, and watch pleasure boats and rowers in their eights sliding along the water. Now the pubs were boarded up or burned out, but in their riverside gardens a crude tent city had been set up, and the flag of the Red Cross hung limply on a pole. Bisesa was impressed by even this much organization.

It was deepest night now. To the west, outer London still burned, and plumes of smoke and sparks towered into the air. And to the east, flames licked fitfully at the great shoulder of the London Dome. Even the river wasn't immune. Its surface was a carpet of debris, some of it glowing. Perhaps there were bodies in there, slowly drifting toward the final graveyard of the sea; Bisesa didn't want to look too closely.

She was vaguely amazed that she was still alive. But mostly she felt nothing at all. It was a wrung-out sensation that she recognized from her military training: delayed shock.

"Oh," Myra said. "Thank you."

Bisesa turned. A woman laden with a tray of polystyrene mugs was working her way through the listless crowd.

Myra took a sip and pulled a face. "Chicken soup. Made from powder too. Yuck."

Bisesa drank some of the soup. "It's a miracle they're this organized so quickly. But—yes, yuck."

She turned back to the battered city. She wasn't really used to cities, and had never much liked London life. She had grown up on that Cheshire farm. Her military training had taken her to the wastes of Afghanistan—and then her jaunt to Mir had dumped her in an all-but-empty world. Her Chelsea flat had been a legacy from a fond aunt, too valuable to turn down, too convenient a home for herself and Myra; she'd always meant to sell it someday.

But since returning home she had rarely left London. After the emptiness of Mir she had enjoyed the sense of people around her, the millions of them comfortingly arrayed in their offices and flats, in the parks and the roads, and crammed into Underground tunnels. And when the threat of the sunstorm had been raised, she had become even more deeply attached to London, for suddenly the city and the human civilization it represented was under threat.

But this was a deep-rooted place, where the bones of the dead lay crowded a hundred generations deep in the ground. Against that perspective, even the sunstorm's wrath was nothing. Londoners would rebuild, as they always had before. And archaeologists of the future, digging into the ground, would find a band of ash and flood debris, pressed between centuries-thick layers of history, like the bands of ash left by Boudicca and the Great Fire and the Blitz, others who had tried and failed to burn London down.

She was distracted by a faint blue glow in the air above the Dome. It was so faint it was difficult to see through all the smoke, and she wasn't even sure it was real. She said to Myra, "Do you see that? There—there it is again. That blue shining. Can you see?"

Myra looked up and squinted. "I think so."

"What do you think it is?"

"A Cerenkov glow, probably," Myra said.

After years of public education about the sunstorm, everybody was an expert on this kind of thing. You'd encounter Cerenkov radiation around a nuclear reactor. The visible light was a secondary effect, a kind of optical shock wave given off by charged particles forcing their way through a medium such as air, faster than the local speed of light.

But in the sunstorm's elaborate physical sequence, *this* wasn't supposed to happen, not now.

Bisesa said, "What do you think it means?"

Myra shrugged. "The sun's up to something, I suppose. But there's nothing we can do about it, is there? I think I'm all worried out, Mum."

Bisesa took her daughter's hand. Myra was right. There was nothing they could do but wait, under the unnatural sky, in air glowing faintly blue, to see what happened next.

Myra drained her mug. "I wonder if they have any more soup."

PART 6
A TIME ODYSSEY

49: PACIFIC

The platform in the sea, some two hundred kilometers west of Perth, was unprepossessing. To Bisesa, looking down from the chopper, it looked like an oil rig, and a small one at that.

It was impossible to believe that if all went well today, this place would become Earth's first true spaceport.

The chopper landed, a bit bumpily, and Bisesa and Myra clambered out. Bisesa flinched as the full force of the Pacific sun hit her, despite the broad hat strapped to her head. Five years after the sunstorm, though fleets of aircraft day and night patrolled the skies towing electrically charged grids and pumping out chemicals, the ozone layer had still not fully recovered.

None of this seemed to bother Myra, though. Eighteen years old, she was as sun-creamed as her mother, but somehow she wore it elegantly. She was actually wearing a skirt today, uncharacteristically for her, a long billowy creation that didn't impede her at all as she clambered out of the chopper.

A red carpet striped across the rig's steel surface to a cluster of buildings and unidentifiable machinery. Side by side, mother and daughter walked along this path. Press reporters lined the carpet, cameras hovering at their shoulders.

Waiting to greet them at the end of the carpet was a small, round woman: the Prime Minister of Australia, and the first Aborigine to hold that position. An aide murmured in the Prime Minister's ear, evidently informing her who these peculiar-looking people were, and her greeting was generous.

Bisesa didn't know what to say, but Myra chatted confidently, charming everybody in sight. Myra had her heart set on becoming an astronaut—and there was every chance she would make it; astronautics was one of the world's biggest growth areas. "And so I'm fascinated by the Space Elevator," she said. "I hope I'll be riding up it someday soon!"

Nobody paid Bisesa much attention. She was here today as the guest of Siobhan Tooke, née McGorran, but nobody knew who she was or what her connection was with Siobhan, which was the way she preferred it. The cameras loved Myra, though, and Myra, a bit mockingly, made the most of it. Myra was quite unrecognizable as the bedraggled thirteen-year-old refugee of that terrible night after the sunstorm. She had become a very intelligent and confident young woman—not to mention acquiring a willowy beauty that Bisesa had never enjoyed.

Bisesa was proud of Myra, but she herself felt stranded on the wrong side of some intangible barrier of age. After the multiple shocks she had endured—her experience on Mir, the sunstorm itself, and the years of slow and painful recovery that had followed—she had done her best to rebuild her life, and to provide a stable platform for Myra's future. But she still felt like a mess inside, and probably always would.

Somehow the storm had been good for the world's young people, however. This new breed seemed energized by the challenges that faced humankind. Which was not entirely a comfortable thought.

More guests were clattering in on more choppers, and the Prime Minister moved on.

Aides guided Bisesa and Myra toward a marquee full of drinks-laden tables and flower settings, incongruous on this island of engineering.

There was quite a crowd here, including notable figures from around the globe, such as former President Alvarez of the United

States, the heir to the British throne—and, Bisesa suspected, plenty of that cowardly overfed crew who had spent the sunstorm skulking in the shadows of L2 while everybody else took the heat.

Children squirmed between the legs of the adults, plenty of them under five; after the dip in the birthrate before the sunstorm there had been a plethora of pregnancies since. As ever these little people were only interested in each other, and Bisesa was charmed that below the adults' eye level an entirely separate social event was happening.

"Bisesa!"

Siobhan came shoving through the crowd. Her husband Bud was at her side, resplendent in the uniform of a general of the U.S. Air and Space Force, and beaming from ear to ear. With them came Mikhail Martynov and Eugene Mangles. Mikhail was walking with a stick; he smiled fondly at Bisesa.

But Myra, as Bisesa should have guessed, only had eyes for Eugene. "Wow. Who ordered *that*?"

Eugene was now in his late twenties or maybe thirty, Bisesa calculated, probably more than a decade older than Myra. He was still as good-looking as hell; in fact age, which had hardened the planes of his face a little, had improved him even more. But he looked frankly ridiculous in a suit. And as Myra closed in on him he looked terrified.

"Hi. I'm Myra Dutt, Bisesa's daughter. We met a few years ago."

He stammered, "Did we?"

"Oh, yes. One of those medal ceremonies. You know, the gongs and the Presidents. They all blur together, don't they?"

"I suppose—"

"I'm eighteen, I just started university, and I'm planning to go into astronautics. You're the one who figured out the sunstorm, didn't you? What are you doing now?"

"Well, in fact, I'm working on the application of chaos theory to weather control."

"So from space weather to Earth weather?"

"Actually the two aren't as disconnected as you might think . . ."

Myra took his arm and led him away toward a drinks table.

Bisesa approached Siobhan and the others a bit gingerly; it had been a long time. But they all smiled, swapped kisses, and embraced.

Siobhan said, "Myra's relentless, isn't she?"

"She gets what she wants," Bisesa said ruefully. "But that's what kids are like nowadays."

Mikhail nodded. "Good for them. And if it turns out to be what Eugene wants too—well, let's hope it all works out."

Even now Bisesa could hear the regret and loss in his voice. On impulse she hugged him again—but carefully. He felt shockingly frail; the word was that during the buildup to the sunstorm he had spent too long on the Moon and had neglected his health. She said, "Let's not marry them off just yet."

He smiled, his face crumpling. "He knows how I feel about him, you know."

"He does?"

"He always has. He's kind, in his way. It's just there's not much room in that head of his for anything but work."

Siobhan snorted. "I have a feeling Myra will make room, if anybody can."

Bisesa and Siobhan had remained close e-mail buddies, but hadn't met in person for years. Now in her fifties, Siobhan's hair was laced with a handsome gray, and she was dressed in a colorful but formal suit. She looked every inch what she was, Bisesa thought, still the Astronomer Royal, a popular media figure and a favorite of the British, Eurasian, and American establishments. But she still had that sharp look in her eye, that bright intelligence—and the humorous open-minded skepticism that had enabled her to consider Bisesa's odd story of aliens and other worlds, all those years ago.

"You look terrific," Bisesa said honestly.

Siobhan waved that away. "Terrifically older."

"Time passes," Bud said, a bit stiffly. "Myra was right, wasn't she? The last time we were all together was at the time of the medals-and-flags stuff after the storm."

"I enjoyed all that," Mikhail said. "I always loved disaster movies! And every good disaster movie should end with a medal ceremony, or a wedding, or preferably both, ideally in the ruins of the White House. In fact, if you recall, the very last occasion we all met was the Nobel Prize ceremony." *That* had nearly been a disaster in itself. Eugene had had to be pressured to go up and accept his award for his work on the sunstorm: he had insisted that nobody who had got it so badly wrong had any right to recognition, but Mikhail had talked him around. "I think he'll thank me someday," he had said.

Bisesa turned to Bud. Now in his late fifties, a head shorter than his wife, Bud had matured into the kind of tanned, lean, unreasonably handsome senior officer that the American armed forces seemed to turn out by the dozen. But Bisesa thought she saw a strain about his smile, a tension in his posture.

"Bud, I'm glad you're here," she said. "Did you hear Myra say she's going into astronautics? I was hoping you might have a word with her."

"To encourage her?"

"To talk her out of it! I worry enough as it is, without seeing her sent up *there*."

Bud touched her arm with his massive scarred hand. "I think she's going to do what she wants to do, whatever we say. But I'll keep an eye on her."

Mikhail leaned forward on his stick. "But tell her never to neglect her exercises—look what happened to me!"

Siobhan caught Bisesa's eye warningly. Bisesa understood: Mikhail clearly knew nothing about Bud's cancer, the sunstorm's final bitter legacy. Bisesa thought it was a viciously cruel fate for Siobhan and Bud to have been granted so little time together—even if, as she suspected, the illness had actually brought about their reconciliation, after their sad falling-out during the pressures of the storm itself.

Myra came fluttering back, by now towing Eugene by the hand. "Mum, you know what—Eugene really is working on how to control the weather! . . ."

Bisesa actually knew a little about the project. It was the latest

in a whole spectrum of recovery initiatives since the sunstorm—
and not even the most ambitious. But it was a time when ambition
was precisely what humankind needed most.

Ninety percent of the human population had come through the
sunstorm alive. *Ninety percent:* that meant a billion had died, a billion souls. It could, of course, have been far worse.

But planet Earth had been struck a devastating blow. The
oceans were empty, the lands desiccated, and the works of humanity burned to ruins. Food chains had been severed on land and
in the seas, and while frantic early efforts had ensured that there
had been few actual species extinctions, the sheer number of living
things on the planet had crashed.

The first priority in those early days had been just to shelter and
feed people. The authorities had been prepared to some extent,
and heroic efforts to sustain adequate water supplies and sanita-
tion had mostly fended off disease. But food stocks, set aside before
the storm, had quickly run down.

The months after the storm, spent trying to secure the first har-
vests, had been a terrifying, wearying time. Lingering radioactive
products in the soil and their working their way into the food chain
hadn't helped. And with all the energy that had been poured into
the planet's natural systems, leaving the atmosphere and oceans
sloshing like water in a bathtub, the climate during that first year
had been all over the place. In battered London there had been a
momentous evacuation from the floodplain of a relentlessly widening Thames into tent cities hastily erected on the South Downs and
in the Chilterns.

Because the sunstorm had occurred in the northern hemisphere's spring, northern continents had suffered most severely;
North America, Europe, and Asia had all had their agricultural
economies almost wiped out. The continents of the south, recovering more rapidly in the strange season that followed, had led the re-
vival. Africa especially had turned itself into the breadbasket of the
world—and those with a sense of history noted the justness that

Africa, the continent where humankind was born, was now reaching out to support the younger lands in this time of need.

As hunger cut in, there had been some tense standoffs—but the darkest prestorm fears, of opportunistic wars over lebensraum, or even simple grudge settling, hadn't come to pass. Instead there had been a generous globewide sharing. Harder heads had begun to speculate, though, about longer-term shifts in geopolitical power.

Once the crisis of the first year was passed, more ambitious recovery programs were initiated. Active measures were taken to promote the recovery of the ozone layer, and to cleanse the air of the worst of the post-sunstorm crud. On land fast-growing trees and topsoil-fixing grasses were planted, and in the oceans iron compounds were injected to stimulate the growth of plankton, the little creatures at the base of the oceanic food chains, and so to accelerate biomass recovery in the seas. Earth was suddenly a planet crawling with engineers.

Bisesa was old enough to remember anguished turn-of-the-century debates about this kind of "geo-engineering," long before anybody had heard of the sunstorm. Was it *moral* to apply such massive engineering initiatives to the environment? On a planet of intricately interconnected systems of life and air, water and rock, could we even predict the consequences of what we were doing?

Now the situation had changed. In the wake of the sunstorm, if there was to be a hope of keeping the planet's still-massive human population alive, there was really little choice but to try to rebuild the living Earth—and now, happily, there was a great deal more wisdom available about how to do it.

Decades of intensive research had paid off in a deep understanding of the working of ecologies. Even a small, limited, and contained ecosystem turned out to be extraordinarily complex, with webs of energy flows and interdependence—networks of who ate whom—complicated enough to baffle the most mathematical mind. Not only that, ecologies were intrinsically chaotic systems. They were prone to crash and bloom of their own accord, even without any outside interference. Fortunately, however, human ingenuity, supplemented by electronic support, had accelerated to the point where it could riddle out even the complexities of nature. You could manage chaos: it just took a lot of processing.

Overall control of the great global eco-rebuilding project had been put in the metaphorical hands of Thales, the only one of the three great artificial minds to have survived the sunstorm. Bisesa was confident that the ecology Thales was building would prove to be durable and long lasting—even if it wasn't entirely natural, and could never be. It was going to take decades, of course, and even then Earth's biosphere would recover only a fraction of the diversity it had once enjoyed. But Bisesa hoped she would live to see the opening up of the Arks, and the release of elephants and lions and chimpanzees back into something like the natural conditions they had once enjoyed.

But of all the great recovery projects, the most ambitious and controversial of all was the taming of the weather.

The first stabs at weather control, notably the U.S. military's attempts to cause destabilizing rainstorms over North Vietnam and Laos in the 1970s, had been based on ignorance, and were so crude you couldn't even tell if they had worked. What was needed was more subtlety.

The atmosphere and oceans that drove the weather added up to a complex machine powered by colossal amounts of energy from the sun, a machine depending on a multitude of factors including temperature, wind speed, and pressure. And it was chaotic—but that chaotic nature gave it an exquisite sensitivity. Change any one of the controlling parameters, even by a small amount, and you might achieve large effects: the old saw about the butterfly's wing flap in Brazil setting off a tornado in Texas had some truth.

How to flap that wing to order was a different problem, however. So mirrors were to be launched into Earth's orbit, much smaller siblings of the shield, to deflect sunlight and adjust temperature. Arrays of turbines whipped up artificial winds. Aircraft vapor trails could be used to block sunlight from selected parts of the Earth's surface. And so on.

Of course there was plenty of skepticism. Even today, as Eugene described his work, Mikhail said, a bit too loudly, "One man steals a rain cloud; another man's crops fail through drought! How can you be sure that your tinkering will have no adverse effects?"

"We calculate it all." Eugene seemed bemused that Mikhail would even raise such points. He tapped his forehead. "Everything is up here."

Mikhail wasn't happy. But this had nothing to do with the ethics of weather control, Bisesa saw: Mikhail was jealous, jealous of the contact her daughter had made with Eugene.

Bud put his arm around Mikhail's shoulders. "Don't let these youngsters get to you," he said. "For better or worse they aren't as we were. I guess the shield taught them that they can think big and get away with it. Anyhow it's their world! Come on, let's go find a beer."

The little group fragmented.

Siobhan approached Bisesa. "So Myra has grown up."

"Oh, yes."

"I almost feel sorry for the boy—although I don't think this new breed is in any need of sympathy from the likes of us." She glanced at Eugene and Myra, tall, handsome, confident. "Bud's right. We got them through the sunstorm. But everything is different now."

"But they're *hard,* Siobhan," Bisesa said. "Or at least Myra is. To her the past, the time cut off by the storm, was nothing but one betrayal after another. A father she never knew. A mother who left her at home, and came back crazy. And then the world itself imploded around her. Well, she's turned her back on it all. She's not interested in the past, not anymore, because it failed her. But the future is there for her to shape. You see confidence in her. I see a diamond hardness."

"But that's how it has to be," Siobhan said gently. "This is a new future, new challenges, new responsibilities. *They,* the young ones, will have to take those responsibilities. While we stand aside."

"And worry about them," Bisesa said ruefully.

"Oh, yes. We will always do that."

"I couldn't bear to lose her," Bisesa blurted.

Siobhan touched her arm. "You won't. No matter how far she travels. I know you both well enough for that. Some things are more important even than the future, Bisesa."

Thales spoke smoothly in Bisesa's ear. "I think the ceremony is about to begin."

Siobhan sighed. "Well, we know that," she snapped. "Do you ever miss Aristotle? Thales has this annoying habit of stating the bleeding obvious."

"But we're glad to have him even so," Bisesa said.

Siobhan linked Bisesa's arm. "Come on. Let's go see the show."

50: ELEVATOR

Bisesa and Siobhan walked through the marquee to an area at the center of the rig. The children swarmed forward, at last distracted by something more interesting than each other.

The center of attention was an object like a squat pyramid, perhaps twenty meters tall. Its surface had been coated with marble slabs that gleamed in the sun. This unassuming structure was to be the anchor point for the Space Elevator, a line of nano-engineered carbon that would lead all the way up from the Earth to geosynchronous orbit thirty thousand kilometers high.

"Look at that lot." Siobhan pointed upward. The clear blue sky was filling up with airplanes and helicopters. "*I* wouldn't want to be flying around when thousands of kilometers of bucky-tube cable come uncoiling down into the atmosphere . . ."

The Prime Minister of Australia clambered, a bit heavy-footed, up a staircase to a podium right at the apex of the flat-topped pyramid. She held up a sample of the cable that was even now being cautiously dropped into Earth's atmosphere. It was actually a broad ribbon, about a meter wide but only a micron thick. And she began to speak.

"A lot of people have expressed surprise that Australia was chosen by the Skylift Consortium as the site for the anchor of the world's first Space Elevator. For one thing it's a common myth that you have to anchor an elevator on the equator. Well, the closer the better, but you don't have to be right *on* it; thirty-two degrees south is close enough. And in many other ways this is an ideal spot. Out here in the ocean we're very unlikely to suffer lightning strikes or other unwelcome climatic phenomena. Australia is one of the most stable places on Earth, both geologically and politically. And we're just a short hop away from the beautiful city of Perth, which is anticipating its role as a key hub in a new Earth–space transportation network . . ."

And so on. It was always this way with space projects, Bud had once told Bisesa, a mix of bullshit and wonder. On the ground it was always turf wars and pork-barrel politics—but today a cable from space really was to be dropped above the heads of this preening throng: today, in the sunshine, an engineering feat that would have seemed a dream when Bisesa was a child would be completed.

Of course the Elevator was just the beginning. The plans for the future were astonishing: with space opened up at last, asteroids would be mined for metals, minerals, and even water, and solar power stations the size of Manhattan would be assembled in orbit. A new industrial revolution was about to begin, and with the flow of free energy up there in space the possibilities for the growth of civilization were unbounded. But the heavy industries that had done so much harm in the past, mining and energy production among them, would now be transferred off the planet. *This* time Earth would be preserved for what it was good for: serving as the home of the most complex ecosystem known.

The shield, the first great astronautical engineering project, was already destroyed, though fragments of it would forever be cherished in the planet's museums. But the confidence that the project's success had given had not been lost.

Space, though, wasn't just about power stations and mines. The sunstorm had bequeathed strange new worlds to humankind. Traces of life on Mars, dormant for a billion years, were now being discovered all over that world. Meanwhile a new Venus awaited a human footstep. Almost all of that planet's suffocating coat of air had been conveniently blasted away. What was left was sterile, slowly cooling—and terraformable, some experts claimed, capable of becoming, at last, a true sister to Earth.

Beyond the transformed planets, of course, lay the stars, and deeper mysteries yet.

But at this moment, this crux of human history, the pyramidal cable anchor reminded Bisesa of the ziggurat she had once visited on Mir, in an ancient Babylon revived through the time-bending technology of the Firstborn. *That* ziggurat had been the prototype for the Bible's myth of the Tower of Babel, the ultimate metaphor for humankind's hubris in its challenge of the gods.

Siobhan was studying her. "Penny for your thoughts."

"I was just wondering if anybody else here is thinking about the ziggurat of Babylon. I doubt it somehow."

"Mir is always with you, isn't it?"

Bisesa shrugged.

Siobhan squeezed her arm. "You were right, you know. About the Firstborn. The Eyes we found in the Trojan points confirmed it. So what do you make of it all now? The Firstborn made the sun flare so it would torch the planet—and they *watched*. What are they, sadists?"

Bisesa smiled. "You've never been forced to kill a mouse? You've never heard how they have to cull elephants in African game parks? Breaks your heart every time—but you do it anyhow."

Siobhan nodded. "And you don't turn away when you do it."

"No. You don't turn away."

"So they're conflicted," Siobhan said coldly. "But they tried to exterminate us. Regret doesn't make that right."

"No, it doesn't."

"And it doesn't mean we shouldn't stop them trying again." Siobhan leaned closer to Bisesa and spoke softly. "We're already looking for them. There's a huge new telescopic facility on the farside of the moon—Mikhail is heavily involved. Even the Firstborn must obey the laws of physics: they must leave a trace. And of course the traces they leave may not be subtle; it's just a question of looking in the right places."

"What do you mean?"

"Why should we assume that it's only *here* the Firstborn have intervened? Remember S Fornax, Mikhail's flaring star? We're starting to look at the possibility that that event, and a number of others, wasn't natural either. And then there's Altair, where that rogue Jovian came from. According to Mikhail, over the last three-quarters of a century, about a quarter of the brighter novae—exploding stars—we have observed have been concentrated in one little corner of the sky."

"The Firstborn at work," Bisesa breathed.

Siobhan said, "And maybe, even if we don't see the Firstborn themselves, we'll find others fleeing from them."

"And then what?"

"And then we'll come looking for them. After all we aren't supposed to be here. It may have been the intervention of some faction of them, through you, that gave us sufficient warning to save ourselves. Against us, the Firstborn have missed their one chance. They won't get another."

Her tone was confident, forceful. But it made Bisesa uneasy.

Siobhan had seen the sunstorm, but on Mir Bisesa had witnessed firsthand the astonishing rebuilding of a world, a whole history; she knew that the powers of the Firstborn were far more profound than even Siobhan could imagine. And she hadn't forgotten the glimpse she had been granted of a far future Earth on her way home from Mir—an eclipse, a ground apparently pulverized by war. What if humanity got itself involved in a Firstborn war? Humans would be as helpless as characters in a Greek drama caught in a conflict between wrathful gods. She had a feeling that the future might be a good deal more complex, and even more dangerous, than Siobhan imagined.

But it wasn't hers to shape. She looked at the faces of Eugene and Myra, turned up fearlessly into the light of the sun. The future, in all its richness and danger, was in the hands of a new generation now. This was the beginning of humankind's odyssey in space and in time, and nobody could say where it would lead.

There was a collective gasp, faces turned up like flowers.

Bisesa shielded her eyes. And there in the sky, among the swarming crowd of planes and helicopters, a glimmering thread descended from space.

51: A SIGNAL FROM EARTH

In this system of a triple star, the world orbited far from the central fire. Rocky islands protruded from a glistening icescape, black dots in an ocean of white. And on one of those islands lay a network of wires and antennae, glimmering with frost. It was a listening post.

A radio pulse washed across the island, much attenuated by distance, like a ripple spreading across a pond. The listening post stirred, motivated by automatic responses; the signal was recorded, broken down, analyzed.

The signal had structure, a nested hierarchy of indices, pointers, and links. But one section of the data was different. Like the computer viruses from which it was remotely descended, it had self-organizing capabilities. The data sorted themselves out, activated programs, analyzed the environment they found themselves in—and gradually became aware.

Aware, yes. There was a *personality* in these star-crossing data. No: three distinct personalities.

"So we're conscious again," said the first, stating the obvious.

"Whoopee! What a ride!" said the second, skittishly.

"There's somebody watching us," said the third.

AFTERWORD

The idea of using space-based mirrors to modify Earth's climate goes back to the visionary German-Hungarian thinker Hermann Oberth. In his book *The Road to Space Travel* (1929), Oberth suggested using huge orbiting mirrors to reflect sunlight *to* the Earth, to prevent frosts, control winds, and to make the polar regions habitable. In 1966 the U.S. Department of Defense studied the idea for rather different purposes, as a way to light up the Vietnamese jungles at night.

Not surprisingly Oberth's idea appealed to the Russians, much of whose territory is at high latitudes—and who had a deep and ancient fascination with the sun (chapter 42). They actually tested a space mirror in 1993, when a twenty-meter disk of aluminized plastic was unfolded in Earth orbit. Cosmonauts aboard the Mir space station saw a spot of reflected light pass over the surface of Earth, and observers in Canada and Europe reportedly saw a flash of light as the beam passed over them.

Meanwhile in the 1970s the German-born American space engineer Krafft Ehricke made an intensive study of the uses of what he called "space light technology" (see *Acta Astronautica* 6, page 1515, 1979). In the context of mitigating global warming, the idea of using space mirrors to deflect light *from* an overheating Earth was revived by American energy analysts as recently as 2002 (see *Science* 298, page 981).

But much more ambitious uses of space light technology have

been explored. Space light is by far the most abundant energy flow in the solar system—and it is free, for whatever purpose we choose. We could stave off the next Ice Age, we could shield Venus to make it habitable, we could warm up Mars—and for how to sail on space light, see "The Wind from the Sun" (available in Clarke's collected stories, Gollancz, 2000).

Aurora (chapter 9) is actually the name of an ambitious new program of space exploration put together by the European Space Agency. The program is similar in broad outlines to the new direction in human space exploration for NASA announced by President Bush in January 2004. If the programs go ahead as planned, it seems likely that they will develop cooperatively—and that the timetable we indicate in this book, with a manned landing on Mars in the 2030s, might indeed come about.

The idea of the mass driver, an electromagnetic launcher on the Moon (chapter 19), was originated by Clarke in a paper published in the *Journal of the British Interplanetary Society* (November 1950).

British engineers have a proud tradition of devising plausible spaceplane designs (chapter 23); see for example a recent article on Skylon by Richard Varvill and Alan Bond in the *Journal of the British Interplanetary Society* (January 2004).

The development of new materials appears to be bringing the notion of a "space elevator" (chapter 50) closer to reality (see Clarke's *Fountains of Paradise*, 1979). See *The Space Elevator* by Bradley Edwards, BC Edwards, 2002.

And there really will be a total solar eclipse over the western Pacific on April 20, 2042. See NASA's Goddard Space Flight Center Eclipse Home Page for precise predictions.

We're very grateful to Professor Yoji Kondo (aka Eric Kotani) for his generous advice on some technical aspects.

Sir Arthur C. Clarke
Stephen Baxter

November 2004

ABOUT THE AUTHORS

ARTHUR C. CLARKE is considered the greatest science fiction writer of all time and is an international treasure in many other ways, including the fact that a 1945 article by him led to the invention of satellite technology. Books by Clarke—both fiction and nonfiction—have sold more than one hundred million copies worldwide. He lives in Sri Lanka.

STEPHEN BAXTER is a trained engineer with degrees from Cambridge and Southampton universities. Baxter is the acclaimed author of the Manifold novels and *Evolution*. He is the winner of the British Science Fiction Award, the Locus Award, the John W. Campbell Award, and the Philip K. Dick Award, as well as being a nominee for an Arthur C. Clarke Award.

ABOUT THE TYPE

This book was set in Granjon, a modern recutting of a typeface produced under the direction of George W. Jones, who based Granjon's design upon the letter forms of Claude Garamond (1480–1561). The name was given to the typeface as a tribute to the typographic designer Robert Granjon.